AVID

READER

PRESS

ROSENFELD

A NOVEL

Maya Kessler

*Translation from the Hebrew
by Maya Thomas*

Avid Reader Press

NEW YORK   LONDON   TORONTO
SYDNEY   NEW DELHI

Avid Reader Press
An Imprint of Simon & Schuster, LLC
1230 Avenue of the Americas
New York, NY 10020

First Avid Reader Press hardcover edition November 2024

Avid Reader Press and colophon are trademarks of Simon & Schuster, LLC

Simon & Schuster: Celebrating 100 Years of Publishing in 2024

For information about special discounts for bulk purchases, please contact Simon & Schuster Special Sales at 1-866-506-1949 or business@simonandschuster.com.

The Simon & Schuster Speakers Bureau can bring authors to your live event. For more information or to book an event contact the Simon & Schuster Speakers Bureau at 1-866-248-3049 or visit our website at www.simonspeakers.com.

Manufactured in the United States of America

1   3   5   7   9   10   8   6   4   2

Library of Congress Cataloging-in-Publication Data has been applied for.

ISBN 978-1-6680-5345-4
ISBN 978-1-6680-5347-8 (ebook)

To all my girlfriends

ROSENFELD

1

Get Out of My Sight

»

He's sitting by one of the white tables on the lawn, talking to his business partner. They laugh at something, but stop when everyone's asked to quiet down. The lighting dims and he watches the movie projected on the screen by the stage. Up until that moment, he has no idea that there's such a thing as me. Up until that moment, I have no idea that there's such a thing as him. But we're soon to find out.

It's mid-September and I'm in the middle of a rough patch. I feel stuck and I don't know what to do to change that, so I'm pissed off at everyone and everything. There are still some joyful moments, such as this wedding of my two friends, Tom and Alison. They're now sitting in front of the screen, roaring with laughter as they watch my movie along with the other guests. Once it's over, everyone applauds and we go straight back to the dance floor, but then Tom tugs at me and says, "Come, they want to meet the director."

"Come where? Who's they?"

"My mom's friends."

"No, no, too drunk for introductions!"

He clears a path through the crowd and the scattered tables across the lawn and I trudge behind him.

"They're in biotech. Marine biotech."

"Biotech? What does that have to do with me?"

But Tom doesn't reply since we've already reached the table where the "distinguished owners of Delmar Bio Solutions" are seated—at least that's what he announces as he stands behind me, gently placing his hands on my shoulders and shoving me toward them. "This is our girl, Noa Simon."

"Pleased to meet you." A handsome bearded man with short gray hair and a confident handshake grins at me, examining me with glimmering eyes. "Richard Harrington."

The other one is clean-shaven, his full head of hair combed back, a big, fat man dressed in a white shirt—or, on second glance, pink—one button excessively undone, exposing a hint of his tanned chest. He looks at me and gives a polite smile, leans in heavily and shakes my hand—"Teddy Rosenfeld"—then leans back again.

Richard says that my movie was really something special, that he's seen numerous wedding videos, but this one "had a different kind of flare."

"So, you're a filmmaker?" Richard inquires while Teddy lights a cigarette.

I tell them that I'm in the industry, but I haven't made my own film yet. Richard pulls up a chair and invites me to sit. Teddy stays silent, surveying me with brown eyes and a serene smile that makes me want to pick up the folding chair and smash it over his head.

I take a seat, and Richard asks me what I'd like to drink, as though we're at a restaurant rather than a wedding. He asks if I've ever made corporate films, then briefly tells me about Delmar and the work they require. I'm working on a daytime television show and I don't have time for another job, but I hear him out and ask the right questions. I'm trying to understand what they're offering, even as I doubt it matches up with my own aspirations. Richard is hearty and charming. Teddy's no longer involved in the conversation, so much so that he faces the stage the way people do at the beach, pivoting to make sure their direction faces the coming sunset.

Richard, on the other hand, is still engaged. "To be honest, we're already in talks with an agency. But you've got something going on, I can tell you that!"

"Thank you so much."

"So not only can you make films—now we know you're also charming!" I like Richard's smile.

"As are you both! Well, mostly you. Teddy is obviously the less charming between the two of you."

Teddy turns his head toward us at the sound of his name, looks directly at me and says, "What's that?"

"About seventy percent less, give or take," I add.

Richard bursts out laughing. "She's razor-sharp this one. Had you figured out in no time."

Teddy looks at me. "What did you say?"

"I said you're not as charming as Richard."

"Richard is incredibly charming, not exactly fair competition."

"True, you never stood a chance. Why'd you even sign up?"

Something changes in his expression. Maybe I pissed him off? I offer a mischievous smile. He gives me a weird look, but then finally turns to face me.

"Noa." I remind him of my name, in case he'd forgotten it.

"I know," he says quietly.

The music suddenly stops, and the new silence is accompanied by the deafening shriek of microphone feedback. The newlyweds' siblings have prepared some entertaining content: a song-and-dance routine. The guests stay in their seats but listen enthusiastically. A sudden interruption midconversation—is this even interesting? The three of us form a unified front. I stay put and listen, the moment enabling me to somewhat process the situation. I now realize just how much I've had to drink. I sense a kind of slight, uncontrollable tremble through my body, which then turns into a shiver. Teddy notices it. The siblings have reached the chorus again. His eyes remain on me until he sharply turns them elsewhere. I feel a little overexposed, but I'm still enjoying sitting at the table with him, as though we're just two people who happened to stand next to each other during a moment of silence. I watch him: while the table blocks my view of his shoes, I see his legs spread apart, the extravagant wristwatch, palm serenely placed over his knee, ringless fingers.

The song comes to an end and everyone applauds.

"So, how come you haven't made your own film yet?" He was listening after all.

"Because I haven't managed to write it yet."

"Haven't managed? What's it about?"

"It's not something I can explain in a minute."

"How can you write something you can't even pitch?"

"It's complicated."

"Do you know what you want? You need to know precisely what you want."

"Absolutely disagree. If you know precisely what you want at the start, you will ruin the creative process."

"I don't know anything about the creative process."

"I can tell."

"You married?"

"No."

This exchange is happening very swiftly and our eyes are locked throughout.

Richard hasn't kept up with us. He tries to resume the lighthearted chat, gesturing to me: "All right, well, come by the office and we'll have a chat, maybe we'll manage to get something going."

"Sure, I'll give you a call and we'll set a time," I hear myself saying.

"Here you go." Richard hands me his business card. Old school!

Tom's mother then appears, draping her arms around Richard's neck. "I see you've met our Noa. What a great movie! Totally brilliant! This is what I call talent!"

Richard beams with joy. "Yes, we've just met! And we're trying to steal her away to make films for us at Delmar. What do you say about that?" Richard and Tom's mother start talking, and I lean over the table, reaching for Teddy's pack of cigarettes.

"Pass me one." My hand doesn't reach.

"For you, anything."

I look at him and say in absolute seriousness, "Careful now."

He hands me a cigarette and places his hand on his heart, smiling. I bring the cigarette to my mouth and place it between my lips with care. My heart's pounding. We've hardly uttered a word, and I already feel like I'm going to pounce on this man and pull him over to me and I won't loosen my grip, I won't let go, until I swallow him whole, until there's nothing left. In my mind's eye, hyenas leap, their teeth tearing through the exposed flesh of a carcass. His eyes are still fixed on me, and the smile is still there. He tilts his head to the right, gesturing for me to come sit next to him. I get up, circle the table, and take a seat.

"Noa." He says my name.

"Yes." I grab his lighter and light my cigarette.

"The meeting's over. You're free to leave."

"Then why did you call me over here?"

"What's that?" He genuinely didn't hear me, but he then adds, "To part company quietly."

"I don't feel like parting company just yet."

"All right." He allows me to remain by his side and glances around. "How are you finding the wedding so far?"

"I find it delightful and moving. And you?"

"I find it delightful and moving too," he says dryly.

"Can't wait to see how you look when you're not delighted and moved."

He looks at me and laughs. "You're sweet. You are." He retains his smile, displaying a disorganized set of teeth, canines slightly pointing inward, somewhat obscuring the other teeth. I find that mouth so beautiful.

"Well?" I'm impatient.

"Well what?"

"Well, what are you saying?"

"What am I *saying*?" He pauses and I tense up. "Don't listen to Richard."

"Richard said lots of things. Which part shouldn't I listen to?"

"Don't come to work for me."

"Really? That's what you're saying?"

"Yes."

"Then who's going to make all your marine biotech blockbusters?"

"Don't know. Don't care."

"Okay." I pull the ashtray closer. "What makes you say that?"

"Sorry?" He leans in a bit, to hear better.

"I'm asking why would you say that?"

"Why do you think?"

"Well, I guess you have something against me. Or for me."

His eyes are on me. "That's right."

"You only met me three minutes ago."

"Which was enough."

"You're despicable."

"You have no idea." He smiles.

One of the waiters interrupts our conversation but I'm stuck formulating my reply. By the time his eyes return to me, I'm quick to attack, my face close to his. "No, you have no idea. You have no idea who I am and how despicable I can be. Sitting here as if you've claimed ownership over being a dick."

He doesn't bat an eyelash. "You should listen to me."

"Don't want to."

"What do you want, then?"

"I want you to tell me what you have against me or for me."

He smiles again. "I'm all for you."

"So?"

"What?"

"Tell me what you want."

He looks at me, his face lacking any and all emotion, and speaks quietly. "I told you what I want."

"Then say it again, because I didn't get it. Be explicit."

"I want you to get up right now and get out of my sight because I'm dying to fuck you."

Yes. There it is, that's what I was after. "That's more like it."

My friends call me from afar to join them on the dance floor.

"It's okay. Go on," he says.

"Okay, I'm going, but I'll be back," I place my hand on his knee, crossing yet another border, passportless. "And Teddy, don't you dare leave this wedding without telling me."

"Wouldn't dare."

"I mean it."

"Okay." He means it too.

"Good. See you." He watches me as I walk away.

We're dancing. Laughing. And he's there, a colossal weight of a man, right on the other side of the lawn. I occasionally glance in his direction. I can't tell if he sees me, but I sense him watching the whole time. Or maybe not? I drink some more and need to pee, but I'm not sure I can risk it. I don't want to waste another second. And how do I even look? It's been hours since I last checked myself in the mirror—typical that everything would have smeared by now. And what if he goes home while I'm in the restroom? I can't bear the thought. I confidently walk across to their table. Teddy's in the same position, just like he'd promised. Richard isn't there; maybe he went to stand in line for the chocolate fondue.

"Did I miss anything?" I sit beside him, sweating from the dancing.

"No."

"Did you miss me?"

"Yes."

"Good. I have to pee."

"Oh yeah? So do I."

"Lovely. Shall we both go then?"

"Yes."

He rises from the chair and stands tall. He looks at me from above and we walk toward the restrooms. I'm a little too drunk; I keep missing fragments of seconds, tiny skips of time. Once we reach the restrooms, he opens a door to one of the stalls. We walk in, and he glances outside before he shuts the door. We're together, alone. Top secret.

"Free at last!" I call out and hug him. He holds me and it feels so natural that I press myself into him, my head leaning against him as I shove my hand through his shirt and momentarily stroke his bare chest and neck. "Need to pee."

I pull down my pants and underwear and sit on the not-so-clean toilet, but I don't care right now. The stall's really small; he leans on the door and doesn't take his eyes off me.

"Nothing's coming out. It's the excitement. Happens to women too, difficulty peeing in certain situations."

"I know."

"Of course you do."

The trickle begins and we both fall silent and listen to it, looking at each other and smiling. Done. Still sitting down, I take his hand and place my face in his palm. Something happens in that moment, I can sense it. He raises my chin, runs a finger across my jawline, then my lips, and my tongue gently glides over his thumb.

"My turn." His voice is deep and cracked.

I rise, wipe and put my pants back on. We swap places: he stands with his back to me, unzips his pants and takes his cock out. I stand behind him. "You're blocking my view!"

"Nothing to see here, ma'am, go on home."

His arm is leaning against the wall and I peer from under it. I speak to his cock in a hushed shout, as one does when talking to someone at a loud party.

"Pleasure to meet you, I'm Noa!"

"Forget it, he can't hear a thing." Teddy pees and I'm satisfied.

"Very nice. Next time, I'm doing the holding."

"We'll see about that." He zips up his pants. "All right, let's go."

"What? No. Not yet. No way."

"Yes way. Let's go."

"No, no, no! There's a whole world out there."

"Same as here. Out."

"But you said you wanted to. You told me."

"And I also told you to get out of my sight. Come on."

I look at him and feel sorry for being too drunk to persuade him. I attempt it nevertheless. "Nobody knows you're here."

"You and I know, which is plenty."

"Teddy . . . you know this doesn't happen every day."

"I know that. Now forget about it and go back out to the dance floor, find yourself a nice guy and marry him."

"What? Why?"

"Why what?"

"Why do I need to get married?"

"That's usually how it goes."

"Not for me."

"Is that right? How old are you?"

"Thirty-six."

He nods his head, then points at the door. "You go look for him, and then I'll come to your wedding and we'll go pee together again, deal?"

I realize that I'm not going to win this one. "Fine. But then I'm doing the holding."

"Fine."

He stands there, motionless. I do too. He runs his eyes over my body, all the way up until he reaches my eyes and stops.

"I can't. I wish I could, but it's not the right time." He's talking as though he's at a business meeting. I extract his use of the word 'wish' and smile seductively.

"Behave yourself." He means it.

"Okay. But let me tell you, you're making the wrong call here, and there's no woman in this world, in your entire lifetime, who's wanted you as much as I want you."

He suddenly turns serious, leans toward me, his face right above mine. "Enough. Out."

He opens the door, and we exit without anyone noticing. I glance at the mirror to see what he's been looking at. I go over to the bar and ask for some water. I drink and watch as Teddy returns to his table. He's talking to Richard, still standing. They chuckle, and then he picks up his cigarettes and keys and says goodbye. No, this is not happening! The entire sum of my joy vanishes at once, everything is consumed into a great black hole gaping within me and there's no point in anything anymore. How can he just stand there and talk to Richard when I'm still here, when we're still here and we can steal away to a stall or a car or an empty street without anyone ever knowing? How can he leave without making sure he can reach me if he wants to? I suddenly feel very tired.

❯

The following morning my head hurts. I can't stop thinking about him, repeatedly recalling our glorious, all-too-short encounter. Teddy-Teddy-Teddy. I make coffee. Teddy Rosenfeld. Google—there he is. The Delmar Bio Solutions website. Oceanography. I read and learn that the company develops underwater monitoring systems, something about multispectral cameras, something about measuring bodies of water, something biomolecular. I don't get any of it. It seems to be a serious, global corporation, very active, with offices abroad. Here's a photo of him. My heart pounds. He's really something. Smart, quick, beautiful, fat, sexy, despicable, not mine, somewhat mine, enough. The way he said 'enough,' as though I were a child who didn't know when to stop. Well, if he doesn't let me in, then he's better off dead. Oh no, what if he dies? And how old is he? Who does he have? A wife, kids? How do I find out? He's got *me*, but he won't let me in.

Even though he saw. He saw who I am, he loved me immediately, he understood everything. He knows I understand too. I hate him for knowing we both understand, yet still letting me go. How dare he not call me this morning—he can easily get my number—leaving me on my own with the weight of our meeting. Is he thinking about all this? Does he even remember? Of course he does. My entire existence is reduced to the need for being the object of his desire, and all other components of life become redundant.

Later on, during my Friday coffee date with friends, I'm still wrapped up in it. I anxiously wait for Sharon, my best friend in the whole wide world, to be done with her errands and join us, and then I wait for her to finish her casual conversations with everyone and become mine and mine alone, sitting right next to me. Now I can be with Teddy again as I tell her about him, about how he said 'Yes' when I asked if he missed me, how he said 'I wish' and 'Behave yourself.' She likes him. My heart skips a beat when I quietly repeat those words, 'Get out of my sight because I'm dying to fuck you.'

>

My joy turns into severe distress during Friday night dinner at my dad's house.

Whenever I'm here, at this house in the suburbs, I feel the need to confirm that I'm just momentarily passing through and I'll soon resume my own life—a life that is the complete opposite of the vast emptiness filling these rooms. My dad's had a wife for years now—Mina. A quiet, desolate type, fair features and faded hair, not a color in sight. Even her eyes are hueless. Mina's actually harmless and nice enough; she and my dad get along well, and I have a good, drama-free relationship with her.

My brother, Roy, lives with them. He's three years younger than me. He occasionally babysits dogs or plants for people who go away on vacation, or he sleeps over at a friend's place, but I guess living here suits him. For someone who left home at a young age, I find it a bizarre choice to live at your dad's place at the age of thirty-three, but that's just how Roy is.

The clearest advantage of coming over here is that Roy gives me weed. That is, I give him money—usually a bit extra, since he's forever broke—and he takes care of the purchase.

I'm sitting in the kitchen under the fluorescent lights, sipping some water after having refused the juice Mina had offered. Even though I'd lived in this house for years, I still insist on feeling uncomfortable whenever I come over.

I'm holding my phone. It's gone from simmering to boiling, and I have to find a way to write Teddy, talk to him, see him. Explain that I need him to acknowledge me immediately, otherwise something bad might happen. I mean, he's currently somewhere, sitting or standing or lying down. Teddy. All it takes is to think of his name for my heart to start racing, for me to willingly give up everything I have, just to know that he's mine. Especially when I'm here. But I have none of him, and I have to leave it be.

I can't drink booze after yesterday but I shouldn't stay sound of mind, so at least I can get my delivery and get a little high. I go down to the basement—home to my man-child brother, who came out like a pro when he was only sixteen, and maybe since he was so mature for his age back then he remained stuck in perpetual adolescence.

We light up, I mix in tobacco and he doesn't. He tells me about some Austrian he's about to meet tonight, who isn't the guy he'd been with last week, of course, and most likely won't be the guy he'll meet next week. And despite the nature of his love life, in a strange and even logical way, maybe even more than I do, Roy dreams of a family life—2.4 children and a pink picket fence.

Banal conversation, awful food, same tiring dynamic at these meals. At least Roy's making me laugh. My dad—or more like the neurotic cloud through which one could spot the man who used to be my dad—is ceaselessly offering up discussion topics, as though even the briefest moment of silence would testify to the lack of connection among the four unfortunate people sitting here together, around the chicken in instant chicken broth. Mina comes to the rescue and tells us about a Gloria Estefan concert. The central narrative involves a mix-up concerning seat numbers.

But who am I to say anything? It's not like I got married and had a family and now they can come over to my place for a nice Friday night dinner, under a warm light.

›

It's only in the middle of the night that I suddenly get it.

I wake up on the couch at my place, certain that I should quickly eat something sweet and follow it up with something salty. Then, while smoking the remainder of a joint, I come up with the notion of emailing him. It's not that I don't have ways of getting his number, but that seems like an invasion of his privacy, while a mere email is clearly fine. And anyway, Richard had invited me to their office, so I can set up a meeting and just show up there during the week. But it's Friday night, and twenty-four hours ago we were standing together in a tiny stall, and I want a sign of life right now.

Their website doesn't have any personal email addresses, so I find Richard's business card. His email address comprises his initial, then last name, then at sign, company name dot com. If that's the case then Teddy's email must have the same structure. Give it a try. It's 2:13 a.m., a fine hour.

In the subject line I write: Urgent Matter

My heart accelerates. I type:

> Present resolution has not been
> found acceptable by both parties|

I then revise:

> One of the parties has found the
> present resolution to be unacceptable.

> For your immediate action.
> Best, Noa

Another sip of water. Another drag. Send.

That's it, it's sent. Done, over, behind me. Actually ahead of me.

Shit. What have I done? How can I fall asleep when I'm waiting for a reply? And what if he never replies? What if he's asleep? And why am I like this? Why wasn't I granted the kind of personality that can just let go? I freeze, staring blankly. The immaculate silence of late-night hours. What a stupid thing to do.

And then that sweet sound, and the phone's light, and the notification on the screen about a new email, with his name. My knees are trembling. Open it, quick.

> party's demands are

Not even a question mark. But he replied! What are my demands? I answer quickly without overthinking.

> Must hold meeting at
> earliest convenience

Silence. I'm fired up, don't know what to do with myself. I go out to the terrace. He replied! It's cold outside. Walk back in, put the phone down, can't keep holding on to it, sprawl on the couch. *Ping.*

> Okay

Followed by:

> Where are you ?

I can't believe it. What madness is this? He's my kind! And with a question mark! Took the trouble. Is he actually going to come over now? This can't be real. Maybe I should tell him to meet me at a bar? But it's the middle of the night, where can we even go? I send him my address. I'll go downstairs, we'll have a chat in his car. What's my actual plan?

> Coming

I can barely contain the excitement of my success. I look around, the apartment's a little messy. Where do I start? Sip of ouzo straight from the bottle. What will he drink? I have nothing worthy of him here. Pick up scattered socks, empty the ashtray, quickly do the dishes, pause to look in the mirror, clean off makeup smeared under my eyes, put on some lipstick. Go to the bedroom. Straighten the blanket, tidy around. Start to fold the pile of clothes. Take off my shirt, deliberate between two bras.

The quiet knock on the door makes my pulse rush. How is he already here? Forget the bra, quickly back into the T-shirt. Fuck. I can't believe I'm going to open the door and here, there he is, standing tall, well-dressed, in the entryway to my home. Teddy Rosenfeld.

"You beautiful thing," he says, almost gloomily.

I shift to the side a little and he comes in. I shut the door behind him and mumble, "It's all right if I lock the door and throw away the key, right? You wouldn't mind, would you?"

"Nice place, got a terrace too, huh? Very nice. It's pretty, you have good taste. You own it?" He talks fast, I forgot about that.

"No, rented. And I'm a bit tired of it."

He stands in front of me. I'm grinning, pleased. He grins too, must be infectious. We're now both standing, smiling in the middle of the living room. There they are, those teeth I missed so much.

"I can't believe you're here. Can I get you something to drink?"

"Water. Just walked up a lot of stairs. You don't have an elevator."

"It's three flights."

"Felt like five."

"Right."

Teddy wanders around my apartment, inspecting each and every item. A glorious creature has suddenly invaded my home at 3:00 a.m. He scans the book titles on the shelves, looks at a photo of me and Roy as kids, his hands held behind his back for some reason. What animal does he resemble? None. I hand him a glass of water. He drinks and his eyes shift to me, glancing at my bare nipples under the T-shirt. After a look at the bedroom—it's small, so he doesn't even go in—and a quick tour of the terrace, we're back in the living room again. He sits down on the couch with surprising, wonderful ease. I sit down too, cautiously.

"Okay, I'm ready," he says.

"Me too."

"Then go ahead. You said that one of the parties has found the resolution unacceptable."

"That's right, and by the way, the fact that you find it acceptable is also unacceptable."

"So what are you proposing?"

"That the parties negotiate."

"Yes, I got that part. You'll need to specify what your party would find acceptable," he continues, amused.

I feel like a fencer who wants to take off their helmet, put down their sword and tell their opponent, You know what, let's just fuck.

"First of all, it's unacceptable that you tell me not to come work for you."

"Okay, what else?"

"Second, it's impossible that I react to you the way I did and then you just walk away from it. And your reaction to me too."

"Eloquently put."

"I'm tired and confused."

"And what's the reason for that?"

"You are."

"Exactly. So as the one representing my side, I feel the need—and don't get upset now—to guard *your* interests, so that you don't wind up tired and confused in the best case or in a continuous nightmare in the most probable case."

"Of course I'll get upset."

He laughs, leans on his elbow and looks for a lighter to light the cigarette already in his mouth. I get up to fetch one and continue talking. "Your assumption that you guard my interests by withholding yourself from me is misguided and simply wrong, as it makes me miserable."

"You're miserable already?"

"Yes."

"You're fast."

"Yes."

"Had a rough twenty-four hours, Noa?"

"Yes," I say proudly. "And you?"

"See, that's exactly what I mean." He takes a drag and looks at me.

I'm crazy about him and his straightforwardness. "Have the last twenty-four hours been rough on you?" I'm pushing my luck.

"No."

"Of course." I deserved that but I won't give in. "But you did think about me. Say you did or I'll destroy you."

"Yes."

"Yeah?" I'm not yet satisfied.

He looks at me. "Yes, I thought about you."

I smile a victorious smile, and then turn serious. "Let's talk for real for a minute."

"Okay."

"Where are you at?"

"How do you mean?"

"Family? Relationship?"

"I'm not available." Shit, shit, shit.

"Married?"

"Not quite. Long story." There's hope yet.

"Then tell me."

"What do you need to know?" He ashes.

"Can't you just speak frankly?"

"I am. I'm not going to unload my entire history right now."

"Okay, but you do need to tell me things. Like, some things."

"I have two boys." He looks me straight in the eye. "Well, they're not boys anymore. Two sons."

"How old? What are their names?"

"Adrian's twenty-six, Milo's twenty-one."

"So really not boys anymore! Show me pictures."

"You want to see them? Really?" Something in his face changes when he mentions his boys.

"Yes."

"Hang on."

He pulls out his phone and then the glasses in his breast pocket, searches for photos. I watch him as he transforms in front of my eyes. I take the cigarette from his hand. He looks through his phone. In the meantime, I examine the elongated strands of hair slightly curving over the back of his neck. I want to touch it. He finds a photo and shows me.

"That's Milo, my sweet boy. With his dog, Xerox." His sweet boy Milo really is sweet, and he's got Teddy's eyes. Same smile, same dimensions.

"He does look sweet. Looks like you. And Adrian?"

"A photo of Adrian . . ." he mumbles to himself. "Not an easy task. Wait."

He searches through his phone, and I take the opportunity to inspect every inch of this man's beautiful face.

"Here, that's Adrian." The photo shows a young, skinny guy with a serious gaze. "Adrian's brilliant, a true talent."

"It's nice for me to see them."

"Is it?" He's not entirely certain for some reason.

"Yes. And your wife?"

"Which one?"

I just look at him and wait for him to continue. He puts the phone down, takes a breath and answers, speaking quickly. "My first wife, Alice, Adrian's mother. Then there's Monique, Milo's mother, who wasn't my wife, we never married. Then there's Lara, my second wife, soon to be ex."

"Oh."

"You asked."

"That's right, I did." I try to gather my thoughts. "So what's the deal with Lara?"

"It's over, we're over." He runs his hand through his hair. "Finished."

"When?"

"Not too long ago."

I'm flooded by a sense of alienation. Up until that moment, I hadn't really accounted for his past, all the women who ever loved him, whom he loved. The fifty-five years he's already lived. And who am I? I stub out the cigarette, slightly extending the act in order to hide from him for a moment. He notices.

"You ask too many questions."

"What else is there for me to do?"

"Don't know."

"Is that why you said 'I wish' and 'it's not the right time' at the wedding? Because of Lara?"

"It's not the right time for a number of reasons, I won't get into that now."

"Why should I care about now?"

"What do you mean?"

"I'm looking at the bigger picture."

"Oh yeah? Is that what you're doing?" Him and his smile.

"What, so there's no room for me in your life?"

"No."

"Nothing?"

"Nothing. And you're gorgeous. You are."

"Then . . . let's be something else."

"I don't know anything else."

"We can be friends."

He smiles and closes his eyes, leans his head back and rubs his forehead. "I'm beat."

"You're here, at my place. Is this an illusion?" I glide my bare foot up, lightly nudging his thigh, as though checking whether he's real. He places his warm hand on my foot, caressing it. Shivers run through my entire body.

"God, your skin," he says quietly.

I sit up and lean into him. His scent. It's a wonderful, enthralling scent. I get closer to his neck, run my lips over it, tasting him. "What is it about you? Why am I so attracted to you?" I ask.

He turns to face me and we're very close. His mouth is an inch away from mine. He casually runs his hand up my spine, holding the back of my neck for a moment, before sliding it all the way back down to the exposed gap between my shirt and waistband.

"So what do we do?" I ask quietly.

"Nothing. I'm leaving." He pulls his hand away.

"We're not going to fuck?"

"No." He's way too resolute.

"You come over in the middle of the night and there's no fucking?"

"Can you believe it?"

"No, I can't."

He leans over, about to get up. I rush to stand first. "No, you can't be leaving now. It's tragic and it makes zero sense."

"Tragic!" He gets up. "Remind me how tragedies end?"

He walks toward the door, I follow him. "Then I'm coming over to your office. I'll set up a meeting with Richard."

He gets to the door and turns to me. I stare at him, awaiting approval.

"Do whatever you want." He keeps his eyes on me. "Just do me a favor, will you? If you do come, wear a bra, because I won't be able to do this again. Good night."

He opens the door and steps into the hallway.

"Teddy, c'mon."

"Go to sleep."

"I won't be able to fall asleep now."

"Then stay up."

He shuts the door behind him. I turn and look at the living room. He forgot his cigarettes.

›

It's noon on Saturday and his cigarette pack is the only evidence he was here. I go out to the terrace and light one. I'm Teddy, a very important man, smoking a cigarette. What's so important about me? Unclear.

I want to remember everything, what he said and what I replied, don't want to lose a single detail. Why does that even matter to me? I can recall his scent, how his skin felt.

Am I really going to his office? Because then I'll get to see him. Do I even want to work there? What have I got to do with a job at some office?

It's afternoon and I decide to leave the house so as not to lose my mind. Ever since my childhood I always found these hours to be unbearable.

Mornings are good because there's hope, noon is pleasant because there's still potential for something incredible to happen, evenings are calm because you can already let go of all that exhausting hope and also be glad that nothing terrible happened, and nighttime is immaculate freedom. But afternoons—a disgusting time of day. It's even worse during weekdays, that time when everyone leaves work and goes back to their families, traveling that same familiar route, and if they don't do drugs then I really have no idea what incentive they could possibly have.

I go downstairs and walk toward the movie theater. This is a thing I do. Once I arrive, I stand there and inspect the movie posters—not in an attempt to choose what movie to watch, heaven forbid, but rather to remind myself that people make movies and that I don't. Then I take the long way back home.

During my first year at university I made a short, a drama which came out so bad that it paralyzed me, and I then spent the following two years only working on other people's productions. Then I wrote a script during the summer between my third and fourth year. A comedy. We shot it, I produced. It was my final project and it worked. It opened doors to festivals around the world and even won first prize for a student film at the Toronto International Film Festival. There was great joy. Naturally followed by a huge crash.

It's hard to believe that ten years have passed since then and I'm still just walking potential aiming at a singular, all-too-rare scenario. I sometimes think that I've attached myself to chronic failure and am still refusing to let go. One might call it *megalomanic depression*: there's a voice in my head telling me I'm good, and there's another saying that I'm not worthy. Both are strong; both are correct. Which one do I trust more? But, in the meantime, still on my way back home, one of the movie posters sticks in my head, and I tell myself the story I'd like that movie to tell, fully aware that I'd have enjoyed the real movie far less.

In the evening, I feel proud of myself for having managed to keep from writing him during the day. Before I go to sleep, I decide to call Richard in the morning and set up a meeting.

›

But the following day I postpone my phone call to Delmar. It's the first day of the workweek, and who am I to bug them now? My visit is surely in the dampest basement of their priority list.

"Who do you think you are?!" the actress roars with demonstrated intensity as the soundman pulls the headphones away from his head, still maintaining his frozen expression. I peer into the director's monitor through the little gap between him and his assistant.

"Should we ask for a less exaggerated take?" she whispers to him, rightly so. There's no way he thinks that this is usable—who talks like that?

"No, it's great." The director stands up. "Cut!"

The first assistant director appears out of nowhere as usual. "Cut! So we have it?" She then looks at me. "Noa, why aren't you on the crew monitor, how many times do I need to tell you?"

"Sorry, you're right, you're right." I quickly walk away and head for the prop warehouse to organize the items for the following scene. Maybe it really is time for me to leave this place.

›

The next morning I take a short break, put my sunglasses on and leave the studio. I light a cigarette and call Richard.

"Delmar Bio Solutions, how can I help you today?" The voice of a young woman who sounds like she couldn't help anyone, not today and not ever.

"Hi, this is Noa Simon, I'm looking for Richard Harrington."

"Richard? What's your name again?"

"Noa Simon."

"Okay, regarding what?"

"He asked me to set up a meeting with him."

"Regarding what?" she repeats with the exact same intonation. Bitch!

"Regarding film work. Can you please put me through or have him call me when he's free?"

"Yes, one sec, I'll write it down. Hold on." What is she doing there?

Going to get a pen and paper? "Hello? Okay, yeah, what was the name again?"

"Noa Simon," I mutter icily.

"What's the number?"

I give her all the details, hang up and cuss. I glance at the business card and regret not having called Richard's cell phone. I don't feel like joining that company if this is the kind of person they hire to man their desks.

The rest of the day is strange and upsetting. I feel like I want to leave my job, this show, and at the same time I'm filled with horrific unwillingness to start something new, at my age, at some desolate company with fluorescent lights and mean-girl gossip and lunch breaks with depressing, uninspiring chitchat. I'm better off staying here; at least the people are more like me. Almost all of them fantasize about making their own movie or series someday. Maybe a presence like Teddy's could help me advance in life, or at least not stay stuck in one place. I get tired and go for a nap on the bedroom set during lunch. I fall asleep despite the ruckus around me. A moment before the lunch break ends, my phone rings, waking me up.

"Hello?" I answer, disoriented.

"Miss Noa Simon! How are you? It's Richard Harrington speaking!"

My heart is racing because I just woke up from a nap but also from the thought that Teddy might know about Richard calling me, maybe he's involved, maybe he's even sitting right next to him with his amused smile.

"Hi, Richard. I'm good, thanks, how are you?"

"Not bad at all! I was glad to see you called. When are you coming to visit us?"

"That's just it, I wanted to set a time. When works for you?"

The first AD calls everyone back from lunch and I want to get away from the noise, so I walk in the opposite direction as the rest of the crew. I leave the dark studio and come out into the bright noon light without my sunglasses, having left them on the fake bed.

"Whenever you want! We're here. Come by today, tomorrow, whatever works."

'We.' My thoughts ping-pong between today and tomorrow, trying to figure out what's best for me. I obviously want to go there right this minute. I don't want to wait until tomorrow, get ready and try to look pretty and then show up and Teddy won't even be there. And maybe it's better if he's not there. Though I really feel like seeing him right now.

"Well, what time are you there till? I'm at the studios till five. Your offices are in the city center, right?"

He gives me the address and tells me he'll be staying at the office late today, so he'll wait for me. So I guess it'll just be him? I go back in and am met with a scolding from the first AD.

"Where's Noa, for the love of God?!" And then once she spots me: "Seriously, sweetie, are you insane? We were back three minutes ago!"

Traffic jam. Of course. Now I'm really antsy about getting there. I am assessing various offices in my mind's eye, picturing hideousness illuminated by green fluorescents. Horrifying. The cars drag by slowly, it's 5:45 p.m. Now I'm envisioning a beautifully designed office, expensive furniture and rare artwork on the walls. Light a smoke.

>

The building's tall and its exterior makes it hard to guess which of my imagined options is the right one. 26th floor. Elevator with a mirror, put some lipstick on. I look like I've come from a full day's work, and something about my beaten appearance makes me happy.

The office isn't all that bad, leaning more toward the nicely decorated look, though lacking any rare artwork. Most important: the lighting's pleasant. Is he here? He isn't? I swiftly survey the place. A thoroughly kempt young woman is sitting behind a curved table at the entrance. I walk over to her. She lifts her head and smiles courteously.

"Hi! Are you Noa?" She's nice and I nod my head with relief. "Richard is expecting you. He's in his office, follow me." She gets up and leads the way in her impressive high heels, and I no longer feel pleased with my appearance, I now feel more like a dirty kid after a Girl Scout meeting hurrying after her elegant mother.

"What would you like to drink?"

"Just water, thanks." I wonder where Teddy's office is. I think I can pick up his scent.

"Here we are, this is Richard." She lightly knocks on the door. I walk in and he gets up, comes around his big black desk, reaches me and gives me a warm hug.

"Noa! It's great to see you again! Did you have trouble getting here? Any traffic?"

He has two plain armchairs at the side of the room. We sit down. The view from the window is gorgeous, and it's almost completely dark outside. The young woman from reception returns with water and a jug of iced tea. They have glass cups, not paper or plastic.

The conversation with Richard flows pleasantly. We talk about the type of work they require and how to get me involved. I try to figure out if they really need someone for this position, and Richard tells me about the media department he wants to set up for the company. I feel good and I like the way he treats me with respect. It's insane that this is all based on a wedding video. After half an hour's chat I allow myself to bring up Teddy's name.

"What about Teddy, does he know about all this?"

"Teddy? Oh yeah, sure, of course he knows. He doesn't really deal with the media aspects and all that. But he'll obviously weigh in, and he'll have thoughts on the rate."

I don't have all that much oxygen right now. I look at the door. "Is he here? In the office?"

"No, he's out."

He's out. I'm jealous of wherever he is right now and I would kill to know if he knew that I was coming, but I keep myself from asking. I feel a little bit calmer knowing he's not here, alongside the disappointment of not getting to see him, of him not getting to see me.

Richard and I decide that he'll talk to Teddy and they'll try to define the role and come back to me with an offer. He walks me out and we pass by another big room. The door's open and I can see only a bit of it, but I know it's Teddy's office, and I feel bad that I can't go inside and just be there for a while, go through his things, search for secrets, examine his handwriting, sit in his chair.

When I get downstairs to the lobby I locate the company sign among the various names on the board. I take a photo of the name "Delmar Bio Solutions," and without overthinking it, I email it to Teddy.

I come out to the parking lot, light a cigarette and head to my car.

〉

Back at my place, even after a long shower, there's still no reply. What does this mean? I already know he's the type of guy who checks his emails the moment he gets them. I roll myself a joint, call Sharon, and tell her about the last few days' events. Afterward I watch two episodes of a series and nearly fall asleep. Brush my teeth, plug my phone in to charge in the living room, and get into bed. The second I close my eyes, I hear the ping. I know it's him. I get up and go to the phone. I was right.

> How was it

Immediately reply:

> It was good. Sounds really
> interesting and I was treated
> nicely. And you weren't there.

I sit down on the couch; the apartment's dark. He replies straightaway.

> Good

He's giving off the feeling that he approves. I don't fully get it. I need clear validation. I take the fleeting opportunity for a dialogue, think up some sort of phrasing that won't push his back against the wall.

> Would you rather not
> have me working for you? |

I type it but I don't hit send. It's too risky. Not that I don't have some serious misgivings regarding this job. But I don't want to present him with all these emotions. Enough. I'll go to sleep and won't reply this time. Good night, Teddy, I reply in my mind.

I get back into bed, but sleep is now a distant thing. Maybe he's angry at me because I disregarded what he'd said. Maybe 'Good' was said in a dismissive tone and I'd just misread it. After twenty minutes of anxiety, I return to the couch.

> Are you angry?

I ask in a simple, direct manner, aware of the fact that I might come across as somewhat childish.

He answers immediately.

> No . Everythfing's fine go
> to sleep

I smile and start crying, because he understands what I'm going through and chooses to calm me down and even writes me something intimate like 'go to sleep.'

> Okay

I get into bed and cry until it's hard to breathe, so I force myself to stop and really go to sleep.

+

My dreams have a repeating motif of movement: it's a sensation I hate, like trying to walk in the ocean, the great pressure of water compressing against my body and I can hardly move forward, just very slowly and with effort, so I desperately search for bodies to grab on to in order to pull myself ahead. The problem is that not everything in my path is steady enough. Everything that looks anchored, a rock or some furniture, dislocates the moment I grab on to it, so I stay in the same place.

>

At around 11:00 a.m., while carrying a pile of props through one of the studio hallways, my phone rings. Unknown caller. My heart skips a beat. I put everything down on the floor at once and answer as fast as I can.

"Hello."

"Noa, it's Teddy."

"Hey." No oxygen.

"You busy? Where are you?"

"At work, filming."

"Very industrious. What do they pay you there?"

"Teddy . . ." I interrupt his fast way of talking. "This is our first phone call."

He laughs. "That's right. Write it down so we'll remember to celebrate it."

"Tattooing everything, don't worry. All the dates of our important moments, right here on my thigh."

"I don't want to talk about your thigh."

"You want to talk about how much they're paying me?"

"Yes."

"Okay. I make . . . something like 45K."

"And how much of that do you clear?"

"Don't know. A lot less?"

"You're really something. Well, listen, come work for us for 100K. Settle everything else with Richard. You'll be in charge of your own schedule, you report to Richard, and to me, of course, which is the same thing. And do me a favor, don't talk to other people about how much you make, keep it between us. You get budgets approved by me, and you'll have an expense account for travel, equipment, whatever you need." He pauses and I'm breathless. "Are you there?"

"Yes."

"Good, best of luck. Happy to have you."

"Thanks . . . happy to be had." Am I?

There's a silence and I realize I'm the one who's supposed to fill it with words, but I can't. I never imagined that this is how it would be. It's too good, something doesn't add up. I hear him taking a deep breath.

"Okay, well, talk to me if you need anything. When can you start?"

"I'll have to give my notice here and see how quickly I can leave."

"Okay, do what you need to do."

"I'll talk to them and let you know."

"No problem."

I want to say more things, but I can't get beyond the only words in my head:

DAMN
I
LOVE
YOU

I'm standing in the dark hallway all wide-eyed, and I feel as though the hand of God has suddenly appeared from above and chosen me. "I just want to say," I start, but am suddenly unsure about the phrasing, "that if after a few months we see that it's not working out for some reason, then I'll understand and, I don't know . . . You shouldn't feel obligated, if it doesn't work out."

He keeps quiet for a moment and then says, "Okay."

"Okay. Thank you."

"Don't mention it. We'll be in touch. Bye, Noa."

"Bye."

What was that? We spoke on the phone: he called; he doubled what I make; it's happening.

After a moment of astonishment and excitement, I'm suddenly overtaken by a dreadful sensation. All the joy dissipates, and instead I feel a huge loss. I walk into the prop warehouse, put the stuff down and sit on a dusty chair, trying to gather my thoughts.

Of course. How have I only just figured this out? There's no more Teddy and me. There's no more something that never existed, even though it did, a little bit. Now I'm not allowed to tread in that direction at all; now he'll be my boss and I'm supposed to behave and respect boundaries and he'll be close to me without being mine. He'll be in front of me, falling in love with women who heeded him and didn't come to work for him. Now all of a sudden I think the reason he didn't want me to work for him to begin with is that maybe he did intend to sleep with me and be with me for a bit, but not if I'm his employee. He said that so explicitly, how did I not get it? I'm such an idiot.

2

Don't Burn Any Bridges

+

nothing will come out of this ❯ be authentic ❯ nothing will come out
of this ❯ be authentic ❯ nothing will come out of this ❯ be authentic ❯
nothing will come out of this ❯ be authentic ❯ but nothing will come out
of this ❯ so be authentic ❯❮

❯❯

I start work on October 9.

On my first day, Teddy isn't in.

On my second day, I see that the door to his office is shut. An hour
goes by until it finally opens and he comes out, accompanied by two
British guests. Our encounter is very brief.

"You here already?" he asks matter-of-factly as he passes me, then
turns and adds with a minimal smile, "Welcome aboard."

He's in England the following few days and I'm fine with that, it
allows me time to concentrate. I need to get to know the material, plan
things. The loss I'd felt during our phone call has now completely faded
away.

At the beginning of my second week, something strange happens.

I'm sitting in the boardroom watching old Delmar promotional
footage on my laptop. I've situated myself there because I've not been
given a permanent desk yet. Maureen, Teddy's secretary—an irritating individual—is using various excuses to delay the matter, and even

though I'm not sure why she's doing that, I still don't feel like listening to her explanations, mainly because her perfume is vile. Three board members enter the room a few minutes before 11:00 a.m., Maureen and her perfume following suit. I immediately get up and start clearing my stuff from the table, which still doesn't prevent her from telling me directly, "Noa, you'll need to clear the boardroom, weekly meeting's starting soon."

Thank you so much for enlightening me, really.

"Good morning!" Richard walks in, tanned and fresh as a daisy, as though he'd just spent the weekend on his yacht with this month's playboy bunny. "Ah—so you've already met Noa Simon? We've just acquired her!" he boasts, winking at everyone as they smile back at him. "Noa's a very talented filmmaker, she'll be setting up our media department."

He introduces me and I shake everyone's hand, trying to focus on new names and simultaneously collect my stuff. Out of the corner of my eye, I see Teddy through the glass as he strides toward the room.

"You joining our meeting?" Him and his sexy backdoor smile— good luck getting back to work after that.

"No . . . I'm just getting my things, excuse me." My office persona is different from the person he'd met at the wedding. Despite the voices around us, he manages to speak quietly and only to me.

"How are you?" he asks genuinely, looking straight into me.

"Okay." I give a shy smile, and he stays planted in front of me.

"Why don't you have your own desk?" he asks, as if I'm the one at fault.

"I'm getting one today," I improvise. He should be asking himself that question.

"What's that?" He points.

"That's my laptop."

"Your own laptop?"

"Yeah."

"Why did you bring your own laptop? What make is this? How old is it?"

"I don't know, maybe six years?" Why is he interrogating me?

He goes pensive for a moment. Someone asks him something, Teddy replies, and I take the opportunity to sneak out of the room. I don't feel comfortable interacting with him in front of everyone, especially not this morning when he's exceptionally handsome.

I place my things in a corner and go downstairs for a smoke. Maybe I'll get another coffee. A ping interrupts my thoughts. I check my phone. The name Teddy Rosenfeld appears on the screen.

> Where'd you go

That's what he writes? Maybe he's a dimwit. Or a genius dimwit.

> Downstairs for a smoke.
> Aren't you in a meeting?

> I am. Come get me when
> you're back up

> I don't feel right
> interrupting the meeting.

> Come by the boardroom
> I'll come out

I stub out my cigarette and go back in. Goddamn building, repulsive elevators, it's just not for me, working at this sort of place. I go to the kitchenette for a glass of water first, then I head toward the boardroom and stop in the hallway, so he can see me through the glass. He notices and immediately gets up and leaves the room, shutting the door behind him.

"Listen, go ask Maureen for the key to my apartment. I have a laptop for you to use, go get it." He's nibbling on cashews and offers me some from his hand.

"Isn't she in the boardroom with you?" I grab a single cashew.

"No, she's back at her desk, go get it."

"I don't want to."

"Don't want to what?"

"Don't want to go to Maureen and ask for a key to your apartment."

"Why not? You know what, I'll give you my key and you give it back later. Come on." He's already walking away, and I follow him, feeling a bit out of control. We pass Maureen, and her eyes lift away from her screen and follow us without her head moving.

This is the first time I'm in his office. He lifts his jacket from his chair to retrieve the keys.

"What sort of laptop do you have? I'm not following," I say.

"A new one, a good one. Go get it so you have it here and you don't have to carry yours back and forth every day."

I look at him, not managing to fully understand his move.

"I can ask IT to issue me a computer."

"You want to stand in line at IT?"

"Okay. Just bring the new one here tomorrow."

"Why tomorrow?" he asks, and eats another cashew, utterly convinced that this is precisely what should be happening right now. "Here, Matt will take you, Matt!" I turn around and see the company driver leaning on the reception desk.

"Aye, aye, Captain!" Matt rushes over to Teddy with a wide grin. "What do we need?"

"This is Noa, have you two met? Take her to my place, she needs to get something, then bring her back here. It's this key"—he shows me a set of keys and hands it to me—"I need to go back in. Thanks." He walks away with his cashews.

›

I'm sitting next to Matt because I'd find it weird to sit in the back once I've met the driver. He asks some questions, makes casual conversation. He's the type who enjoys talking for talking's sake: he'll turn left here because the road's closed ahead, these radio guys aren't what they used to be, look at that shithead blocking the entire lane.

I text Teddy.

> Are you for real?
>
> What's wrong
>
> Sending me to your place? You didn't even explain where the laptop is
>
> Get there call me

I get out of the car and walk toward the building.

"Noa." He answers the call using my name.

"What's the code to get in?"

"Two-four-oh-six-star. You in?"

"Wait." I push the numbers, the buzzer goes. "There."

"Good. Go up, ninth floor."

"Say."

"Yes?"

"Where are you, still in the meeting?" I get into the elevator and press 9.

"No, I'm in my office."

"Your elevator has signal?"

"Yeah."

"So we won't get disconnected?"

"We won't. When you get there ring the doorbell, check that no one's in."

"What do you mean? Someone might be there? I'm not going in."

"What's the matter?"

"Why did you send me over to your place when you're not there and when someone else might be there—and like who, housekeeping?" The elevator door opens. There's his door, I can see it, ROSENFELD.

"No, Betty's not in today."

"Who's Betty, the cleaning lady?"

"Yeah. Milo's there sometimes. What's the problem?"

"You are not sufficiently sane."

"Just ring the doorbell, he's probably at his girlfriend's."

I ring the doorbell, wait, hear Teddy telling Maureen something in a businesslike tone. "I think there's no one home."

"Good, get in, office is to your right."

"No alarm, Teddy?" I inquire while pushing the key in and opening the door.

"There is, yeah."

"Good thing I asked."

"On your left as you go in, four-nine-two-five-two-six."

The alarm's off and I shut the door. Hello, Teddy's house. Shit, this place is way too gorgeous. I guess I hoped it'd be impressive but tacky, so that he would seem less perfect, but I'm doomed. This apartment's so gorgeous he should go fuck himself.

"Beautiful," I say quietly, peering left toward the vast living room: paintings, books, pleasant lighting, plants, large wooden dining table, glass doors leading to a balcony facing west, iron stairwell leading to yet another floor.

"Whatever you do, don't go upstairs. There's a lady living up there who's missing a few screws."

"What?" I freeze, and he laughs. I hear a loud argument commence through the phone.

"Found it?"

"Wait." I enter his home office, very tidy.

"You see a black cabinet?"

"Yeah."

"There's a box inside with a MacBook, see it?"

"Yeah." I find the pretty box. "How many of these do you have lying around?"

"As many as you need. Take it—wait a sec, Noa—no, no, Phil, they've got biomolecular indicators there, they'll have to bring someone from Hexa-Labs for that sort of installation—Noa, what else? You okay there?"

I close the box I'd started opening. "Yes. Anything else I should take? Charger? Mouse? I don't know."

"Yeah, take the mouse, there's a box on my desk. Charger's in the laptop box. Found the mouse?"

I grab it and leave the room. Instead of walking to the front door I intentionally continue through the hallway and reach his bedroom. Huge bed, spacious room, and the loveliest corner: a window reaching all the way to the floor, an armchair, and a low coffee table. And a view. What a view. "Teddy! This is beautiful."

"What is?"

"Your bedroom, this little corner with your philosopher's armchair."

"How'd you get there, got lost on the way out?"

"No, I came over to look at your bedroom."

"What did you do that for?" he asks slowly. I can hear voices still arguing in the background. Why is he keeping me on the line?

"I want to get naked and get in your bed. Just for a couple of minutes, then I'll get dressed and go back down to Matt."

He falls silent and I wait.

"Okay," he approves, and I'm not entirely sure he's heard what I said.

"I'm really going to do it."

"I see." Oh, he heard all right. "This isn't easy for me."

"Nothing you can do about it."

"Come on then, let's get it over with."

"I'm taking my clothes off, putting you on speaker." I quickly get undressed and under his covers. "There, I'm in." I can hear that he's with me even though he's not saying anything. "What are you doing?"

"Concentrating."

I burst out laughing. "It's cozy here! I can smell you."

He stays silent for a moment longer, then quietly and quickly says, "Okay, enough now, get out of there, it's driving me crazy."

"Crazy how?"

"Get out."

"Okay. I'll just leave a few drops of pee, so you'll know I was here." I'm amused.

"What did you say?" I think he heard me the first time.

"I said I will pee in your bed."

I hear him taking a deep breath. "Sure, do what you need to do."

I get up and put the phone on speaker again while putting my clothes back on.

"You remember the alarm code?"

"No."

"Four-nine-two-five-two-six."

"Okay."

"See you soon."

I'm sitting next to Matt and smiling. I think about the fear I'd felt before going into his apartment as opposed to the way I behaved once inside.

I'm trying to figure out when it actually happens, how does it work, that moment when I just shift all of a sudden.

When I get back to the office I go straight to him.

"Idiot," he says, but his eyes are smiling.

I bat my lashes with exaggerated innocence as I hand him his keys, stalling my fingers over his for a moment. "You're messing with the wrong people."

"I'm starting to realize that."

"Thanks for the laptop."

"You're welcome."

›

Three days later, I see his first wife.

I already have my own desk. Maureen had let me choose between two desks situated in the main work area and I chose the better one, meaning the one overlooking Teddy's office. I'm sitting there trying to understand how the new laptop works, but my attention's lost when I notice an attractive, well-dressed woman standing with Teddy in front of his office. I watch them from afar. They're talking and I can see the years they've spent together. She's laughing at something, and he introduces her to an employee who happens to pass by. He places his hand on his first wife's shoulder when he introduces her and a swell of jealousy overcomes me. Despite the distance, his eyes momentarily come across mine. I give him a little smile, as though saying I know it's her. He smiles at me, then turns to look back at her.

››

An eventless week passes until one day, at around 2:00 p.m., Teddy comes out of his office all of a sudden—full-blown presence—and calls out for Richard to gather everyone in the boardroom. He ransacks the cupboard and pulls out glasses and drinks, pours high-end whiskey, everyone must partake immediately. And if anyone doesn't want to then they can get back to work or go home. Naomi, an engineer I've befriended, compliments the whiskey and immediately receives two bottles. The room becomes filled with contagious excitement. I walk over to Richard to ask why we're celebrating. Teddy's on the other side of the room, cheerfully talking to some employees. Richard says nothing's happened to justify this event.

"So what I'm witnessing is the CEO's psychotic episode?"

Richard laughs. "Let's just say that even if there is a reason to celebrate, he's the only one who knows what it is."

At some point Teddy walks up to me. "And how about you?"

"I'm okay. Trying to acclimate."

"Seems to me like you've acclimated just fine."

"What are we celebrating?"

"It's in your honor"—he's making it up on the spot—"but it's a secret. We won't tell them."

I gather up the courage. "You coming for a smoke?"

"Yeah okay. We can smoke in my office, let's go."

We leave the boardroom. I'm glad I offered and he accepted and we can smoke in his office and get some time alone. He leads and I follow—but dammit, Jamie's right behind us.

Jamie feels right at home in Teddy's office. He opens the window and she picks the big armchair. She's sexy: tanned skin and lightened hair, peroxide dry. She dresses corporate style: pencil skirts, high heels, lace bras peeping through her expensive button-downs. She acts carefree and yet is filled with self-importance, as if she's totally overworked but she still went out drinking last night and so now she has a sexy little hangover.

Teddy doesn't seem troubled by the scenario; you could even say he's pleased. That annoys me, but I don't want to give myself away, so I concentrate on looking as though none of this is on my mind. For all I care they can think my head is a desolate wasteland with an occasional tumbleweed passing by—as long as they have no idea they're all I can think about. The charm that emanated from Teddy only ten minutes ago has faded, especially now that he's got Jamie out of his chair. She stays to lean over the armrest, occupying her territory. We're already smoking, I lean my shoulder against the window frame, and the three of us have a casual chat about nothing in particular. Teddy asks her to press a painful spot on his back for him, around the shoulder blade area, and she eagerly complies and says something that obviously means she's done this for him before. He enjoys it, indulging in the pain relief, and I watch them, knowing fully that this little display is for my benefit.

What I see before me now is a Teddy that I'm able not to like; I know this defense mechanism of mine—immediately shift to hating someone to avoid any uncomfortable feelings. So I concentrate on not hating. The cigarette's nearly done, but I'm not going to leave them on their own, because what point does this interlude have if I'm not here to witness it? I owe him this. I consider how it would have been if it were only the two of us, but I'm forced to stop fantasizing when Jamie hugs Teddy and kisses him on the cheek.

"What a boss, huh?" She looks at me with a genuine, radiant smile and adds, "Best boss ever!"

I'm not charmed.

I don't bother answering, and he gives me an amused look, which obviously irritates me, and now we're stubbing our cigarettes out to go back to the boardroom. The ceremony has come to an end, everyone please rise for the national anthem.

+

I had friends who were boys growing up, it's not like I didn't. It just took some time for me to figure out how it would work. For example, during the summer break between seventh and eighth grade, I went with a friend to Backwoods Kids summer camp. On the first day there, she threw up and went home. I remained on my own and thought—I'm screwed. How will I survive without her? I was wrong. The days were glorious, totally guilt-free, and full of discovery: holding hands with tough-guy Johnny, falling in love with sensitive Greg, having an affair with the pretty boy from the Italian exchange group, who for some reason constantly walked around with a toothbrush stuck in his mouth. It was wonderful. Except for one not-quite-wonderful thing that also happened there.

Over that summer, my mother renewed her attempts to reconnect with me after a few years of my adamant refusal to see her. When she heard I was going away to summer camp, she called and suggested she come for a visit. Why would I want that? This was a no-parent zone. I declined. But one day, as the bus brought us back to the campsite from a day trip, I saw her standing in the car park, waiting for me with her then boyfriend. Greg asked me, "Is that your mom?" I immediately said, "No!" and he said, "But you have the same hair."

I did not take it well. I actually didn't take it at all. I didn't even take a popsicle when she brought an entire box of those orange ones for everyone, an act I interpreted as an attempt to ingratiate herself with my friends, so I'd look like an ungrateful daughter.

I asked her to leave.

After she cried and drove off, the security guy at the entrance to the campsite told me something along the lines of "That's your mother. No matter what, she'll always be your mother." I stood there for two hours trying to defend myself: my mother had done terrible things and didn't deserve my time; I had told her not to come and she did anyway; I'd only just started trying to trust her again, so why ignore me when I'd explicitly said no. "She's just repeating the same mistakes!" I raged. It was already evening, and all I can recall is that he was gentle and patient and quiet, and repeatedly said, "Don't burn any bridges," and that we stopped talking because the camp guides sent one of the kids to tell me that the entire camp could hear me shouting.

»

"What's up with you? Are you pissed off?"

"Yes."

That's the beginning of a conversation that leads to us leaving the office in the middle of a workday, three weeks after I started there.

During this horrid Monday, the last day of October, I realize that one of the projects' deadlines has been postponed because "the project's being deferred," according to Hailey—she's a project manager working closely with Richard—who then adds, "I'm pretty sure I told you." No, you didn't tell me, you fucking bitch.

I'm in the office kitchenette wondering how to kill my hunger, because I've been so annoyed that I haven't eaten anything since this morning. I feel useless and anxious, and something about these feelings reminds me of my dad's incompetence, which is a shame because this association feels extra uncomfortable when it merges with the image of Teddy as he enters the room.

"What's up with you? Are you pissed off?"

"Yes."

"Why? What happened?"

"Nothing, someone pissed me off is all."

"So you're not nice to me because someone pissed you off?"

"What? No, I'm not nice to you regardless," I say icily. He gives me a smile.

"Okay, so what's the plan?"

"Wait for this stupid day to be over."

"Who pissed you off?"

"Doesn't matter."

"Well, day's ending soon."

"It's one o'clock."

"So what should we do?"

What does he mean? What's with him today? "What's with you?"

"Nothing, you're too good."

"You are too."

"I'm good too? Then let's go, we're leaving. I'll make a quick call and we'll go. No, forget it—I'll make the call on the way. Come on, you have a bag? Jacket? Something?"

I'm looking at him, not fully understanding what he wants. The truth is I do understand what he wants, but I don't allow myself to consider the possibility that we're about to spend some time together, so I refuse to cooperate, even on the level of comprehension.

"Where are we going?" The surprise makes my voice come out all flat.

He's already walking away and I'm following him yet again, seeing nothing but his back and barely hearing him saying, "As though it matters where we're going."

In the elevator I stand a little too close, filled with intimate excitement, like a kid who just found treasure on the beach a moment before she calls everyone to come see. We hail a taxi, I go in first and he follows, he gives the driver an address I don't know.

"You hungry?" he asks.

"I was, now not really."

"Aren't you cold?"

"I didn't dress right today. So, food? We can go eat, sure."

"Yeah, we're going to this great place, you've never heard of it, and that's a good thing. Japanese, really great."

"That's twice great."

"You keeping count?"

I nod and look out the window. His phone rings. He holds the phone slightly away from him, glances at the screen, and answers with a short, aggressive "So?" He continues the conversation, and for some reason I feel like I have license to do as I please. I stroke his neck, and before I even manage to think I'm pressing my face into it, smelling him, getting handsy. He allows it and I stay close to his face. He eyes me and it suddenly becomes too intense, too sexy, and I pull away a little bit, but I have to maintain our contact, so I lay my head on his thigh, my back to him. He caresses me, running his hand from my hair to my back, from my back toward the front of my waist, repeating that final movement while still focused on his phone call. I close my eyes. His touch is incredible, I don't want that hand to ever part from me; his fingers gently glide over my back, and I wonder how it makes sense that he knows to touch like that, being the self-absorbed type that I think he is.

Over at his secret restaurant, we're sitting at the bar, chatting with the chef as he cuts fish and serves us tiny, exquisite dishes. Another sake and another Japanese beer, another dish. The fish is delicious, the chef and Teddy obviously know and like each other, and even though I feel a little out of my league, I'm really enjoying myself. I'm tipsy and I'm finally with him.

"You realize how delicious this is?" he asks.

"Yeah. You realize how pushy you are?"

"Pushy? How?" He's amused by me.

"I don't feel like repeatedly saying how everything is so deliciously delicious."

"Yeah, okay. You're right."

"Yes."

"Okay, anything you do want to say?"

"Lots of things."

"Yeah? What do you have to say about how fat I am?"

There I was, convinced that this feature doesn't bother him in the slightest—I mean, how could this man be self-conscious about anything? "I say you're perfect."

He smiles his smile and I swear that I'm in love. Very much so. At least for now.

"We're going to have to fuck, you know," I say.

"Fuck? Not a chance."

"Really soon."

"Forget about it."

"Can't."

"Then go home."

"You are fucking me today."

"Oh, yeah?"

"Yeah. In half an hour."

"Is that so . . ."

"Most definitely."

I see the spark in his eyes, and then I see it dying down, overcome by a more rational look.

"And what if I tell you that I think it's not a good idea because I know what'll happen afterward?"

"Then I'll tell you that it's a great idea and that there's no choice in the matter and I'm not going to wait anymore!" I wave my finger in his face, watching his look softening again.

"Wild thing," he says. He grabs more sashimi. "You need me to give you the speech?"

My heart rate doubles. "Which one? The one about how I won't suddenly become your girlfriend tomorrow and you're unavailable and not interested right now and so on?"

"Yeah, that one. You need it?"

"No."

"And what about you?"

"What about me?"

"Future-wise."

"Don't know."

"What do you want? What would you want?"

"Nothing. You fuck me and then I die. No future."

"And you work for me . . ." he recalls, and takes another bite.

"Then I'll stop working for you. It's not going anywhere as it is."

"You've only been there for three weeks—"

"Four—"

"Three. The fourth started yesterday. Don't try me, I remember things. You shouldn't leave, you're going to get some interesting projects with us."

"But you do know that doesn't really interest me, right?"

"The work doesn't interest you? Maybe not at this stage."

"No, there won't be a stage that'll interest me. That's the truth. I'm grateful for the opportunity, don't get me wrong."

"Why doesn't it interest you?"

"Because. It's not the kind of subject matter I have in mind."

"What kind of subject matter do you have in mind?"

"You know, men, women. He says this, she replies as she would, and so he fucks her real good. That's about it," I say dryly, and he smiles and looks at me. "But don't assume that I'm not motivated to make good movies for you guys, and it's obviously challenging and I really appreciate—"

He interrupts me: "I know you appreciate it, don't worry."

"So, you see what I'm saying?"

"Yeah, you want to make real films."

"Yes." I look at him. "And I want other things too."

"What other things?"

"Now."

"What's changed in the last two minutes? I'm still your boss, aren't I?"

"Okay. But I won't not-fuck you just because you're my boss. That doesn't make any sense either."

"Perfect sense."

"No, no sense. So there you have it, nothing you can do about it. It's already happening, this thing."

He leans on his elbow, sips his Japanese beer, his face in front of mine.

"Tell me more about 'this thing.'"

"Being together when we can, fucking loads and coming here to eat, and you talk to the chef and ask if I like the delicious food, and we'll be together all the time, most of the time, all the time from morning till night, and watch TV in bed and eat some more, and go on weekend getaways and family gatherings."

He's obviously amused. "Just what I had in mind."

"All right, then how about this: I go on with my life. I meet nice young men, potential fathers, continue as usual as though you don't exist, and at the same time—"

"I do." He finishes my sentence and I look at his lips and really want to kiss him already.

"Yes. Just like that. I get what you're saying and why I can't fit in your life right now, but it still doesn't eliminate the option of being with you for as long as I can. So I'm taking responsibility for myself and my dark, childless, family-less future, and you get to simply enjoy my company. It's a good deal."

"You're bullshitting me."

"You have my word."

"You can't promise that sort of thing. Not to mention you're too drunk to make any promises."

"Teddy, even if I did have a bit to drink, which I'm not ruling out, I still won't have you say no. It's torture."

"What's torture?"

"Seeing you all day long and not touching you."

He pauses for a moment but keeps his eyes fixed on mine. "Yeah, it's torture."

I smile with relief. "See? You want it too."

"Of course I do."

"Check please, now," I say.

He laughs. "I'm a mediocre lay, you'll be disappointed."

"That's okay, so am I! Mine's this tiny." I illustrate with a narrow gap between my thumb and index finger.

He smiles and releases a gentle sigh, turns his head to the side and then looks at me again.

That's it, he's all mine.

We leave after the check and goodbyes in Japanese. Sayonara, sayonara, I sing in my mind, pleased that it's happening. So that's how it goes, he doesn't grab you in the elevator or on the street after running toward you in the rain, but rather two adults just get up from the table and get into bed and fuck on a Monday at 2:54 p.m.—such wonderful simplicity. Where are we going, actually?

"Let's go to your place," he says.

He hails a taxi, but it passes us. I turn the other way, looking for a taxi too. I really didn't dress warmly enough.

"Should we Uber it? There's another one," he says, and the second taxi halts and we're both inside.

"Where to?" the driver asks, and Teddy gestures for me to answer.

This ride is different from the last one. Strangely lucid—and I'm drunk, which I wasn't before. I did drink on an empty stomach before all the fish joined in. His presence is different now. He doesn't touch me, but he's here. He's quiet. He's not on his phone. I stay faithful to my side of the seat and the slight distance turns me on, and the thought of him wanting me is driving me insane.

We get out at my street, where everyone is behaving like extras on the movie set for *Just Another Monday*—moms and dads walking their kids home after kindergarten and school.

"Come here for a sec, I need cigarettes," he says.

"Let me."

I go in the store and he stays outside. I buy us the cigarettes he likes and hand him the pack, excited to see him again after an entire thirty seconds of being apart.

We get to my building's stairwell. I turn to him with a huge grin. "You didn't remember the stairs when you said 'let's go to your place,' did you?"

"I remember everything."

"Oh yeah? What color's my door?"

"Don't remember."

"Ha!"

"Gray."

"That's right! Impressive."

I wait for him on the second floor. "You'll have to walk all the way back down afterward."

"We'll see." He reaches me, remaining two steps below me, our faces almost at the same height. I unbutton my pants and my thumb slightly pushes down my underwear. He looks at what I'm showing him and comes up to my level, stands behind me, and quickly runs his hand down my stomach, smoothly pushing his fingers all the way to my pussy, and I feel him and he feels how wet I am and then I shift a little and he puts his middle finger in, deeper, and releases a restrained sigh that excites me. I move and he takes his fingers out, smells and tastes them. Yes please. I give him a little kiss on the lips. Must have more of that.

We enter. I glance around the apartment having remembered it relatively tidy, and indeed it's only relatively tidy. It's much more urgent to tidy myself up. "I'm going to shower."

"No."

"Yes, just for a sec."

"Why would you do that?"

"Because I feel like it."

"You give me a taste and then change the dish? No way. Where's your bed?"

"I think it's over there on the right."

He laughs and sits on the bed. "There's your bed."

He wants me this way. I like that. I climb over him to the other side of the bed, sit in front of him and light the remainder of a cigarette from the ashtray. He wants to smoke it too. He's got his feet on the rug, looks around, inspecting the room. Takes off his wristwatch and places it on the bedside table.

"Take your shoes off," I say.

He takes off his shoes without leaning down and comes closer to me, places his hand on my throat and kisses me, as though tasting me for a moment, and then we kiss and it gets intense all at once because I feel all the weeks and hours and minutes I've wanted this, and my heart pounds because he's kissing me the way I need him to kiss me.

I stop for a moment. "I really waited for this."

"Me too," he says plainly, and I'm touched that he's waited to kiss me, who am I to have him wait to kiss me? But there you have it, I can sense through each of his movements how much he's waited for this. He stays seated in the same position, his hand shifts to the back of my neck and he pulls my head slightly back while his other hand strokes my breasts and then rises up to my face and holds my jaw and opens it and kisses some more and it's demanding and arousing and I kiss him and feel how the lack of satisfaction this whole time has already become permanent background noise, and now he's with me and we're touching and he's mine but the noise is only amplifying and maybe it's actually more like hunger, which can only get satiated once that cock goes where it belongs. I take my shirt and bra off; he looks at my body and goes for my breasts. I lie on my back, he's on top of me, making sure to lean on his side so as not to crush me to death with his colossal weight.

"Yes. My favorite kind of nipples. Why would you do this to me. Now I'll never let you go." That's what he tells me, and in return I reach my hand and feel that excellent cock still covered by pants, slide my hand down to feel his balls, as exciting and wonderful as I'd imagined them to be. It feels good and right and amazing touching him; I'd spent such a long time imagining my hand holding him there.

"Now I'm going to ask you some questions," he informs the minuscule distance between our faces.

"Okay." I smile. I'm enjoying this so much that I'm jealous of myself.

"I need some information first. Just the basic facts."

"So, let me show you where it hurts. Okay, I can provide information and tell you that I have an IUD."

"That's good to know."

"Good. What else?"

"Do you need to be on top to come?"

"Oh, that sort of info?"

"That too."

"I can come in all sorts of scenarios."

"How do you come when you're alone?"

"On my belly, want to see?"

"Yes."

He moves aside and I roll onto my stomach, raise my ass and shove my hands between my legs. From that position we remove my pants and underwear. He strokes me, puts his hand between my legs and gently shifts my hand aside, skipping the line.

"God you're so wet. It's all for me?"

I roll onto my back, we unzip his pants, he pulls them down and his underwear too, and at long last I get to meet Teddy's cock. What a cock. What a scent. The scent alone makes me wet. I roll on my side and slightly lift myself, holding his cock and giving it little kisses and then licking it from top to bottom and all around, and then I realize Teddy's there too, so I look at him and see that he's looking at me and smiling.

"Took you a month and a half, you idiot," I tell him as his cock is pressed against my lips.

"A real idiot," he agrees, and gently caresses the side of my face with his fingers. His cock isn't completely hard right now, and I lick it and put it in my mouth and cup it from below, and his lovely scent increases. His cock gets harder in my mouth. I lick the tip, the upside-down heart-shaped summit, then I push his entire cock deep inside and start sucking him off like nothing else exists in the world right now, nothing but my mouth and that cock. His moans get louder, his vast hand cradles my face from the side.

"What are you doing to me? What is this?" he says almost mutely. "I need to fuck you."

He shifts over and flips me on my back and lies on top of me, his face over mine. I feel his fingers on my pussy. I kiss him and his lips are on mine, at first it's just his tongue delicately stroking mine, and then he kisses me all of a sudden and at the same time I feel his cock going in, not quite all the way, and then he changes something in the angle and there—it's in. Teddy's inside me, his cock's inside me, he is on top of me and I want this, precisely this. Now we're not kissing anymore because we're fucking instead, and then—on top of all this goodness—he starts talking.

"You see, I knew it, I knew this is how it would feel to fuck you," he says quietly right next to my face. "From the moment I saw you I knew exactly how my dick would feel in your pussy, I knew this is how it would feel, and ever since then I've known it and constantly had to think of your pussy and your ass. And then you take your clothes off and get into my bed naked when I'm not there to fuck you? That's what you do?"

And every word, every sentence, pulls me deeper inside, and I can come any second now but please make this last forever, this glorious thing. He stops moving all of a sudden but stays inside me. We're both sweating, especially him. He strokes my breasts and kisses me again, and I move so that he'll continue fucking me and he presses down on me and doesn't budge.

"Fuck me," I whisper in his ear, the delicious saltiness of his sweat on my lips. He looks at me, a deep, concentrated look, his face almost frozen, and I can sense the madness coming back, and this time it gets higher and higher and higher and I tell him that he's fucking me and I push him and turn us around and sit on him, but he immediately resumes control and sits up and grabs my hair and tilts my head back, and it gets very intense and he thrusts more and more and he says he can't take it anymore and I hear the two of us groaning, almost shouting, and I'm on my back again and he's on top of me and I feel him getting closer and I know he's about to come, and the thought of how close he is makes me orgasm. And when I come, he comes too, and it's simply much too good and unbearable and almost improper. Motherfucker.

I lie next to him, serenity surging through my body, and my brain relaxes and expands until everything feels possible and I become filled with countless ideas, and I know for certain that out there, there are fields and oceans and lakes and rivers and pipes in the walls around us. And there's nothing scary or heavy about it because everything just makes perfect sense.

And then the silence gets weird. I open my eyes and look at him. He's lying there, staring at a blank spot.

"What does it matter?" I ask, not entirely understanding what I mean. What sort of question is that? What am I talking about? His eyes shift onto me.

"What was it earlier, 'he says this, she replies as she would,' and then what?"

"Then he fucks her real good." I laugh. He does too.

"Can you get us some water?"

"Yeah, sure."

"But don't go."

How I love my apartment right now, the ultimate lair. I go to the kitchen, delighted that this man whom I want so badly is lying in my bed and that we've just fucked one of the most amazing fucks I've ever fucked. I open my barren fridge and take out a bottle of water. I find the cigarettes I'd gotten us in his jacket pocket. Now I'm cold. I quickly lie down beside him, only then realizing he's actually remained rather dressed, and I still cover us both with the blanket. He takes the bottle.

"You didn't bring me a glass?"

"No. Should I?"

"You savage. No, never mind."

He downs a third of the bottle in three gulps. I light a smoke and he takes it. It's getting a little dark outside and the apartment's somber too. I try to get to the bedside lamp, leaning over him but unable to reach it. He turns it on. When was the last time someone who isn't me turned this light on? He smokes, his hand resting on my thigh, heavy and pleasant.

"So what do you say?" I ask casually.

"What do I say about what?"

"About what just happened. Or are you used to these sorts of standards?"

He eyes me from the side, as though trying to decipher some cryptic code, and I immediately regret my pestering question. I try to think of something to say in order to withdraw it, but then he says, "Don't worry. You're something else."

I fall silent for a moment. He looks away from me. I lie on my back and talk to the ceiling. "Sometimes you don't answer my question but rather the essence of what I mean. I like that. You bypass what's being said and get straight into it—like you overtake the knights and speak directly to their king."

He stays silent, takes a deep breath. I glance at him and he looks like he's somewhere else. He strokes my thigh and gives a big yawn. "I need my phone."

I grab it from the kitchen table, can't help myself, press the screen. Wow, this phone's seen a lot of action, texts and missed calls and emails and constant updates and stock market figures. "You have dozens of messages."

"I need my glasses too."

I go over to his jacket, already knowing the glasses are in the inside pocket. Rush back under the blanket, lie on my side and gaze at all this beauty. His face is quiet as he reads, a delicate vein of concern at the corner of his eye.

"I'm making a quick call, okay?"

"Sure."

After the phone call he stays lying down and on his phone. I feel so good that he stayed, and something about how he isn't paying too much attention to me is strangely a relief. I'm just lying down and he's next to me in my bed and entirely mine.

Until he leaves.

›

It's morning already.

Twenty-sixth floor.

I'm seeing him soon.

The door to his office is open, but there's no one there. He hasn't come in yet. I'm not going to ask when he's supposed to arrive. I need to show him that I know my place, know how little I'm allowed to demand from him.

A bit after 11:00 a.m. I hear Maureen talking to him on the phone, and I gather from what she's saying that he's on his way to the airport. So I won't see him today and probably not for the next few days. He didn't say a word about a trip.

Richard calls me in and asks to set up a meeting to talk about something he wants me to do. I stand at the entrance to his office and suggest that we sit down now, but he says he can't and we set a time for tomorrow.

Each hour that passes without hearing from Teddy adds another layer over the memory until it becomes blurry and inaccessible. I go back to my apartment. At least over here there's still a chance of feeling him. I lie in bed. I can't find his scent on the sheets anymore.

What is this, kindergarten? You're over fifty, haven't you realized by now that the day after your cock went for a visit inside some lady, you should really talk to her so that she doesn't feel like shit?

›

Wednesday, gloomy and rainy. I wake up, shower, have a coffee, and drive to the office. Hair still wet and it's cold in my car.

Richard asks me to make a pitch film for some investors they're about to meet to raise funds for a major project the company's developing. "Need to think outside the box," he proclaims.

"What are you talking about, Richard?" I chide him gently. "Everyone thinks outside the box. Nowadays it's far more original to think inside the box."

I leave his office with a pile of papers and forms with stats, start to read and get to know the material, and neglect to notice I'd stopped waiting—until I get a text from Teddy. My heart stops, naturally.

So

That's what he writes.

So what?

So tell me

Tell you what?

About you . what you're doing

Working

On your film

That's a question. I'm starting to get it.

No, on your film, Delmar's.
For investors.

Work on your own film

They'll fire me

Cunts

It seems he truly doesn't care about the Delmar films. And he says nothing about what happened or about having gone abroad. I decide to end it with his cunts. This is good enough for now.

That lasts till nighttime, when I need a different sort of attention from him.

I'm going to visit my grandma
tomorrow morning.

He sees the text and answers straightaway.

Didn't know you have a grandma

You don't know anything about
anything yet. |

I revise:

You don't know anything about
anything.

Who's mother is she

Nurit's mother.

Nurit 's your mom ?

He question marked.

Yes

    Mom's mom

He doesn't know my story.

    Where does grandma live

    Jerusalem

    How you getting there

    My car.

    No

    No what?

    Call me

    Now?

    Yes

    The usual number?

    Yes

I'm overtaken by a swell of warmth. I've been granted permission—more than that—given explicit orders.

"Noa," he answers.

"Teddy." I'm much more excited than I'd have liked.

"What's up? Listen, take my car. Or you prefer Matt to drive you?"

"To Jerusalem?! No, no way, I can drive and there's nothing wrong with my car."

"I've seen your car."

"And I've seen yours."

"Good, and which one do you think is more appropriate for a drive on the highway in the rain?"

"They're both fine."

"Go to my place, Milo's home now, I just got off the phone with him, I'll ask him to come downstairs and give you the car keys."

"As if. I haven't even met him yet." The word 'yet' managed to squeeze itself back in.

"You're a pain. Fine, forget it, I'll get a key over to you. When do you want to leave in the morning?"

"Benevolent dictator, that's what you are."

"No idea what you're talking about. When do you want to leave?

When you want to leave call Matt, he'll pick you up with keys to my car."

I smile, touched by how important this is to him and startled by how extreme he can get.

"Okay? Good," he decides for me. "Bye."

"Wait! Teddy." I'm stalling.

"What?"

"You must miss me by now, terribly, I can only imagine it's hard on you."

"Very."

"The distance must be killing you, is what I'm saying."

"You're right. And you?"

"Me? Nothing."

"Not a thing?"

"Totally blasé."

He laughs, and I can see my shimmering smile reflecting off the darkness in the window.

"I need to go. Speak to you soon." As though we'd spoken before.

>

I'm driving to my grandma's place in Teddy's car. I'm not used to driving a quality car, it's like riding a strong, well-bred, super-obedient horse. I listen to music, and I'm not cold; the car whizzes over inclines without a hitch, and since I seem important, no one dares to overtake me.

My grandma has lived in the same apartment ever since I can remember, at the bottom of a hill on a central street in Jerusalem. A small, modest apartment, a remnant of European culture standing silent among the old building walls, windows facing the street. I used to sleep over and spend the nights listening to buses exerting themselves up the steep road.

I don't visit her much, only once every few months. For the last few years she's had a carer from Sri Lanka living with her—she's the one who opens the door for me. Grandma's very old. She's sitting at the dining room table, slowly eating her lunch. I kiss her and smell her scent, which is the sum of all the scents she's ever had. I'm genuinely happy to see her. She's happy too, asks me if I'd like to have something to eat. I say no and make myself a cup of coffee. She wants me to tell her about my life. I give her some general, positive outlines.

"I'm fine, I started a new job."

"Oh! Great, that's great, where?" She speaks slowly.

"It's a company that deals with marine mapping, they have this bio-technology that knows how to identify all sorts of currents in the sea, and then they use the information in a number of fields."

As she listens, she squints her eyes into two narrow crevices, as though blinded by the sun. "Very interesting," she rules, her hand rising for yet another slow voyage from the bowl to her mouth.

"And I'm in charge of making in-house movies and developing the media department, but we're still in the planning stages."

She asks about the terms of employment, it takes her a while. It's better to extend my reply, saves her asking, and I already know how her mind works.

"Really good terms. They pay me double what I made in the last place, and they even include expenses and insurance and all. And I don't have to work fixed hours either, it's an ideal job," I explain, and she listens attentively. "Take another bite in the meantime."

"It's so interesting . . ." What you're telling me. ". . . what you're telling me."

I keep quiet for a moment so that she eats, then I continue the story and mention Teddy. Little rascal's onto me straightaway.

"You find him interesting, this man?"

"I find him interesting, this man, yes."

"But it's no good . . ." Since he's your boss. ". . . if he's your boss."

"Yeah, what can you do. I knew that when I started working for him. I actually drove here in his car, he didn't want me to take mine in this weather."

"Oh!" Her eyes suddenly light up. "So he cares for you."

She pauses our conversation, turns to her carer, and asks her to clear the table and bring her some pudding. I use the time to take a photo of her, and she gripes about how she's "not pretty enough for photos any-more." I send Teddy the photo. The pudding arrives, I don't want any, thank you, thank you so much.

"And how's your brother? He came to see me last week."

"Then you saw him last, maybe you can tell me how he's doing." I laugh and she does too. When she laughs I can feel it in my heart.

"He's in love," she rules decisively, not a hint of romance in her tone, but no deprecation either.

"Oh yeah? With who?"

"A guy from Austria, Thomas."

"Okay, Grandma, well I suggest we don't get too attached to Thomas."

"He gave me the impression of being a . . ." She pauses to swallow for a moment, then clears her throat and continues. ". . . very nice young man."

"The Austrian? He brought him over?"

"Yes."

"Is that so . . ." I'm surprised. A ninety-five-year-old woman is more informed about my brother's sex life than I am.

"And your father? And Mina?"

"Dad's fine, I think. The usual."

Message ping. Teddy.

> Very glad to get this photo
>
> Grandma Diana.
>
> Lady D

"Is that him?" I like how she realizes straightaway that I'm texting him now, in front of her.

"Yeah. Would you like him to come over for a visit too sometime?" Why am I offering this? Maybe because he said he was glad to get her photo.

"Maybe." She's not enthralled by the idea. "But it was very tiring, Roy's visit."

"Then maybe not." I withdraw.

She squints her eyes again. "I'm worried about you."

"I know. But there's no need. All is well."

›

It's only on Sunday that Teddy remembers to come back from England and show up at the office. We've not seen each other for almost a full week, but maybe since I was so preoccupied with him, now that he's finally here I can't manage to connect my Teddy with the man standing in the office next door. Am I still crazy about him? Maybe I'm over it? I think I'm not attracted to him anymore.

I stay in my seat, drinking my now-unfortunately-cold coffee. After a few minutes, he walks over to me and stands next to my desk.

"And here you are."

"Here I am," I say, smileless, feeling cozy within the indifference clotted all around me.

"Why are you sitting so low down?" He's referring to my habit of sinking down low in office chairs.

"Thanks for the car."

"No problem." He lightly touches my desk. "How's your grandma doing?"

"Same, she's very old."

"Your dad's parents no longer with us?"

"Yeah." I look at him, the back of my neck pushing against the edge of the seat.

"What does your dad do, what industry's he in?" His fingers gently tap on the desk, not too far from my hand.

"My dad's a chemist, an academic." I want to touch his hand.

"So your parents are divorced?"

"Yeah, long time ago."

"And your mom? What does she do? Where does she live?"

"I'm not in touch with her."

"What do you mean?"

"Just what I said."

"What does 'not in touch' mean? How long now?"

"Since forever."

"What does that mean? I don't get it."

"From a very young age. Can we stop the interview now?"

He goes quiet for a moment, looks at me. "Anything else you'd rather be doing?" He lifts my pen, passing it between his fingers absentmindedly.

"Yes."

"What's that?"

I stay motionless and just lower my gaze, fixing my eyes on his cock through his pants, more or less at my eye level, then look up at him again. He slowly smiles at me, then gently shakes his head, places the pen back down and leaves.

Yeah. I'm definitely still crazy about him.

3

There's No One after Me

»

Things go wrong. I know that and I get that. It's how I react to the wrong that isn't right; a reaction of a person I do not wish to be.

From the moment Richard tasks me with my mission, I work on the pitch film around the clock, researching the subject, writing drafts, finding ways of relaying the points and in an entertaining manner no less. A meeting is set for me to present Richard and Teddy with my idea. The night before the meeting, I edit a rough sketch to explain what I plan on doing, because people don't know how to imagine things, so the more you demonstrate, the better you're understood. I only finish at 4:00 a.m. Set an alarm for three hours' time and go to sleep.

The meeting goes brilliantly. I manage to make them laugh, and even though he's not as enthused as Richard, Teddy seems pleased with me. They're glad to have me on board, and I'm enjoying every minute of it.

But four days later, at the next meeting, the concept crumbles into a pile of nothing thanks to the limited brains of the extended team. And as if that's not enough, Teddy and Richard are just sitting there listening to their employees' banal, bland ideas. Genuinely listening! And their positive reactions to these imbecile suggestions are even worse: not only are they not defending my concept, the one that had charmed them, but now they're also getting it up for any idea offered by Jamie or Phil.

I feel contempt for Teddy for allowing this to happen. His reactions are exposing the fact that he never understood my idea to begin with, so I avoid any eye contact with him. At a certain point he gets up and leaves the room.

Afterward, Richard tries to calm me down. I'm so angry I'm almost trembling. The real frustration here is with the fact that they're doing actual damage to the film.

"You have to understand, these are people who have been employed here for a very long time and they know the material inside out."

"But they don't know anything about film."

"Correct, and that's what you're here for, and again, you did a great job and we'll continue improving it together."

"But it's on you to mediate, to filter through their ideas. Because their notes weren't coherent, they didn't even make sense, so I have no clue where to go from here."

Richard looks a little lost. Enough, this is going nowhere and I feel too exposed. I want to go down for a smoke and be on my own for a moment. I mumble a thank-you and tell him I'll work on a new version and set up another meeting with their assistants.

Richard smiles. "Cheer up! It just goes to show you've tickled their imagination!" His joviality annoys the shit out of me.

They can tickle their fucking clits for all I care, I think as I leave the room. I'm not a creative-writing master class; I need to make a good film and they're getting in my way. I grab a cigarette from my bag and quickly leave the office. While waiting for the elevator, I notice Teddy through the glass door and realize he's on his way out too. He pauses for a moment. My heart's pounding: on the one hand I'm hoping the elevator stalls and we can have a moment alone; on the other hand— he's better off dead than standing next to me when I'm like this. The elevator arrives and I get in but he's already close, so I'm forced to hold the door open for him. The door closes behind him. The silence doesn't even last three seconds.

"Your behavior's unprofessional." He's chosen to say something direct and delivers it in a curt tone, without bothering to look at me.

"You liked the idea four days ago—"

"And you're too sensitive," he interrupts me.

I can't think of a reply, my heart's racing. "That's how creatives create things. Need to have feelings—"

"That's beside the point."

"Then what is the point?"

"That was no way to conduct yourself in front of clients."

So he's a client now? "Fuck all the clients in all the world," I mutter.

"Like I said, unprofessional. If you want to continue working here, or anywhere else for that matter, you need to stop acting like a little child." His brief glance insults me to my core.

"And you need to understand that—" I realize the direction this is heading in and I halt. The real nightmare is that I know he's right, and right now I find his precision unbearable. "Right. Thanks." I don't mean it.

"You're welcome." He does mean it.

The elevator stops at the fourth floor and two people enter. We're at the back.

"I thought I'd get some support."

"Support with what?"

"I don't know, dealing with everyone there." Ground floor.

"You'll get it when you deserve it."

And he gets out of the elevator and walks away, and I hate him and decide to quit right there and then.

›

Better off not going home in this state. I feel like seeing Sharon, so I join her wherever she's at. And where is that? The playground in the park, unfortunately. An afternoon filled with the ruckus of insatiable urban kids. We manage to swap half a sentence at best; she's got her hands full with her three children, almost like an ER doctor. I try to help, taking charge of her eldest, but she wants her mommy, so we swap and I take the middle kid. He wants to get to the top of the big slide through a pipe with a ladder in it, but it's only for over-three-year-olds or those with adult supervision. I'm the adult supervision. We're inside the pipe, children are screaming. There he is, sliding with delight, a matter of three seconds, and then back to the starting point again—a matter of four minutes. I get tired after two rounds. My eyes search for Sharon so she can put me out of my misery and also hear everything I have to say about my doomed creative fate at Teddy-the-son-of-a-bitch's company, about how he'd behaved in the elevator and about the huge mistake I'd made taking this job. But there's zero chance for us to talk. I see her standing with one of the playground moms having a very smiley chat. Is that where I'm supposed to be? And what about those who never want to chase kids around playgrounds filled with demanding brats and dedicated mothers? What should they do?

I watch from the side and an inner voice speaks—it's all worth it, it makes sense, it's natural, possible. Children give meaning, continuity, hope. This, it's love. And in order to reinforce all that fine potential, my mind starts projecting lovely images of children in pajamas; of a vast field covered in soft grass and children running and laughing and I'm with them; of hugs and kisses and drawings and cakes and boots in puddles and sentences uttered by little people still examining the world, and it's you who's supposed to teach them about it all; of the bedroom of a child who's just woken up from a sweet nap.

These thoughts make me sick and that throws me back to reality, and I suddenly realize that the kid is no longer on the slide. I quickly look around and I see him vigorously jumping on the duck-themed swing. For some reason he's now shoeless. When and where did he take them off? I fight the need to get away from here. I love Sharon. I'll help her get everyone back to her place and I'll stay for dinner.

〉

It's raining the following morning and there's a meeting I'm attending because I didn't quit my job after all. I'm not sure why they wanted me to join, but right now I prefer this to going back to my beaten and bruised pitch film. Our distinguished bosses are also present, along with at least six other people from the office. Teddy, as usual, spends the entire time on his phone, absently present. The boardroom is vast and bright, and I look out the window at the gray day. Except for a cold "good morning," I didn't get any personal acknowledgment from him. It's been two weeks since he came over to my place, including two weekends where I did nothing but try to understand how he could want to be anywhere without me. And then there was the good meeting where I'd presented my idea, and then yesterday's shitty meeting where the idea was destroyed, and then the stabbing incident in the elevator.

They're talking about a bid that Delmar is about to go for, and I don't understand most of what they're saying. Jamie's very involved in the conversation. I'm not sure what her official title here is. She's young, yet pretty high up in the company hierarchy and mostly walks around filled with self-importance, a sexy shade of preoccupied. Next to me is Hailey; I still haven't forgiven her for that 'I'm pretty sure I told you,' a sly and self-serving type coated with a sweet voice and an everyone's-pal kind of attitude. Hailey and Jamie always act like they get along really well, but it's clear that they're in a constant power struggle. From what I've gathered so far, Jamie is Teddy's protégée, while Hailey keeps her distance from him.

Phil's saying that if the merger contracts aren't sealed then they can't go for the bid.

"Hexa-Labs isn't obligated to British regulation, that's the beauty of this timing." Teddy gives him an explanation which sounds completely vague to me but seems to be clear to everyone else. Phil's still troubled. "By the time we get their signed approval the bid will be over. Everything's a mission with them."

"We already got it, I have it." Teddy resumes messing with his phone.

"What? When?" Phil's confused.

"I think we need to get Coleman in the loop," Jamie says as she pushes a strand of hair behind her gorgeous ear. "He's very well-connected there."

"Absolutely not," Teddy dismisses her and looks at his phone. "Coleman doesn't need to know anything, and you're not going to say a word to him. Or did you already?"

"Teddy." She allows herself to address him with what seems to me like a brash tone, but maybe it's just her sexy voice. "He'll get it for us within a second. We need to get him involved, I'm telling you."

"No. You're wrong."

Hailey nears her shoulder to mine and quietly says, "Wow, she has no shame."

"Who's Coleman?" I whisper to her. I have no idea what I'm doing at this meeting.

"One of the major clients. He's Jamie's."

Richard explains to Jamie that Coleman has no incentive. I try to listen and understand what's being said when I suddenly feel a vibration in my pocket. I check and see a text from Teddy. I slightly turn my chair to the side so Hailey can't see my phone.

> Better today

I glance in his direction; he's sitting a few seats away from me, doesn't look at me.

> Are you asking or saying?

"Does he know?" Teddy reclines and asks Jamie, who in turn leans forward, elbows planted on the table as her delicate golden necklace flutters over her collarbones.

"It's a small industry, of course he knows," she replies.

"No, he has no way of finding out," Teddy rules decisively while typing something on his phone, "and that's how it needs to stay."

Messaging me, as it turns out.

> Asking
>
> Yeah. Better.
>
> Good . join me for lunch
>
> Are you asking or saying?
>
> Saying

A gentle rush of excitement washes over me and I try to hide my joy.

> Then okay.
>
> What are we having
>
> Whatever you want.

I wait for a moment and then I can't hold back anymore.

> Just us though.

He explains the bidding process to everyone and they listen attentively. I get a little tense, sneak a glance, and see that his phone's placed in front of him. When he finishes he points at Jamie. "You, stay here after the meeting, I want to talk to you." Only then, five minutes after the deed, he looks.

Thats the plan

Relief. We'll finally be alone again. Appetite? Gone.

〉

The meeting's done and I go back to my desk while Teddy and Jamie stay in the boardroom. Less than a minute and he's out.

"Let's go."

At the restaurant, we're sitting in a booth, I sit across from him. He eats and I order only ouzo, despite his appalled reaction. I feel like what happened yesterday is still hanging between us. He's behaving strangely and I can't figure him out.

"So what's up?" he asks after finishing with his phone and in between bites.

I quickly define a guideline for myself: no making faces, no whining, no talking about the past two weeks—and stay authentic. That's the mission. "As good as can be."

"You really not hungry?" He leans back and wipes that beautiful mouth of his, sips from his soda.

"Really and truly."

"Calmed down since yesterday?" He continues eating.

An irritating, condescending question, but better off moving on. "Yes."

"What was difficult about yesterday?"

"At the meeting? Or the elevator?"

"The elevator?"

"Yeah, what you said to me afterward." Damn. Why can't I keep my mouth shut.

I see his expression changing. He hides a smile, a kind of genuine, embarrassed one emerging from within. "Okay, you're not as strong as I thought, far from it." He takes a sip. "That little talk in the elevator, that broke you?"

"It didn't break me," I protest, "just hurt me."

"Hurt you? Jesus, you're a kid. I'm ending this."

No! I freeze by the mere thought. "No, no, don't even think about it."

"I'm absolutely thinking about it."

"Why? Why would you end something so obviously good?"

"Look at how you get after two sentences."

"How do I get?"

"We haven't even started yet. I'm not doing this."

We haven't even started yet—that is the scariest, most dreadfully wonderful, correct thing I've ever heard. "Exactly, we haven't started yet. And we're not stopping now. I don't even have that option in mind."

"I've been talking to you about nothing *but* that option from the very beginning."

"Who stops after one fuck?"

"Noa."

"Do you regret it? Our fuck?"

He takes a second. "No."

"And the one coming up?" I ask seriously, and he smiles, surprised, but I continue, poker-faced: "I don't get this insanity. Is that why you invited me for lunch? Is that 'the plan'?"

"I already know how this'll play out." He's almost talking to himself. "I'll destroy you. I know that."

"You won't destroy me. And even if you do—this is what I want."

"I have no doubt that you think this is what you want."

My phone rings: it's my dad. I silence the call and take another sip; the drink scorches my throat. Get a grip, girl, this is a test, it's yours to win.

"And what if I'll be the one doing the destroying?" I say.

"Sounds swell to me. Want some dessert?"

What a bizarre conversation. I'm not in control.

"You're missing something here, you just don't seem to get it," he says without looking at me.

"Are you for real?" I attack, and now he's looking. "How can you possibly say that I don't get it? I get it all, I'm just reacting, for fuck's sake!"

"Look at you!"

"Look at what? What do you see?"

"I see. I see you."

"Speculation."

Phone rings again: Dad again. I put it on silent.

He goes on. "You're too fragile, if I'm being honest. Putting aside how annoying you are, I don't want you getting hurt."

How annoying I am?! No, don't get stuck on that. Don't want me getting hurt? This is a trap. I need to flip this around, come at it from his angle. "And what do you want?"

"Me? I want quiet."

"As if. You don't want quiet," I dismiss him. "This isn't the behavior of someone who wants quiet. I felt you at my place and I've felt you ever since, and I haven't stopped thinking about you. I understand you have a voice that says 'forget it,' but it's not the only voice, there are others and I can hear them." He's finally listening and I keep going. "And I'm supposed to react. You shove a hand in front of my face for me to blink—you wouldn't be interested if I didn't blink. I'm only doing what I'm supposed to be doing. That was the deal."

"Our deal doesn't entail you saying to me 'fuck all the clients in all the world.'" He is so sexy, this man.

"Okay, I shouldn't have said that. But still, that's not a significant violation."

A waitress heads toward our table; seems to me she's been eavesdropping this whole time.

"Everything okay, guys?" Why would she refer to us as 'guys'? "Would you like anything else?" she asks in an overly high pitch, looking at the table rather than us as she puts down a small toothpick container.

"Thanks." He smiles at her. "You can clear the table." He doesn't seem as relaxed as he was.

She clears the table and walks away. I look him straight in the eye. He looks back at me, and I feel like this is the first time he's really seeing me since we got here. I get up and move to the bench next to him.

"Noa, go back to your seat."

"No," I reject his command, "Teddy, I did precisely what I was supposed to do from the very first moment and all the way to now."

He turns to me, grabs on to the table as though he has to hold on to something. "What do you want?"

"You. For us to continue what we started. Why are you doing this?"

"Doing what?"

"You know what."

"Teddy Rosenfeld!" We're suddenly interrupted by a man's voice.

"Werner! What are you doing in my part of town?" Teddy quick-draws with a smile.

I don't know if it's intentional or not, but his thigh presses against mine as he turns and shakes the suited man's hand, exchanges a few sentences with him. The slightest touch and I'm immediately flooded, returning to this bond we have, recalling the things he said when he fucked me.

"What are you, an idiot?" I ask when the suited guy walks off and Teddy's eyes return to me. Our faces are close.

"Judging by my invitation to come have lunch with me, yes, I guess I'm an idiot."

"And say that I did let you push me away, what then? You'd be alone? That would last all of fifteen minutes. And then what? Someone else who isn't me comes along? What are you going to do with someone else now?" His jaw tightens, and I refuse to let go. "Then you might as well stick with me. You won't find anyone who's better suited for you than I am. What would she have that I don't? Success? You don't care for that because it has nothing to do with you. Talent? You're in good hands. Beauty? I'm pretty enough for you. Big tits? Okay, maybe, but that's not a good enough reason."

He looks at me and takes a deep breath. "Don't make this any harder."

I ignore him and continue my manifesto. "Money? You have enough. Humor? No competition here. What? What could *she* possibly have that would make *you* move even an inch?" Our lips are close, I can feel his taste. "Nothing. It's me, Teddy. I saw the list. There's no one after me."

It looks like he's about to suffocate me. Or kiss me? He leans his elbow on the table, closes his eyes for a moment, and rubs his forehead.

"You cunt." He says it quietly and I know that if this was indeed a test—I've just passed with flying colors.

>

We're waiting for a taxi, infuriating drizzle of rain.

"Come here." He leads me to an abandoned gap between the restaurant and the nearby building, hidden from the street, pushes me to the wall and presses himself against me. It's incredibly arousing and he starts kissing me all at once, more and more and even when he stops he doesn't move an inch away and his mouth's on mine. "Don't forget what I told you."

"What?"

"It's not going to happen with me, this thing that you want."

The taxi's arrived and the app pings. He backs away but keeps me pressed against the wall.

"And one more thing," he adds, and gives me a cold look. "I won't have you talking shit about your beautiful breasts ever again."

This time I'm awarded his bed, and after he takes off his wristwatch, he fucks me as though he hasn't fucked in years. He licks my nipples, making me go crazy and wet, then goes down on me, shoves his cock in my mouth and lifts my chin, groans, fucks my mouth while his fingers wrap around my throat. I'm on all fours with my ass up and he's fucking me hard, he's almost violent, but he doesn't hurt me, demanding yet precise. It's not like the previous fuck, the first one; this one's less for me and more for him and this change draws me deeper in, and we're both sweating and our scent fills the room, and the view from the window is a gray afternoon.

We stop for a bit, look at each other, and I slap his face just for fun or maybe to balance something in his aggression, and he laughs and kisses me and gets up with his giant undershirt and no underwear—cock in fabulous intermediate mode—and goes out to pee.

I think about Tom and Alison's wedding, when we'd only just met and went to the restroom together. It reminds me that I still have a little tin box of cocaine in my bag that I haven't touched since that night.

"I'm going to get a beer. Want one? I don't keep any ouzo in the house." He puts on his underwear. I get up and stretch across the philosopher's armchair, pick my bag up and put it on my lap.

"Beer's fine, thanks." I find the little tin box.

"What's that?" he asks.

"Coke. Want some?"

"No."

"Can you get me something to line this on?"

"Come take whatever you need. Just put something on."

"Yeah." I put on my underwear and pants and long-sleeved shirt.

"So what's really upstairs?" I look at the stairs leading to the floor above as we enter the living room.

"That side leads to the guest room and the roof. You can get to the roof from Milo's room too, which is on the other side."

"Does he sleep there?"

"Rarely."

"Then where does he stay?"

"Mainly at his girlfriend's. They stay over here sometimes, but not much since she's gotten her own place." He turns on the kitchen light.

"What's her name?"

"Daria."

He pours some water and takes out a couple of beers from the fridge. I look for a plate. "What a lovely kitchen. When did Milo's army service end?"

"Six months ago."

"And what's he doing now?"

"Who knows. Hangs out."

"And you don't get on his case to do this or that, study?"

"Not yet." He leaves for a moment and I look around. Everything is very homey; this house has a woman's touch. He comes back with his glasses and phone in hand, reads. "I was planning on going back to the office after lunch. You're a troublemaker."

"Found a plate. Got a straw?"

"A straw?"

"A drinking straw."

"No, I don't have 'a drinking straw,'" he imitates my diction with amusement and kisses me on the lips all of a sudden. "You're sweet."

"You got money?"

"Money I do have."

"Cash. I need a bill."

"Take it from my wallet."

Back in the bedroom, I'm on my knees on the rug, pouring a tiny pile of cocaine onto the plate. He's typing something on his phone and muttering swear words. That reminds me to check my phone. Eight missed calls, seven of which are from my dad. This doesn't mean something bad happened; that's just how he is. If I don't answer him, then he just tries over and over again. I prepare a few fabulous lines and snort one. Delightful. He comes over and sits on the armchair, places his phone on the table.

"Delicious?"

"Yes!" I smile and wipe my face a little.

"Okay then let me do one. Haven't had any in ages."

"Great. Do one, I want you to do one." I hand him the plate. He leans in and snorts two lines in one go, the fatso.

"So you and Lara lived here together."

"That's right, detective." He reclines.

"And she left?"

"Yes."

"How can anyone leave this house?" I do another line.

"This house? How can anyone leave this man, that's what you want to be asking."

"That is a given."

"It's my house, what do you mean 'how can anyone leave it'? She's the one who moved in with me."

"Then who's the woman who made this house the way it is?"

"I'm the woman. And Monique, Milo's mother."

"And where is she now, Monique?"

"Back in her home country."

"Which is?" Snort another line.

"Denmark, that's where we met."

"Really? And Milo? Does he get to see her?"

"Milo? Sure, all the time. They're real close. She comes for visits, he flies over to her. No problem."

"She got any more kids?"

"No. Just wanted the one."

"One from you."

"Yeah. We got a good one."

"And what's it like between you two?" I pass him the plate, tighten the rolled bill and hand it to him.

"Me and Monique? Great. We're good, always were." He snorts a line immediately followed by another one.

"How come she didn't stay with you? With you and Milo?"

"She wasn't looking to stay to begin with." He gets up and lights a cigarette, opens the window. "She's a free spirit, one of a kind, unique. Very talented." He better shut up like now.

"Then where did Milo grow up?"

"He was born in Copenhagen, been here since he was ten. I lived between here and there. Then we all moved here, so I bought this place and Monique renovated it with me."

"It's a gorgeous house, Teddy."

"You're gorgeous, Noa."

"Me? What do I have to do with it?"

"Nothing."

"So that was my weekly compliment? That's what you waste it on?" I light a smoke too and stand next to him. He leaves his cigarette in his mouth and lifts my shirt with one hand and strokes my breasts and my nipples, shifts the cigarette from his mouth to his hand, leans in and presses his mouth on me for a moment, takes a breath and straightens up again.

"Want another one?" he asks.

"Another what?" I lost my concentration.

"Another compliment."

"Yes, please."

"You'll appreciate this one."

"Go right ahead."

"I really didn't think I'd continue this with you." He stubs out his cigarette in the ashtray.

"That's because you're an idiot. And that is not a compliment!"

"It's not?"

"Of course not! You know it isn't."

"I disagree."

I give a smile of relief mixed with coke, which is already giving me a nice buzz. "But hey, since you're surprisingly cooperative, let me ask you this: you told me you and Lara are still married, officially. Not that it matters, I'm just trying to get the general gist."

"When did I say that?"

"When you were at my place. The first time."

"Well, that's changed since."

"So the 'unavailable' title's changed too?" I stub out my cigarette.

"What do you want with titles now? Forget it, I got all sorts of trouble, don't you worry."

"I'm not your only trouble. I didn't think I was."

"Right now, you're my most outstanding trouble." He smiles, and those teeth face me yet again.

"Now that's a compliment!"

"I need to pee."

"I'm doing the holding this time!"

"You and your nonsense. Leave me alone."

"You're not being supportive about my penis envy. I'm suffocating in this house!"

He laughs. "All right, monster, let's make your dream come true." He heads toward the bathroom and I quickly follow him.

I stand next to him, pressing against his side. His armpit's close to the back of my neck and my right hand's holding his heavy cock. He pees and we watch the stream as it hits the water. He turns to look at me, gently kisses my neck.

"I love your smell," he says.

He finishes peeing, I shake it, he laughs and puts his cock back in his underwear.

"Good job," he praises me, and I give a pleased smile. "Now it's time for your cold shower."

"No, no way!" I shriek and try to run but the fucker's already got my arm and he's taking my shirt off.

"Come on, don't be scared, just for a minute, it'll be fun."

"No! I hate cold water!" I try to break free but he won't let me out.

"Take your pants off."

His commanding tone overthrows me. I take off my pants and underwear and stand naked before him.

"You're very beautiful. All right, now get in here." He situates me inside the spacious shower. "Arms to the sides." He presses me against the cold tiles. "You're not allowed to move, stay still." He grabs the showerhead. "Just spread your legs a bit."

I slightly spread my legs apart. He turns the water on with the coldest, strongest stream and showers me immediately, from my throat all the way down. He doesn't move and I try my best not to scream, dying for him to stop, but he stalls, looks at my body, shoves his hand in his underwear and touches his cock, the water's freezing and my nipples harden, my entire body's covered in goose bumps. He turns the water off, presses against me with his clothes, warming me up, kissing me; my arms are obediently pressed against the tiles. He caresses my frozen breasts, runs his hand between my legs, disconnects me from the wall and leads me to the bed, places me face down, and then lies half on top of me and shoves his cock between my legs. I try to get him in but he moves away.

"It stays out, use it like it's your own dick."

I'm on my stomach and he's somewhere there, and his hard cock is between my legs and I press it to my clit and feel its entirety, warm and wet, and it's my cock now, and out of that thought, which is getting further away from us and into chambers I'd never before visited with characters I'd never met, I get closer and closer and his fingers are inside me and I groan and when he says something like "That's what I want to hear, don't want to hear anything else from you other than that," then, of course, I come.

He moves away and I turn onto my back, and he's on his knees on the bed, rubbing his cock and looking at my body. I lean on my elbow and hold his balls with my free hand and watch his beautiful face as he comes on my stomach.

It's getting dark outside. I grab my phone to call my dad. Teddy comes out of the bathroom, grabs his glass of beer, and sits next to me, feet on the floor. I hit Call. He drinks, then hands me the glass. I drink, and he looks at my face inquisitively, his jaw tightening.

My dad picks up. "What on earth is going on, Noa, where did you go? I've been calling you over and over again and you're not answering."

"I was at work," I say, and look at Teddy. He takes the beer back.

"Work? Okay, I see. Well, listen, I want you to find some time for us to meet, okay? I need to talk to you about something."

"About what?"

"Yeah, not over the phone. Everything's fine, everything's fine, but I want us to find some time and it's pretty urgent—"

"Sure," I interrupt him so that he doesn't repeat himself because he's starting to get on my nerves. "We could do lunch on Thursday."

I hang up and don't give another moment of thought to the mysterious 'something.' I've got something much more important right here in front of me.

Teddy places the empty beer glass on the bedside table. "So you're my final one, that's what you're saying."

I give him a genuine, almost shy smile. "Yes. And you're my first." We laugh.

"I need to lie down, move over a little."

"Can I stay?"

"You can do whatever you want."

He grabs the remote and turns on the TV, and I relax into his bed's comforting warmth. Get up, snort another line, and go back next to him, and I feel unburdened, nothing but silence for miles.

»

I stupidly let my dad decide where we're meeting for lunch, and he's picked a restaurant I wouldn't even enter for a napkin. The place is putridly unventilated; he's already waiting inside.

"Why this table?" I ask.

"What's wrong with this table?"

"It's tiny, it's right at the entrance to the kitchen so the waiters keep passing by, and I'm supposed to sit with my back to the door, and I hate sitting that way."

"Then come here, take my seat! What's there to see here? I came to see you. I think the table's fine," he says, but doesn't get up.

I give up and sit down. While we wait for the food, he prattles on about unimportant matters, until I ask him directly, "What did you want to talk about?"

"Oh, now? Why don't we eat first?"

"What is it?"

"Yes. Okay. Well, look, I was contacted by your mother."

"Okay," I say in a practical tone, aware of the fact he'd kept the word 'mother' for the end of the sentence.

"So, the thing is, she wants to make some sort of move, but as part of our agreement she requires my signature."

"For what?"

"The apartment where she lives right now is rented, but we have a joint asset that she got in our divorce settlement at the time."

"Yeah, the city apartment." Does he seriously think I don't know about that?

"Yes. Right, that's it, the city apartment."

"Okay, and?"

"So, look, she—" He pauses and considers his wording. "She wants to organize her will and inheritance. And the thing is that because of the rift between the two of you, she doesn't feel connected to you, and she doesn't . . . she wants Roy to inherit the apartment." He looks at me for a brief moment and immediately continues. "Now, I won't accept an unequal division, even if you're not in touch with her, it has nothing to do with it. Inheritance is inheritance, and it shouldn't be divided that way."

"I don't have a problem with it, makes sense to me."

"Don't be such a smart aleck, Noa, you need to take some responsibility here too, and remember that you don't have a lot of options, you need to show some maturity here—"

"No, not interested. I don't want to inherit anything from her."

"Well, the important thing is that she said that if you get back in touch then she'll reconsider, or feel differently, or God knows what, but since you haven't seen each other for years now—and this is her words, not mine—she says it wouldn't feel authentic."

"No problem, she doesn't need to leave me anything."

"No, that's just not right! This inheritance is from both of us. That is what was agreed on and I'm not going to back down." He's tapping his finger on the table in an embarrassing display of assertiveness.

"I don't want anything from her, Dad. It's ridiculous."

"Yes, but you must understand that I don't have all that much, and your grandma's still living in a rental, so there are no other assets."

"I don't need anything from you or from her or from Grandma," I say dryly.

"Well, Noa, I'm sorry to tell you that's not how it works."

"I'll determine how things work for me."

"No, I won't have her leave everything to Roy." He's talking to himself more than to me. "I won't agree to it."

"It's a dated divorce settlement, it's irrelevant, that apartment hasn't been yours for years." My leg starts twitching.

"I'm asking you to try here. Cooperate."

"No! It's not a matter of cooperation, I don't want anything from her, and I'm not interested in renewing contact with her, and this whole thing is sickening." There, I'm starting to get angry. Well done, Dad.

"I hate to tell you, but I can understand her." He gives me his puppy-dog eyes even though he's choosing to taunt me.

"Great. Then you get back in touch with her," I retort.

"Oh, come on, I don't see why we have to keep going around in circles here."

"I don't appreciate this kind of bullying and I don't want to get any money or assets or anything from her."

"Well . . . then we need to figure out what we'll do."

"No, no 'need to figure out' and no 'what we'll do.' Everything's fine, she can leave it all to Roy, I'm happy for him, I'll be fine."

The waiter suddenly towers over us and interrupts the conversation. "Who's having the house salad?"

After that, we talk about other things. I hate each and every minute that passes and I can't wait for it to end.

>

How am I supposed to go on working now? I can't concentrate on work. My thoughts wander and I get tired. There's the closed door to Teddy's office. What would he say about her choice? He'd probably never do such a thing. But what do I even know about him? I don't know what kind of dad he is. I decide not to tell him about any of this, and one could almost think that my thoughts have an effect on reality, because the door suddenly swings open and there he is.

"Tell me something, do I look like an idiot to you?" he shouts with pure rage, and I get all tensed up, only to realize that he isn't talking to me. I look back to see whom he's addressing. People are staring along with me as he walks toward Jamie, who's leaning her sweet round ass on the desk while having her typical whispery chitchat with Maureen. "You have any idea what you've done?" he yells at Jamie. "Or are you too stupid to realize what you've done?"

The look on her face is a dead giveaway that she knows what she's done. She goes a little pale, but quickly comes to her senses and looks him straight in the eye. "Teddy—" she starts to say with her vocal fry, but he interrupts her.

"You asked me and I said no, but you think you know better than everyone, don't you?" He doesn't lower his voice. "In my office, now!"

Jamie maintains a proud expression and gives him an 'after you' gesture. He turns and walks away and she follows.

The door shuts. His office door is made of glass, half of it transparent and half frosted. I can see where they are in the room: she's sitting on the guest chair, usually situated in front of his desk but now a couple of feet farther away, and he's standing between her and the desk. She's leaning back, both of her high heels firmly on the ground at a short distance from each other, and she's slightly shifting from side to side on the swivel chair. The blend of the circumstances and her body language is off, almost intimate, which immediately puts me into a jealous mode.

He called her stupid in front of everyone. What did she do? How do I find out? Will Teddy tell me? Their conversation lasts a good while. At a certain point, Jamie sits up, the high pitch of her replies can be heard through the wall, but I can't make out her exact words.

I see Richard looking troubled as he heads toward Teddy's office. He knocks on the door and goes in straightaway, then shuts it behind him. After less than a minute the three of them come out, quickly pacing in single file. Jamie picks up her purse and her leather jacket, and they leave the office. Despite how pointless this will most likely be, I try my luck with Maureen.

"What was that all about?" I remind myself not to breathe through my nose.

"Huh?" Maureen plays dumb.

"What happened?"

"What are you talking about?"

I can't stand her! I decide to leave it alone and concentrate on work but instead find myself marching straight over to Hailey's office—her door's always open, of course, since she's got so much going on that she has nothing to hide. Hailey and I very obviously dislike each other, but seeing as she's taken the hypocrisy oath, she's usually nice to me.

"What's up, Noa?" She smiles and immediately starts rambling about not having had her lunch yet and how I look and how she feels.

"Did you see what happened with Jamie?" I ask.

"Yes, I actually did, saw and heard the whole thing."

"What was it about?"

"Oh, don't you worry about it, honey, it's totally none of our business. Do you need anything? Because I really need to get going!"

Two hours pass. Punching. Punching, that's what I'm imagining, me beating him up.

What is it now? What's my problem? So she screwed up—like I give a fuck—and she's probably in anguish too. Then why do I want to be in her shoes? What does it take to get told off around here? I'm entertained by this, so I text him.

I want to be told off too.

This is, of course, a moronic notion since the chances of getting the desired reply are slim versus the serious chances of no reply, something that I never manage to fully prepare for and can totally ruin my day. I'll look at my phone every twenty seconds and touch the screen every time it goes idle to see if I got any texts; sometimes I'll unlock my phone and check the texts again—in case it's one of those rare yet precedented instances where my phone didn't notice it received a text and therefore didn't notify me. Eventually, I get tired of waiting and leave the office, and in an attempt not to lose my mind I plan to catch a movie with Alison.

We're sitting in the dark theater. A light flashes inside my bag.

Trust me you dont

I can feel the oxygen resuming its course through my veins. That's what junkies are like, I realize now. The drug rushes through my veins and I'm a person again, until the next fix. There are so many things in this world—I look at the vast screen—so much hardship, hunger, degradation, desperation, death, and occupation, and what's all that compared to this? What kind of shallow person spends an entire day preoccupied by some man's attention to her? Take all that energy, get out there, and do some good in the world. Humanitarian aid, anonymous donations, help the poor, save children from starvation! What do you do instead? Think incessantly about Teddy Rosenfeld and if he'll reply and what you'll write back. So after all those thoughts, I give a dead-end reply:

Okay.

Which, as the case usually goes with dead-end replies, gets a reaction straightaway.

Where are you

Now, the dose already in the bloodstream, the junkie lies back with a smile.

At the movies.

Then why aren't you watching

I smile to myself. His sweet mind.

I am.

I want him to tell me what happened. It's all making sense now: I've never gotten the sort of emotional reaction out of him the way Jamie did today. Why wouldn't I be jealous?

I hope he'll ask me to come over and I imagine myself there, and we're lying in his bed as he tells me everything.

The movie's over. I text him from the rear stairwell leading out to the street.

Fin.

It's already evening. Alison zips up her jacket and asks if we're going to hang out and talk for a bit. I check my phone. There's a text from him.

How was it

She can tell I'm distracted and she puts her hand on my shoulder. "Okay, put your phone away for a minute and let's go sit somewhere, need to tell you something."

What does she need to tell me? I look at her, and she smiles that smile of hers that bares only her bottom teeth. I point at her stomach and she nods her head in excitement. I hug her tightly—but not too tight—and shower her with questions. How's Tom, and what week are you in, and how can you sit next to me for two hours at the movies and not say anything about it. I'm very excited for them and I can't believe there's going to be a kid who's the combination of these two individuals, and I already have love for this baby. We sit down at a café nearby and talk about everything she's going through; during these moments I identify with her so strongly that I can genuinely connect with the convenient logic of the customary way: woman + man = child.

After we say goodbye, my excitement turns into a strange kind of mood. The street's full of people. I walk and text Teddy.

Free to talk?

Yes

"Hi."

"Hey. How was the movie?"

"Don't remember." I hear that he finds that funny. "Where are you?"

"Where would I be?" His voice is quiet and peaceful and calms me down.

"At home?"

"At home," he confirms.

"I was with Alison, my friend who you actually know, now that I think of it."

"Don't know your friends."

"You were at her wedding."

"She married Judith's son?"

"Yeah."

"Okay."

"So that's it. And she's pregnant. She just told me."

"I see."

Now I'm the one laughing. "See what?"

"Your point."

I light a cigarette, which stalls me for a moment. "I'm happy for them, you know. Very much so."

"I know. I know you are. Of course you are."

I go quiet. He stays quiet along with me, I can feel him. I take a risky turn. "What happened with Jamie?"

"Forget about it."

"Tell me. Please, tell me."

"No, I'm not getting into that." He takes a deep breath.

"Are you still mad at her?" Maybe he will get into it after all.

"Incredibly."

"You called her stupid in front of everyone."

"She really is stupid."

"But in front of everyone?"

"She's stupid in front of everyone."

"Why?"

"Because she's way out of line."

"What did she do?"

"She handles one of our biggest clients and she gave him information that he then leaked, and that can screw up the England bid we've been working on for months now."

"Coleman."

"That's right."

"I see. But she thought it would help the bid, so she meant well. Her intentions were good."

"I don't care."

"Shouldn't you care?"

"No. Not at this stage."

"So what's going to happen? Is she staying with Delmar?" I reach my street.

"No."

"Seriously? That bad?"

"Had it up to here, she hasn't been right for us for a while and now she's doing actual damage, you know?"

"Okay. She's still lucky."

"Why's she lucky, Noa? Because I told her off?" He pays me back with my own words, and I'm moved by his ability and willingness to see right through me.

"Yes."

He's amused. "Bullshit. Didn't feel so lucky in the elevator, did you?"

"Also true."

"Complained about it afterward."

"I didn't complain at all."

"Fine. You have no idea how unlucky she is right now."

She's unlucky *right now.* Then when was she lucky? It suddenly dawns on me. I pause, knowing that I have no way of verifying the theory I'm currently developing, not now.

I don't want to stay silent for too long. "I'm home."

"All right. Good night."

No, that's not what I wanted. So many mistakes.

"Good night." I stub out the cigarette and enter the building.

»

During the weekend I rewrite the script for the pitch film. It's challenging, but I manage to incorporate most of the team's ideas—just not the horrendous ones—while almost preserving my original concept.

At the start of the week, my meeting with Richard goes well. We review the revisions, and he's pleased and just asks that I make a few minor corrections, none of which bother me. I feel elated and gloomy at the same time. I must learn how to compromise, I know that's my problem—I mean one of my problems—and stop looking for external validation, and concentrate more, be more focused, and stop being angry at everyone all the time just because that's what I'm used to, and sit down and write my film, and accept that I am what I am and completely and entirely change!

"So what's the budget? How much do you need?"

I lift my eyes away from my laptop. There he is, Teddy, standing by my desk again, this time in short sleeves.

"I don't know yet."

"Roughly."

"I don't want to just throw out a figure. I'll sit down with the producer and we'll get a budget together and I'll hand it in."

"Okay, no problem. How are you?"

"Fine." I look at him and hold on to my hands, so I don't touch him.

"I can see that." He smiles at me and walks away.

Thing is—some days I just have to. It literally hurts between my legs and it takes over my entire body and my mind. And now I'm sitting here, still able to smell him. Ten minutes pass, during which I can't stop thinking about him and his cock—and there it is, a message ping.

What are you doing

Yes, good question. I'll send an honest reply.

Thinking about you.

Come here and think in front of me

And then what? That'll just drive me up the wall. I see that the coast is clear. What does he actually want? Another text.

Cmon

He wants me to come. I go into his office, shut the door.

"There." I sit on the chair in front of him.

He reclines and runs his hand over the back of his neck. I look at his inner arm, fair and smooth, and I want to touch it.

"What's with you?" he asks.

"What's with me?" I look at him tauntingly, my legs stretched out before me, one on top of the other as I shake the bottom one in defiance.

"Why do you look restless?" He examines me with a sympathetic gaze.

"You know why."

"Do I?"

"I believe you do."

He goes quiet for a moment, looks at me. "Maybe tonight."

"Maybe now."

"Can't now."

"Can too."

"I have a meeting in"—he glances at his wristwatch—"less than half an hour. Can't leave the office."

"No need to even leave the building."

"Where?" he asks.

"The stairwell."

"You're out of your mind. Way too risky."

"Not our floor. All the way up, there's a quiet area. I checked."

"You checked? That's how you spend your time at work?"

"Yes, among other things."

We look at each other, silent and smiling.

I mouth, "I want you."

"Behave," he answers quietly.

I look at him. He looks back. I take a breath. He gives a serene little smile. I shove my hand in my pants and continue looking at him. His eyes follow my hand and his calm is receding. I put my fingers in until I find what I was looking for, pull my hand out, and stand up. He looks at me tensely and shakes his head almost unnoticeably, but I'm already leaning forward and reaching my arm out all the way to his face and he immediately grabs my hand and presses it to him and inhales deeply.

"Who behaves like this?"

"The media department."

He pushes his chair back and gets up. "All right, show me your place."

I straighten up, heart pounding. He leaves the room and I follow. We cross the main work area and reach the office's glass door. He opens it, we come out, and now I'm the one leading the way.

"Need to take the elevator up first." I push the button.

"Very thorough."

"Don't want you saying I'm unprofessional," I say.

He's standing in front of me, calm in a way that makes me want him even more. The elevator arrives and we go in. I grab hold of myself and keep my distance, otherwise I might pounce. We reach the top floor.

"Come on." I lead him out to the vacant stairwell and climb up two more flights of stairs. He follows me up, not too fast, not too slow.

"What the hell were you doing up here?" He laughs as we reach the abandoned, secret spot inside this gigantic office building.

I stand facing him. "It's not like we can do anything we want here, but still."

"What do we want?" he quietly asks, and pulls me to him, softly placing his hand on my neck, pushing his fingers through my hair, and turning my face to him, kissing me, smelling and kissing my neck, pressing me against him in a way that immediately turns me on as my hand reaches between his legs. There's that cock. He puts his hand on mine and presses it so that my hand can feel a whole lot more now. He disconnects and takes a slight step back.

"We can't fuck here." It's actually me declaring that. I can't see it happening under these conditions.

"Open your shirt and show me your breasts," he says, and I unbutton my shirt and stand in front of him, and then I push my bra under my breasts and they're out.

He stays still, just looks at me and my body, and then unzips his pants and takes his cock out—the latter only now learning about this urgent board meeting. I reach out, grab it, bend down, and put his soft cock in my mouth. His scent is gorgeous. I put one knee on the floor, but his cock is too high up when I'm on my knees, so I stand up and bend forward with my legs straight and suck him off, and he puts his hand on my back and slides it over my ass till he reaches between my legs, and I groan and want him to press right there over my pants, and he's already hard as he takes my hand and places it around his cock. Now he's using my hand, he presses tightly and it's arousing and we continue like that for a few moments until he stops and turns me with my back to him, strokes my breasts, puts his hand in my underwear, I lift my ass and that move turns us on, I hold on to the rail and he lowers my pants and my underwear down to my knees, places his cock on my ass, I want him to go in but there's no way it'll work, I feel him running the tip of his cock over my pussy and then he pushes it and I spread my legs farther and lift myself a little higher and apparently there is a way because there it is, he's in now.

How I've missed his cock inside me, heat rising from between my legs, through my heart, and all the way up to my brain, which is very excited about him fucking us right now.

He goes in deeper, I feel him inside my internal organs, everything is sensitive there today. "Your pussy's too much."

"Too much what?" I ask, and look back at him.

"Being inside you. I can't explain how it feels."

He's pounding me harder and it's getting intense. I shut my eyes. It's unbearable and amazing at the same time. I know I can't come in this state, but it doesn't matter, the pleasure of having him fucking me like this is fuel for many future orgasms. A door slams a few floors below us. We really should stop. It's no good here, just had to feel him for a moment. I better leave him unsatisfied if I want to see him tonight.

"Let's stop."

"Let's not." He leans forward, his hands on the rail. I look at his extravagant wristwatch, which he usually removes beforehand.

"So you're stopping?"

"No. Can't and won't." He keeps going and that's understandable.

We're in the elevator and he's standing there smiling and glowing, and I must be too. I smell my hand, our strong scent.

"This hand is going to be glued to my face all day." My words come out muffled with my hand covering my mouth. He takes my hand away from my face and nears it to his, smells it too, kisses it, and lowers it down.

"Come over tonight?" he asks.

I slowly nod my head and smile—so there you have it, even though he's not unsatisfied, I'm still invited over. He smiles at me and looks at the elevator screen. We're on the twenty-sixth floor.

Back at the office I'm sitting at my desk, my body still feeling what just happened, thinking about how everyone around me has no idea, but can maybe sense that Teddy just fucked me in the stairwell ten minutes ago, that his cum is here with me, that I'm in the midst of an emotional and physical celebration. Teddy passes by me with Richard, shoots me an intimate look.

›

But in the evening, when I text him that I'm coming over, he replies:

Wont work out

I'm already dressed and ready to go. Sit back down on the couch. The disappointment's weighing on me, so heavy that I can't move. I need to get used to the idea that we won't be seeing each other tonight. He didn't even tell me until I prompted him. Disgusting. I quickly reply.

Okay

I try to remove the disappointment and change into some sweat-pants. Take it easy, it doesn't always work out. I had a great time with him upstairs today. I'll see him tomorrow morning, we'll be together tomorrow night.

The following day at the office I realize that he's out of reach. He's busy and seems agitated, so I stay away from him. I decide to give him some time and wait for him to initiate. But the hours pass by and he doesn't text me or call me over, and at some point I realize that he's left.

It's difficult not to text him in the evening, but I hang in there. Well done, Noa.

The same situation continues the following day. I know that it has nothing to do with me and that he has nothing to offer right now. The whole thing gets me down, so I sink into work. When I get back home, I feel like it doesn't make sense anymore and I text him.

How are you?

Time goes by and no reply from him. I can't even cry, I just feel this terrible emptiness. It takes so little for me to be unable to find any point in life, unable to see anything that should keep me here.

At night I get these exhausting dreams about Sharon and another friend of ours; we're supposed to sleep somewhere, we have no beds and no mattresses, and everyone's pregnant and I'm pregnant too, and despite the sinister tone, we laugh about my pregnancy.

My car dies on the way to work and I have to leave it on the side of the road and wait for a tow truck and it's raining. It hasn't even been a month since I proclaimed to him that my car can go all the way up to Jerusalem—and here it is, expiring on the side of the road in Tel Aviv.

In those moments of distress, when I'm supposed to call someone and ask for help, I'm aware of the option of calling Teddy, but I don't do it. Doesn't make sense to ask for help if he's not even talking to me. I'm experiencing his disconnection as abandonment, understanding and sympathizing with him for choosing to abandon me, because I really am repulsive and there's no reason for wanting to stick with me. The moments we've had together seem illogical, incomprehensible. No explanation.

I arrive late to the office, soaked from the rain and pissed off, and sit at my desk. I have a meeting with the producer and the cameraman I'd taken on for the project, they're both friends of mine from university. Maureen authorizes me to use the boardroom. They arrive, I make them some coffee, and we sit down to work on the budget. Teddy shows up at the office while we're working. I spot him and Jamie through the boardroom's glass wall as they arrive together.

Why is she here? Our eyes meet and my stomach convulses. They stand there talking for a moment, and then she walks away and he heads in our direction. He comes in and I introduce him to my friends. As he shakes their hands, I pick up some of his scent. He's nice to them and makes them feel comfortable. Before he goes out, he puts his hand on my shoulder.

"I need to talk to you."

"Sure, no problem." I try to keep a steady voice. "I'll come by in a bit."

"Thanks. Good luck, guys."

After they leave, I walk over to his office. I'm in a delicate state, broken but not interested in revealing it, mainly because I must maintain a professional demeanor and not allow my mental state to influence the project. Maureen's at her desk, his door's closed.

"Hey, is Teddy here? He asked me to come see him."

"Huh? Yeah, he's inside, wait a sec." She gets up and knocks on the door, Teddy replies, she peers inside and talks to him from the entrance.

"Noa's here, you called her over?" How dumb is this scenario.

"Yeah," I hear Teddy say, "let her in."

Maureen gestures for me to go in and I do, shutting the door behind me.

"How did the meeting go?" He looks amazing, which is unfortunate.

"Went well, we'll have a budget in a few days' time."

"Sit down for a minute," he says, and points at the guest chair, and I feel it rising inside me, feel like I might burst out crying and really don't want to cry in front of him, because he'll fling me down all twenty-six floors and rightly so. "You okay?" He gives me a brief yet piercing look.

"Yes. You?" I summon all my strength, sit down on the chair in a noncommittal manner, very different from how I'd sat there but three days ago, at a different time in life.

"I'm fine, I have some tricky matters to attend to." He runs his hand through his hair. "But we'll get through it."

"Everything work out with Jamie? Is she back?" I don't look at him.

"No. She came by to sign some papers and just came up to say hi."

I nod my head, trying to keep my eyes on a certain spot between us.

"Noa." He says my name in a tone that reminds me that he can see into my soul. I need to get out of here.

"Okay." I get up, clutching the production file in my hand. "I'll send the budget over, and if you need any clarification, then let me know and we'll go over it."

I'm talking with a nice, courteous smile. He takes a little breath and continues looking at me in the same way, but I'm already headed toward the door.

"If you need anything just let me know," I add a vague sentence lacking any and all context, but that's just what comes out. Maybe he says something else, but I'm already out the door and I know that what just happened is not good. I know that he could see I'm broken, that I didn't manage to hide a thing, that maybe it would have been better if I was the one sitting before him rather than that stupid person I was portraying. Shit.

I go straight to the restroom, not even passing by my desk, get into a stall and shut the door.

What were you thinking sitting in front of him at the restaurant and telling him that you're strong and that he wasn't going to break you? He doesn't reply for two days and you're completely distraught. This is who you want to be? How much of a pathetic loser can you be? Why would he ever want you? Why did you think he ever did? He called you over to see that you were okay, that you don't just collapse when he's unavailable, but there you go, you showed him that you do. If nothing else happens, we'll be stuck with Noa while he gets to go on living with Teddy. That's not fair.

I want to get out of the office before anyone sees me, most of all before he, the one who sees all, notices me. I quickly gather my things and go down to the parking lot, look for my car, can't figure out where I'd left it until I recall that it died this morning. I go out to the street, quick steps away from the office building, can't manage to hail a taxi, so I start walking. Heavy traffic on the roads, the rain messes with the drivers here. People crowd under a bus stop, and I just keep on walking, disregarding the fact that I need to cross the city to get home. I'm getting drenched, but I don't mind that, and at some point I also stop minding the pain.

When I get home I shower and sit down on the couch.

Think about it:

There's Delmar, and despite everything it's a fine and interesting job and filming will start soon and you'll be the one directing and no one else, and there are your friends and your family—sort of—and there's you and your body and you're healthy, and there are ideas and there are books and TV shows and movies you haven't watched yet.

And then there's Teddy.

Whatever you can take—that is, whatever he's willing to give—take it. Because he's singular, one of a kind. And you *can* give something back to him, so maybe you're right. Maybe there really isn't anyone after you.

4

My Sort-of Family

+

I'm not sure how to describe the landscape of my soul, but I guess that a satellite view would reveal a host of black holes. For example, I can wake up in the morning and everything's fine, but I don't want to exist. And nothing can deaden the thought that I really should hang myself, or choke or cut my own head off—doesn't matter how, as long as I manage to sever my mind from my body and from this world.

During such mornings, reality's coated by a murky layer, but I know that I'm seeing the truth, that this is reality in its most absolute, primal form—unlike all the other moments where there's hope or gratification, moments that are a complete lie.

»

Tonight works come over tonight

I get this text on Monday afternoon, five whole days after that conversation in his office. He hasn't come by the office, and we haven't spoken, not even over the weekend.

'Come over tonight,' as if it's obvious and clear that I can and want to come over. He assumes that I'm on hold until the moment he snaps his fingers. But maybe that's exactly what I've committed to with all my declarations. I'm not sure how to reply. My heart rate accelerates again, it's incredible how I can just return to this state with him within a mere few seconds. I decide to reply in a professional manner, since I'm also pissed that he's not showing any interest in the project.

I have a budget, not final but
an estimation.

Good bring it

No, not enough. I need more than that, something has to be said. I take the risk:

Why come over tonight—
ask me if I want to come.

Want to come over ?

Yes.

Is that better ?

Yes.

So tonight we'll see us. That's good. I feel unsettled but I know that once I'm there and he behaves the way I like, I'll get to be myself again.

❯

I knock and he opens the door. He's on a call. He returns to the living room and I shut the door and follow him. The call seems work-related, and he sounds annoyed. I go for a smoke on the balcony. I can't see him, but at a certain point he gets angry and raises his voice. Not that I don't like it, listening to him getting upset is a form of pleasure. I wonder if I'll get a different side of him once he's done. Though I can already tell—I shouldn't have come.

I finish the cigarette. Twenty minutes more, he's still on the phone. It's getting cold on the balcony. I go back inside but don't know where to be without disturbing him. I search for his eyes and ask with a little hand gesture if I should go. He motions 'no' with his hand. I go to the bedroom to get out of his sight, sit on the bed, and turn the TV on. Don't know how long that goes on for, since at a certain point I fall asleep.

"Noa." He's sitting next to me on the bed trying to wake me up, his hand on my back.

"Yeah." I open my eyes, disoriented.

"I need to go."

I quickly come to my senses and sit up. "Okay, I'll get my things."

"No, no. Stay here, I'll be back later, don't go. Just didn't want to go without telling you. Go back to sleep."

"Where are you going?"

"Come here for a minute." He hugs me and kisses me on the lips. It's been a week since the last time.

"Where do you need to go? What time is it?"

"It's ten. I need to go for an hour, maybe two."

He doesn't want to tell me. Stay? Leave? I don't know what to do.

"Stay," he answers my thoughts.

"Okay." I look at him.

"Good. I'm heading out." He gets up. "Make yourself at home."

Weird. An hour, maybe two? Where's he going? Well, it doesn't matter anyway—the twisted bottom line is that I'm here and he's not and he said stay. Just like the first time I came here, when he'd sent me to go fetch the laptop. Could it be that I felt closer to him back then? After getting a little high, I wander around the apartment. Go up to the strange room upstairs, find nothing of interest and come back down. Consider peeking into Milo's room but feel uncomfortable about it so I don't.

Now what? I lie on his bed and watch a movie—more like stare at one—and try to figure out this man. After midnight, I text him.

> Hey, maybe I'll just go and
> see you tomorrow

Not so clever since I don't really want to go back home now.

> Back in 30

What should I say? I'll let him be. I get that he would've preferred to be here right now and that's good enough. That's a good enough reason to wait patiently.

He shows up at 1:15 a.m. and finds me sitting in the middle of his bed.

"Survived?" He doesn't immediately come up to me.

"Yes. Now can you tell me where you were?"

"I rather not." He takes off his wristwatch.

"Such terrible conditions!" I shout and pound my fists on the bed. He grins, then takes off his jacket and shoes and pants.

"I did warn you."

"You did."

"There you are." He sits next to me and grabs my face with one hand and my neck with the other and kisses me and we kiss and I close my eyes and feel his entirety within seconds, his scent, his taste, and I open my eyes so I can see him, how I've missed this son of a bitch, how much waiting do I need to endure.

"I don't feel like fucking yet. Would you believe it?"

"With you? No." He leans on the pillows, leaves a hand on me.

"You're right, I do feel like it. But I feel more like talking than I do fucking."

"Oh my." He leans his head on his arm.

"No, a nice talk, you know. A light chat."

He laughs. "What do you want to talk about?"

"I want to find something out."

"What?"

"I had a thought and I'd like to find out if it's true."

"What thought?"

"Okay." I scratch my face, considering my words and quickly compromising. "You and Jamie."

He looks at me. "Well?"

"That's it, that's the question."

"You want to find out if I fucked Jamie?"

"Yes."

"Why do you ask?"

"Shit," I immediately say and he laughs. "That reaction means you did."

"Right," he confirms.

"Really?"

"Really. Why wouldn't I?"

"Exactly, why wouldn't you? I get it, she's very attractive. And does it still happen sometimes?"

"No, no. Not anymore." He smooths his hair back and gives me a warm look. We smile. I try to figure out the time frame.

"When did it happen? When you and Lara were still together?"

"Yes."

"And Lara knew?"

"No. Why would she know?"

"So what happened?"

"Why do you ask all these questions, monster?"

"Because I want to know."

"Why?"

"Because it turns me on."

"Yeah right. Fat Teddy fucking that little shithead. She really did a number on me with that bid. You know what, it's unbelievable how I keep finding myself in these situations with women after giving them everything they wanted—and then they go and fuck it all up." He runs out of air. "It's unbelievable. You'll be the same, you're halfway there."

"Pretty good chances."

"I know! And here you are, and now would be the time to send you home, but instead I want to fuck you. Even though you're a pain." He proclaims all of this beauty in the exact same position, not moving an inch, arm shoved under head, one foot over the other.

"Then tell me what went down with her. Who initiated it?" Suddenly either option stresses me out a little. If he was the one who'd initiated, then that means she won something that I hadn't; and if she was the one, then it means that I'm just like all the others.

"We met at a wedding, if I'm not mistaken . . ."

"Extremely amusing," I mutter, and he smiles.

"It was in New York, we were drunk. I fucked her in the lobby restroom, even though we could have gone up to the room, now that I think about it."

"More."

"More. Well, you of all people should know how this works. This and that all evening long, and then at some point she showed me that she wasn't wearing any underwear."

"Classic," I say with a smile.

"Yeah," he agrees. "So that was it, we just got up and went out to the lobby and into the restroom, I fucked her from behind, came on the goddamn floor like an idiot. Not very interesting."

"She didn't come?"

"You think I remember?"

"You remember everything."

"Not that."

"Did you kiss?"

"Yes."

"And then after that time, did it happen again?"

"Yes."

"A lot?"

"Yes."

"A hundred times?"

He laughs. "No."

"And did it go any further?"

"No, pretty much the same every time."

"Did you come on the floor every time?"

"No." He smiles.

"So it was the same as us?" My heart's pounding.

"No."

"What's the difference?"

He looks at me. "I didn't have any feelings for her."

Warm excitement rushes through my body. I stand up on the bed. "I win I win!"

"You're a real piece of work."

"Made you feel!" I call out, and leap onto him.

"Why would you even compare, huh?" He's laughing.

I lie on top of him, hug him with all my might. He puts his arms around my waist and I look at him.

"And why did she do it? Because she wanted you?"

"Yes."

"Like I want you?"

"You said no one wants me like you want me."

"That's right! Very true. But it wasn't for some kind of personal gain?"

"No."

"Okay. Thanks!" I end the discussion.

"That's it? Done?"

"For now, yes. Now we may fuck."

He laughs and hugs me. "Praying for a fast recovery from your mental disorders, honey."

〉

I wake up in the middle of the night. Darkness. I lift my head, Teddy's lying next to me. I hear a car alarm from afar. I touch him and he turns his head to me, and it takes me a moment to see that his eyes are open.

"Teddy?"

"Yeah?"

"You're not asleep?"

"I am."

I cling to him and he hugs me with one arm, gently caresses my back. I park my hand at the bottom of his stomach, just before the valley.

"Me too." I go back to sleep.

In the morning we're drinking coffee in the kitchen. I quietly follow his movements, trying to learn the order of things. Maybe this is a good time to talk to him about the budget? "So what about the pitch film? You have a few minutes to talk about it?"

"Yeah."

"One sec, I'll bring the spreadsheets."

"No, no spreadsheets, tell me how much."

"Why? I have it all ready for you."

"Bottom line. How much?"

"It annoys me that you're not showing any interest in it." I feel the need to mention this, or maybe I'm stalling.

"If you knew how much I have on my plate you wouldn't get annoyed."

"So tell me."

"Not now. What's the budget? Say the number."

"Around two hundred grand."

"Really? Two hundred grand?"

"Yes. See? I knew you'd be surprised, that's why I wanted to show you the Excel sheets"—I'm getting nervous—"so you'd understand the requirements and how it got to these costs. It also includes postproduction, which is a major part of the budget."

"No, no, leave me out of it. Fine."

"What do you mean 'fine'?"

"Fine, you have it."

"What? That's it? I want to show you all the beautiful tables and charts! We worked so hard, we color-coded."

"I don't need to see. You got your approval."

"Okay. Cool." I feel relieved. "Thank you. It'll be great to have a proper budget to work with. And you'll raise loads with it. A small fortune!"

He smiles at me and his phone rings. He looks at the screen and answers. "Hey, how are you?"

I pick up the newspaper to give him some privacy, but I'm eavesdropping. His tone of voice is different from usual. I can clearly hear the person on the other end of the line.

("Listen, I looked into the loan situation.") "Yeah." ("And it looks like it'll work out with the bank, I'm going to need a guarantor signature though, that's for sure.") "No problem." ("So should I come to the office?") "Whatever works for you." ("I might come by your place this evening, does that work?") "Yeah, no problem, just let me know."

He tosses the phone on the counter with an agitated move. He's silent, clears the mugs and washes them. I join in and tidy up alongside him. "Who was that?" I ask quietly in case he doesn't feel like answering.

"Adrian."

There's something strange about how he speaks to his son, about what he's like after the call. I'm missing some vital information and I have so many questions, but I realize that this is not the right time. This realization leads me to decide to leave and not go to the office with him. Do something on my own and give us some space.

"I'm heading out," I say.

"Aren't you coming with me?"

"No, I'm not coming in this morning. I'll come by later."

"Okay. Where you headed?"

I'm surprised and flattered that he's asked. "I think I'll go for a swim, and I have to run some errands."

"Isn't it too cold for a swim? I thought you hate cold water."

"Heated pool."

"Right. Okay, well have a swim for me too." He picks up his phone and a few papers from the counter.

I go to the bedroom, put my shoes on and grab my bag. "Bye, talk later!" I call out when I'm at the front door.

"Wait, I'll walk out with you."

I wait and he does a few last things, turns on the alarm. In the elevator we stand a couple of feet away from each other. He looks at me and seems troubled.

"So how does it work?" I ask. "If, say, I want to come over to your place, who do I talk to?"

He gives me a tired yet warm smile. "Come over whenever you want."

"Well then I'm just going to go right back up." I make believe that I'm about to press 9.

His smile widens. "You're sweet."

We get out of the elevator, and before he heads to the parking lot he turns to me, puts his hand on my cheek and kisses my lips.

"Bye, see you later." He turns and leaves.

I did good. I do love him.

>

I'm swimming and thinking about all the things I still don't know about him and then about all the things I do know: a long list of hard data, made of tiny subjective bits of information I've gathered.

Teddy's a hard worker. He works all the time. He doesn't do it for the money, he's got plenty already. He does it out of commitment. Furthermore, it satisfies his need for control, as well as other vital needs—challenge, creativity, purpose.

The pool's edge, breath, flip, water pushes in either direction, other side. The images come up in sync with my breaths: Teddy's phone tossed onto the kitchen counter, Jamie without any underwear in a New York hotel bar, me broken in the office restroom, my dad at the stale restaurant, "I hate to tell you, but I can understand her."

+

In the beginning, there were visitation agreements.

I didn't like it. I was nine, and I didn't like the fact that we were meeting twice a week for an afternoon designed for our togetherness. Before she left, she had been there all the time, in her way. That was the default. But then, afterward, everything changed, and she shifted from being a mom who's always there, yet not necessarily focused on me, to being a mom who's overly focused on me, yet not always there.

Almost never there, in fact. When I go to sleep—she's not there. When I wake up in the morning—she's not there. When my stomach hurts—she's not there. When I get back from school, she won't be coming home from work soon. She'll come home, all right, but not to my home. And where am I when I'm at her place? She'd organized a room for us with nice wooden beds and clean sheets and toys, but I don't like this room or this apartment, and I don't understand why things that I know from my own home are now here. The soft towel, the striped hat, the plates with the little flower prints. This isn't right, it'll pass soon, it'll go away. This won't last, I won't have to come here again.

But I know that she won't be coming home anymore. That there's no return from where she's at, where they're at. And I don't even want her to come home! Because even though sometimes she's joyful and soft and kind, sometimes she's the complete opposite; sometimes she's harsh or angry, and I'm scared of her anger and I feel like I'm in her way. So this is for the best. But then why meet twice a week and every third weekend?

During the first year, when she realized I didn't feel comfortable at her place, she used to ask me where I wanted to go. My answer was always the same: the model home showroom. It was a massive store comprising showrooms simulating homes: living room beside living room beside living room, kitchen kitchen kitchen, bathrooms. She'd take me there and we'd play.

She seemed comfortable with the time frames, arrive for pickup, return. I hated the walk from her car to my doorstep, just eight stupid feet, don't know why they troubled me. At night I'd wake up crying. I have no memory of that, my dad told me about it. Maybe he just made it up. He also told me about the times we'd waited and she never showed up, when he'd found me waiting in the street, sitting for hours on the curb, as well as one time when he saw me sitting in the middle of the road: "Noa, what on earth are you doing there?!" and I replied, "Waiting for a car to run me over." But maybe he made that up too, or just took a single occurrence and mythologized it because that's how he'd experienced it.

I remember when she told us. It was hard. My dad wasn't there. I remember she sat us down and told us that they were breaking up. I remember saying "I can't believe it" over and over again until she angrily silenced me, because it must have been very annoying.

》

Two days go by, and on Thursday afternoon I'm scouting for a location with a small crew in preparation for filming. We're standing in the middle of a huge, abandoned hangar. The cameraman climbs up a rusty staircase leading to the gallery. "Noa, come take a look from up here." I climb up and check the camera angle he's suggesting. "What do you say?" he asks, then takes a few steps away to check another option. I don't rush after him and instead I check my phone and, in a moment of recklessness—without the assessment or approval of any internal committees—I text Teddy.

> What about tonight? May I
> come over?

I look at the phone. Come on, be 'Read.' There, he's seen it. Now he's typing. Shame he doesn't type as fast as he talks.

You may!

He approves and even marks his exclamation.

I'll quickly go home, shower and get ready, get to his place and when he opens the door, I'll kiss him. Everything goes as planned, but when he opens the door I feel like I'm not supposed to kiss him. I hear voices inside the apartment, and then an excited dog appears behind him, black-and-white fur.

"Come in, Milo's here with Daria. Come say hi."

My heart's pounding, I did not prepare for this. I follow him in. Milo's sitting by the big wooden table; Daria's standing next to him drinking a bottle of beer.

"This is Noa Simon." He's introducing me with my full name?

"Hi!" That's me, warm and incredibly friendly, shaking Milo's hand as he clumsily rises to his feet.

"Nice to meet you," Milo says politely and smiles, giving me a boy-ish, flaccid handshake. "This is Daria, my girlfriend." He states the obvious and sits back down. We shake hands and she smiles, little white teeth.

If I got thrown into a truck full of sweaty movers, I'd know precisely what to do in order to make a good impression and win their immediate appreciation. But this scenario? All I can think of is things like, So, yeah! I'm the one currently fucking your dad!

Teddy breaks the silence: "You want a beer?"

"Yes!" I reply to his trivial offer with disproportionate enthusiasm. "So this is the famous Xerox?" I reach out to pet the extremely cute dog.

"Oh, so you've heard about him?" Milo asks in a proud tone, and I nod my head.

They're talking about Daria's studies. She wants to study psychology and she's deliberating between two places. Teddy leans on the counter, listens to them, shares his opinion. He's barefoot and homey, I haven't seen him like this before. I listen and pet Xerox.

"Tel Aviv University doesn't really do it for me." Daria rolls her eyes.

"Noa studied film there," Teddy says, and looks at me. "Right?"

This confuses me since I definitely know I've never mentioned that, not to him or to Richard. Not that there's anything to hide, but I never submitted a CV and never gave them this information, or anything else, for that matter.

"Yes, I did my BA in film there." I feel Teddy's eyes on me. "But it was a long time ago. Ages," I immediately add.

Half an hour later we're saying goodbye to them at the front door. Teddy gives Milo a strong embrace and kisses his cheek. He gives Daria a kiss too, a polite one.

"Why did you not tell me they were here?!" I ask quietly the second he shuts the door behind them.

"It would've just stressed you out."

"True."

"So there you go, it's behind us." I appreciate his use of plural.

"They're very sweet. Milo's gorgeous."

"I think so too." He smiles. We sit down on the big, soft couch in the living room.

"How do you know where I studied?"

"You think that's difficult to find out?"

"No, of course not. But when did you look me up? Before I started working for you?"

"What's it any of your business?"

"Tell me!"

"Will not."

I kiss him on the lips. "I missed you," I say.

He kisses me and strokes my neck, kissing there too.

"When and what did you find out about me? I demand to know," I ask as the little kisses continue.

"You don't need to know everything." He gets up from the couch. "Let's go out for a smoke." He heads to the balcony. I follow him.

"So that was Milo. Next up—Adrian," I summarize.

"Good luck with that." He laughs and then we go quiet. Sounds emerge from the street below: distant music, honking cars, fragments of conversations, and bursts of laughter. City center on a Thursday evening.

"Tell me a little bit about Adrian," I say in a soft tone, staying cautious.

"Not much to tell. He's very different from Milo."

"Different how?"

"Complete opposite."

"What does that mean?"

He scratches the side of his jaw, thinks for a moment. "What does it mean? That he's a putz."

"Seriously?"

"What can I say? I love him with all my heart, that boy, I do. But he is a putz."

"Why?"

"He's . . . Look, there's no doubt that he's smart and diligent. But he's also stubborn and arrogant. And the worst thing is that I think he lacks a sense of humor, which doesn't really make sense considering his wonderful parents."

"Yeah? What's Alice like?"

"Alice's fine. You saw her not long ago, when she came by the office."

"Yeah, I know."

"Alice's great, she's a close friend of mine."

"She remarried?"

"Yeah, long time ago. Her husband's fine too." He gets up.

"Wait, tell me more." I stay seated.

"Okay. You want another beer?"

"Yes."

"I'll buy some ouzo, promise. The cheapest one on the shelf."

I give him a smile and he goes, leaving me on my own. This evening is far different from what I'd had in mind. In fact, it's much better.

›

"All right, what do you have planned?" he asks.

He has no idea, but this is a terrible question to ask me on a Friday morning. That is to say, I have no plans: I'll be leaving now, this place and him, back to the silence and void of the weekend, because if I don't make the effort and plan ahead with someone then I'll surely be sitting at home, smoking, watching content and sleeping and that's all she wrote.

"I'll see, I'm not sure yet." Ask me to stay with you today, please ask me to stay with you today.

"Do me a favor, Noa, will you? Press my back over here." He sits on the chair and points to a certain spot on his upper back. I know this backache of his, and I of course recall that moment at the office when he'd asked Jamie to press it for him. But he's never asked me to do it until now. I take on the task and stand behind him.

"Like that or harder?" I ask as he moans with his eyes shut, focused.

"Harder."

"Like that?" I press into his muscle but he doesn't react, so I intensify the pressure and make it real strong. We stay like that for a few minutes, with me leaning my entire weight into his shoulder blade while he's moaning and quietly concentrating.

"I need to leave soon. You want me to drop you off on the way?" he asks.

"No, it's cool," I answer, and decide as I go, "I'll meet some friends."

I go straight to the café. I don't spot any of my friends, and after I text a few of them, I realize that no one's planning on coming by. I have a coffee on my own and then slowly walk home. The sun's out even though winter officially started today.

At home I work for a bit, but then I feel like resting. I watch two movies. Once the second movie's end credits start, I go out to the roof. The sun's weaker now and the temperature's dropped. The city's quiet, a radio's playing in one of the houses, kitchen sounds from the apartment across the street. I think about my dad. It's unkind of me to hardly ever visit them, the last visit was a month and a half ago. Maybe I'll tell him that I'll come by tonight.

"Hello? Hello? Yes?"

"Hi, Dad. It's Noa." As though he has another daughter.

"Noa? Hey! Sorry, I didn't see who was calling, can you hear me?"

"Yeah, yeah, I can hear you. What's up?"

"Fine, everything's fine. Wait, I don't know if there's any signal here."

"There is, I can hear you just fine. Where are you?"

"Well, see, we went on a trip with Miriam and Mordechai, we're

just a few minutes away from the Dead Sea. Hello? Can you hear me?"
How can a man who's a gifted chemist, an outstanding lecturer, be so
incompetent at a simple phone call with his daughter?

"Yes, I hear you. Good, have a great time then."

"I'm sorry? Yes! Thanks, thank you. And you, what about you? You
okay? Everything okay?"

"Yes, everything's fine."

"Good, well, we'll be back tomorrow around evening time, so—wait,
did you call because you wanted to come by today?"

"No, no, just wanted to see how you're doing."

"Oh. Okay then. So let's talk, we'll talk later—tomorrow. I'll call
you."

"Okay."

"That was Noa," I hear him telling Mina. "She's fine, she sounds
fine. Why are you tailgating that truck? Look how close you are . . ."

I hang up and call Roy. He doesn't pick up but then texts me that he's
at rehearsal with his theater group in Jerusalem. I ask him if he'll be visiting Grandma since he's already there. He replies that he'd suggested
that, but she said that she's too busy. I reply with a laughing emoji.

Great. Now what?

What am I going to do with myself tonight? I can stay right here
till Sunday, maybe even after. There's no one waiting for me anywhere.
Absolute freedom, profound loneliness. I look at my phone. How much
time I waste waiting to hear from him, it's dreadful, I have to stop.

I call Sharon and ask her what they're up to tonight. She says they're
going for dinner at her parents' place. I immediately invite myself, but
then I must hold the phone away from my ear since she's cheering and
rejoicing very loudly. We say we'll meet there.

>

Sharon's sister, her two brothers, and their families—they're always
glad to see me. I have adopted this family. Everything that was lacking
in my home could be found here. All the good things that never happened there, happened here. It's not like I don't know the issues she has

with her parents, but still, this is a real home, the kind you walk into and can just let go, and there will always be someone to catch you.

Late afternoon, and even though it's a bit cold we sit in the yard before dinner. It feels pleasant. I love being with Sharon, we sit almost on top of each other on the bench swing, commiserating over the endless longing of our adult lives. I feel like one of them—I partake in mutual jests, only compliment dishes I genuinely find tasty. After the meal we stay seated around the vast messy table; the kids are already running around in the yard, the babies are tired and their mothers are caring for them. I try to imagine Teddy joining me for such a dinner. Bringing him here makes much more sense than bringing him to my dad's place.

What am I thinking, bringing him here? Why would he come over here, or anywhere for that matter? I must be getting confused, wanting more than I should.

After I help clear the table, I sit down for a smoke. Sharon's brother joins me. We have a little chat, and I go back to my thoughts about Teddy being here. Why not think about it? Just play with it in my mind? Okay, imagine it—I allow myself—so he's charming and funny and witty as usual, and everyone thinks he might be a bit old for me and they wonder about my choice, but then they're charmed and they realize why I of all people chose someone like him; he shows interest in all the conversations, he's great with the kids; he's the most successful person at the table. I'll sit next to him on the bench swing and he'll stroke my back.

These images bring up conflicting feelings. On the one hand, maybe I could want that. On the other hand—revolting. I walk over to my bag and grab my phone. Missed call from Roy, nothing from Teddy.

last seen today at 8:53 PM

Ten minutes ago. So close, I can sense the proximity through the short span of time. Where is he? What's he doing? Got people over for dinner? How does this man's life look? I so want to be with him right now. I keep from texting him, put the phone down, and return to my sort-of family.

>

On Saturday morning I wake up in a good mood. I have coffee on the roof, water the plants, and remove the dried leaves. Go for a swim, come back home, and everything suddenly seems much simpler. What's your problem? You want to see him? Text him.

How do you look on a Saturday?

Come see for yourself

How easy.

He opens the door for me, wearing different glasses from the ones I know. He looks beautiful—wild, unshaved, T-shirt even though it's not warm out and long sweatpants. He smiles at me.

"I brought wine."

"I can see that." He takes the bottle and reads the label.

"Yeah, you probably have something better, and if you feel like wine, you'll drink your own. Anyway."

"We can drink yours." He puts the bottle down and heads to the utility room. "Just a minute, I need to move the clothes to the dryer."

I follow him, watch as he leans down and pulls wet clothes out of the machine, shakes them and puts them in the dryer.

"You do your own laundry?"

"Yeah, Milo's and mine. But Betty does the sheets and towels and upholstery and God knows what else, she puts everything in the laundry, that woman." He straightens up and points at me. "Should I do yours too? Take it off."

Once we're back in the living room, I'm standing and he's in front of me. Saturday silence, dryer's working.

"Hey."

"Hi."

He leans down and puts his hand on my neck and kisses me. My body's pressed against his and it feels like my insides are pushing to the front, crowding in to get as close as possible to him. We kiss with our eyes open, and just like the first time, he kisses as though he's tasting me, like the beginning of a kiss over and over again, and it starts and within a second it gets intense and it turns me on but I don't want to scorch it.

"Okay." That's me, moving away from him. "Let's drink yours."
"Wise choice."

He goes to get a bottle and two glasses, and I sit down on the couch and feel at ease and happy to be at his place and hope I can stay here until tomorrow or until thirty years from now.

+

I fell in love with film on my first-ever shooting day; I should really say I fell in love with moviemaking. What is it that makes me feel so good on a set? I'm fascinated by how loads of people work together to reach a communal result. I love being part of a busy team, where everyone knows their roles, passes by one another in a practical manner. Everyone works hard to compose all the elements that need to appear before the camera lens, to capture this complex creation's single moment of existence.

The set overrides reality, that is to say—a film crew entering a place gets additional rights that its inhabitants don't usually have. The crew's energy creates an enclosed atmosphere and a flexibility that bends the local rules into a small autonomy, like that time we filmed at a huge police station, two floors of which were vacant and rented for filming purposes, and between takes we smoked weed as the floors above and below us housed a multitude of cops. This sort of thing happened in other places too, like the parliament, courthouses, army bases, religious sites.

That same flexibility also occurs between people, no matter their familial status. Not all, but most people do partake in the never-ending flirtation summer camp of shooting days, where there's more leniency than usual. This is without a doubt a playground for people like me, who enjoy the dynamics enabled by the set, that instant intimacy: just utter a couple of sentences, add a look and a spoonful of light touch, and mix well.

»

Mid-December, the third and final shooting day of the pitch film.

We're shooting at the hangar. I glance at my phone between takes. I would love for Teddy to come visit me on set, but he doesn't show up, as can be expected. "I don't have the time"—that's what he told me, unlike Richard, who visited set on the very first day, excited and proud.

A little before lunch break, and a moment after the assistant director announces, "Camera rolling, stand by for action!" I see Teddy walking into the hangar, accompanied by two men I'd never met: one in his fifties, not too tall, the jacket, the pants, the shoes—everything looks oversized, and the whole thing creates a pleasant and disarming impression; and a younger-looking guy, one could even say he's attractive but only to a point considering the preppy look. My guess is that this is Wills, the Delmar VP of operations in the United States, who's visiting for a few days, and probably one of his senior staff members. Matt the driver appears behind them.

"Noa?" That's the assistant director who's waiting for me to call action.

"Oh, sorry," I whisper. "Action!" I shout.

"Action!" he repeats much louder.

During the shot I watch the monitor closely. The camera's mounted on the cameraman as he advances toward the actor, I indicate something on the monitor to the assistant director, and he nods and passes the message on through the radio. I sneak a glance at my visitors, who are standing to the side very obediently, quietly waiting for "cut." I'm amused by how they're following orders given to them by a junior production assistant who hasn't the slightest clue that this is the company CEO.

"Cut," I say quietly.

"Cut!" the assistant director announces through the radio, and within a millisecond the motionless crew thaws into a bustling beehive.

My eyes and Teddy's meet, but on my way to him I'm stopped for questions, notes, adjustments; an actor needs the restroom, a production assistant hands me a soft plastic cup of too-cold water. Teddy introduces Wills—I was right—and Frank Clancy, the Ivy League hottie. By way of apology, I make a joke about how they were made to stand in the corner, and they say how impressive and professional the set seems.

Wills is friendly, the conversation with him flows smoothly, and Frank looks at me with smiling eyes.

"Noa, we need you!" The assistant director approaches us. "We need to cue second camera, when should I cue him?"

I excuse myself and invite them to stay for lunch. Teddy claims that they really came here only for the free meal, we all laugh, and I turn to my assistant director and quietly tell him that this is the CEO and ask that they take good care of them, and then I go off to give notes for the next take. Before we start shooting, I call Teddy over to the honorary position at the director's monitor so he can watch too. He stands next to me with his hands in his pockets, his face serene and beautiful. My man. I love having him there next to me, slightly behind me, my body lightly touching his with the kind of casualness no one would notice but the two of us.

"Stand by, first position!"

My "Action!" the assistant director's "Action!" and a quick glance at Teddy, who gives me a secret smile, eyes back at the monitor.

This take is much better. During it, the gaffer—he's the guy in charge of lighting—quietly stands next to me, and since this is our third day filming, it's already been dozens of times that we—the gaffer and myself—have been standing like this by the monitor during a take, and he feels comfortable touching me as he indicates a dark area on the monitor and quietly tells me that he'll adjust the lighting for the next take. I guess that's all I needed. This moment is pure joy, it's just a shame that what I'm filming isn't a feature I'd written, but even that doesn't matter now, as Teddy sneaks a glance at the masculine hand stalling over the back of my neck. Though my eyes are firmly fixed on the monitor, I can see everything. I turn my head slightly in Teddy's direction, the gaffer's hand still there, because how could he know who the man standing behind him is.

"Nice?" I ask Teddy.

He gives me that smile I love, the restrained one that holds underneath it a vast smile that doesn't break the surface.

"The nicest ever," he says quietly, giving me precisely what I want.

As I walk them to their car, I manage to get him alone for a moment.

"What time are you filming till?" he asks.

"We're supposed to finish by seven, but we'll be later than that, I think. In any case I'll stay here for longer, and then we might do some wrap drinks, so I don't know."

"I'm giving you a key, come over afterward." He separates his apartment key from the rest and puts it in my hand. I look at him with a huge grin. "Don't piss me off now," he adds.

"Heaven forbid."

"Good. See you later."

"But aren't you going to need a key to get in?" I smile.

"Got a spare in the car." He gestures for Frank to sit next to Matt and gets into the back seat with Wills.

I manage to catch his eyes before he shuts the door. "I'm not sure I'll make it."

"Whatever works out. Bye. Good luck."

I shove the key in my pocket and go back to the set. I feel so damn good.

>

Filming finishes late, breaking the set takes another hour, and the drinks end only around 1:00 a.m., so I forgo the opportunity to use the new key and go home instead.

The following day I wake up at noon. I'm beat and it takes time for me to recover. I drive through the pouring rain to return some filming equipment and get back to my place. Teddy texts me that he's busy this evening. I lie on the couch and fall asleep.

I wake up. Pitch black outside. What time is it? Almost midnight. Two texts from Teddy.

Asleep already ? Having dinner
close to you

And the first one, half an hour earlier:

You home

I reply that I'm at home and ask if he's coming by.

Three texts in one go.

OK

Finishing dinner

Be there soon

He hardly ever comes to my place. Maybe he'll stay over?

I'm still deep in sleep mode and I can't manage to wake up and tidy the messy table in front of me, dirty ashtray and leftovers. I lie back down on the couch, pull up the blanket and nap until I hear a knock on the door.

"Look at this face." He says when he sees me.

"Yeah . . ."

I go in and he's behind me, shuts the door. He's beautifully dressed and smells as lovely as ever, a pleasant combination of his own scent mixed with alcohol. I sit back down on the same spot on the couch so that he doesn't hog it. He goes to pee, I hear the flushing. Half-asleep, I smoke some of the joint awaiting me in the ashtray. He returns to the living room and sits next to me, places his hand on my knee.

"You're exhausted. Go back to sleep."

"No, I'll wake up soon. I want to be with you for a bit."

"Okay."

"Who did you have dinner with, Wills and Frank?" I ask, my eyes almost shut.

"Wills. Frank's taken off already."

"It was great that you came to visit the set."

"You're sweet when you talk in your sleep."

"You're sweet when you're here. Why are you here?"

"I came by for a minute, I'll head off soon."

"Sure. Just for a minute."

"Yes."

I open my eyes and look at him. Something is different, maybe him, maybe he's different.

"Come here," he says.

He turns my face toward him, caresses me and then comes closer and kisses me. A long, soft kiss, surprisingly sexy, after which we stay close, me with a grumpy-tired face and pursed lips, him with a calm face.

"Stay over," I say.

"No. You can come over to my place if you want."

"I feel like having you stay with me."

"Why?"

"Because I love you."

"Ah."

"I love you."

"It'll pass."

"It won't."

"So it won't. Why do you love me?"

"I love the way you are in life, your attitude. I love being next to you."

"Okay."

I release a little laugh. "Some reactions you got there."

"You love my reactions too?"

We smile.

"So you'll marry me?" I ask.

"Of course I will."

"Good. Just wanted to make sure."

"All right, let me take you to bed."

"Escort services."

"Exactly."

He gets up from the couch with his typical weightiness, pulls me up, and then puts his hands on my back, as though he's pushing me into leading the way. Once we reach the bedroom I turn to face him.

"Wait, but if you're not staying, then I'll come over."

"You're already in bed."

"I'm still standing!"

"So let's get you in bed."

"I need to get ready."

He sits on my bed, doesn't take his shoes off. "Do what you need to do."

I look at myself in the mirror, washing my face. How ugly am I! It's incredible. I wonder if he sees what I see when I look at myself. I turn off the light and go back to the bedroom. He's reading something on his phone, holding it away from him and squinting since he doesn't have his glasses on.

"Should I read it out to you?"

"No, nothing important."

I lie down next to him, situating my head on his shoulder. "You know I've never told you that I love you?" I say with my eyes closed.

"You told me five minutes ago."

"Yes, but *before* that I never did. That's what I mean."

"Doesn't matter."

"What doesn't matter?"

"If you said it before or not."

"Oh, I thought if I love you or not." He doesn't reply and I continue: "Because it matters to you if I love you, it's significant information."

"I know you love me."

"Good."

"And it's a shame too, of course."

"Of course, a real shame," I quickly agree.

"Since there's no future in it."

"Only the present. Present perfect."

"And you're wasting valuable time on me."

"Procreation time?"

"Yes."

A deep and heavy conversation is suddenly emerging out of a quiet, serene moment.

"I have no idea what I'm supposed to do with that right now," I say.

"That, I can't help you with. I can buy you a baby if you'd like. That I can do."

"Ha, then it might as well be yours and mine."

"No."

"No."

"I don't want to, Noa. You know that."

"I know. I don't really want to either. I don't know."

I sit up in bed, sleep has escaped me all at once. He puts the hand holding the phone on his thigh and looks at me.

"Want a blow job?" I ask in a casual tone, and he smiles, surprised. I smile too.

"No."

"No kids, no sleeping here, no loving you, no blow job."

"See? I need nothing. The perfect man."

"Not my cup of tea."

"What did you want?"

"What did I want?"

"Yes. What did you want from me?"

"This! For you to be here, in my bed, with me and mine, to love and to cherish."

"Then you got it."

"And you? Why are you here? What is it that you want?"

"Nothing."

"I was asleep on the couch. I didn't call you crying and say, Come over, Teddy, I need you."

"You just happened not to call today." We laugh and he adds, "Monster."

"No, not true."

"I wanted to see you."

"Why?"

"Because."

"What do you mean 'because'?"

"Just because."

I fall silent for a moment, not managing to understand myself. "You staying over?"

"No."

"Then go."

"That's it?"

"Yes," I say, and immediately regret it.

"All right." He gets up. "Come walk me to the door."

"I can't, I'm completely naked." I swipe my shirt off, followed by my underwear.

Already standing, he turns and sees my naked body. "Fuck."

"What is it?"

"Look at you." He sits down again, facing me. He puts his hand between my collarbones and runs it all the way down, using not only his fingertips but his entire palm, and stops at my pubic bone. I gently push my body against his hand; he pushes back and with his other hand takes my arm and holds it up, revealing my armpit, so that he can lean down and have his face close to it. I turn my head and look at him, see his tongue and then feel it slide over my armpit. It turns him on. The hand on my pubic bone moves farther down between my legs, not really touching anything, just staying there. He moves from my armpit to my nipple, grabbing it between his lips and that triggers me, my pelvis pushes up again and he pushes down again, and I want him to touch me, want him to touch my clit, but he avoids it, tormenting me. He lets go of my arm so that he can play with my wet and hard nipple, as he moves to lick the other one. He stops and straightens up. We look at each other. I sit up and he grabs my face and kisses me so hard that I can feel myself get wet just from his kiss.

"Fuck you," I say quietly.

He smiles and suddenly pushes me back down to the bed, holds my thighs and spreads them open. I'm dying for him to touch me, he can feel it in my body and see it on my face. He licks his fingers and gently caresses my clit, makes me moan and shut my eyes. I feel him move around, his fingers are still there and then it's his mouth, tripling the intensity and now I truly need him to get his dick involved in this wild carnival he's having here.

"Come on." My voice is begging on my behalf.

"What is it?" he repeats my words. "You think I'll fuck you now, after all those things you said?"

I smile and open my eyes to look at him. "Yes. I think you will."

He gets on top of me, my hand goes for his cock but his hand gets there first and he's already taking it out and before I even get a chance to hold it—he's inside of me. He locks his eyes on mine, pushing deeper slowly till the pleasure shuts his eyes and he starts fucking me. Like, properly fucking me. So proper that I soon get to the point that I must flip over because—with all due respect to the faithful missionaries—I know it will feel even better. His movements are strong and accurate, accelerating. I'm getting what I need right now, my body senses it and my mind knows it, though no matter how content I get, in a weird way, it also feels like waiting.

We fuck for a good while and suddenly he stops.

We catch our breaths for a moment, he pulls out.

"What happened?" I'm still facing down.

"Enough."

"No coming? You don't want to come?"

"No."

"Okay." I turn over and look at him, trying to figure out if something made him stop. I don't want to say anything. He's right, enough words have been spoken tonight, and maybe enough of the fucking too.

He stands up. "You're good? Finish yourself off for me, will you?"

I smile, a bit relieved. "Maybe."

"Come walk me to the door. Naked."

I get up and watch him pick up his keys and cigarettes from the table and open the door. He turns to me and pulls me into his arms.

"Good night, monster." He gently kisses me on my lips.

"Good night, Ted. A man worth loving." Guess I still have some words left.

He smiles his amused smile and disappears down the stairs.

I shut the door, flooded by both love and emptiness. I go to the bathroom, put the seat back down because he didn't, sit and pee, then I manage to think up a better slogan, so I rush to my phone and text him:

TED. Sperm Worth Spreading.

He replies:

Apparently not !

I confirm:

Apparently not.

He signs off:

Good night my dear

»

Two days later and it's Friday again. Why there must be weekends at the end of every week is beyond me.

It's a beautiful morning outside, but I'm not in a good mood and I stay in bed. I want to know when I'm seeing him next, I won't be at peace until I find out.

> Busy having people over for
> dinner tonight?

He replies half an hour later; I'm still in bed.

> Yes you're invited

I like that he's invited me but I'm also concerned that I may have forced him to invite me. I feel the need to rectify the impression I've made.

> That's not what I meant.
>
> Call me

"Hi," I say in a lukewarm voice.

"What are you up to? Where are you?"

"Home. In bed."

"Why aren't you in my bed?"

"Aren't I?"

"No."

"Right." I smile. I mean, he does know that I tried him last night and he never replied, so his playing coy right now is stupid, and still, I'm glad to hear him and even more glad to hear him say all that.

"Come over for dinner, not sure yet who'll be joining, but just come."

"Okay. I'll come."

"Good. Don't bring anything and don't ask me whether to bring anything."

"Okay. Should I bring anything?"

"I'm crazy about you. Come by at eight. Bye, I need to go."

"Bye."

He's crazy about me. What should I bring?

›

I dress nicely and put on makeup for dinner. A message pings and I need to stop for a sec and go check who it's from. It's Roy, he notifies me that he's in Tel Aviv and can meet up, since I've almost run out of weed.

I'm sitting in the car waiting for him at the street corner where we'd said we'd meet. I wonder if he knows about Nurit's inheritance plan. No, there's no way she told him, he can't handle that sort of pressure. Roy's in touch with her, but he knows that he's not allowed to talk to me about her, ever, in any sort of context, so I don't really know what the nature of their relationship is, I can only imagine it. He also knows that he's not allowed to talk to her about me.

The idiot's late, which means that I'll be late to the dinner, and that's making me nervous. When he shows up, we exchange fewer than ten words and I head straight to Teddy's place. I'll probably meet Adrian tonight. I think I'll feel comfortable with Milo, even though we'd met only for a short while, but Adrian's a whole different thing.

I'm at the front door holding the expensive bottle of gin I'd bought, and I ring the doorbell because I don't want to use the key when his kids are around. Milo lets me in, he's in a cheerful mood. I can hear chattering and laughter. I walk in, and then I notice a woman standing at the entrance to the kitchen with a wineglass in her hand. Teddy's in the kitchen, and he comes out when he hears me. He's wiping his hands with a small kitchen towel as he stands next to her, placing a soft hand on her back and introducing her as "Monique, Milo's mother." He introduces me as "Noa." Strangely enough, it feels right that he doesn't give me any sort of title. I shake Monique's hand, a bit embarrassed. She gives me a hearty smile; her hand is soft and warm.

Only then do I glance toward the living room. Milo and Daria are there, and a man's sitting across from them, tall and fancified with a well-kempt mustache—Emile, "a dear friend." I look back at Monique. Wild and fair red hair, Scandinavian features, enviable clothing, jewelry. There's something glamorous about her.

Teddy returns to the kitchen and she follows him, and judging by their dialogue I realize that she's the one who'd made the food. This realization deepens my discomfort. I place the bottle of gin on the table and sit down in the living room. Shake Emile's hand and ask Daria how she's doing. Milo and Emile talk between themselves in Danish. Daria looks at Milo as he speaks.

Teddy and Monique join us in the living room. Monique places two little bowls on the table, one with some special cheese she's brought from Denmark, the other with olives. Teddy reclines on the couch with his glass of wine and she sits next to him, not too close. They look good together, big man and petite woman. And there's their son. Why did I come here?

"What are you having, Noa? Wine? There's Campari too, grab some, it's in the kitchen."

"Okay," I say, and go make myself a drink. Maybe he should have served me one? No, why should I feel like a guest? He's right, I'm better off making it myself. I go into the kitchen and hear them laughing. They switch from Danish to English, but I still feel uncomfortable. I feel offended that he didn't tell me Monique would be here. Why is he doing this to me? I pour some Campari and add orange juice from a jug standing near the bottle. Teddy walks into the kitchen. He puts his hand on my back and leans in, kisses me on my lips, red wine flavor.

"Don't do this again, please," I hear myself saying, and my heart starts pounding way too hard.

"Do what, not kiss you again?"

"Stop it," I mutter impatiently.

"What's the matter now? What do you want?" Now he sounds impatient too. Too fast, give me a minute.

"I want you to tell me if your ex, the mother of your child, is going to be at a dinner that I'm invited to." My voice is trembling. "That's the least you could do." I'm grossing myself out. Why am I making a scene now? 'That's the least you could do'? What a sickening thing to say.

"Fine," he says coldly and checks on her food.

How do I get myself out of this? Why did I even say anything? The pathetic person that I am. "I'd have still come," I add on a positive note. "I just need to know these things." Am I tearing up now? God.

He glances at me and takes a baking pan out of the oven. "Why does it matter?" A swell of laughter rises from the living room. He smiles warmly, probably understanding the joke.

"Because. It matters to me."

"Does it make you feel threatened?" He faces me and I realize that I have to deal with what I'd brought upon myself.

"Maybe. I don't know."

"Then it shouldn't. Get over it," he says, and goes back out to the living room.

I push tears back and rush after him so that I don't stay in the kitchen on my own. Teddy sits down in the armchair this time, and now the expected seat for me to take is where he'd sat earlier, on the couch next to Monique. She turns to look at me and smiles. Milo looks so much like her. Teddy's talking to Emile, and I get an opportunity to talk to her alone.

"I'm happy to meet you," I say.

"Yeah? Oh, that's nice! How do you know Teddy?" She has a thick accent. I gather from her question that he hasn't told her anything about me.

"I'm . . . Well—"

I strangely get stuck midsentence. To my surprise, she gives an understanding smile, as though telling me, It's all right, you don't need to explain anything. I smile back with relief, and she looks at me inquisitively. I need to somehow extend our private conversation.

"How long are you here for?"

"Just a few days. I had a chance to come see Milo, and Emile said he would join, so . . . ! Everything worked out, eventually."

I'm moved by the way she pronounces her son's name. I decide to give some more away: "To be honest, I had no clue you were going to be here tonight." I then smile with embarrassment but keep my eyes on hers. So blue.

"Oh, really? What an idiot!" She sends Teddy a quick glance, indicating the idiot in question. She's fabulous! We're in cahoots.

"I know! And I found myself in the kitchen, telling him shit like 'Don't you do that again.'" I mockingly mimic myself.

"Oh no! Well, all I can say is that I know what it's like to be under the influence of Mr. Rosenfeld, believe me."

My honesty's worked. What a great talk, what a sweet, completely harmless woman.

I'm in the kitchen helping Teddy set the table, counting silverware for seven people, but there are actually only six of us.

"What about Adrian?" I ask.

"What about him?"

"Isn't he coming?"

"Don't think so."

"Where is he tonight? At Alice's?"

"Don't know." Maybe he does know. My questions seem to bother him. I decide to leave it alone, but when I get back to the living room, I sit next to Milo and take the first opportunity I get to ask him too. "So Adrian's not coming?"

"Is he supposed to?" He raises his eyebrows.

"That's what I'm asking," I say with a smile.

"Oh. I don't think so," he says, his voice clogged, as though I've just asked him something very abnormal, and then he adds in a clarifying tone, "He doesn't live here anymore."

"Yeah, I know, of course. But still, Friday night dinner . . ."

He shrugs. "He hardly ever comes, Dad probably didn't even tell him."

Why did I assume that Adrian would be here tonight? And why doesn't Teddy talk to me about him? It doesn't matter. You're here now, right where you wanted to be. So just be.

The evening continues. After dinner, Monique comes out to the balcony with me and we smoke together. I compliment her on the food and on her contribution to this gorgeous home, and she quietly gossips about Daria, hinting that she thinks Milo's gotten stuck on someone she doesn't sufficiently like. But she does like me.

After I have some more to drink, I step up my game. Emile has the best sense of humor. He laughs so hard that he cries when I tell him that as a child I didn't have a Ken doll, so I had to settle for a relatively flat-chested Barbie, and I'd also cut her hair, but she still wasn't masculine enough and I couldn't help but see Tammy, her former self, in her, so I drew a little mustache on her, but then she looked like Hitler, and at that point I pretty much gave up and just played with my Barbies with Tammy-Hitler playing the male characters. Teddy looks at me affectionately. I'm glad I've managed to get over it like he'd asked, and furthermore to justify the fact he's allowed me to come over.

Six bottles of wine later, Daria's tired and goes to bed. Milo stays in the living room, sitting next to Monique. It's nice to hear him speaking Danish, like witnessing another version of him. Emile and I are talking, and Teddy sits down on the couch next to me, joining our conversation. When Emile gets up to have "a last little drink for the night," Teddy smiles at me, reaches his hand to my face and strokes my cheek, even though we're not alone. I'm lucky to be sitting here, to be part of this thing that feels like it's beyond space and time; I suddenly realize that this is how I have always imagined Friday night dinners. This is closer even than the way it is with Sharon's family. This is how it's supposed to feel. I am in the place where I should be.

After everyone leaves and Milo goes up to his room, Teddy and I are already drunk and tired. We get into bed. I turn onto my side and put my hand on his neck, where I've wanted to touch him all evening long.

"You're not going to fuck me?" I ask slowly, not all that sharp anymore.

"Were you the one who brought that gin bottle, the one on the counter?" he asks with his eyes closed.

"Yeah."

"Then no, I'm not going to fuck you."

"Asshole." I smile.

"Tomorrow. I'll fuck you tomorrow."

"Fine," I say, close my eyes, and fall asleep straightaway.

>

On Saturday we go with Monique and Emile to the museum. Milo joins us but Daria doesn't. After the exhibition we stroll along the boulevard. Monique and Milo walk a few feet ahead of me, arm in arm. Even though she's smaller than him, you can tell that he's her cub.

During lunch, Monique tells Teddy—in English and in a way that I'm meant to hear too—thank God she doesn't have to spend this whole day with Lara.

Teddy reacts with his poker face, or rather doesn't react at all, but this seems to be a continuation of an old dialogue between the two.

What is the deal with Lara?

5

The Scariest Mountain

»

And then, a few days later, this happens:

I'm sitting at the office working on the film. There's a scene about Delmar's history, so I'm looking for photos taken here in the past. Richard has given me an old hard drive to go through. One of the folders has photos from an event they hosted a few years back, and I see Teddy. Standing next to him is one of the most beautiful women I've ever seen in my entire life.

That's Lara. I know it. This is not good. No one wants *this* to be the woman who came before them—she's painfully beautiful. Not just beautiful, she's literally stunning. Bright smile and green eyes, a short top revealing a great deal of her fair, heavenly body, long skirt, big earrings, tattooed arms. She appears in only four photos: standing next to Teddy and smiling while casually holding a glass of champagne; hugging Richard, the two of them smiling at the camera; a photo of her on her own, blurry background, she's laughing with her pearly white teeth, looking at the cameraman with her glimmering eyes. The last photo is of other people, but you can see in the background, Teddy and Lara standing facing each other, a moment that just happened to be caught on camera. I examine the photo and feel like I'm looking straight into their relationship. He's standing there looking at her—they seem to be midconversation— she's in front of him looking up, and her smile and her eyes on him and his eyes on hers, and the whole thing's documented for posterity, and passes back and forth between them over and over again for all eternity.

I copy the photos, eject the hard drive, grab my laptop, and march over to his office. He's sitting behind the desk, looks up at me.

"What's this, Maureen just lets you barge into my office?"

"Maureen's not here," I announce curtly.

"Oh, right."

I place my laptop before him with Lara's photo filling the screen. "This is Lara, right?"

"That's right, detective."

"This is the woman you were married to? This? This stunning woman? What is this? I'm going home."

"Yeah, go home because my ex-wife's a very beautiful woman."

"That's right, I'm going." I pick up my laptop.

"So long," he says.

"Who even looks like that?!"

"Lara does." His eyes return to his computer screen.

"This is wrong, you two should have never split up," I say, serious.

"Get out of my office."

"Okay, okay." I retreat. "Tell me when you're ready because I'm coming with you."

"Okay."

⟩

Later on in the car I immediately bring it up again. "So how did it go? What happened? What happened with her?"

"Who's asking?"

"She's too stunning to understand how anyone would ever have let her go. What do you do with such beauty? What did you do? Take her on walks?"

"Are you aware of how infantile you sound?"

"Yes. Why did you break up? What went wrong?"

"All sorts of things. She had a hard time."

"Hard time? What could possibly be hard for a woman like her?"

"You have too many complexes."

"This is not a complex. This has nothing to do with my complexes. This is objective."

"My dick is objective."

"Your dick, your beautiful dick, was married to her for four years! It went in and out, in and out, of her beautiful pussy for four years!"

He laughs. "Yes. And . . . ?"

As Teddy's driving, he's holding the back of the passenger seat, as though his free arm needs its own real estate. This gives me the feeling of a pseudo-hug, so I allow myself to further investigate. "You miss her?"

"No."

"And what about her? Did she like breaking up with you?"

"Absolutely. Loved every second of it. Drop it, will you?"

"That's it? Time's up? Tell me what happened. Why did you marry her?"

"Why? Because I'm an idiot."

"Because it was important for her?"

"For her, for her family. Marriage, prenup, the works."

"Prenup? Jesus. Why don't you have a prenup with me, now that's the real question here."

"Because you're a wild creature, you don't count."

"Luckily."

"Lara's aristocracy. Came from money."

"Oh."

"Loads of money. Her father wanted a prenup, I didn't really care."

"And what did she want?"

"Bottom line? She wanted me to show up her dad."

"She wanted to have the upper hand?"

He clears his throat and nods his head. "Yes. Something like that."

"And you fell for her just because she's beautiful? How could you be with someone who has no sense of humor?"

He laughs. "Monster. Why do you assume she has no sense of humor? That I really couldn't do."

"Because a woman this beautiful and aristocratic can't even begin to understand what humor is and why it's even necessary."

"Nonsense. You know, I think you'd have liked her."

I think about Lara and I know he's right. "Would you believe me if I told you that, in a way, I can love any woman you've ever loved?"

"Yes," he says candidly, and adds, "I can believe that."

I fall silent, pleased about our little moment of understanding, feeling the possibility of loving through his eyes. But then I recall all these shitheads surrounding him. "Except for . . ." I emphasize every syllable and he smiles.

"Here we go."

"These girls you hire to work at your office, who you think are so hot you can't see how dumb they really are! It's beyond."

"You think I find them hot?" He stops at a red light and I finally get the look I've been waiting for.

"I think that you think they're 'fine.' "

"Yeah? You watch from the side and think, Wow, he really has the hots for Maureen?" His eyes return to the road.

"Yeah, let's take Maureen for example. Can't you smell her perfume? Have you no senses whatsoever?"

He turns to look at me again, his eyes piercing me. "You're talking to me about Maureen's perfume?"

"Yes."

"I can't stand the way she smells."

"Really? Yes! I'm very glad to hear that."

Green light.

"Now you listen to me, you obsessive little creature. All these girls you don't like, these are exactly the type of girls I need around me. Because I really don't need your type around me."

"Why not?"

"Because you interfere—"

"Good!"

"And you annoy me—"

"That's my job."

"And you drive me crazy."

I look ahead, the smile etched into my face. "I can't tell the difference between who you really are and who I've made you out to be," I say.

"None of it is me, it's all in your head. I'm just some fat man that you insist on messing around with. But one day, one day you'll wake up in the morning and see me without the illusion, and it'll be hilarious. I'm really looking forward to that day." He laughs and leans back.

"Is that what happened with Lara?"

"No," he gets serious, "it wasn't hilarious with her."

›

Waking up at his place in the morning, he's not in bed, he's never there when I wake up. There's a good smell of fancy shaving foam. He walks in and hands me a mug. I sit up, still dazed from the night, the light in the room is bright. I sip the hot coffee and watch as he finishes getting dressed. There's something about the symbiosis with him, he knows how to be together. Sometimes it doesn't make sense, it contradicts other facets of his personality. Maybe that's why when he does disconnect, he completely disconnects.

Last night is crawling up my consciousness: we enter his apartment after the Lara talk, which leaves me in a cheerful yet strange mood, and he needs to finish something and goes to his office. I roll a joint, smoke a bit, then grab the ashtray and walk over to him.

"Teddy!" I say in a performative tone.

His eyes shift onto me, I've broken his concentration. I continue with the same tone:

"You're going to need to meet my dad. We'll do a little get-together, a few brief competitions, a tournament if you will. Just so we can determine who's the best out of the two."

"Then I'm getting a coach."

I resume my normal voice. "We haven't fucked in a week. A whole damn week."

"Coach said to reserve stamina." He continues reading. I look at his eyes as they scan line after line at a fast pace. I get down on my knees, press my cheek against his stomach, stroke his balls over his pants.

"I'm mad about your balls. My plan is to marry them, buy a house in the suburbs, catch a movie at the drive-in and share a vanilla shake at the diner. Me and those testicles."

"Where did you get the impression that my balls are a couple of Americans in the fifties?"

He gets up, pulls me onto my feet. "Let's go," he says quietly, and we go to the bedroom.

I take all my clothes off and lie on my back. He kisses my neck, my breasts on his way down, spreads my legs, his hands are on my breasts and his tongue moves slowly and heavily but without pressing too hard and then he flips me over, torso on the mattress and ass raised right at the edge of the bed. I hear him unzipping his pants and it turns me on, the anticipation, knowing it's happening now. He's putting his hard cock inside, lifts my ass higher up. His hands grab my breasts and he's fucking me. And more. I turn my head and look at him over my shoulder, and he keeps going and looks at me, the pace of his moans accelerate and synchronize with mine, and it feels so good, so good that I consider stopping just so it doesn't end, but I don't stop and we continue like that, a span of time strangely compensating for all the moments he hasn't been inside me, and it keeps going, addicting, hypnotizing. I look at him and turn onto my back so we're face-to-face again.

He wipes the sweat from his face with the back of his hand. "Even when I'm fucking you I think about wanting to fuck you."

I smile and he runs his hands all over my body, kisses everything he comes across. I open my eyes and look at him. "Teddy," I slowly say, "where have you been?"

"Spread your legs for me."

I do as he says and he makes himself hard and goes in again and fucks me until I come, and after a few moments, he comes too.

We're lying in bed, our faces close. One inside the other, not a single gap felt. The room's filled with our scent and we're naked and sweaty and I can feel these swells of intensity gushing into me, as though everything he's ever been through becomes a part of me, and I'm the sum of all that I am and all that he is. Everything he has is mine too now, the way he views the world, what he deserves, what he has to offer, and his rare, shameless giving; I wonder if returning to my reality and life with this addition might be a variation of happiness.

❭

Later on in the morning, we're in the kitchen when his phone rings. I can recognize his tone now when he talks to Adrian. This time I can't hear what Adrian's saying, but the context's easy enough to understand: (.. .. ..) "Okay. I'm not alone right now." (.. .. .. ..) "That means Noa's here." (.. .. ..) "You want us to do this later?" (.. .. ..) "Okay." He hangs up.

"Adrian?"

"Yeah. He's coming up."

"Okay."

I know there's no point for me to suggest something silly like leaving or waiting in one of the rooms, nothing I can do about it. It is what it is and there's tension here.

"Be right back," I say, and go to the bedroom to put my bra on and fix myself up, since my appearance is a dead giveaway that I'd spent the night at his dad's place. I hear the doorbell and the echoes of their words. They're standing in the living room when I join them.

"Nice to meet you," Adrian says from afar, glancing at me for no more than a couple of seconds. He doesn't really even say that, more like he recites something that he knows he's supposed to say.

"Hi." I'm not ingratiating at all, only barely smiling, distant. The complete opposite of how I'd been when I met Milo.

Adrian talks to Teddy while we walk toward the big table and they're already in the midst of a dialogue concerning shares, as though they're picking up from where they left off another time. As they talk, I can see the similarity between them—the same pace of speech, same mind running too fast.

"You want some coffee?" Teddy asks from the kitchen.

Adrian sits down and I join him at a safe distance of a few chairs away, on the other side of the table. "No thanks. Get me some water."

"Noa, another coffee?" Teddy talks to me very naturally. Adrian grabs the newspaper lying in front of him.

"No thanks." No idea why I said no, I actually do want another coffee.

Teddy pours water into a jug and takes three glasses out of the cupboard. I glance at the balcony, spot my morning joint in the ashtray— and all I feel like doing is going outside to smoke it. If Adrian's a smoker, then I can ask him to come out for a cigarette, but I don't know if he smokes, and anyway, I have nothing to offer him.

"You want something to eat?" Teddy checks with Adrian, and I think of how he's the dad who feeds him, his baby, then kid, then young man, and what it means to be his woman, how could he be trusted with such a delicate thing as a child? I can already see darkened mountains and lightning storms up ahead in the distance.

There's a drizzle of rain so I go out to the balcony to rescue the joint, and since I'm already out there I just stay and smoke it. In any case, it doesn't really matter whether I'm sitting with them. From outside, I can see my reflection in the glass more than I can see them. It doesn't matter, I repeat to myself as I take a deep drag, hoping to get high even though it might put a dent in my communication with Adrian, that inexplicable king of ice.

That means Noa's here.

That means Noa's here.

I need to go back in. Someone's turning off a vacuum cleaner in the apartment next door, white noise ends. The glass door isn't shut all the way and I can hear their conversation from afar.

"Another Lara?" That's Adrian.

"We're not doing this right now." That's Teddy.

"Not now and not ever. Does she know?"

I can't hear Teddy's reply. Who's 'she'? Does 'she' know what? I feel nauseated. How can I go back in now? I light up the end of what's left, inhaling the smoke. I want to call Adrian outside and ask him, What? What is it with you? I get what's uncomfortable, your dad's not with your mom, but that's old news. Now any woman he ever has will need to deal with your five-year-old behavior? What's the plan? What's 'another Lara'? Do I look like Lara to you? I'm a miserable kid from a stupid, ugly suburb, with an underachieving dad and a mom who I have no clue what God was thinking when he decided she was worthy of carrying a child. Who are you to have any say at all?

That means Noa's here.

But Adrian's the child here, and you're on the dad's side. You need to adjust your attitude, take responsibility. If it were you in Adrian's shoes, what would you want that goddamn Noa to do now? Stay out in the cold, the bitch. Come back in and read the room, maintain surgical precision in each and every move, not do anything that can later contribute to frustration and anger and hatred toward her.

I go back to the table and sit down with all these thoughts. I'm tired. This whole time they've been talking between themselves, mergers and investments. Adrian's eyes move around at great speed, occasionally coming across mine ·· and then quickly shifting away. I quietly wait, and when Teddy says he'll be back in a minute and gets up, maybe to make a phone call, he leaves me and Adrian alone and that's good, because I only stand a chance with him if we're one-on-one.

"Adrian?"

"Yeah?" He shifts his bird-of-prey look in my direction.

I stall for a moment but then manage, "I was looking forward to meeting you."

"Oh, yeah?" he challenges me. "Why?"

I smile in embarrassment. "I don't know." My eyes make an escape to the side and back to him. "What a shit question."

He seems surprised, his eyebrows slightly frown. "My question's shit?"

"Yes. Your question's shit."

He looks down. "Right."

"So I've convinced you? You're convinced?"

He continues leafing through the newspaper with indifference, but I can see the slight smile he's trying to hide. The moment I get this sliver of understanding, I calm down, as though someone has just put on a song I really love.

Teddy returns, Adrian continues where they'd left off. They're father and son again, and the son's telling a story that doesn't really interest the father, but the father's interested in showing interest. I look at Adrian's mouth and see Teddy's, that unique arrangement of teeth sloppily duplicated in his mouth; the hands and the long fingers, the same nails; same wise eyes. I keep sitting there, present and mute, trying to understand why he'd asked if I'm another Lara and whom he meant when he'd asked if she knows, and at the same time I'm thinking how special Adrian is and glad that he said 'Right,' even if he didn't mean it in the way I chose to take it.

"So, did you enjoy meeting him? Had fun?" Teddy asks after Adrian leaves, hugging my shoulders.

"I like him."

"Yeah? I'm glad you can see what I see." He doesn't look glad.

"He's just an introvert, but he's interesting. And you know, he resembles you in a way."

He stands there looking at me, and there's an odd little moment that I can't figure out, because I feel repulsion and attraction at the same time, and they're both strong.

"'Another Lara' meaning what?" I dare to ask.

He replies with genuine, pure anger: "It means you should shut up and leave it alone."

Have I hit a raw nerve? Something doesn't add up. Feels like I've been here too long for him to keep me in the dark.

»

Pouring rain. I'm standing in line at the café beneath the office building. My phone rings, it's Roy.

"What's up, Royo?"

"Very bad."

How dramatic can a person be? "What happened?"

"Our investor's suing us."

Three years ago, Roy and his friend Neri tried to develop an app. Neri, who comes from money, managed to raise the funds, but they had trouble with the development and the whole thing fell apart.

"What do you mean 'suing you'? Can they even do that?"

"Turns out they can! I'm in an actual nightmare." He gives me all the details and I realize that he really is in a tricky situation.

We decide we'll meet for lunch somewhere nearby.

"So what does it mean exactly?"

"Let's start with the fact that regardless of this situation, I've got a thirty grand overdraft, not including loans, okay? Now, his investment is over eighty grand, and I'm sorry but I really don't see what I'm supposed to do about this. Not to mention the fact that Neri has his shit together, he got a lawyer, but because of our beef he's now putting all the blame on me."

"Okay, you're not going to give eighty grand back because you don't have eighty grand. So that's not an option," I say confidently as I watch the inheritance conversation with our dad glide by the corner of my eye, like the shadow of a ghost.

"What do I know?"

"But isn't there a contract to protect you from this kind of thing?"

"There is a contract, yes."

"And did you read it?"

"Of course I read it! But I didn't get any of it. It was like reading a manual for a particle accelerator."

"Great."

"I'm really sorry"—who's he apologizing to?—"but I really don't know anything about this sort of stuff."

"And why would Neri put all the blame on you?"

"Neri's an asshole, if I told you the stuff he's done, you'd literally drop dead."

"So what are you thinking of doing?"

"Flee the country."

"Come on."

"I don't know, I really don't."

"Okay, well there's no point talking to Dad."

"Dad? I'd rather get an enema in front of everyone at my high school reunion than talk to Dad! Just the thought of him lecturing me about how right he was when he'd warned me, no, no . . . I'm not even going to tell him about it." He raises his chin in defiance.

"So what are we going to do?"

"I don't know, there's a lawyer I might meet for a consultation."

"So you do have someone who can give you advice?"

"Yeah, but she deals with real estate, she's just a friend."

"Who is it?"

"A friend."

"Your friend?"

"Not exactly, it's through someone . . ."

I know that tone. I recognize the tremor of his vocal cords when he's talking about—or more like trying not to explicitly mention—Nurit, our mother.

"Nurit's friend?"

"Yeah," he says quietly.

"You need a lawyer who knows this sort of stuff. And what about money? Can she help you?"

"Yeah, but she's not doing all that great right now, I don't know. She said she could help with like two thousand, maybe three."

"That won't cover anything," I rule dryly, aware of my icy tone.

Roy walks me back to the office. The rain's flooded the streets and my boots get soaking wet. When am I finally going to get a pair of boots that don't soak through? I've finally managed to save a bit now that I have this job and also because my expenses have seriously dropped, since Teddy just takes care of everything.

"I can give you around ten grand. But what does it matter how much money I give you if you don't have a lawyer?" The thought of the inheritance passes through my mind again. This is why I can't stand that woman. She messes me up.

"First of all, if you gave me ten grand that'd be awesome, and I don't understand how you even have that kind of money, and besides I'm in the midst of an anxiety attack. Luckily I downed two bottles of Rescue Remedy an hour ago, otherwise I'd be sprawled in that puddle right now."

We continue walking in silence.

"How's Thomas doing?"

"He's a sweetheart! I'm in love."

"Yeah, of course you are."

"No, for real, I swear."

"Good." I smile and think that maybe Thomas could help him with some money, but I guess if that were an option then Roy would have already asked.

"Grandma's got the hots for him." He smiles.

"Yeah, she told me. She could help you a little bit too."

"No, I don't want to ask her. Not again, I can't."

We say that we'll talk later, and I head back to the office.

+

Grandma Diana, Nurit's mom, is the only grandmother I have left. When I was eleven, I was lying in bed in the room where we slept when we stayed over, and I spotted a book on the shelf with a title that intrigued me.

"Grandma, what is that book about, *Mater et magistra*?" I was under the impression that this was a book that could teach you magic. She sat down on the bed next to me.

"Which book?"

I pointed at the shelf. "That red-and-white one."

"Oh! It's Latin for 'Mother and Teacher,' referring to the role of the Church. And what about you and your mother?"

That was disappointing and oppressive, mainly because during that time I was already fervently refusing to see Nurit, and any mention of the subject would get to me straightaway. I told my grandma that if she wanted me to continue coming over, she should never ask me that and never talk to me about it again.

And so she never did.

›

Oh no, I think in the elevator after my meeting with Roy, since I already know I want to consult with Teddy about the whole thing. I'm nervous to talk to him about financial affairs because I have no idea what that'll do. Up until now, he hasn't been keeping score at all; on the contrary, I've experienced nothing but generosity and giving from his side, and that's precisely why I'm nervous, for him to think that I take his wealth for granted. But he'll know what to do. He's the big boss. My stomach turns and my socks are wet and my brother's fucked again, life has knocked him down again. Nurit can only get him a lawyer who's not an expert in the field. Great, really. You can see why she feels guilty toward him. In any case, she won't be his salvation, nor will her inheritance. I'll help him.

Teddy's in the office's main work area talking to Phil, and unfortunately for me—or for my brother—he looks pissed off today. They go into his office and shut the door.

I wait for almost an hour, and then Phil comes out and I think this might be the right moment, even though I feel the timing isn't right and I should wait for the end of the day, but he's going to a dinner tonight and I'm not supposed to come over. I tread cautiously toward the open door, delighted by the fact Maureen isn't at her desk.

Maureen isn't at her desk because she's in the room with Teddy! When did she manage to get in there? They're standing and she's writing down some instructions he's giving her. He notices me the second I walk in the room, so I can't sneak back out and now I have to say something.

"Sorry to disturb. Can I have a word?"

"Yes." He's got a tough expression on.

"It's not urgent, it can wait." I immediately withdraw.

"No, come in," he says in that same tone, and looks at Maureen. "Okay? We clear?"

Maureen nods her head and walks out, leaving a trail of her perfume behind her. I shut the door and come closer to the table. He sits down.

"What is it?" His attention isn't on me, he's checking some papers on the desk.

I carefully sit in front of him, and I have no idea why I've arrived at this moment so unprepared. I had a whole hour—why didn't I think of phrasing?

"Are you pissed off?" I don't know how to begin this without acknowledging his state first.

"Yes."

"What happened?"

"Doesn't matter."

"We can do this later."

"What is it? What do you need?"

"Money." Is that seriously what I decided to say? "Help . . . advice," I add. I should be stoned to death.

"What do you mean 'money'? How much? What kind of help?"

"Roy, my brother, he's in trouble—"

"What kind of trouble? What did he get himself into?" He's quick, this man.

I tell him everything I know in a few stuttered sentences. "Can that even happen? An investor demanding their money back, suing?" I question the expert.

"Anything can happen."

"It sounds surreal to me. Eighty grand!"

"Got to check the contract. First have him talk to Werner, he's a lawyer specializing in IP, this sort of lawsuit probably relates to concept and rights." His practicality moves me.

"Who's Werner? Is he your lawyer?"

"One of them."

"Lots of women, lots of lawyers."

"Yeah, goes together." He almost smiles.

"Werner." I recall the suited guy we saw at the restaurant that time. "Teddy, Roy can't afford Werner, or whoever, and I can give him some money, but it'll still only be enough for fifteen minutes, half a consultation—"

"I'll pay Werner, don't start with your nonsense, don't worry about it." He goes back to his papers but continues talking to me. "Have Roy tell him it's on me. And another thing, you want us to transfer some money to him, so he calms down a bit? What's his deal, what sort of debt is he in?"

"Not something you can just fix." My leg's twitching.

"What are his debts, how much?"

"I don't know, I don't know." I'm stressing, my palms are sweaty.

"How much?" He's starting to lose his patience.

"He said around thirty grand, but that has nothing to do with this, I just wanted to consult—"

"Okay, let's transfer, I don't know, forty, fifty grand over to him first of all, and we'll talk to Werner and figure out what the deal is."

"What?"

"Tell him, tell Roy to call him right now. Take his number from Maureen."

Forty, fifty grand? People don't just give away that kind of money. What is this? "I don't get—"

"Have him call Werner today."

"Teddy, that's a ton of money. That kid will never be able to pay you back."

"Noa"—he's sharp as a razor and I'm not breathing—"don't piss me off. The money doesn't matter. Let's just transfer whatever helps him right now, he doesn't need to pay it back."

"What do you mean 'doesn't need to pay it back'?"

"I don't like these investor types. Who's the investor?" He checks the time. "I'm getting a call soon. Ask him, have him give you a name."

"Okay." I quickly get up to clear the room for him. "Thank you so much."

"And have him come talk to me, Roy. I want to hear exactly what happened."

"Yes. Sure. I'll set a time with him."

"Tomorrow evening, my place."

"Okay. And should I join? Do you want me there too?"

"Of course I want you. There. Too."

"Wow, and this is when you're pissed off. What if you were in a good mood?"

"He'd be getting less!" This time he's really smiling at me as he picks up his ringing phone.

"Thank you, Teddy," I say almost muted. He's already on the call.

〉

This is how problems get solved.

This is how I wanted it to be, after all.

And when things happen the way I want them to—that's the worst. I don't like having something to lose.

〉

"Holy Mary-Kate and Ashley!" Roy looks around in awe. "What is this insane apartment?!"

"Yeah, I know." I'm tense and I use a harsh tone with Roy. "Did you talk to Werner?"

"Huh? No. I left him two messages and he hasn't called me back yet."

"And you mentioned the name Teddy Rosenfeld?"

"No."

"But I told you to! Why is it so difficult for you to do as you're told?" I'm too agitated for the delicate encounter ahead. Teddy's in the shower, he'll come out soon with his hair all combed back, and my brother will finally get to see his big sister's boyfriend.

"And they let you stay here in all this beauty?" Roy hugs me and quietly asks, "Say, what's the story with this Teddy person?"

"What do you mean?"

"I don't know . . . You tell me."

"I don't understand the question." I do but I'm not comfortable with this situation and I'm losing my patience with Roy. "Want something to drink?"

"Yes, please."

"Did you bring me some weed?" I hand him a bottle of beer.

"Yeah. How have you run out already?" He goes back to the chair where he'd left his jacket, pulls out a little baggie and hands it to me. "Here you go."

"Thanks. Oh yeah, and—" Up until now I haven't told him that Teddy wants to give him a ridiculous amount of money. I wanted to give him the news face-to-face. "I have some great news."

"Bad news?" He misheard me, the poor dear, having just sipped from his beer. The scared look on his face for that brief second contains the very essence of his existential tragedy. Inheritance, donation, whatever it is—I always feel like he doesn't stand a chance.

"*Great* news," I correct him, tears almost forming in my eyes. "Teddy wants to settle your debts."

He swallows the rest of his sip. "Excuse me? What?"

"Excused. Teddy wants to settle your debts. And that's what's going to happen."

"What's going to happen? What are you talking about?"

"He's helping with your lawsuit and funding your lawyer, and on top of that," I speak slowly, trying to hide my emotions, "he also wants to transfer enough money for you to close out your debts. And, crazily enough, you won't have to ever pay it back."

"What? Why? Why would he do that?" His big eyes open wide, dumbfounded. "What the fuck?"

"That's how Teddy is."

"You told him how much we're talking here?" His voice slightly breaks with the height of the question.

"Yes."

"You're fucking with me, right?"

At that moment, Teddy comes in and joins us. He shakes Roy's hand and says he's glad to meet him. We sit at the big table, I roll a joint and Teddy questions Roy and asks for details about the investor and how things went down. Roy's so excited that I think he's about to faint. When Teddy hears that Roy hasn't spoken to the lawyer yet, he doesn't tell him off, but instead he immediately makes the call himself, even though it's already evening time.

Roy and I listen in like two little kids.

I'm so in love with him that I might throw up. Roy's sitting next to me, staring at him with a hypnotized look—just like anyone who's ever been privy to this wonder—and I suddenly feel genuine happiness. This is the first time that Teddy's meeting someone from my family.

It's strange.

No, not 'it,' *me*. I'm strange.

⟩

A few seconds after we say goodbye to Roy and he goes out to the street, a heavy downpour begins. Typical—it's my brother's luck, after all. But maybe what happened this evening could change the course of the universe? I look out into the dark and see him running through the rain until he disappears down the street. I know, the day will come when all of this will no longer be mine.

Teddy comes over and stands by my side, hands in pockets, and looks out the window with me.

"What am I supposed to do with this kind of unrestrained giving?"

"Who are you asking?"

"You."

"Me? I don't give nice answers."

"I'm still asking."

"Say thank you and shut the hell up."

I turn my head and look at him. "How can I say thank you when I'm shutting the hell up?" I ask without the slightest hint of humor.

"Start with the thank you," he instructs.

"Thank you," I abide.

"And now shut the hell up."

I bow my head. The rain stops. I recall Roy's eyes when he heard the good news, that baffled look, and I'm flooded by a terrible sadness. It takes over my thoughts and fills the air all around me. It's not the demand to shut up that makes me sad; it's the gratitude that I feel. My eyes start stinging and the tears plummet down. He looks at me and places his hand on the back of my neck—not quite places, more like grabs it possessively—and leans in toward the side of my face.

"Do me a favor." He doesn't sound like he's making a request, but he isn't dismissive either.

"I can't," I say with my head still down, the crying relentless.

"I don't believe that."

"Okay."

"I don't believe that you can't."

"Okay."

"Because I don't need you standing here crying. And you should be fine not talking to me about it beyond what's necessary."

"Why can't I talk to you about it?"

"Because I don't want to."

I lift my head to look at him. His hand is still on my neck. I understand what he's asking of me. "Okay," I accept the terms, holding my head high.

His eyes are still fixed on me. "Yeah?"

"Yes," I confirm, as though I'm the older sister of the girl who was crying here a moment ago. He slowly nods his head.

"That's what you were taught? To feel uncomfortable when you get presents?" His grip loosens and he lets go of my neck. "Where's the sense in that? Parents who don't have enough to give their kids teach them to feel bad when they get something. What's the point in that?"

"That they learn how to get things on their own?"

"And what do you think just happened here? You got Roy what he needed, all on your own. So there you have it. Easy as pie."

And after his pie, he turns and walks away, leaving me to stand by the window, without him.

»

Sunday, New Year's Day, and Teddy's in his home office on a telephone interview for the radio. He tells me in the morning that he's not going to the office today, and I wonder whether to go in myself or stay home. Meanwhile, it's already noon. The pitch film is in its final editing stages, so the next step is with an editor at a postproduction studio. Betty's cleaning in the kitchen. I walk around the vast apartment and up to the room on the top floor. It has its own balcony, one with nice potted plants, not an insect in sight, and from there I climb to the roof. It rained last night, so there's nowhere dry enough to sit, nothing but tarred surfaces and metal ventilation squares, but the view is great.

What radio station did he say? I try listening to the interview. His deep voice moves me, knowing that it's him. I'm trying to understand what they're talking about. Something about submarine systems. The interviewer asks and Teddy replies. How come Richard isn't interviewed too? Richard. Does he know about Teddy and me? Two months now. I can't figure out what they're saying and it makes me feel tired. Or maybe it's stupidity that I'm feeling? The interview ends and I get thirsty, so I go back down to the apartment.

Back inside, I see Teddy standing in the kitchen talking on the phone, but I keep walking all the way to the front door and I come out, press for the elevator, and I'm not sure why I left. My head hurts and I realize that I forgot to drink. The elevator arrives and I go in. No phone or cigarettes, no keys.

I walk down the street and sit on a bench, watch the passersby. I'm overtaken by extreme exhaustion, and I can't explain to myself why I had to come downstairs, why I couldn't just stay there and look at his face after having heard him on the radio.

Everything's fine, I tell myself, but I remain frozen in the same contorted position, tilt my head back without having anything to lean it on, close my eyes. In a way, I'm asleep right now. Like a rhino standing motionlessly in the sun with its eyes shut.

Suddenly all my muscles loosen at once and my body drops, which wakes me up. I'm not sure how long I was out for, maybe it's been only three seconds, maybe a few minutes. I get up slowly, hardly managing to keep my eyes open, and walk back to the building.

"Where were you? Why'd you disappear?"

"I went out for a minute."

"I called you. Why didn't you take your phone?"

I don't reply, sit down on the couch. He's doing his own things, doesn't ask any more questions. I try to think about what to do with myself— maybe I'll just go to sleep? If I were alone at my place right now, that's what I'd do. That's the truth. But I can't just get into bed in the middle of the day, or maybe I can, but I don't feel like figuring out explanations— even if I'm not asked for any, I end up preparing them anyway.

"I need to go to my mother's apartment."

His mother's apartment? All I know is that his mother passed away a few years ago and he doesn't talk about her much, just like he doesn't talk about anything much. This is the first time I'm hearing about her apartment.

"Come with me."

"Where is it?"

"Downtown. King George Street."

"What is it, a rental? You rent it out?"

"No, it isn't rented out."

"Why do you need to go there?"

"I need to take care of something. You coming? Let's go. Are you ready? Get dressed."

>

In the parking lot, when we get closer to his black executive car, he says, "You drive."

"Me? Why?"

"Because I don't feel like it. Do you mind?"

"No, it's fine, no problem."

Once we're in the car, he leans toward me a bit and moves my seat forward. This creates a physical proximity that we haven't had for a few hours now. I'm still in a weird mood.

"What is it, monster?"

"Nothing."

I start the engine and carefully come out of the parking lot. I try to concentrate on driving, but then I start staring and immediately tell myself to stop and keep my focus on the road. I'm tempted to stay within the stare for another brief moment, and I think about how this is similar to my situation with him, that I'm stalling despite the danger—and then Teddy's voice as he answers his phone forces me back to reality.

"You tell him, you tell him." He gives vague orders to someone on the other end of the line. "Okay, go ahead and tell him." He points at the right-hand lane. "Take that exit." After he hangs up, he looks at me. "Did you talk to Roy?"

"Yeah, he's supposed to have an appointment with Werner in a few weeks. Hope it'll work out."

"It will." He goes back to his phone.

There's traffic, even in the fast lanes, and we slow to a crawl before the exit leading downtown. I guess that we humans still have an animalistic instinct; otherwise there's no explanation for how we know, before even turning our heads, that the driver in the car next to us is looking at us. I look back at him, trying to quickly assemble all the data he has on me from his point of view: he can probably tell that the man sitting next to me owns the car, and that I'm his half-lover, half-employee, and that he just asked me to do the driving this time.

>

Teddy's mother's apartment is located in a nice little area downtown. We park in her private spot, or more like his. I raise the hand brake and turn off the engine.

"You know you don't have to lift that, right? With these cars, once you're in park there's no need."

"Thanks for the tip."

The elevator's small and we're close to each other but not touching.

"You didn't grow up here," I speculate.

"No. But she lived here for a very long time."

We get to the front door and he looks for the right key. Inside it feels heavy. The air in the apartment is stale, and it's dark and unpleasant. The smell is musty, I feel it in the back of my throat. He shuts the door behind him and goes over to open the windows. Something is off about this place. I look around: piles of cardboard boxes, mostly still open, containing dishes, photo albums, old devices, papers, books, and countless other things. There's a photo of his mother on the wall, age sixty perhaps, looking at me with Teddy's eyes. An attractive woman with strong features, resembling his, but finer. Her huge son walks around calmly, goes to pee, turning on and off the faucets in the bathroom and the kitchen. Something about this moment is more intimate than anything we've experienced so far, but not necessarily the nice kind of intimate.

"How come she lived in this sort of apartment?" This is not how I'd imagined Teddy's mother's house.

"What do you mean?"

"I don't know. Didn't you want her to live somewhere more . . ." I search for the words but he replies before I manage to find them.

"You think it mattered what I wanted? I wanted a lot of things, but she did whatever she wanted. I asked—I told her I'd get her a new place in the city center, closer to me, but she wouldn't hear of it."

I look at all the boxes and then it hits me: the boxes don't belong here. They're surrounded by a wholly organized apartment: the living room furniture's all in place, not in some pile or covered with sheets; the bookshelves are packed full of books, paintings on the walls, and everything else too—it's all frozen in time. And this unboxed apartment has been joined by another apartment's boxes.

"What are all these things? Are the boxes not your mom's?"

"No."

"Then what, are they your things?"

"George's."

"Who's that?"

"My father. Deceased too." He walks away from me and picks up a framed photograph from the shelf. "Look, that's me."

There's a young Teddy, maybe twenty years old, much less attractive than he is now. Two Scandinavian-looking guys next to him: one is tall and very impressive, the other one a little chubby, intriguing. Teddy's a lot thinner than he is now, even though he wasn't all that thin back then either.

"Who are they?"

"That's Nico"—he points at the impressive one—"and that's Søren. Sweethearts."

"Where are they from?"

"Denmark."

"Friends of yours and Monique's?"

"No, they're my brothers! Sort of. Long story."

"Your brothers?"

"Not biological. My mom got with their dad." He puts the photograph back and I look around. From where I'm standing, I can see the edge of the bed in her bedroom. I walk closer and peer inside. The bed's made. He hasn't touched anything. I go to the kitchen, afraid to see a sink full of dirty dishes still waiting for her to come home and wash up. He follows me in.

"You're insane," I say.

"What's insane, what do you want?"

"I'm being serious."

"What's the problem?"

"You don't see what the problem is?"

"No, I don't. What am I supposed to do with this stuff? Rent some storage space and put it all there? I don't have the time. So this is the storage space. What's the difference?"

"You need to keep a few things and the rest, you know, donate, sell."

"Anything here you want to buy?"

I smile a little, but keep going. "No, really. Tell me what the plan is."

"The plan? I'm going over to Shlomo's, the neighbor, to pick up the mail."

"Okay, but what's the deal with this apartment? What are you going to do with it? Nothing?"

"Yes, nothing. Someday. I don't have time for it, too busy." He turns to leave. "Wait here, I'll be back in a few minutes."

I stay put and don't want to touch anything, so I remain motionless. What the actual fuck? He might as well walk in right now and open the fridge and eat something out of some pot, this psycho who's kept his mom's place like some sort of historical museum, and then went the extra mile and shoved all of his dad's life into it too, thus actually making it a postmodern museum, come to think of it. I need to get out of here.

›

On the way back, I don't want to drive. I don't quite know why, but I'm mad at him. I think that this is the first time I don't understand him. He disgusts me, driving his car with a toothpick in his mouth; maybe he did eat something out of some pot after all. I'm silent. He's silent too.

It just doesn't make sense to leave everything untouched, and it makes even less sense that he doesn't understand why that's a problem. It gets a little dark and the cars turn their headlights on. He's not even close to coping with her death. I don't want to judge him, but I also can't help it. It's not like he lacks the means to take care of it. If he isn't going to deal with it, then he should at least be aware of what that means.

I look out the window. We're back in the city center. Traffic's heavy, everything's dense and gross. This city can be so ugly sometimes. What am I doing with this man? Tapping his fingers on the steering wheel, whistling some tune. Such an aggravating human being. He notices my look.

"What, Noa?" he asks.

"What, Teddy," I repeat after him dryly. "Nothing."

"Since when are you so quiet?"

I swallow. I have no way of answering that without revealing my thoughts. "I don't know what to say." I go for honesty, which probably won't pay off.

He falls silent and I can't read him. What's wrong with me? What does it mean, him taking me there, to that apartment? That he's revealing himself, that he is letting me see his weaknesses, his complexes, the decay. And here I am, repulsed. Instead of feeling love, instead of being supportive. I look at him. I'm not sure I want to be supportive.

"How would she feel about it?" I ask, and immediately clarify, "Your mom?"

"I'm sorry?" He really didn't hear me.

"What sort of woman was she, your mom?" I take advantage and try from another angle.

"My mom? The finest woman there ever was. Smart woman, the smartest. Every day, I'd kill to talk to her. Every day." Each word is more grating than the last.

"You've never talked about her until now."

"What's that?"

"Never mind." I can't decide how to run this conversation.

"You said I never talk about her? I told you she passed away seven years ago."

"Yeah." The car before us stops to park. A cat perks up on a low wall nearby and looks straight at me. "And how would your mother feel about the fact you haven't taken care of her things all this time?" My words are dripping with rage.

"I don't understand the question."

"What's there not to understand?" I raise my voice.

"How would she feel about it?" He repeats the question, perhaps trying to find the answer. "I don't know, she doesn't. She's dead. What does it matter, how she'd feel about it?" He sounds amused by the whole thing. The road clears and he continues driving.

"I don't know, maybe it's undignified." Great, Noa, why not run barefoot through a minefield?

"'Undignified'?" he echoes, though this time I can hear a hint of agitation. "I don't understand what you want. There's no such thing. No dignity, dead is dead. And throwing her things away is dignified? Selling—what were you bullshitting about? Selling her things, that's dignified? What are you talking about? She's gone. No dignity, no difference. It doesn't matter to her anymore, that's for sure."

"Okay, Teddy, it's debatable what is or isn't dignified, but that's not the point right now." We reach his building's parking lot.

"I don't think there is a point, except for you being annoying all day long."

I make a real effort to ignore his snide comment. "And what about you?"

"I've not been annoying all day long."

"I mean that you're not dead. You're still alive. So it should matter to you. What does it give you, having that monument, that King George memorial site? How do you feel about the fact that it exists?"

"Are you doing therapy on me right now?"

"Come on."

"I don't feel anything. You're putting meaning onto meaningless things." He turns the engine off. "Are you coming up or going home?" His preference isn't clear from his tone, but I can only assume that right now he wants me gone.

"I'll come up to take the laptop and I'll go."

"Okay."

In the elevator we're both agitated. Not even a foot separates us, but I can feel every inch as though I'm a microscopic cell for whom this distance is immeasurable.

>

I'm sitting in my living room, smoking and drinking a cup of tea, even though the kettle produced scale-flavored water as punishment for not using it enough recently.

Maybe he's right. What difference does it make if his mom's apartment is packed up or not? What would I do if my dad—and Mina too, for argument's sake—passed away? I know the answer: I'd go to their place and pack it all up. But why? To complete the action. To close it down. So not a single thing could reach out and touch me. I'd want to have it behind me, to not have it anymore.

That doesn't sound good either.

So he's the opposite. He doesn't want to put it behind him, he wants the apartment to exist, for his mom to live forever. And that's his right. It's his right to keep her in that mausoleum, but then he shouldn't assume he can have my love. I'm not interested in loving a little boy. I can't be in love with a man who's still nursing at his mother's breast. It repulses me.

Why did he take me there? Because he doesn't know who I am. He doesn't know that I'm the devil incarnate, the death angel of motherhood, that I despise every umbilical cord that isn't immediately severed the second the opportunity presents itself. That I find dependency sickening. Maybe he's even kept the umbilical cord, his and hers, the one that connected them back when he was still inside her. It's probably there in some Tupperware in the freezer, next to the placenta, which he's also kept, and every time he visits he cuts off a tiny sliver, fries it in his mom's frying pan, and eats it while filled with delight. That way they'll stay united for all eternity. Maybe he ate her too?

I disgust myself. I'm the rotten one. No compassion. Good thing I'm not a mother, God help that potential child, save him from being born.

They say he's merciful, God, so he should make sure I never have any children.

Remember that, Noa, remember that you're not supposed to be anyone's mother, because sometimes you get a bit confused. You forget. But don't you dare. You don't need it. You can't! You can tell your stories, that's harmless enough. It won't be as harmful as you, a heinous bag of worms disguised as a woman, would be to another human who depended on you.

Teddy.

He doesn't have a clue. He has no idea how dreadful you are. He thinks you're nice, you're sweet, you're like Lara, or Monique, or Jamie or whichever one. Did he take them there too? Lara, for example? Of course he took her there. He fucked her there too, I know it. And she leaned back, her shimmering white neck stretching as she laughed: It's so fun to fuck in your dead mom's place, so wild am I, so open to new experiences.

No, I'm not another Lara. And if he doesn't know that by now then he'd better find out.

If anyone's looking at my apartment from outside right now, they must see flashes of light and shadow moving across the little window at the very top of the tallest tower of a castle on the scariest mountain in the kingdom.

6

Damages

»

A beautiful fondant tiger lies on a fondant tree trunk, its paw dipping in a blue sugar pond, on the cake inside the box on Sharon's lap. We're in her car, on the way back from the suburbs to the city. We long ago discovered that these errand runs are a great opportunity for us to steal a few hours of quality time.

Fifty minutes earlier, I'm waiting for her outside my building. She pulls up and I get in, quick kiss. She drives for a few feet and then stops.

"You drive," she orders me.

"Sure! Apparently that's all the rage right now."

We swap and I sit at the wheel. I'm already being honked at, so I immediately start driving, and only then do I fix the seat, buckle up, adjust the mirrors.

"What's all the rage right now, you driving?"

"Yeah, I've got five stars, want to see the top reviews?"

"I would, please advise," she says in a matter-of-fact tone that makes me laugh.

"I'll fax it over"—I make her laugh too—"by end of day!"

This span of time is good for her: she returns calls, chats with her sister-in-law about a medical procedure her brother's about to undergo, then a short work call. We barely manage to get a word in between calls, but as usual, being together is pure joy.

We get a bit lost in the neighborhood where we're supposed to fetch the cake, but eventually find the house and take off with the extravagant loot. *Happy Birthday Dori* written in chocolate letters beneath the tiger. Now that the treasure's been secured, she wants to know how things are going with Teddy Rosenfeld.

"Depends when you're asking."

"And where are we currently?"

"Right now? Knee-deep in mud."

"Why? Give me a recap." She licks a bit of icing off her pinkie finger. "Where are you up to?"

"Last time you told me about how he's helping Roy."

"Right."

"Can't stop thinking about that."

"Can't start thinking about that," I say.

"How come?"

"It's . . . tiring."

She laughs. "It is quite exhausting."

"Want to hear something genuinely repulsive?" I ask.

"Yes I do."

I tell her about the previous day at his mother's apartment. Much to my delight she also gets creeped out, validating my reaction.

"But whatever, he'll take care of it at some point," she suddenly defends him. "Can't judge people in these situations."

I stay quiet for a moment, dreading feeling deserted if she doesn't see it the same way I do.

"I don't know . . ." I try to push aside my need for her allegiance. "We're going around in circles, everything's repeating itself. But not quite the same, because it keeps getting deeper."

"Then it's not circles, it's more like a spiral. You're almost in the same place but at a different coordinate."

I like that image.

Sharon pulls her hair up into a ponytail. "And the sex?"

"Not enough. I don't know, unclear there too."

"And when you do?"

"When we do it's beyond amazing."

"Really?"

"Never had anything like it before."

"Then hold on to that cock and just leave the whole apartment thing alone. What does it even matter?"

"Right, what does it matter?"

>

Tuesday morning, two days after King George, I wake up with a nagging headache. No text from Teddy, our silence crossing into another day. I down a Tylenol with my coffee. The source of my tension is obvious: only two days left to finish editing the film before I present it to the office. Every time I think about it, my stomach drops.

I'm with the editor in the postproduction studio and we're focused on the work. Throughout the day, not once do I check to see if he's texted. By nightfall, I realize that I won't be hearing from him today either. So I guess we're not talking.

How do I get back to him? And why, even? What happened?

The following day, final editing session. My phone lies motionless on the desk. The editor and I argue over one of the cuts, message ping. Teddy Rosenfeld.

Where's Noa ?

A smile overtakes my face before I even manage to think of a response. Why am I smiling? Because he's the one who broke the radio silence? After a calculated ten-minute wait, I reply.

Editing the film. Showing
it tomorrow.

Wonder if he remembers the screening at all. The beauty of it is that after I send that text, he doesn't reply or continue the dialogue. I have no patience for another silent twenty-four hours, so I text him again after half an hour.

How are you?

Tired

That's all you've got? That you're tired? I decide not to dignify that with an answer.

A few long hours pass and the session comes to an end. The editor and I are in the parking lot, smoking a cigarette next to our cars. The film's almost done, just one final adjustment that he'll do from home. He wants to get there in time to see his daughters before they go to bed, so he takes off. I get into my car and try to figure out what to do.

It starts drizzling, almost 8:00 p.m. Another evening without him? Four months since I'd met him, two months of sleeping together, two weeks since we last fucked, three days of silence. And a partridge in a pear tree.

I text him.

> What are you doing?

I look at the phone, he sees the text, now he's typing.

> Waiting

> For?

> You

Oh yeah? He's waiting for me? I find that hard to believe. And what if I hadn't texted him, he would just continue waiting? I think about him over at his place. Drive over there now? Walk in, be with him, talk, fuck. Yes, obviously. Why am I contemplating? I mean, he's waiting for me.

Without replying, I drive over. I get there quickly but can't find parking for nearly an hour. The waiting time is wringing my nerves because I don't want him to text me again, I want the next text to be mine when I'm already outside his front door. Just as I finally find a parking spot, he texts me.

> Still busy ?

I rush to his street and text him from the elevator.

> No. I'm here. Open up.

I send the text and wait by the door. He takes a moment, so I use the opportunity to breathe and fix myself up. Take off the jacket, hold it in my hand. C'mon, open up already. I knock on the door. There are rustling sounds from within and then he opens up. He looks at me and smiles. I smile too, but maintain the seriousness I've kept for the past few days.

"There's our beautiful Noa," he says softly as I walk in.

"There's our son of a bitch Teddy," I answer with a curse that sur-
prises me.
"Of all the curses in the world, you had to pick the maternal one?"
"Sorry, it was an accident."
"Why didn't you use your key?"
"Didn't feel like it." I put my bag down.
"How are you?" he asks.
"Fine." The apartment's warm so I take off my sweater. "If this was
my place I'd have to keep my sweater on."
"No heating there?"
"There's air-con and a little heater."
"Good thing you're here then."
"Maybe." I look at him, he smiles.
No real encounter yet. We're maintaining distant energies: I'm
reserved and he's Teddy.
"Finished the film. Almost."
"And you're pleased?"
"No such thing."
He laughs and takes a seat. His interest seems superficial, so I decide
not to elaborate. I'll wait for tomorrow. And what now?
"I need something. Mind-altering. Don't feel like smoking, don't feel
like drinking."
"Then what do you feel like?" He really is being nicer than usual.
"Coke?"
"Can't help you with that."
I grab the phone from the table. "I'll text someone."
"Lovely. Will he be joining us?" He seems amused.
"No, I'll go down."

     Hateful Eight 500
     Double Trouble 900

That's what the dealer replies. I put my sweater back on and grab my
jacket. "Where's the nearest ATM?"
"Two blocks from here. How much do you need? I've got cash." He gets
up and walks over to his jacket, shoves his hand into the inner pocket.
"Why? I'll walk over there."

"Here. Is that enough? Take it."

"Fine." I take the bills as though I'm the one doing him a favor. "Thanks. Be right back."

As I wait for the dealer, I think about the last few minutes, our encounter, what was missing. He's being nice to me, behaving himself. But he's not taking me and kissing me and making me his, and anyway it's clear he doesn't need it. Yes, that's what's missing, his need. I think about his cock, up there in his apartment, inside his pants. Maybe I should go up there and address his cock directly, have a heart-to-heart. There's the dude, double trouble.

❭

"Want some?" I stall the question for as long as I can, since I assume he won't want any.

"No, not today."

"Okay."

I still feel a bit disappointed, snort his lines too. I get high pretty quickly. My heart's pounding. Front teeth fossilize, jaw clenching over and over again. I fill my lungs with air. My palms are sweaty.

He's sitting there, relaxed, watching me. "How's the mind?"

"Altered."

"That was the point."

"It's a stupid drug," I say, and light a smoke near the balcony door. He walks over to me and takes the cigarette from my hand, smokes. We haven't stood this close until now. I look at him and feel the speed running through my veins. He's wearing a button-down shirt, his chest peering through the collar.

I don't need to touch him either. It's probably his fault. I look at him.

"How come you don't want to fuck me?"

He looks me in the eye. "Don't know."

Despite the rejection's sting, there's a sense of elation for having been right.

"But you waited for me to come over." I'm covered by delicate sweat, accompanied by slight nausea.

"I did. Not so I can fuck you."

I sigh. The cigarette burns out and Teddy goes back to his chair by the big table. I circle him, pacing back and forth between the table and the kitchen.

"So if there's no fucking, what should we do?" I ask, frenetic.

"What do you want us to do?" He takes a sip from his wine.

"I don't know." I put what's left back in the little tin box. "Maybe tell me a bit about your mother, about Denmark. Your nonbiological brothers."

"All right." He's cooperating, to my surprise. "What do you want to know?"

"Tell me the story. Don't you know how to tell a story?"

He smiles and takes a deep breath and I think that maybe I should ask a more precise question, but then he starts telling me about how when he was four, his mom, Henia, met a hippie stoner musician in Denmark named Martin, and they fell in love and left their families to be together. Martin left his wife and two sons and moved to Israel, and Henia brought Teddy along to live with them. Teddy's dad was crushed by the whole thing. He took Henia to court and tried to get full custody, but Teddy didn't want to leave his mother and he loved Martin. Whenever Henia went to work they'd hang out together; he remembers those years as an exceptionally happy time. But then Martin's ex-wife got sick and the three moved to Denmark so Martin could be with his boys.

"So they took you there and told you that these were your new brothers?"

He laughs as he talks about his past, and I examine the spark in his eyes. He tells me that he met Søren, the younger of the two, first; Martin came by with him one day after a hospital visit. He wanted the boys to get to know each other and play together, but they couldn't talk because they didn't share a language. Nevertheless, Teddy recalls that they bonded very easily, he even remembers making Søren a sandwich. He scratches the back of his neck, and I get to see his inner arm, which turns me on as usual, and suddenly I'm attracted to him again.

He met Nico only after their mother had passed away. Martin took

Teddy to their home, Nico was in his bed. Martin opened the door and marched Teddy in. Nico didn't acknowledge their presence, and it was only after his father scolded him that he deigned to sit up on the bed and look at Teddy.

"I have a crystal-clear memory of that moment, I even remember what I was thinking."

"What were you thinking?"

"I thought, What a beautiful boy."

"Really?"

"Yeah. And then he stood up, walked over and slapped me across the face, and hard."

"No way!"

"Yeah." He starts laughing. "And by the time poor old Martin realized what was happening, the kid had beat the living crap out of me, face, chest. Fists."

"My God."

"And I didn't put up a fight, didn't hit back. Nothing. My nose started bleeding, my mouth. I just stood there smiling."

"Smiling?"

"Smiling! I was proud of him." He's really laughing now, delighted over the harsh memory.

"What's so funny?"

"The story is. We laughed about it for years."

I take a deep breath. The influence has worn off a bit and my heart rate's back to normal. "So your mother and Martin didn't stay together?"

"It lasted a few years." He stretches. "So, did I tell you a nice story?"

I look at him and feel the distance again. I don't want to give in. "You didn't get to the part where we find out that there's this apartment on King George."

He looks at me and I wait for him to say something before I go on, if I go on.

"What does that have to do with anything?" he asks, and then at once he changes his tone. "What do you want?"

"I want you not to be pathetic."

"Pathetic?"

"Yes. It's pathetic and I don't get it. I mean, I do, but I don't accept your choice."

"I don't need you to accept my choice."

"Didn't think you did. But I'm still going to say I find it sick."

He takes a deep breath. "You can say whatever you want, Noa."

"Then why did you take me there?"

"I don't know. Guess I shouldn't have."

I go quiet. I don't like this conversation and the way I'm conducting it. This isn't the right conclusion, that he shouldn't have revealed it to me. Rather, maybe he's asking for something. I decide to leave it alone. I feel drained.

"I want to go to sleep," he says, and I recoil, but don't manage to say anything since he continues straightaway. "You're tired too, right? Go to bed, I'll come in a bit."

I freeze. He's not sending me home, but he is sending me to bed.

〉

I undress in the bedroom, neatly placing my clothes on the armchair. I keep my underwear and T-shirt on and go into his bathroom, where all the good smells are. The toothbrush I was given on my first night here awaits me in its cup, facing down in discernible sorrow. I climb into bed and lie on the side that isn't his, cover myself and stay motionless for a few minutes. Not a single movement, not even to scratch or shift position.

Something isn't right.

He'll come soon. What will I do then? I picture him in the living room. This man. What do I even have to offer him? Why is he letting me in? And why doesn't it feel like I'm in?

Rustling sounds from the apartment, the lights go out. He enters the room, heavy shadow. I lie there frozen. If I'm pretending to be asleep, then I should put more into it, loosen the body, make my breathing heavier. But I don't, I just keep still and think about all the times he's seen me asleep so he must know what it looks like, and then I think about the fact I've never really seen him asleep. I'm always the one sleeping, lying beside him, and when I wake up he's not there anymore.

If so, the mission is clear. This might take a while, but I'll get there.

He finishes getting ready and lies down, the mattress shifts beneath me as he situates himself. Even though he didn't touch me before, the possibility still exists for him to suddenly hold me. Every night, when I go to sleep in my bed alone, I lie on my side and yearn for that embrace, and maybe I can have it now, if I ask, but no. There's no point because I know I'm alone. And being alone by his side is much worse than being alone on my own.

These thoughts aren't good for my plan because they weigh me down; the tears come up and seep through my shut eyelids and I must keep still. Can't have him realize I'm crying. How annoying can I be, really? I have my back to him, but I know that the little light next to him is on and the phone's still in his hand.

Eventually, it happens. He turns off the light. His breathing extends, body goes limp. I wait in silence for him to fall into deep sleep, and only then do I open my eyes. The tears have already dried.

Move slow. Sit up. Carefully turn my head back and freeze again, so as not to shift the air. Slowly turn my folded legs to the other side and then lower my feet to the rug, shift my weight, and rise. Take a few soft steps and carefully sit on the armchair, next to my pile of neatly folded clothes.

The view's perfect from here.

There you are, helpless.

I'm sitting in front of you, watching you, and you have no way of knowing. Not when you're asleep. Should I not have said anything? I have no reason to be with you if I'm not honest. Also, what have I got to be scared of?

You're not so threatening when you're sprawled like that, like a whale. How much damage could you possibly do?

›

All night long I feel the distance between us, in my sleep.

When I wake up in the morning he's obviously no longer in bed, which immediately makes me feel like I've lost the advantage I gained in the nighttime. To even the scales I plan to shower and already be dressed when I come out to the living room, but while I'm under the stream of water, he enters the bathroom. He's already dressed and ready for his day, as was expected.

"What time are you screening your project?"

My heart skips a beat. Good morning, heart.

"At eleven. In the big boardroom."

"Okay." He leans on the doorframe and looks at me. He's seen me shower before, many times, but this feels different, my naked body in front of his eyes.

"What?" I ask somewhat hostile, since I can't figure out his mood, and since I still have remnants of coke rushing through my bloodstream.

"I'm thinking about what you said yesterday, about how pathetic and sick I am." His tone has changed from last night, and I suspect that maybe it does matter to him what I say.

"I said that *it* is sick, not that *you* are sick." I try to redeem myself while shampooing my hair. "And that I don't want you *to be* pathetic, not that you *are* pathetic."

"Yes. But it's interesting that you allow yourself to even say something about it at all," he says, and stares at some random spot on the wall, like an actor delivering a line he's learned by heart. "Given your own predicament."

"What's that supposed to mean?" I rinse off the shampoo, close my eyes.

"That maybe we should start by hearing from you. What's the deal with the ban on your mom?"

I fall silent for a moment, surprised. His words seep into me like venom. "Why are you calling it a 'ban'?" I open my eyes and give him a cold look.

"I don't know, isn't she banned from your life?"

"No. What an annoying choice of words."

"Then how would you call it? Wouldn't want to annoy you, heaven forbid."

"I don't call it. I don't think about it."

"Why don't you think about it?"

"Because there's nothing for me to dig up there." I pour soap into my palm, Teddy's soap.

"You don't say."

"Great. Getting back at me for yesterday, is that what this is? Because that's even more pathetic."

"Why won't you see her?" He ignores what I said.

"I told you, I know who she is and there's nothing there for me." I wash the soap off my body.

"That's a narrow and unacceptable outlook." Now he's way out of line.

"Who are you to determine anything, what's acceptable or unacceptable, really, you're just—" I turn off the water. "This is my business. You took me to your mother's apartment, so I talked to you about it, but that doesn't mean you can talk to me about my shit."

I come out and angrily grab the towel he hands me, mad at myself for not realizing that by discussing his mother, I've sentenced myself to endure the same. But this isn't the same. I dry myself and dig an even deeper hole as I quote him:

"Not all mothers are 'the finest woman there ever was,' Teddy, and in my case we're talking about a woman who made our lives miserable and continues to do so."

"Sounds to me like you're exaggerating."

"How do you know if I'm exaggerating or not?" I rage. "What do you even know about me and her and what we've been through? What do you even know about my home, about my dad, you've never even been to dinner there."

"I'm sorry, did you invite me over and I just never showed up?"

"You're invited! Come anytime!" I storm out of the bathroom and walk over to my little shelf in his huge walk-in closet. "Why would I invite you over to that house, with Mina's disgusting food and my dad's ingratiating attempts to get on my good side? It looks nothing like your life."

"Does it look like yours?"

"No! And you know that! What do you want?" I shout at him while putting my underwear on. He stands at the entrance to the walk-in closet, blocking the passage as well as most of the light.

"None of this is you telling me what happened with your mom."

"None of your questions are actually asking that, and stop saying 'your mom'!"

"What do you want me to call her, then?"

"By her name, if you have to mention her at all."

"Then tell me what happened with Nurit and why you're angry."

"There is no way I'm telling you when you ask me like that." I put my bra on.

"What do you need in order to tell me? Want us to hold hands on the beach at sunset?"

That's a strike; now I'm truly insulted. I look for a clean shirt, but I can't find one on my shelf.

"Fuck you. You insensitive shit."

"So now my sensitivity's the issue?"

"Now? It was the issue from the start." I find pants, but my legs haven't dried yet, making it harder for me to dress quickly.

"Am I too aggressive?"

"You're too repulsive."

"Right, you're the aggressive one."

"There's just no way I'm going to stand here now and tell you about everything I've been through." I move to exit the closet; he lets me through.

"What have you been through? Why do you make everything so mysterious and dramatic, and then when someone does show interest in your mysteries you get hysterical?" I settle for the T-shirt I wore yesterday, and he continues. "How long can you beat around the bush? Just talk already."

"I told you I'm not going to talk to you about it right now."

"When's best for you to talk? Should I get Maureen to set a meeting?"

"Really, that's what you have to say to me right now? This is the most dreadful way anyone has ever asked me about my past, just so you know."

"Great, honey, I feel honored."

I look at him with pure hatred. How have I never noticed how ugly he is? Standing there peacefully, protected by his clean clothes. I sit down, put on my socks and shoes.

"Why aren't you speaking with your mom?"

"You're calling her that again."

"With Nurit."

"I told you, because I have nothing to say to her."

"A partial and evasive reply. Answer me."

"Fuck off. What does it matter to you if I'm speaking to her or not—" I stop talking because his expression darkens and he walks toward me until he's towering above me.

"It matters to me that you're dense and stupid and you don't understand what a mother is." He raises his voice. "And you don't get that it's time you look her in the eye and finally realize that she's a person, and considering how things are with you, there's no way she's not hurting about it every single day, a pain that you can't even come close to understanding, a pain you insist on causing her for nearly thirty years! Over what? What happened? What did she do? Whatever it is, do you realize that it's nothing compared to what you're doing to her?"

"What I'm doing to her?! It's amazing how much empathy you have for a person you don't even know, how you defend her and destroy me, and for no apparent reason."

"The reason is apparent, and I'm not destroying anybody." He's stopped shouting.

"I was a kid, Teddy! I'm the kid in this story!"

"I know, and you're not a kid anymore." He looks at his phone for the first time since this conversation started. "All right, I have to get going. You ready?"

›

We take his car to the office. I drive and loathe him. Good that I can do two things at the same time! He's on the phone and I'm flooded with thoughts. How dare he talk to me like that, he blames me for the whole thing—I can't stand him. And I don't want to be in a relationship with anyone because it means that there are moments when you have to sit next to them and contain all of your loathing and stay nice and pleasant, and then even fuck. If he thinks I'm ever fucking him again, he's wrong.

He finishes the call and starts going through his emails. The radio's off, the car's quiet, except for the windshield wipers moving back and forth at a steady pace.

"You want me to come with you to meet her?" he asks. He must have no idea who I am if he's suggesting such a horrendous idea.

"No. I want you to stay out of my business."

"I won't have it."

"What do you mean 'you won't have it'?" I'm so agitated I almost laugh.

"You'll regret it, she won't be around forever."

"Nor will I, luckily."

"Exactly."

"And excuse me, how do you even know if this is hurting her? You're a parent so you know? The world has never seen shitty parents?"

"Because I'm a parent, yes. And also because she's your mom."

"For fuck's sake!" I pound on the steering wheel with both hands.

"Your mother—Noa! You, the person that you are. This thing that you are, it didn't just appear out of nowhere."

I simmer in silence. I'm done talking to him. Now she's also getting credit for all the good things about me? He looks outside, then turns and looks at me for a second, but it's long enough for me to see one thing clearly: there is no love there.

›

At the office I try to concentrate, but can hardly manage it, because I'm fuming.

I can't stand him, so I don't care that he's been talking to Hailey for ten minutes just a few feet away from me. Teddy and Hailey have a professional relationship, but for some reason they seem closer than usual today. At least that's what it looks like from where I'm sitting. Their casual chat goes on and on and judging by her body language—and his too, frankly—they're clearly enjoying themselves. So that's how it goes, huh, Teddy? Just a word, just one comment about a sensitive subject, and you take revenge?

He must be impressed by how beautiful her eyes are, by her big tits, her smooth, tanned skin. They seem to be amused, and the cunt touches his arm and laughs out loud, making sure the entire office can hear her joking around with the CEO. Enough, just stop talking. Where's Jamie when you need her?

And what now? I want to leave but I can't, I'm presenting the film to the team soon. I text the editor to check if he's finished exporting the final version.

Uploading now. 20 mins

Okay, more waiting. And these two morons are still flirting away right in front of my face, too far for me to hear anything, but close enough for me to see everything.

›

We turn off the light in the boardroom. My heart's pounding, we're starting. Need to turn the volume up a bit. That's it, at this point there's nothing else to do but let go.

I observe everyone as they watch, the projector's light gently illuminating their faces. Richard is hypnotized with a smile at the ready, mouth a little gaped. Phil is concentrating, making sure there are no content issues. Naomi, the engineer I like, and two of her team members seem to be enjoying it. Hailey is watching attentively, and I can't tell what she's thinking. Yes, watch closely, even though you and your opinion are of no interest to me. You're welcome to connect the dots and realize that Teddy's close with Noa, and Noa's made the film, and if the film's good then Teddy will appreciate Noa even more.

Teddy.

Reclining in his seat, his body only partially turned toward the screen, noncommittal. Typical. I see his eyes from the side blink, focused stare ahead. Unlike earlier, he's now beautiful. His face is calm, lips pressed together. He's not smiling. He didn't read the script because he doesn't 'have time for that,' so he's seeing it all for the very first time. Love the film I've made for you, Teddy. Please. It's a matter of life and death.

There's an amusing bit and everyone laughs. Richard sends me a wink and I smile at him. Look at Teddy again. Those who don't know him couldn't tell that he's smiling right now. But I do know. The second time that everyone laughs, he looks away from the screen and our eyes meet. I think he's pleased. Good. But don't assume that I don't despise you anymore.

Done. Applause, compliments, a few notes. Phil says he thinks the film should be played at the convention next week. A discussion ensues around the matter, Teddy's on his phone of course, uninvolved. Hailey's not sure that it would be a wise move. Despite her faulty reasoning, Phil goes quiet, but then Naomi comes to his rescue and counts off several reasons to go ahead. Richard is persuaded and decides to use it. Teddy's getting up. On his way out he touches my shoulder.

"Excellent film," he says and walks out.

〉

After the screening, I leave the office without telling him. I take the elevator downstairs, each floor further distancing me from the joy of success and getting me closer to the rage of this morning's conversation.

Ban. That's what he calls my way of coping with the fact that the woman who gave birth to me isn't fit for motherhood. That's what he has to say to me. And it's only for the sake of retaliation. I'm starting to realize who he is, how alienated, how brutal. How cruel.

Excellent film. Fuck you.

I'm in the street, the rain's stopped and the air's cool and crisp. The sidewalk beneath the office building's wet and the café chairs are leaning forward over the tables. I'm going home.

When I get to my apartment, I turn on the little heater and take my shoes off. This whole thing's gone way too far. I shouldn't be in this sort of relationship with Teddy, it's a mistake. There's nothing for me there.

Someone who loves me—that's what I should be looking for. Someone who uses great care when asking me about why I'm not in touch with Nurit. Who respects my answer and hugs me and tells me he understands, and that it hurts him to hear I'd found myself at age nine with a mother who didn't reply when spoken to, who shut herself away in her bedroom for days on end. The smell in that room was disgusting. And then, after everything collapsed, she wasn't in the bedroom anymore. The smell remained.

To be honest, I don't remember everything; not the breakdown (just recall screaming, shouting, crying, her and him too, and Roy so tiny, only six years old—I remember him crying a lot, also remember shouting at him that he was a crybaby, screaming for him to stop crying; when I grew up, my dad told me how I'd cared for him, but all I can remember is how mean I was to him), I don't remember the depression days, or how the household managed after she left.

I didn't hate myself. Not sure how, but my self-hatred appeared only later on. I hated Nurit. Loathed her. When did I develop my hatred toward her? Was it right after she left? Or maybe before? Maybe I'd stopped loving her when she didn't get out of bed, a pathetic depressed lump beneath the blanket. You might as well have shoved a few pillows in there, they'd be just as functional as she was. At least you can lean on pillows.

This one afternoon, I was sitting in her car and looking out the back window. This was around two years after the divorce. Roy wasn't with us, we were alone. We weren't getting along that day, I don't remember why, but I do remember us waiting at a red light at the crossroad leading to my house, and I'd decided to count down from ten, and that if the light changed before I reached zero—I'd never have to see her again. If it didn't change and I'd reached zero, I'd continue meeting her.

When I got to two, the light changed.

Roy continued seeing her on a regular basis. She'd come to pick him up, and I'd look through the window and see her car drive off with Roy inside. It seemed easier for him to cope with the fact that she'd completely abandoned us. She'd even dared to judge me for my decision: showing up angry, threatening, ignoring, shouting, stalking me outside school. Begging, sending letters, trying to entice me with all sorts of bribes. But I refused. I didn't want to be in the same room as her. When she realized that nothing she did made a difference, she changed tactics. Maybe she'd decided to give me some time to calm down. She continued writing letters and passing messages to me through various people, but nothing helped. I won.

Dad tried to help too. Help her, me. Tried to persuade me to meet her, but very quickly folded since I was incredibly strong and stubborn, and he was, and still is, weak and nonauthoritative.

A few years later, he met Mina. She came into our lives in a very minor, drama-free way, through the back door. She never tried to create a deep bond with me, she was always scared of me and kept her distance, or maybe she was just smart enough to leave me alone. It was convenient for me that they were together because I felt more comfortable about being absent from the house. At a friend's place, on the street, at school, on the army base—didn't matter where—there's no place like any other place but home.

I wake up from a loud noise, like beaten metal. I'm on my couch, it's dark and raining outside. It takes me a moment to realize where I am. I get up and look out. The wind's disconnected an aluminium board from the roof and it's now bashing against the wall outside. There's nothing I can do to make the noise stop. Back on the couch I think of Teddy, but then remember everything, and when I look at my phone I'm battle-ready again. Three missed calls from Teddy Rosenfeld. Ha! I smile and think about not returning his call, not showing up at the office on Sunday or any other day of the week, maybe never. That way he'll know that he can't treat me like this, that I'm very strong, and I don't need him as much as he thinks I do. Got texts too:

Where'd you go

And then another one, a few minutes later—

Not answering

Check what time he called. Three in a row, shortly before the text asking or notifying me that I'm not answering. No, I'm not. It doesn't matter to him anyway.

If I were to conduct a little midterm assessment, it's clear that he and I shouldn't be together, that I'm better off staying away. I'm filled with renewed energy, a clear understanding that I need to move on, and I actually feel relieved. I imagine someone else, something else, sense myself without him, and maybe it feels nicer. That's it, a conscious decision, a choice; I'm beginning to end this.

›

The following morning it's Friday. I call Roy because I'm about to run out of weed. "Hey, what's up?"

"How you doing?" I retort.

"Fine, but you're catching me at a bad time, we have the premiere today. Are you coming? They're probably coming too. Dad." Dad includes Mina.

"Right, it's today."

"And Thomas will be there!" He lightens his tone. "Just come! I'm really sorry, I have to go. Okay?"

"Wait a sec!"

"What?"

"Got some weed on you?"

"A bit, yeah. Just come. Got to go. Bye!"

How do I get to Jerusalem? Take my car? Don't want to risk getting stuck. Public transport? No way. And if I'm already there then I can visit Grandma after the show. I'll just take my car.

From the exit to the highway and all the way to the hills leading to Jerusalem—my brain refuses to let go; Who were you waiting for the other night, Teddy? Me? Right. Then keep on waiting, because I'm not coming back. You had me, and you blew it.

The car has made it! The entrance to the theater is actually a parking lot. I see my dad and Mina, they're standing in one spot and looking around in awe, as though they've teleported from another dimension and just happened to land straight into a fringe theater premiere. I wave at them.

"There's Noa!" my dad announces to Mina.

I reach them. "I'm in this dimension too!"

"What dimension?" My dad tries to hug me in his lanky way. "It's so great you're here, we weren't sure you'd show up. So you made it. Great! You look great."

"How did you get to Jerusalem? We'd have picked you up." Mina tightens the scarf around her skinny neck. "I can't believe how cold it is."

"This coat's perfect for this kind of weather," Dad boasts, patting his windbreaker. It's far more suited for cycling than the theater, but I notice a buttoned shirt beneath it, and I imagine how Mina ironed his festive shirt so that he could look dignified for Roy's premiere. That moves me.

I meet Thomas inside the theater, shake his pale white hand as my dad and Mina sit between us on the gray plastic chairs. He introduces himself with a thick Austrian accent, pronounces my name with pointy edges. I smile at him and we say we'll talk after the show.

The performance is nice, not my favorite medium, that's for sure. I spend a considerable amount of time coming up with what I'll say to Roy afterward. Seeing him onstage is always accompanied by a sense of tension about him screwing up.

My dad watches attentively and nods his head every time he gets something. He occasionally whispers an explanation or insight to Mina. She's sucking on an herbal lozenge which she'd offered Thomas (who took one) and me (who declined) earlier on. My foot starts twitching. The lady next to me glances at it and I stop. Now I need to concentrate on keeping my foot still.

What's Teddy doing now? Friday, 3:12 p.m. I check to see if he's online.

last seen today at 2:25 PM

The lady next to me eyes my phone and releases a reprimanding huff in my direction. I put the phone away.

Outside, after the applause and congratulating Roy and the rest of the sweaty cast, Thomas and I talk. He tells me that he's returning to

Vienna soon, and I think about his relationship with Roy coming to an end, as expected. I try to find a spot to roll a joint with the new weed Roy gave me. Thomas doesn't smoke, but he helps block the wind with his slender hands. He has a very clean smell.

Mina and my dad ask if I want to join them for dinner somewhere in the area. I politely decline and say I'm going to visit Grandma. They leave and I stay with Thomas and with Roy, who's hardly available to hang with us. It's getting dark, so I say my goodbyes and drive to the center of Jerusalem.

This weed got me too stoned, and I feel a little indifferent and gloomy. I fix my grandma's remote control. I help her caretaker hook up the printer. I have no idea what she needs to print. Grandma looks tired and old. The only moment her existential suffering pauses is when I rub her dry, swollen feet.

I drive home.

Once I'm back, I start feeling the need, or needing the feel. It makes me think about texting him, which then leads to thinking about what I'd write, if I would.

If he really is worried about me or wants to see me, then he can do something about it in less than sixty seconds. I need it to come from him. Because if everything falls apart the moment I loosen my grip, that means that there's nothing here, that it's only me keeping myself on board, like a street cleaner grabbing on to the back handles of a garbage truck, which will drive away whether he grabs hold or not.

❯

Describe obsession;

Sunday noon.

I'm working from home, preparing a list of revisions requested by the team during last week's screening. I haven't seen Teddy or spoken to him since then; his messages remain unanswered. He didn't try again, not even over the weekend. And where is he now?

Who the fuck cares where he is? What am I doing, missing him?

It doesn't seem to matter to him whether he's talked to me, seen me; knows where I am or what I'm doing. Maybe I'm no longer alive? This is the best thought of all the thoughts I've had today. The notion of freeing myself from existence calms me down. I imagine his phone ringing and he picks it up: Noa's dead, she died on the spot. The thought of him at home, sitting down on his bed and holding his face in his hands, that's my favorite. Yes, cry, I'm not here anymore, I died on the spot, you fucking idiot, and where were you when I was alive? How can you give up on me? How are you not demanding to see me? Don't you understand that I'm all you really have? Maybe you have some things, but it's only me that you truly have, not even your kids, not even yourself.

Sunday evening.

So what I'll do is starve you and me and this relationship. Because I have no other choice. You lost me. Go on back to the life you had before me. Welcome back to a world that doesn't include me.

Monday, late morning.

The film's done. I send it to Phil. Now what? Sharon invites me over to hang with her and the kids. I know it'll be a distraction, and yet I find myself preferring to be alone. I'd probably want to come over if she had time to talk about my turmoil. But she doesn't, and rightly so; the lives of parents make more sense to me sometimes, because they're not in the center of it all, they don't have the dubious privilege of delving into their inner world, a sickening egocentric feast. You'd think that people only have children so they don't lose their minds. And then they lose their minds from the having of the children. Still better. Is it?

Monday night.

I don't see the point in living. What am I supposed to wait for? He'll never get out of my heart, my mind won't ever let go. I won't be able to escape the shitstorm of loving him. How right he was back then, at the wedding, it's so hard for me to think about it, replaying in my head. *Listen to me.* Why didn't I?

Tuesday morning.

The convention's today. The film will be played on a loop at the Delmar stand. I deliberate whether to go. I'm almost certain Teddy won't be there. So what's the point in going? I don't have anything to do there anyways. And if he does go? He'll be busy and we won't get a moment alone, and even if we do—I have nothing to say to him. I'm not going.

Tuesday afternoon.

A phone call from the office number makes my heart skip a beat. I pick up, feeling my pulse at the bottom of my stomach. It's not Teddy, it's Richard: "Loads of praise for the film," "Huge success," "Shame you didn't drop by." And all I want to ask is: Teddy?

Wednesday morning.

I'm going crazy. Why would you let me continue life without you after you've shown me how life can be with you?

Wednesday afternoon.

I shouldn't stay inside. I go downstairs and start walking. I walk all the way to his street. Maybe I'll see him leaving or coming back home. I sit and wait, lurking. No luck. Not a trace. Maybe he's abroad? Richard didn't mention him when he called yesterday. I write to Richard—Is Teddy in town? |—but I don't send it. Why would I ask him that? Just let go.

Wednesday night.

Now I prefer the distance; I remind myself that being with you is hell, because being with you just means holding back my love for you. So what's to miss?

It wasn't like that from the start, I remember how free I felt. So where is that freedom? How did I lose it?

And what am I doing now?

I feel like the way out is clear, and I'm meant to take it. And this way isn't even my choice. All other options are gone as far as he's concerned. And what about his body? Where's his goddamned body? Isn't it asking for me?

Thursday morning.

I can't cry. Can't be indifferent either. I'm in absolute anguish, and the only way to survive is through obsession. I try to wean myself, quit messing with it, stop trying to figure out where he is and what he's doing.

But I should be honest with myself: I don't want it to end this way. If I need to see him that badly then I can solve that. I'm anxious about going to the office because I know it's a bad idea. But how can he not call? It's obvious to him that I'm hurt and angry, and he just goes on with his life, undisturbed. Madness.

Thursday, 6:30 p.m.

I leave my apartment and start walking toward his place. When I arrive, I look up, then ring the downstairs buzzer. My heart is pounding wildly. No reply. I have a key, but I won't go in. I sit at the entrance to his building. It's cold and dark. I can wait in the lobby, but I don't mind the wind chill. I sit on the low brick wall. People pass by, returning to their homes. Time crawls by and I stay seated.

Shortly before 8:00 p.m., a taxi arrives and stops in front of his building. He emerges from the back seat and stalls for a moment with the door open. My heart stops—maybe he's not alone? He turns toward the seat and pulls out his briefcase, then shuts the door. He's alone. As he walks toward the entrance he notices me.

"What are you doing here? Why are you sitting outside?"

I stand up and he stops in front of me.

He looks at me, I say nothing. He gently nods his head, his eyes cold, and says, "All right. Let's do this."

›

In the elevator, I sense that he's also gone through something this past week, something's shifted. I look at him. For some reason I haven't managed to visualize his face over the last few days. When he looks up at me, I try not to look away. Is this better than sitting at home obsessing over him? We walk into his apartment, and he shuts the door but stays in the entranceway, placing his things on the console. I stand there not knowing what to do, so I shove my hands in my pockets. The apartment isn't heated yet. I don't understand why he's still standing there when he usually walks straight to the big dining table.

"Yes, Noa darling"—unusual phrasing—"what was that all about?"

I'm scared to talk. Scared to tell him that I've checked if he can do without me, and I've found that he absolutely can. "I don't know."

"You don't know?" he repeats after me. "Then why don't you go home and come back when you do."

My heart sinks. He's mad at me. "That's what you want? For me to go?"

"No. I don't want you to go. Why would I? It's wonderful having you here."

"Okay." I'm about to die.

"You'll undress soon too, so why would I want you to go?"

"What?"

"Yeah, I know you. But before that, why don't you tell me"—he briefly touches the dent between my collarbones with his finger—"why you didn't answer when I called."

"Because I was angry at you," I say in a soft voice.

"What does that have to do with it?"

"I was angry, so I didn't answer."

"What were you angry about?"

"What you said about Nurit. I don't want us to talk about it."

"I'll talk to you about whatever I want to talk to you about. And I won't have you ignoring my calls. Even if you're angry. It's irrelevant."

"You will have me ignoring your calls. Just like I have you ignoring mine."

"No, I won't have you ignoring my calls, is that clear?"

"Don't know."

"Again with your 'don't know.' What do you know? How to make me fuck you? Is that what you came for? All right, I'll fuck you. Take your clothes off, I'll fuck you right here, you won't even have to reach the bed."

"That's not what I came for, Teddy, stop it."

"I won't stop it. You want to go? There's the door."

"I don't want to go."

"Then take your clothes off."

"What do you mean? But I'm cold. It's cold here."

"I don't care."

I'm confused and don't know what to say. "Are you angry with me?"

"Yes. Take your clothes off, I won't ask you again."

I take off my jacket. What does he want? Does he really feel like fucking me right now? I pull up my sweatshirt along with the T-shirt underneath it. I'm braless. Why do I need to strip here? I feel the cold air on my breasts, my nipples. I pull my feet out of my ankle boots, pull down my pants and underwear and toss them on the pile of clothes now gathered on the floor.

An unfamiliar sensation floods me as I stand there naked. I feel exposed and it really is cold. I look at him, unable to recall anything from this agonizing week. And he's a stranger, not quite Teddy, and I don't feel quite like Noa. He stands facing me, his expression is apathetic as he surveys me with his eyes.

"You understand what I'm saying?"

"Yes."

He comes closer, almost touching me, his fingers gently gliding just above my skin. His face is near my shoulder. "There's your scent." He closes his eyes and I switch on. My scent, it matters to him. He nears his hand to my lower stomach. "And your pussy." His finger hovers only momentarily over my pubic hair, but I can feel it deep inside.

"Anyone else fuck you this week?" He looks at me from above.

"Since when do you ask me that sort of thing?"

"Answer me."

"No."

"Shame." His lips are beautiful, and he's beautiful and I want him to kiss me. He takes a step back. Is this punishment? Is this a ritual?

I ask quietly, no admonishing, "What do you want?"

"I'm not sure I want anything from you."

I swallow hard. He's standing there completely dressed and I'm naked and he's not sure he wants anything from me?

"That can't be," I hear myself saying, glad to discover Noa's here and she'll help me handle this.

"Why's that?"

I look down at my body and start raising my eyes in his direction, but my gaze doesn't reach his eyes because it stops on his cock still in his pants. "I can make your cock hard without even touching it."

He smiles. Not a calming smile, but still one that reminds me it's him. A swell of warmth runs through my body as I recall what it's like to be with him, and how this encounter is different from the one I had in mind, minding the gap. I maintain my distance from him, maybe five feet, and start talking, unsure what I'm going to say until the words come out of my mouth.

"Putting me aside, my body didn't understand where you'd disappeared to. My pussy, what am I supposed to tell her every night, every morning, when she asks where you'd gone, where's your cock, why aren't you fucking us?" I slightly spread my legs apart, feeling the cold air between them. He looks at me, a quiet look. I walk up to him and do something strange, press against his side, kind of like a dog rubbing against him. "I want you to take me and fuck me and pound me. Hard." I speak with a normal, almost practical tone, but I've allowed my lust to take over. "I want you on my mouth and my ass and my nipples and in my pussy, which you know better than I do."

And there he is, I can see Teddy behind his eyes, and I know he's not as angry as before.

"Sit down."

I shove him to the wall and push against him. He's still standing and I press my stomach forcefully on his cock still in his pants. He's pretty present already, so I turn my back to him and now it's my ass against him, pushing back and shifting forward, as though I'm fucking him with it. He's moaning and then he places his warm hands on my waist and all at once he takes the movement from me and makes it his own, and I feel what I'm supposed to feel, I feel his need.

"Sit."

I turn to face him and point at the floor, manage to get him all the way down. Once he's seated, I spread my legs apart and bring my pussy near his face, lean my arms against the wall, feeling how wet I am as he closes his eyes and takes a deep breath. He looks up and reaches his hand to my breasts, his touch on my nipples stings and arouses me and they harden, and then he grabs my ass with his other hand and gets my pussy closer to his mouth, and now it's the warmth of his tongue and I look down and see him from this strange angle, his whole body, stomach and legs, sitting like that must be hard, his cock must be hard, but I look back up at the wall in front of me and close my eyes and concentrate on his mouth until I release a deep moan.

"Your taste . . . how can you taste this good, tell me."

Games and rules and restrictions—I don't care about any of it. I sit on him and my hands are already unzipping his pants. He slides forward a bit and we take his cock out, and I've pretty much succeeded, it's pretty hard and I haven't seen it for too long, and I'd thought about it a lot, so I shift back and lean forward and put as much as I can into my mouth all at once, and as my lips tighten and soften intermittently I watch his hand spread open on the floor, that hand that belongs to me, and I'm turned on by how he's keeping it like that to maintain his balance. I stop and rise, sit on him and shove my hand between us, grab his incredibly hard cock and put it inside me. Now there's no more need for hands, he's inside and I move above him and he groans and my hand's behind my back, straightened and reaching all the way down to his balls. He's setting the pace again, he never lets me fuck him, he's the one who'll do the fucking. He looks at me and I look at him, and then he kisses me, his hand comes up to my face, his finger goes into my mouth, and his tongue, and I want him to devour me, or me him, and we kiss and we're not even really in sync, but it doesn't matter because we're so incredibly close right now.

"I missed you, Teddy. Teddy. Teddy. Why?"

"What did you think would happen?"

"You don't hear from me, and you don't even try to find out what's going on? For an entire fucking week, nothing?"

"I can go much longer than a fucking week. Don't try me."

At least he admits he knows exactly what he was doing. His hands are on me and he lays me on my back; the floor's cold and he pulls the rug over to us, and once most of my back is on it, it feels nicer.

"So I'm on my own here? That's what you're saying?" I ask.

"No. I'm here too."

"You're here too."

"Let me fuck you, I have to fuck you," he says, and goes inside me and it's so good, it's beyond good, it's much more than I can take.

"That's what I want, all the time, for you to fuck me. That's all I'm good for, that's all I have to offer the world."

It doesn't end in the foyer. We move to the bed and fuck for a long while, until there's no more distance, until all the alienation vanishes, the bedroom goes back to being my safe haven, my body's hot and so is his, and maybe we're not as angry anymore, and I'm trying to get a promise out of him, a declaration or I don't know what, but I can't get him to say the words I'm looking for, and I actually don't even know what I want to hear, but I feel what I'd wanted to feel even without the words: he waited for me.

7

Meeting of the Minds

»

In the morning, I wash my face and look in the mirror. My eyes are swollen, lips too, but I've somehow woken up pretty. I'm glad to be here. And now what? I find him at the big dining table, reading the paper and eating breakfast.

"Good morning." He smiles at me, and I notice he's dressed to leave the house even though it's the weekend.

"Good morning. You going somewhere?"

"In a bit. I have a meeting."

I make a cup of coffee and join him. Not a word about our week apart, not a word about our night. I look at him for a moment as he eats while reading the finance section. So maybe everything's okay? When do we talk about what we've been through? In any case, I'm not going to risk it. Right now, just act normal. Grab a newspaper, read next to him. I pull a magazine from the pile.

What's this? Who's that, smiling all over the front cover of the pretentious *Gallery* magazine, hair, makeup, and wardrobe, draped in a roll of film—a suitable object to characterize this week's woman of the hour? Why, if it isn't Tamara Klein. And why is she on the front cover? Well, to promote her debut film.

"Tamara Klein." She's one of those girls who are actually sweet—if I'm being honest—yet annoying because everything always works out for them—if I'm being really honest.

"What are you reading?"

" 'I just told myself that I don't need anyone. I sold my car, used the money to move to Berlin, and the script just wrote itself,'" I read out loud in a somewhat sarcastic tone, mostly talking to myself.

Teddy looks up at me. "Who's she?"

"Tamara Klein, we studied film together."

He looks at the front cover. "Gorgeous." He keeps his gaze on her for a moment longer and then gets up to grab some salt for his egg-white omelet. When he's with his back to me, I can't help but give him the finger.

"Good for her. Best of luck." I continue leafing through the article. "Oh, and she has a kid too, of course, 'five-year-old Shira.' Why not? I wonder what little Shira was doing while her mom was writing a script in Berlin."

He sits back down and sprinkles salt over his eggs. "I don't see what the problem is."

"Who says there's a problem?"

"Why does it piss you off that Tamara made her film?" He enunciates her name carefully, dignified.

"Because. Because it's like sitting on a train and watching another train go by and knowing I was supposed to be on it. And I can see her sitting there and getting to the place where I want to be. So it's annoying. And she's a woman, like me, so that's even more annoying."

"Where do you want to be?" He eats quickly.

What kind of game is this? Doesn't he know about my frustrations? This is the first thing I'd told him when we'd just met. "What do you want?"

"I want to understand," he claims, but I don't believe him. "I want to understand why you're pissed off at Tamara for making her film, as though it's in place of yours. What does one have to do with the other? You want to make a film?"

"Yes. You know I do."

"So, what are you doing about it?" He finishes eating and pushes the empty plate away.

"Trying."

"What does that mean?" He places his elbows on the table and leans toward me, antagonizing.

"That throughout the years I've made all sorts of attempts at expressing my ideas."

"I don't know what that means, 'expressing ideas.' Did you write anything? What did you write, films?" he presses me.

"Yes, mainly scripts." I'm getting tense and I get up to look for my cigarettes.

"And, what happened? Why didn't they become films?" He's genuinely trying to torment me this morning. Was yesterday not enough?

"You already know why, so why are you asking?"

"No, I don't know why. Nobody wanted them? Or what?"

"I wrote scripts for movies, for TV, applied for all sorts of funding, producers, channels. Unfortunately, all of the replies I've ever gotten back started with 'unfortunately.'"

Now I'm pissed off. I find the cigarette pack in the kitchen, but it's empty, even though I clearly recall having two cigarettes left.

"Got a smoke?"

"No, I ran out. Smoked yours."

He could have at least left me one. I return to my chair empty-handed.

"And why did you stop trying? Why don't I ever see you sitting down and writing?"

What does he want from me? "Okay, Teddy. Aren't you late for a meeting? Leave me alone."

"No. Instead of leaving you alone, let me tell you what I think about you."

I look at him, irritated, and remember that at least I look pretty this morning.

"You come from nothing and you're going nowhere. That's your story. You got any other plans? I'd be surprised if you do. You complain about Tamara Klein, but I haven't seen you do anything to change the outcome of your situation."

"Okay."

"So, either you're depressed," he continues, "which means you're depressed with me even though you said you were going to be fine, so let's take that into account, or you're bullshitting yourself and everyone around you, and you can't and won't do anything, and then it's just a shame that you're suffering! Might as well just define yourself as going nowhere and move on."

"So you've found another way to hurt me?"

"No, your attitude toward this conversation is wrong." He's enjoying being condescending. "You sit here bitching to me about Tamara's success, and I'm thinking, What does she really want? What does she need to stop suffering?" He gets up and clears his dishes.

"Oh, you're trying to help me! That's what this spectacle is all about! Because you're not helping right now, you're just denigrating me, you're destructive." I stay seated and only slightly raise my voice.

"Own up to what we're talking about, don't go hiding behind your walls."

"I am owning up to what we're talking about! That's precisely your point, that there's no hope, only two options, either I'm depressed or I'm incapable. Which one do you expect me to choose?"

"You need more options? Then how about this." He stands in front of me, wiping his hands with a kitchen towel. "You go ahead and tell me."

I take a deep breath. "I have no doubt that I'll be able to do something. I don't know how good it'll be, I don't know when I'll be able to do it—"

"Noa, 'able' is when you try. How will you be able? What will you be able to do?" He's almost laughing in my face.

"Okay. Right now, I'm obligated to Delmar, it's only three days since the pitch film screened at the convention, how much free time do you think I have?"

"If you think you can get ahead in your career only once you get some free time, then you're not only naive but also an amateur. At least be honest with yourself. And that's what I'm trying to tell you. I don't like it, Noa. I don't appreciate it."

That last sentence breaks my heart more than any of the shitty things he's ever said to me.

"Okay." I decide to change tactics so that maybe he'll appreciate me after all. "I haven't written during the last few months. I can't right now."

"There you go. That's all I'm saying."

"No, no. You're saying a whole lot more and much worse."

"Doesn't matter what I say."

"So now it doesn't matter?!"

"It didn't matter before either. That's what I've been trying to tell you, you and your 'destructive.' No one's out to denigrate you. I just want to open your eyes a little so you can look at yourself and question this convenient notion you have of yourself." His eyes are hard.

"What convenient notion do I have of myself?"

"The way you introduced yourself the first time we met—you gave off a different impression."

I can't even swallow. "I said exactly the same things."

"Why aren't you writing now?"

Enough with the justifications, just tell the detective what he wants to hear. "Because I'm with you."

"Good. Thank you."

"For what?"

"For admitting that you're not writing because you're here."

"You're welcome."

"And when you cry to me about your friend who made it, what am I supposed to do about it?"

"What are you supposed to do about it?!" I'm really shouting at him now. "Nothing. It has nothing to do with you!"

"So just ignore it? Or acknowledge it?"

"Ignore!"

"What is it about me that makes you unable to write?" This lunatic won't let go!

"I'm too busy conducting my research."

"What research?"

"This research." I gesture at us.

"I don't buy that."

I decide to stop talking. It's very unlike me, to shut up in the middle of an argument when the smell of blood is still in the air. My silence quiets both of us. Maybe he's given up, maybe he thinks that he's managed to get through to me. He goes to his office and I hear him talking on the phone, until the call ends abruptly and he stays there.

"I'm going out to buy cigarettes," I say to the huge apartment. Then I get worried that I'll upset him if I go without telling him, so I stand outside his office and say it again. "I'm going out to get some cigarettes."

He looks at me and nods, and I immediately turn and walk away before he manages to shove another insult in my face. I pass through the entrance on my way out, my feet walking over the same spot where I'd lain the night before.

›

I buy two packs, one for him too. I don't want to be at his place right now, but I know that I have no choice, that I already blew my opportunity for a clean getaway, that I'd be as pathetic as him if I went home now just because he's fallen for Tamara Klein and decided to crush my heart when he'd mentioned the first time we met and explained how retrospectively disappointed he is in the loser that I turned out to be. I'm starting to get a serious headache.

When I get back upstairs, he's about to leave.

"Wasn't sure you'd come back," he says when I enter the living room.

"I have a headache." I don't recall the decision to share this bit of info with Teddy. "Got you a pack."

He takes it from my hand. "Thanks. Get some rest, I'll call you later."

"Get some rest at home?"

"No, monster, here, get some rest here."

"Okay."

He kisses me on the lips, and I feel like it doesn't make sense for him to kiss me only moments after he's said those things about me, and by the time this thought ends he's already out, the door slams shut and I'm standing alone in the middle of the living room.

What Teddy is saying isn't new to me. Maybe I hadn't heard it from him until now, but I've heard it from myself for as long as I can remember.

+

I've had stories in my head ever since I was little. Once I realized that I was good at it, that I could create whole new worlds, I taught myself how to live in a parallel dimension—much more precise and satisfying than my disappointing reality—and the stories helped me reach a more complete self. Whenever I felt like I needed a certain kind of attention, I'd make up characters who would satisfy the need. Those fantasies turned out to be my creative genesis.

When I was a little girl, there was this beautiful boy, and he had a pack of dogs and no parents, of course, and he knew seven languages. Since I was the one who made him up, I could invite him over for strolls that led from my school all the way home, and these walks made my existence more tolerable.

As I grew up, my interest tilted toward romantic scenarios. During that time, I first discovered American culture, so I had an entire football team and girls and dramas and making out. I was no longer present in my own stories, there was no need for my character. It was all so clear to me, who the characters were, what they said to one another, the ambience, the houses, the clothes. I imagined something different from the TV shows I was watching, since they didn't fulfill my needs, until one day, a girl from my class returned from a trip to the US and brought back some teen magazine clippings neatly arranged in see-through folders, boys and girls from a new TV show. They were photographed in front of a white background, some standing tall, some sitting on a flipped chair, one with a surfboard: Brenda, Brandon, Dylan. *Beverly Hills, 90210.* Aaron Spelling stole my ideas! At least it made me realize that people might actually be interested in my inventions.

I studied film in high school and tried to use it to tell my stories, but I wasn't able to translate the things in my mind, something always went wrong along the way. So I worked on other people's movies, helped them tell their stories, and kept my stories to myself. I continued inventing characters to keep me company, role-play characters, male alter egos. At any given moment, I could make up the masculine character I wanted to be or have in front of me, and no boy or man could ever compete with my epic imagination. At least that's what I used to think.

»

The day before Teddy goes off to Germany for a round of fundraising for the new project, we're both at the office. I upload the movie file to his tablet and try to show him how to play it.

"Show Phil," he dismisses me.

When I return from Phil's office, I see Adrian standing in the main work area. I know why he's here: Teddy told me they were going to have lunch with the rest of the family for Adrian's birthday. By the time I notice him, we're far too close not to say hello.

"Happy birthday."

"Thanks. You work here?" he asks, and I nod. "I didn't know you work for him."

"Yes." I sound like I'm pleading guilty.

He doesn't continue the conversation. I've forgotten that I shouldn't approach him with a guilty tone. In fact, I've forgotten that I shouldn't approach him at all. But for some reason, I stay next to him and decide to extend the moment and see if we get to a point where he says something. What do you have to say to me, Adrian Rosenfeld? Go ahead, I'm waiting.

He realizes that he's supposed to say something. "Are you joining us for lunch?" he asks dryly, no inviting look, obviously.

"No, no. Of course not," I quickly reassure him.

"Why not?" He's got that wiseass tone.

"What do I have to do with it?" I say honestly. "It's a family thing."

He lowers his gaze and then looks at me again. Is that a taunting look? Is it contempt? "I see. So when he gathers up all of his loved ones and brings them all around to say goodbye, you're not going to be there?"

I'm so surprised that I pause for a moment, but I recover quickly. "Is that today? Fuck, I have Pilates."

He smiles. Not right at me, but a sweet, concealed smile off to the side. The smile of a wise person. He seems pleased that he's dared to tell me what's on his mind. This is good, we should stop here.

"Happy birthday, Adrian." I seal the conversation.

"Thank you very much!" he says way too loudly, almost aggressively.

"Nice try," I add as I walk away, heading toward my desk with conviction but keep on going so that I'll get out of his sight and end up in the accounting department. I stand next to a potted plant with overly yellow leaves and occasionally look out the window, hoping no one starts wondering what I'm doing here.

I'm glad I managed to talk to Adrian, and I'm even glad that he said something mean. I'm happy he allowed himself, but the happiness brings me closer to him and so it turns into empathy, which then dissolves very quickly and morphs into distress. I force myself to concentrate for a moment longer on what I was just told, before I escape the thought; putting aside the hint of my insignificance in Teddy's life, I'm much more disturbed by Adrian's decision to mention—of all the topics in all the world—his father's death.

⟩

When Teddy gets back from lunch, he calls me into his office. I walk in and see that he's not behind his desk, but rather standing close to the entrance. I shut the door. I'm not sure what the people around us know since we're clearly close, but we generally maintain professional attitudes when we're at the office.

"How was it?" I ask.

"Nice. What did you tell Adrian?" As always, he gets straight to the point.

"Happy birthday."

"What else? Is that it?"

"Kind of. Why?" Didn't think Adrian would even mention our talk.

"Because he said you're funny, that you made him laugh."

He thinks I'm funny? I smile and immediately get back to looking serious, and Teddy notices, of course.

"So what did you say to make him laugh?"

"I don't know. Why are you interrogating me about Adrian? We spoke for like ten seconds."

"I'm asking, not interrogating. Why is everything an interrogation to you?"

"Look who's talking!"

"Okay, so you don't want to tell me?"

"I have nothing to tell."

"Then why didn't he shut up about you all through lunch?"

Now that really does surprise me. Why would he talk about me? All through lunch, no less? What did I say? And also—how little does he need? Well, maybe as little as I do; and it's not even what I told him, but rather what he told me, and that is not something I'm going to share with Teddy.

"I'm surprised to hear that," I decide to say. "I really didn't say anything significant, just retorted, but it must have made him feel nice. I don't know."

"What did he say?" he asks, and when he sees my look he adds, "Something about me?"

"Even if he did say something about you, I wouldn't tell you."

"So you two just stood there laughing at me?"

"As much as I'd love to hurt you, Teddy, I'd never use someone else to do it, especially not your children."

Teddy has a lot of facial expressions, but there's one that is the absolute essence of his ego, and that's the one he's giving me right now. How's he going to react, and what about? And why am I not scared?

"So you're saying you want to hurt me?"

"Yes."

He falls silent; his jaw tightens. And that's a good thing, because maybe it means he knows why. The main thing is, I took the focus away from Adrian.

"Okay, well done," he finally says.

"What have I done well?"

"Saying it like that. I mean it."

We stay silent. He seems pensive, his eyes are still on me.

"All right." He suddenly disconnects and goes to his desk. "I told Milo you'll be staying at my place while I'm in Germany," he announces, and sits down.

He hasn't said a word to me about it until now. My foot gets fidgety. How does he always do that? How am I on the bottom again? Maybe I should decline? Yeah, better off declining.

"If you want to. Whatever you want," he adds over my silence.

"Yeah. Okay." Why yeah? Didn't I just decide to decline? I really need to improve my control mechanism, there's a near-psychotic episode going on here.

"I'm not in the mood for this trip." He stretches his arm backward and yawns, then looks at me again. "What did he say? Adrian. Tell me."

I bow my head, "Under His Eye," and rush out, managing to catch a glimpse of his smile as I turn and feel his eyes on my back.

»

Thursday, almost sunset, I'm at Teddy's apartment. He's in Germany, meeting investors. I'm cooking in the kitchen because I've invited Sharon and another friend of ours for dinner. I'm enjoying the gorgeous apartment, listening to music and dimming the lighting, opening a bottle of wine.

Suddenly Milo's standing there, I guess I didn't hear him coming in. Xerox is running around him, and Milo unhooks his leash.

"Hey!" I'm happy to see him. "How you doing?"

"All good. Came to do some laundry."

"Cool. Need any help?"

"No, to be honest, it's not like I'm actually *doing* the laundry." His rhythm of speaking is 50 percent his dad's. "I just leave what I've used and pick up clean clothes."

"Excellent deal."

"Totally." He goes to his room, and I fill Xerox's water bowl.

When he comes back, he sits down to talk to me. He tells me a little bit about Daria, getting along, not getting along. He says that maybe he'll sleep over here one night, and we plan to watch a movie together if he does.

Two minutes after Milo leaves, I get a text from Teddy.

Call me

What is it now? Did I say something wrong to Milo? I quickly replay our talk in my head, but can't come up with anything incriminating.

"Listen"—no hello—"I want to tell you it's going great. This is the smoothest round of fundraising I've ever had. Your film's doing most of the work, I'm not kidding. Phil shows it at the beginning of every meeting and it saves us an hour of explanations. You there?"

My heart rate is way above what it should be. "Yes."

"And in terms of willingness to invest, let me tell you, they watch it, and by the time it's over they're already putting money on the table. And this happened several times today."

I'm glad he can't see me right now because I must look awkward, standing motionless, with my widest smile, so as not to interrupt the universe when it's in the middle of being kind to me. I try to sound normal: "I'm happy to hear that, thank you."

"Aren't you polite all of a sudden."

"It really does make me happy to hear that."

"Yeah"—he takes a breath—"it's working out remarkably well."

"Really great."

"All right. You having a nice time at my place?"

"Yes! Milo just came by to swap his dirty laundry for clean clothes."

"Is he still there?"

"No, just left."

"Sweet boy. Your friends are coming over tonight, right?"

"Yes."

"Have fun. I'm going for dinner, we'll talk later."

"Okay."

"Noa." Will I ever stop getting this feeling when he says my name?

"What?"

"Thank you."

I stall for a moment. "And now, after you've thanked me, are you going to shut the hell up?"

He laughs. "No. Same rules don't apply to me, in case you haven't realized that yet."

"The writing was on the wall."

He laughs again. "Exactly. You're the one who wrote it."

>

I wake up late in the morning. No Teddy to incentivize me; he's supposed to land around noon. I think about the previous night, laughing with my friends. It was strange to have them see his apartment but not him, strange and marvelously convenient. And despite the convenience, I was also illogically hopeful he'd suddenly walk in and they'd get to meet the man behind the name.

I reach for my phone. Text from him.

> Going to Copenhagen from
> here . coming back Monday

My immediate reaction is almost always a curse. I read it and straightaway I say out loud: "Motherfucker." And then I tell myself silently, Another weekend alone.

After having coffee on the beautiful balcony, I come to my senses and decide to try to enjoy the circumstances. I go into the utility room and empty out the sack Milo left. Among his clothes are also lace panties, bras, pink and purple sportswear. I imagine Daria wearing those panties and try to figure out if she finds them comfortable, then I put everything in the washing machine. I make a list of all the errands I've postponed, immaculately tidy up the house, move the clothes to the dryer, and go visit my apartment.

>>

> My meeting with Werner the
> lawyer is tomorrow morning.
> Come with??? (please)

It takes some real expertise to be as exasperating as my brother. I mean, this isn't some spontaneous meeting, and nothing has changed to make him suddenly need me to accompany him—so why wait until the last minute to make this request?

> What time? And where?

> Nine thirty. I think north. Need to
> look up the address, checking now

Wouldn't it be more efficient to just check the address rather than text me all of that? Anyway, going with him means missing Teddy's landing at nine. I wanted to be home when he gets back, been imagining that moment all week long. Teddy, however, hasn't even asked whether I'd be there when he gets back. So maybe there's an advantage to letting him come back to an empty apartment. In any case, I'm not going to send Roy to see Werner on his own if he's asked me to join him.

Yeah, it's north

He confirms, the moron, and sends me the address. We decide to meet there at quarter past nine. I have nothing appropriate to wear for this meeting.

In the morning I'm drinking coffee on the balcony again. Betty's vacuuming the carpets in the living room. It's been a few days now that I've been sleeping in Teddy's bed, showering in his bathroom, feeling as though his home is entirely mine. And now I'm going to a meeting with his lawyer. So maybe I am him? I wish I were Teddy Rosenfeld, going over to see Werner like that, full of charm but able to summon confidence, restraint, and practicality at the snap of a finger.

Roy shows up at 9:29 a.m., panting. I'm standing beneath the humungous building and I don't tell him off when he arrives, I just go straight into the lobby and he rushes after me.

Werner's office is very fancy. Roy and I stand by the reception desk looking like two extras from Les Misérables who just happened to arrive at the wrong set. One of the secretaries asks us to take a seat and says she'll call us in soon.

"Does it make you sad that this couch alone costs more than all the money I've ever made and will ever make?" Roy whispers to me as we sit on the leather couch. I smile. I guess he's right.

"Would you like something to drink?" the secretary asks.

"Oh yes! Don't mind if I do! Got any coffee? I didn't get a chance this morning," he informs her and I feel embarrassed, but she cooperates, giggling politely, and she doesn't even shudder when he adds, "Two and a half—even three—sugars."

When we go into Werner's office, he recognizes me immediately. He points at me and smiles: "We've met before."

"That's right." I smile too, glad he remembers me.

"Come in, take a seat."

We carefully lower ourselves into the chairs in front of his desk.

Werner turns to his computer screen and I notice that Roy seems tense. The giggler walks in and hands Roy his coffee. I start wondering if we're supposed to describe everything that happened from the very beginning, but then Werner starts talking and I realize he's already in the loop. He explains the situation to us in a few brief sentences, clarifies the original contract's lack of fairness, talks shit about all the industry dickheads, and then lists the clauses that make it tricky to free Roy from the agreement.

Roy and I recoil, exchange looks. "Then what are you suggesting? How are you going to get him out of this?"

"The contract is clearly voidable for cause of fraud and deceit. I believe we can prove that there was never animus contrahendi, no meeting of the minds."

Roy's eyebrows raise with wonder. He looks at me, then shifts his gaze back to Werner.

"So you know how to move this forward?" I ask.

"Yes, yes. Absolutely."

"Any chance he'll get out of it without having to pay anything?"

"Oh, yes. I usually manage to get clients out of this type of contract."

Roy and I are excited. There's joy on our faces, and when I see our reflections in the glass window we look like two neglected little kids sunk into the cushioned chairs. If this really were a musical, then this would surely be the cue for Werner's song to begin, but instead of getting up on the table to gracefully perform his number, he wants to go over the clauses that will enable him to nullify the contract. Roy leans down and pulls out a tattered copy from his bag, then asks for a pen so he can mark everything Werner's saying.

"You don't need to do that," Werner reassures him. "I just wanted you to get a general idea of things. From here on out, it's in my hands."

"I'm in his hands! I'm in the hands of that certified, experienced, clever man." The elevator gallops downward as Roy hugs me, jittery and blissful. "Get it?"

"I get it."

"No meeting of the minds! No animus contrahendi! He can animus my contrahendi whenever he wants!"

I smile at him. He's sweet, I'm glad Werner's going to get him out of this. Being Teddy is very convenient.

⟩

Roy and I are walking through the streets. The weather's nice and the sky's blue, even though it's January. Teddy tried calling while I was at the meeting. I call him back.

"You home already?" I ask.

"Yes. Why aren't you here?"

"I was at Werner's."

"That's it? I leave you alone for five minutes and you run off with my lawyer?"

I enjoy that question and the smile in his tone so much that I don't even have a clever comeback. "We just left his office."

"What did he say?"

"That it'll all be fine."

"Good. He knows what he's doing. I'm going to the office, meet me there."

"Yeah?"

"Yeah."

"Okay."

When I get to the office, he's in with Richard, Phil, and a few others. His door's open and their loud conversation echoes through the main workspace. Maureen's at her post. I sit at my desk and take my laptop out. I want to walk in there and give him a hug and get mine in return, but there's no access to be had.

I hear him laughing. I miss him. It's good that he's back, that he's in the room right next to me; I feel like I'm getting more oxygen now.

> Where are you

> Been here a while, I'll come say
> hi when you're free.

> Come in here

I hesitate by the door.

"Noa Simon!" That's Richard. "Has anyone told you that you deserve an Oscar?"

While Phil excitedly reports the film's success, Teddy looks at me, and every time our eyes meet it feels like a lot of information is being exchanged, or like there's understanding or just affection. After I thank them for the compliments I try to sneak out, but Teddy gestures me over in a way that leaves me no choice but to sit in the only free chair in the room and grab the whiskey already poured into a glass and raise it along with the others and hear about how they've raised millions of dollars—and that's not just some generic phrasing for 'lots of money,' but rather the kind of multidigit number that's unfathomable to my little brain, which comes from nothing and is going nowhere.

›

When you start drinking at noon, it kind of makes sense for you to be sitting at your desk with your head down by 2:00 p.m.

"All right, get up, we're all going for lunch." Teddy touches my back and I quickly lift my head and look at him as my eyes try to focus. "You eaten anything today?"

"No."

"Let's go."

"Who's going?" I rise to my feet, trying to stand straight. I am so definitely drunk.

"Richard, Phil, Naomi, and a few others."

"And Noa," I inquire, "she going?"

"Noa's going too, yes." He's a very stable man, no doubt about it.

So much light! I forgot my sunglasses. Everyone's walking on the side-walk. Marching feet, shoes. I see his shoes. I'll follow him.

At the restaurant, he's sitting almost across from me. There's a glass of water in front of me. He's put it there. I drink it. He's talking to Rich-ard as he pours more water into my glass. Naomi's sitting next to me. I look at her and think about her wife; she told me once about how they put their children to sleep and showed me photos of their home, and it made me feel happy and jealous.

"What's up with you, babe?" Naomi leans in.

"I do not remember."

She bursts out laughing. "You had a drink in Teddy's office, I know all about that."

"You had a drink in Teddy's office too!" I whisper-shout. "You all did. Teddy did. And quite a bit."

"But Teddy always drinks. He's what you'd call a high-functioning alcoholic."

"So that's what he is?"

A braless waitress, or a waitress with a very amateur bra, places bread and olives on both sides of the table. Everyone keeps on chatting, but I find it hard to believe that no one's noticing. Now she's talking about the menu and she leans slightly toward the center of the table, her finger sliding over the listed dishes, chipped red nail polish. All of this is happening right next to Phil, who's leaning as far back as he can, his eyes searching for anything else to look at. I look at Teddy and see that he's actually looking at me. Why are you looking at me? Look at her, can't you see? He must see something, because he suddenly smiles at me and I smile too, and my heart's too full and it presses on my chest from within. The waitress leaves and Naomi resumes our conversation.

"Are you coming to Michigan?"

"Michigan," I repeat after her, and I know she's talking about the Delmar trip.

"Yes." Naomi picks an olive from the plate and pops it in her mouth.

"The whole office is going, almost everyone. You should come too."

"What would I do there? You guys have work to do, you're not on holiday."

"Okay, but those gatherings are fun. I've been twice already, it's really nice."

"Cold."

"So what? Come with us, we need you there." Naomi always makes me feel good.

I need Teddy to tell me to come, I answer her in my mind, and look at him. He catches my gaze and points at the bread basket.

〉

I'm already better when we head back to the office. Teddy's walking beside me.

"Hey, I have a question. I want to come to Michigan."

"So what's the question?"

"Can I?"

"Yes. Not sure you'll have anything to do there."

His reaction makes me recoil. I'm employed by Delmar and most of the employees are going, so why shouldn't I? A sense of insult rises within me, but I push it all the way back down. I only just got an Oscar, what's the point in feeling like this again? It's absurd.

"Let me think about it," Teddy says as we enter the building.

The day extends and we leave the office late. In order not to leave together, I usually go downstairs a few minutes before him and wait by the elevators, but this time I walk up to his car. I can feel the entire week he's been abroad, the entire day we've spent together without touching, and when was the last time we even fucked? What are the chances he'll be up for it when we get back home? Zero. No sex tonight.

"Why didn't you wait at the usual spot?"

"I don't know," I say and look at him. "Parking lot's empty."

"You getting in?" he asks as he puts his briefcase in the back seat and stands in front of me.

"I need to pee."

"Why didn't you go upstairs?"

"I was saving it," I hear myself announce.

"Saving it?"

"Yes. Saving it for you."

He stays standing and looks at me, playing with his car keys. "What does that mean?"

I stay silent and look at him. Something in his eyes intrigues me.

"You want to pee on me?" A drop of sweat plummets down his temple. Why's he sweating in January? "Is that what you're saying?"

"It's yours. As you wish."

"As I wish?"

"Yes."

He stalls for a moment, then takes a deep breath. "All right." He puts the car keys in his jacket pocket. "I like this. As I wish?"

"Yes." I'm pleased that my trick's worked but I'm wondering what he's wishing for.

"I want you to pee, just like that, in front of me."

"What do you mean 'just like that'?"

"Just pee. Like you say, release some urine."

"Yes. Where?"

"Right where you are."

"Pee here? That's your wish?" I look down at the smoothed concrete ground, peering to the sides to see if anyone's around or if any cameras are nearby.

"Yes."

I'm a little bit surprised, but I take action straightaway, reaching toward my jeans' zipper.

"No, no. Keep it on."

"So how will I pee?"

"Just like that, as you are. Standing up, in your jeans."

"Oh, actually release urine!"

"Yes." He smiles a little.

"I won't be able to!"

He runs his hand over his mouth, his eyes surveying me. I'm wearing high-waisted, light-colored skinny jeans. An odd wish. I look at him. All right. I concentrate really hard, and for two whole minutes I stand there trying to pee.

"I can't do it." My eyes are open again.

"Shame." He turns toward the car and I immediately stress about my failed mission. "Let's go." He gets into the driver's seat.

I stay out of the car, stand next to his window. He's inside, punching in the code and revving up the engine. He looks at me and opens the window. Even though there's something stupid about this moment with the window coming down, I continue, lean my hands on the roof of the car and close my eyes. I concentrate, remind myself I wanted to pee to begin with, I need to pee, it's all in my head. I take my time.

"Turn the engine off," I say, since the noise gets him further away from me.

Still with my eyes shut, I hear him switching off the engine. I press my clit strongly, over my jeans, my mind associating the arousal with the need to pee, put my hand back on the roof of the car. Concentrate some more. Open my eyes and look at him and then feel it starting and see his eyes descending.

I'm peeing in my pants, a wet stain spreading between my thighs and down my left leg. I push hard so that the stream doesn't stop and I look at him watching it intently. Done. He leans his head back, quietly exhaling with his eyes closed, his hand sliding toward his cock, and suddenly he sits up and looks at me.

"That really turns me on, Noa," he says, and I shift back a bit so he can open the door, and then he puts his feet down on the parking lot concrete, pulls me toward him, and places his hand over the wet stain while his other hand grabs my ass, and now I'm pressed against him. He puts his face on my wet jeans, I feel his warmth. He takes a deep breath, then peels off my jeans along with my wet underwear. I hold on to the roof of the car and push my shoes off my feet, his hand between my legs. He collects my wet clothes and shoes and places them on the passenger-side floor. I go in, climb onto him. Not a lot of space between him and the steering wheel. He reclines the seat and makes some room. He pulls down his pants and underwear and his cock's hard, rock hard.

208 | MAYA KESSLER

I get very aroused, all the blood in my body's rushing to my pussy. I sit on him, his cock's inside of me, and he leans back as far as he can, his big hands are on my waist and he holds me back but close at the same time, and starts fucking me. His movement's confined.

"Don't move," I quietly tell him. "Just me."

He stops moving and now it's just me, fucking him. Starting slowly and then picking up the pace, and he groans and grabs my breasts through my shirt, and then grabs my face and pulls me to him and kisses me. He has a strong taste so I fuck him even harder because he's actually fucking disgusting, and then he pushes me off and shifts me to the passenger seat, lifts his pants and gets out of the car without zipping them. I can feel all the bruises I'll have later. He's already on my side of the car, opens my door, puts my seat all the way back and gets in and lies on top of me, his sweat dripping onto me as he raises my legs up, and now he's the one doing the fucking and I'm almost entirely neutralized, can't move, and he's fucking me hard and then harder and then so hard it starts hurting. When the pain comes, the instinctual reaction is to clench, defend, not allow anything in, but I'm enthralled by this situation and by how wild he is so I try to let go, remembering the way I did earlier so I could pee, and close my eyes and let go some more, and my body reacts to the sensation and I hear myself screaming like someone who's currently being fucked, and feel myself getting closer.

"Noa, Noa, what the fuck are you doing to me? What the fuck is this? It's too much," I hear him saying through my screams as I start coming.

"I'm coming," I manage to say almost inaudibly, and then feel how close he is too, and I get one of the strongest orgasms I've ever had.

›

On the way back I'm naked from the waist down, my wet jeans and underwear are lying by my bare feet. He's driving and the air around us is quiet, whole.

"Maybe you can make us a movie for Michigan," he suddenly says, thinking out loud. "Something for the employees, appreciate all your hard work, et cetera."

"Yes! I can put something like that together. I have the material."

"Talk to Richard about it, he'll tell you what to aim for."

"I definitely know who *not* to talk to about it."

"I appreciate that." He smiles. "You're starting to get the hang of it."

So he wants me to come? Maybe he really does? After all, he likes having me around, even when he's unavailable. Like the night he left me alone in his apartment and went off and didn't even tell me where he was.

"Teddy."

"What?"

"Now can you tell me where you were that night, when you left me at your place?"

He eyes me. "Do I have to?"

"Yes!"

"Why?"

"That's the price for the peeing. It's steep, as you can imagine."

"You settle on the price before, not after."

"Please tell me."

He looks at me. "I went to Lara's."

"Really?"

"Yes." His eyes shift to the road ahead.

"Huh." This surprises me. "But you were on a work call."

"Yeah, there were a number of incidents that day."

"And what happened with Lara?"

"A lot of things."

"Come on, you have to stop keeping everything from me, it's driving me crazy."

"She's pregnant, Lara."

"Is it yours?" I can't breathe.

"No! God no."

I can breathe again. "So? Her boyfriend's? I mean, does she have a boyfriend?"

"Yes, only he's not her boyfriend anymore."

"So she's alone?"

"Yes."

"So maybe you should get back together." Why is that what I'm saying?

"That's why I don't tell you anything." He's onto me straightaway.

"Okay, okay. I won't say anything, keep going."

"Keep going where?" He rubs his eye. "She's driving me mad."

"You're in touch?"

"We talk every day."

"Goddamn it! An entire universe right under my nose and I don't know a thing about it. Mediocre detective." For some reason this whole thing isn't hurting me. "What happened between you two?"

"What do you think happened? I told her from the get-go that I won't get into it, that I don't want any more kids. And she said she didn't either, and that's how it was, fun and fucking and parties and Lara's bullshit."

"Until . . . ?"

"Until she lost her balance and got depressed, and everything became all about me ruining her life and fights and hitting and drama, until I had enough." We reach his street and drive into the parking lot. "How are you going to go upstairs like that?"

"Don't worry, I'll hold my clothes on me somehow."

I put on my shoes without socks and we get out of the car. I hold my rolled-up jeans against my front. There's no one around, and we go in through the back door. The elevator door shuts.

"And then? What happened?"

"Aren't we done with that?" He gently caresses my ass.

"Not yet. You were just saying how you had enough."

"Sounds about right." He takes his hand away.

"So I'm guessing she left immediately, didn't make any trouble."

He smiles. "No, it took a while, but she left eventually, sort of." We enter the apartment. "She met this guy, got pregnant, and then they broke up. So again it's me who has to." He turns off the alarm.

"Has to what?"

"Be there for her." He locks the door behind us and we go in.

"I understand a lot more now than I did before, about us too. Why don't you ever tell me anything?"

"Aren't you on a need-to-know basis, Noa?" He takes off his jacket. We're standing in the living room and I'm still half-naked, but I don't intend to end the conversation.

"How far along is she?" So much information to catch up on.

"She's due in June." He unbuttons his shirt, takes it off and stays in his undershirt. "You staying like that?"

"I'll get in the shower soon. And what about when the baby's born? Is it a boy?"

"A girl." He sits down to take his shoes off.

"Really? Another little Lara."

"Yes." He smiles and gets up, goes to the kitchen and I follow him.

"She wants to raise her on her own?"

"That's what she's saying." He opens a bottle of wine. "Want a glass?"

"Yes, thank you. That's not an easy choice, it's a real challenge."

"That's right. But she's very sheltered, Lara. Don't forget."

"Yes, I know. But still. And what does she need from you?"

He pours us some wine. "Good question. Right now, mainly to drive me crazy."

Back in the living room, he sits on the couch and puts his bare feet on the table. I stay standing because I don't feel right sitting on his beautiful couch in my current state. "Does she know about me?"

"No."

"Better off." I take my shoes off and carefully sit on the rug, take a sip of the wine and then another one, feel the warmth in my stomach. "My heart's pounding, but I'll ask anyway."

He looks at me. "We're not fucking anymore. I only fuck you."

I nod with pursed lips, trying to restrain the joy into an emotionless expression, or at least almost emotionless. "So what happened that night?" I scroll us back to the top.

"When you were here and I left? She felt bad and I was in the middle of an important call. She called, told me, 'I'm getting in a taxi and coming over.' And you were here. So I went over there and stayed with her till she fell asleep, and then I came back."

"Seriously? Jesus. Why didn't you tell me? You could have told me back then, you know."

"If you say so."

"But a week before that we were at the top of the stairwell at the office building, remember?"

"Yes, I remember."

"And then you told me to come over, but later you said it wouldn't work, and then it took you a week to tell me to come."

"Yes."

"So was that because of Lara too?"

"Yes. She did come by that night, and she stayed over."

"Stayed over for the entire week? And weekend?"

"Yes."

"And then you did sleep together?" I place my bet.

"Yes."

"And I just sat at home." I'm smiling for some reason.

"Yes."

"So why aren't you sleeping together anymore?"

"Because I don't want to. When she stayed over here, I didn't really want to either. I wanted you. But that's how it went. That's what was needed."

"I understand that, I think it's beautiful, I do," I say honestly and then point between his legs. "I hope that when I'm pregnant I'll get my fair share of that glorious cock too."

He doesn't find that funny. "I'm not doing that again."

"What, my pregnancy's not going to get the premium package?"

"No more package for you if you keep at it."

"Okay, okay. We're almost done, hang in there," I cheer him on, and continue investigating the most fascinating realm known to man. "So where does she live now?"

"In her luxury apartment." His eyes are closed and his head's leaning on the back of the couch.

"And what is she doing?"

"Who knows? She's doing Lara things."

"Did you really sleep with her and want me?"

"Yes. You."

"Maybe because I was something new."

"No, Noa." He opens his eyes and looks at me. "Because with you I can talk."

My heart skips a beat. I'll pee my pants every day from now on!

"And what should I do?" I ask.

"I don't understand the question."

"With you. What should I do with you?"

"With me? Nothing. What can you do?"

"And if I have a kid? With a man who isn't you?"

"Great. I'll be very happy for you."

"Damn. And you won't be sad if I don't come by anymore?"

"I guess I will, a little." He smiles. "And that's enough for now." That's it, the heavy doors have now closed.

"Okay." I get up. "Thank you for telling me. And thank you for preferring to sleep with me while a beautiful woman such as Lara wanted you."

"Come here."

I come closer and he pulls me to him and hugs me, a strong and long and pure embrace.

8

Like Father Like Cousin

»

"Good morning." He's sitting in the hotel dining room by Lake Michigan. He looks at me for a moment, smiles, and goes back to his phone.

"Good morning." I sit next to him, turning the empty mug over and pouring myself some coffee. He continues reading quietly, doesn't look at me. I wait for him to say something, maybe share what's on his mind or ask where I'd spent the night, but he says nothing. I stay silent too. When I finish my coffee I get up. Let's start by stepping away from this table.

The lobby's decorated in a nautical theme: anchors, boats, ropes. A huge painting of an ancient ship sailing through a gusty sea hangs above the reception desk. I go up to the third floor, look through my purse, and find the key to my room—which I've not entered since we arrived, and it's now our fourth day here. All my belongings are in his room.

A dated, desolate hotel room. Tightened sheets, bed runner with illustrations of shells for guests who don't take their shoes off before lying down to rest. I pull off the ugly cover, fold it, and place it aside. Lift the blanket, take my shoes off, and lie down. What happened here?

»

We're on the flight to Michigan.

I've not been on a plane in a long while. My seat's at the back of the plane, and after we take off I breathe a sigh of relief and let the last three weeks sink in: Teddy's been busier than ever, and I've been working

endlessly on the movie, which we'll screen at the event. This morning, Richard made a last-minute decision not to go, since his daughter's
about to give birth to his first granddaughter.

I sleep for the first five hours. I wake up with an aching neck, try
to get myself together, drink some water, stare. It's dark around me,
people are sleeping. I carefully get up, skip over the woman in the aisle
seat, and go to the restroom. I lock the door and the little light bright-
ens, that familiar, detested smell. Teddy's somewhere in first class, and
I haven't seen him since we boarded the plane. He told me to come
show him the movie during the flight because he hasn't managed to
watch it yet. When I come out of the restroom, I ask one of the flight
attendants how I can talk to someone in first class, and she says I can
only go there by request and that she can't ask until breakfast is served.
I return to my seat.

Two hours creep by, and after they clear our breakfast trays I finally
get approval to go up to first class. I walk in quietly, holding my tablet
under my arm. There's Teddy.

"Did you get some sleep?" he asks in a quiet tone.

"Yes. I couldn't get to you before."

"Well, you're here now. Did you get any decent food? Want anything
from here?"

I show him the movie: he has the headphones and I squat next to
him, trying to stay within his seat's parameters and not disrupt anyone.
My heart rate accelerates intermittently for six full minutes.

"Very nice," he says when it's over.

Back to my seat. Three hours left.

〉

Let's think of Lara again; ever since he told me, I occasionally bring her
up in my mind. Imagine her from the photos and add a pregnant belly.
A beautiful, round white belly with a little baby inside.

Where is she now, this very minute? How was she when she stayed
over at his place for a week? Does she feel at home there? A home in
which she'd lived for years and then left or was asked to leave. He

opened the door for her. How did she walk in? Passed by him as he closed the door behind her? Did they hug? Did he smell her when he hugged her? Did he feel her stomach on his? How can they even manage a hug? And fuck? How did he fuck her that week while I was at home climbing up the walls, and now I know that he already knew; and that this was his decision; and I think it's only fair, I want to see these sides of him. I wouldn't want him to send her home. Shame he didn't tell me, that's all. Could I have handled it? Who here on this plane thinks I could have handled it? Raise your hands, I can't see.

>

After a long flight, excruciating immigration lines, and a brief domestic flight, we land in Michigan. Darkness. I hate arriving at a new place when it's dark, and it's even worse when it's freezing. First cigarette outside the terminal, waiting for taxis. Teddy may have flown first inaccessible class, but he's sharing a taxi with the rest of us. He wants to get in the last taxi, signals me with a look to go with him. The driver flings our luggage into the trunk. I join Teddy in the back seat and we're alone for a moment, but then the door opens and Naomi asks if there's room for one more and we immediately invite her to ride with us. No freedom and no touching, but I can feel his body's warmth, his thigh pressing against mine, the back of his hand casually lying across my little finger. Traffic's heavy and I can see into the apartment buildings along the road, windows into the lives of others. Teddy's on the phone and I look out at the foreign darkness, excited to be in a different country with him, even though we're not alone. I glance at Naomi and see she has her eyes closed. I lean forward because I want his hand on my back, but he doesn't touch me, so I lean back again. He finishes the call and gets another one straightaway. It's Wills. Teddy talks to him and smiles at me, momentarily puts a warm hand over mine.

When we reach the hotel, we're welcomed by Amanda, the head secretary of the US offices. She hands out our room keys. I'm on the third floor, as are Phil and Naomi, not on his floor. They go up to their rooms and he stalls in the lobby, and I figure that I should go up to my room, but he signals me to wait so I sit on one of the couches in the lobby and check my phone. Amanda's fussing over Teddy, and I hope her behavior annoys me just because it was a long flight, since I really don't feel like getting pissed off here. Wills shows up and I'm glad to see him, his warm demeanor calms me down. They decide to meet up later, and Teddy and I get into the elevator together in a way that seems natural and go straight to the top floor, his floor. We walk into the spacious room and if he doesn't turn his attention to me and me alone—chances are I won't survive. I go into the bathroom, leave the door open and pee. He walks in, washes his hands and looks at me through the mirror.

"Come here a minute." I wipe but stay seated.

He walks over and stands in front of me. I lean my face against him, feel his cock calmly resting in his pants as he runs his hand over me, gently stroking my hair. I close my eyes and take a deep breath and then look up at him, my chin still touching his stomach. He looks at me absentmindedly, pushes my hair back with both hands. My eyes smile at him.

"Stand."

I rise up, reach my hands down to lift my underwear, but he turns me around, grabs my hands from behind.

"Leave them down."

He leads me back into the room, runs his hand over my ass. He lays me down, licks me between my legs and I'm aroused, I close my eyes, spread my arms to the sides. We finally have a moment. A good few days have passed since the last time, and now I feel that he wants me, a desire that very quickly intensifies, and then his phone rings. He stops, puts his face close to mine.

"Not enough time." He disconnects from me and goes over to his phone.

He answers the call and sits next to me, starts raising my underwear and I complete the task and stand up to get my pants on too. I don't know whom he's talking to. I sit right up against him, kiss his neck and face, hug him. He strokes my leg, focusing on the call.

That's what it'll be like here, I already know it. But at least I'm by his side.

>

During dinner I sit across from Amanda. I wait for the right moment and ask if there's a projector in the hall where the event is taking place. Twenty seconds of talking to her are enough to realize she can be the flagbearer for Teddy's delegation of insufferable girls. She says she has no idea about a projector—and she does so using five different sentences that carry the exact same meaning. At this stage I try to change tactics, delete the question, and construct a demand; I rephrase and tell her that we'll need a projector for the event because we've made a movie especially for it. She says she has no idea about it. I'm starting to get pissed off, because I might as well have had the same conversation with a goat and gotten the same replies. I use an aggressively polite tone to ask her if she can find out, she says she'll try in a tone indicating it's going to be complicated and chances are slim. I thank her. The wonderful conversation has ruined my appetite and I say that I'm going out for a smoke. Finally, something she does have an idea about! She gives a small, minuscule gesture of repulsion.

>

"Why do you keep that duck-lady on payroll?" I ask him after dinner when we move to the hotel bar for a dreary toast.

"What duck-lady?"

"The head secretary of the US offices." I mimic her tone.

"Amanda? She's fine, what do you want from her?"

Why does he think she's fine? I decide to further inspect. "Did you fuck her once upon a time and now you're scared of a lawsuit?"

"Are you out of your mind?" I love it when his jugular swells up. "Why would I fuck her?"

"Got another explanation?"

"She knows her job and she's good at it. Would you believe it?"

"No. Then who's responsible for getting a projector? What do I need to do, who do I ask? Not her?"

"We'll get you a projector."

Get *me* a projector? Why is he wording it like that? I want to remind him that he was the one who asked me to make a movie and that I've put a lot into it—he saw me working on it day and night—but saying that won't be clever, so I keep it to myself. We're at the bar and he's already in the midst of an overly smiley and swaggery conversation, so I walk away and sit on a barstool. I'll rectify the situation with alcohol. I feel like ouzo, but they don't have any, so I order a G&T and drink fast. My mood isn't perking up, Naomi's nowhere to be found and I have no one to hang out with, the small talk around me is painfully dull, so I go for another smoke.

I stand outside and light a cigarette. It's not as cold as it was earlier, but the wind is irritating. There's no way that it won't work out—all we need is a projector and a white wall. Not even a screen. Frank Clancy, the likable and almost-hot member of Wills's team, comes out of the hotel. I remember him from when they'd visited the set back home. I stare at him and realize he's walking toward me.

"Can I have one of those?"

I hand him one and tell him that I'm glad to discover another smoker. He laughs at himself and says it's because he hangs out with artists and we're a bad influence on him. I say that I'm an artist who doesn't influence him badly or at all for that matter, and he replies politely or flirtatiously, hard to tell. He says he's glad to be here and meet everyone, and I ask where he lives and he says they're in Brooklyn. Since he answers in plural I ask if he has a girlfriend and he says he does. He's a bit embarrassed, says they've been together for three years. Doesn't sound long to me, but it's actually longer than any relationship I've had in the last decade. I ask what she does for a living and immediately regret it when I hear she's an editor at HBO. Of course she is. He looks at me and smiles, then compliments me on the pitch film, and says he's heard they'll be screening a movie I made especially for the event. In a burst of indiscretion, I decide to tell him about the Amanda situation, explaining that not only is she dumb, she's also manipulative. He bursts out laughing and jokes about my brutal reaction.

We go back to the hotel bar. After another drink, I realize there's no reason for me to stay and it's almost midnight, so I find a moment when Teddy's between conversations and he stops in front of me.

"I think I'll go up to the room, is that okay?" I ask.

"Yes."

"I need a key."

He puts his hand in his pocket, quickly passes me the key. "They haven't heard about key cards here, can you believe it? Leave it open for me, I don't have a spare."

I shower and think that this would be a good time for a video call with Sharon since it's now early morning back home, so after the shower I call her, and we talk while she prepares her kids for school. Then I eat everything edible in the room, watch some local TV packed full of blaring commercials and promptly fall asleep.

›

I wake up at 5:00 a.m. I must have had a bad dream about Teddy, because when I see him in bed next to me, I feel like I can't stand him. I turn the other way and try to sleep, but I can't. Instead of the dream getting further away, the distressing feeling just gets stronger. It feels like I don't love him. I get up, look out the window. It's not dawn yet, everything is barren and frozen. I want something hot to drink but it's not worth the noise it'll make.

He wakes up at 6:00 a.m. We don't talk much. He gets in the shower. What will I do all day? What was I thinking coming here? He comes out shaved and dressed, tells me he's going downstairs and we'll talk later.

During the morning, everyone's busy with meetings and I wander around the hotel, feeling alienated. I don't know what to do with myself. I have lunch with them, during which I start feeling an uncomfortable sensation, like a urinary tract infection or just a concern for one— which is even worse than the infection itself, since it's a total mindfuck. I spend the second half of the day sleeping because of my bladder's misbehavior and maybe the jet lag too.

I wake up around midnight, Teddy's not in the room. I pee and try to figure out if there's a problem or if it's just in my head. I drink loads of water for ammunition. Eat some nuts, go for a smoke on the balcony, feel like I'm polluting Lake Michigan's air with my cigarette and I'm cold, so I go back in. More than anything, I feel like smoking a joint, but there's nothing I can do about that.

> Where are you?
>
> You up ? I was in the room
> you were asleep
>
> Yes, I'm here
>
> Go back to sleep
>
> Where are you?

He doesn't reply. I try again after twenty minutes.

> Where are you? Reply
>
> At a bar with wills frank Phil
>
> Alright. See you later

What a worthless day. But tomorrow will be different, because we'll be screening the movie at night. It always speeds up the heart rate, the thought about the moment when the movie starts, the fear of technical difficulties, and then observing the people as they watch and I almost control them: now you will all smile, now you will all laugh, now you will all be moved. I imagine the movie through Wills's eyes, Frank's, Phil's, Naomi's, and even Amanda's. And there's Teddy's eyes too, he's watched it only once and now he'll see it at a festive screening and feel the audience's reaction, so he's got some excitement coming his way.

Even though he said he'd take care of it, I should make sure.

> Hey, is there a projector for
> tomorrow?

No reply. Go pee again. Yes, something is definitely wrong with my body. Great! Why not? Anything else for this fantastic trip? He replies after ten minutes.

> It'll be fine

'It'll be fine' means it's not fine yet. A heat wave of rage rises within me. Six months ago, something like this would be inconceivable, him supposedly not being able to get something together. If he can't do it, it means he's not trying. That is, not telling Amanda four words: "I need a projector." That's all. How complicated is that?

Due to all the nerves and self-hatred and hatred toward him and hatred toward urinary tract infections and generally toward my being a woman—I fall asleep again. I see him coming into the room in my sleep; at some point he lies next to me in bed.

›

Of course, even if I go to sleep ten hours before he does—when I wake up he's no longer around. Maybe I really shouldn't have come. I shower, stare at the dainty marine life embellishing the tiles, try to wash off the stinging sensation and the rage and frustration along with it.

When I enter the hotel dining room I see he's just finished his breakfast and he's getting up along with Wills. Great timing! Lucky man, Mr. Rosenfeld. I approach the buffet and happily discover they have cranberry juice. I pour myself a big glass and join Naomi's table.

"That's your breakfast?" she asks with a smile while chewing on some bacon.

"It's cranberry juice, sweetie pie!" I reply with a performative tone. "If you know what I mean."

"Oh boy, do I. Infection?"

"Serious concern for one."

"Poor thing. You need antibiotics." She pulls over the plate of pastries she'd gotten. "You really picked a place for getting a UTI!"

"Yes, this is the place I picked," I say, and she laughs.

"Got a prescription? How will you get antibiotics here?"

"I don't know," I say in despair. "But hey, guns are easy to get here! So, worst-case scenario, I take out this bladder."

"Yuck, go away! I'm eating."

"Oh yeah, how are the pancakes? I'll get some too."

>

I spend the following few hours trying to resolve the screening matter on my own: I bypass Amanda and approach her higher authority, the manager of Delmar US, a serious woman named Susan, who unfortunately refers me back to Amanda, who's having a hysterical breakdown in preparation for tonight's event. It's enough to stand next to her for just a minute to realize nobody's home. I consider asking Wills for help, but he's very busy and constantly at Teddy's side, so I dare not come near. I wish Richard were here.

I go to the shopping area and buy everything I can to try to get my bladder to stop signaling that we have to go pee as though we've just downed a fifty-ounce bottle of Coke, only to finally reach a restroom and discover a measly few drops.

I go back to the room and take the maximum allowed dosage. I couldn't help but wonder: Can one commit suicide by overdosing on cranberry pills?

In the afternoon, His Majesty appears in the room.

"What are you up to?" he asks and immediately goes to the bathroom, the toilet seat bangs against the wall. He comes out and swaps shirts, looks at me for a moment and then his eyes shift down to the supplements I'd bought. "What are those?"

"Nothing." How will I hide the monster I currently am? "I have some physical discomfort."

"Physical discomfort? Are you sick?"

"No. I think I have an infection, maybe."

"That's unfortunate." He leans over the desk and reads something. Unfortunate, all right.

"Teddy?" At least reassure me that it's worked out.

"What?"

"I don't feel like asking again," I say, agitated.

"About the projector? I didn't get around to it."

I freeze with rage. "So we won't be showing the movie tonight?" I present the worst-case scenario, hoping that'll snap him into reality. After all, there's no way he'll forgo that kind of gesture toward his employees. No reply. "Teddy?"

"I don't think so."

"You don't think so?" I refuse to fathom.

"Yes," he says, and I fall silent as he finishes getting ready. "Can you cope? I need to go."

"Of course you need to go."

"Maybe we'll get it for tomorrow night. We'll see."

"Not interested. The event's tonight."

"Fine, then we won't."

"Then why did I come here?" I want to cry.

"No, no, don't go there."

"Tell me why I'm here."

"You wanted to come! You asked to come."

"Because I thought we'd show the movie."

"You asked way before that."

"And you asked me for a movie—"

"So I asked and it's not working out."

I stop and look at him. "Why are you being like that? Care to tell me?"

"Noa, save me the drama, I know it by heart and I don't have the time."

"Then at least don't be surprised that this is my reaction."

"I'm not surprised and still"—now he's really shouting at me—"I can't always fix everything for you, so give me a break and go do something else and stop bugging me, because I'm working here in case you haven't noticed!"

Wow, such aggression, pretty rare to hear him raise his voice like that. Great, hopefully he'll have a heart attack and die, save us all the misery. Not sure what 'us' means—seems I'm the only one suffering from his existence. Fix everything for me? What's that supposed to mean?

He leaves the room and slams the door. The key flies out and lands on the floor. I get up, lift the key and put it back in its place.

>

I go out for a little stroll. I hate everyone, every person passing by me. They're all preoccupied with the event. I don't know what to do with myself. What do I do? Do I need to pee? Why did I come here, why, why am I stupid? I don't need to pee, it's just this damn infection. Where am I going?

I sit down on the bench outside, in the cold. It's not good for my bladder, the bad feeling is intensifying, but I don't care. I want the pain. I want it to hurt even more. Am I stuck at age sixteen? Is that my deal? It's ridiculous. I don't want to be who I am. I don't want to feel like this again. My fingertips feel the cold key in my pocket. I take it out and place it on my knee. I stare at this little piece of metal that would have existed either way, even if I didn't; there'd still be this room key, at this hotel, on this continent. Even if I die tomorrow, the key remains. It has a round hole in the middle, like a little mouth. It's talking to me: Always remember that you're alone. Nobody's with you. He's not with you, he doesn't know you. He doesn't know who you are and how you're built and how easy it is to take you apart. He could have easily made you feel good, even if the movie won't be screening.

My phone rings. My heart skips a beat, a swell of anger, chock-full with tiny fragments of hope.

"Yes." I answer in his style.

"Where are you? I need to get into the room."

I take a breath. "Coming."

>

I walk across the top-floor hallway and see him standing by the closed door, shoulder leaning against the wall, looking at his phone. He notices me. He looks exhausted, but I don't care.

"Where were you?" he asks since he has nothing else to say.

I stay quiet, motionless. He realizes I'm not opening the door.

"You want to give me the key?" He's calm.

"No."

He examines me with a strange look.

"I need to hear that you understand what the problem is," I say.

"The problem's standing right in front of me." Asshole.

"There's no way you don't understand my frustration."

"Your frustration, that's a problem too."

"No!" I raise my voice, I don't care that we're in the hallway. "My frustration makes sense! Your attitude toward it, that's the problem! There's no way that you genuinely don't get how shit I feel about it not happening because of some mysterious technical difficulty, and there's no one around here to talk to and get it going, and you're busy and I get that, and I've respected that from the moment we arrived as I'm sure you've noticed, so the least you can do is respect my frustration!"

"Can you open the door and continue shouting at me inside?"

"No!" I want to kill him.

He shifts his head to the side in revulsion and then turns and heads toward the elevator. I freeze, only my eyes follow him. He reaches the elevator but doesn't push the button and instead sits on one of the armchairs there. I stay put and cross my arms. He leans back, puts one leg over the other.

"Come here," he says.

I walk over and stand in front of him. He looks at me and my heart's pounding.

"I get your frustration." Maybe now he'll come back to me? "I don't accept your drama, in any shape or form. Doesn't work for me."

"I haven't said a word to you for three days. In fact, three weeks. So what drama are you talking about?"

"I'm locked outside my room."

"And how am I supposed to react? Just keep my mouth shut? That's the kind of person you want around you?"

"I don't want anyone around me, let's start with that."

"That's just plain bullshit."

"And I'm not dealing with this now, not with you, not with us," he continues. "And it would be very convenient if you kept your mouth shut and not lose your mind and not need this much attention. But if you are that interested in getting my attention, I can tell you that I see the way you've set it all up in your head, and I see how you insist on doing anything in order to feel miserable and abandoned, and you know what? That's also the reason why you're not in touch with your mom, right? That way you can keep going through life with your abandoned-child label. You're more addicted to that than you are to your weed."

I look away, maybe because I'm searching for the sign-out button. After all of this, I'm ready to get on the next fucking flight back home and never see him again. I look at him.

"What is this?" I ask.

"What?"

"Where are you?"

"Here, in front of you. Just like you wanted."

"I see."

He checks the time. "This was my thirty minutes of rest."

Thirty minutes? It's not even been five. I bite my lip and give him the key. He gets up, walks over to the room and we both go in. I try to keep my head above water, so as not to drown in everything he said. I decide to stay in the room, even though all I want is to get up and take the stairs all the way down and get out of the hotel and keep running until I vanish.

He takes off his jacket and answers a call on his phone. I take my laptop and sit on the bed, don't look at him, do everything I can in order to focus on my own things. He's laughing with whoever's on the other end, hangs up and gets in the shower.

Message ping on the company's internal system. Frank.

Frank: Where are you? Coming down soon?

Well done for looking and even finding me. I quickly reply.

Noa: I'm still in the room.

He obviously doesn't know 'the room' is Teddy's.

Frank: Any luck w the projector issue?

Noa: NO :(

Frank: For real?

Noa: I know. Shoot me.

Frank: No, you're not to be shot by anyone, especially not by me.

Noa: Please. I'm begging you.

Frank: No no, c'mon. It's just a work event!

He's heartwarming. I can genuinely feel the warmth. Enough with me, a weakling on her knees. And this whole event is still ahead of me. I still can't grasp that the movie won't be screened tonight, and now, on top of all that, I'm forced to carry Teddy's insults.

Frank is typing.

Frank: Still there?

Noa: Yes.

Frank: Let's meet downstairs, I'll cheer you up. Promise.

Noa: OK. I'll get ready, be down in 20.

Frank: Cool. See you soon!

Teddy comes out of the shower. Hate of my life. I go into the bathroom, undress next to him, not paying attention to each other. While I shower I can hear him leaving the room. I assume that he didn't leave the key behind this time. I finish showering, wrap myself in a big towel and go check. The key's here.

I take two painkillers to stop feeling the infection, put on a beautiful black dress I brought with me and some makeup and go downstairs.

>

Frank, all fancy and handsome, is waiting for me in the lobby. When he sees me he smiles and says I look gorgeous. I start feeling a little better. We walk into the event hall together, have a drink, go out for a smoke, drink some more, talk to colleagues. I see Teddy schmoozing from afar, but I have no interest in him. I manage to disconnect. Two and a half G&Ts later, I'm pretty drunk. The rage within me hasn't gone anywhere, but it's starting to morph. Frank's starting to morph too: his eyes glimmer and his gaze deepens, the casual touches become more frequent. Amanda's walking around with a huge smile on her face as though we're all at her wedding. I whisper to Frank that her dress is horrific. He turns to examine the fashion hazard and stands a little bit behind me, almost up against me, and quietly tells me how unattractive he finds her. I appreciate the gesture. We stand on the side and talk shit about her, and my eyes wander to Teddy as he passes through various groups of people and gets them chuckling, then stops next to Serious Susan and talks to her quietly. He stands really close to her, leaning in so that she's the only one who can hear him. She looks ahead and nods, smiles, then turns serious—naturally—and tells him something. I feel like walking over there and shoving him with full force. Instead, I lean in toward Frank.

"I shouldn't get too drunk because I'll definitely do something I'll regret later." I mean Teddy.

"Yeah, same here." He means me.

I check the time and tell Frank it's been only half a fucking hour and we still have the whole goddamn night ahead of us. He asks what we can do, and I know that only a joint can help me right now, and if Teddy thinks I'm a junkie, then surely I should act the part. Frank says that it's a tricky one to resolve, and I announce to him that I'm tired of being unable to resolve things around here. I walk with conviction toward the hotel kitchen and Frank rushes after me.

"What's the plan?"

"Other side of the kitchen."

We walk across the lobby filled with perfumed Delmar personnel and leave through the front door. It's cold outside, but we're already sufficiently drunk to ignore it. We reach the hotel kitchen's back door. My money is in the room so I ask Frank if he has any cash on him. He takes a bill out of his pocket. There's a hotel employee smoking a cigarette, and I approach him with my cheeriest attitude and a smidgen of flirtation. I tell him that I feel bad for asking, but maybe there's a way of scoring us something to smoke; I say that we can pay and then idiot Frank presents the money in his hand—a hundred-dollar bill. The employee's embarrassed and says he doesn't have any. I refuse to give in, plead for him to ask someone, promise we won't tell no matter what, explain that it's risky for us too. He mumbles something and tells us to wait a minute and goes inside. Frank and I exchange excited looks, mainly thrilled about the possibility of success.

The employee shows up again and whispers that he found someone who might be able to help us. We thank him and wait a few tense minutes, and then another guy comes out, one with a bandanna. He's more relaxed and communicative and tries to understand what the deal is. After we explain, he nods and asks us to wait. Frank looks at me with glimmering eyes as the guy disappears into the kitchen.

"I can't believe you."

"Now he'll come out with the hotel manager and they'll call the police," I say with a slightly trembling voice, maybe from the tension, maybe from the cold.

"Are you cold?" Frank asks, and warms my arms for a moment.

The chilled-out guy comes back out—no police escort, luckily for us—concealing a little joint in his hand. A thousand thank-yous and the passing of the hundred-dollar bill. We run off in victory, laughing about this being the most expensive joint we'll ever smoke.

The weed's strong and there's no tobacco mixed in, so two drags in the dark next to the trees and we're already absolutely high. We get a giggle attack when we realize how difficult it's going to be for us to reenter the event in our current state.

"Frank, we did not think this through!"

"No, we did not!"

We hide the magical reefer and go back in, very thirsty. The speeches have already started, so we stand in the back. The first speaker is Wills, he thanks his team and especially Frank, who gets a round of applause as everyone turns and looks at him standing next to me with bloodshot eyes, thanking the crowd with an awkward wave. I feel a bit sorry for him but it's also amusing. I see Teddy looking at Frank, which means he sees me too, but I make sure not to make any eye contact with him. When the crowd turns away again, I gently press against Frank to let him know that if he's disoriented, I'm right here next to him. He presses his arm against mine.

+

Sometimes I think that there are, generally speaking, two main types of relationships between a man and a woman; there are men who are fathers: standing between you and the world, shielding you from it. But they are usually unavailable to play with you; and there are men who are brothers—or maybe better, cousins—standing shoulder to shoulder with you, so there's no shielding, but you get to experience the world together.

Throughout the years, I've had relationships with fathers as well as cousins. I was more in love with the fathers, but long-term relationships—I had only with cousins.

＞

Teddy's the next speaker. I'm not charmed by his charisma, nor by the smiles he elicits or by his wit. While he talks, I notice an elongated metal box hanging behind him, one with a screen rolled inside it. My heart starts pounding. Could he have organized it and played a trick on me? Maybe it's a surprise or something equally repulsive? My lips are dry and I can't even listen; I rerun our earlier fight in my mind with the option of the movie being screened and regret everything I said. I wish I were quiet and introverted and stoic so that people couldn't see every little emotion inside me. Frank senses me tensing up—he is a cousin, after all—and asks if I'm all right and goes to get us some water. I wait to hear if Teddy mentions the movie and at the same time I ask myself—how would he even have the video file? And if he's taken it from my laptop, how would he know which file is the final version?

And anyway, why would he do something like that? As always, it's all in my head. That screen is probably always there, and who knows, maybe they even have a functioning projector in this hall! How stupid can I be? Cancan dancers come out onto the stage one after the other, flinging their legs up in unison while singing at a high pitch, How stupid? How stupid? How stupid can you be?! They stretch out their arms and point right at me.

Frank returns with water and Teddy's still on the stage, sending warm regards from Richard and explaining why he's absent. Everyone raises a toast to Richard Harrington's brand-new granddaughter. Teddy finishes his speech and Serious Susan is up next. I look at him seated at the leadership table, looking ahead and listening to her attentively, or—since I know him well enough—pretending to listen to her. I also see how he discreetly takes his phone out of his pocket, looks at it, quickly texts someone and puts it back in. I take my phone out of my purse. I'm not the one he texted.

What does it actually matter? What difference does it make if the movie's screened or not? It's not interesting, not the movie, not this event, not this company. Nothing here is what I'd hoped for; I'm supposed to be in the real world where films and TV shows are produced, and my boyfriend or actually my husband's from the industry, maybe a British director, with an inspiring accent and a ring on his finger, because he's married to me, so all the girls from the movie set aren't supposed to sleep with him even though they really want to, and if they do then they feel bad when he comes back to me afterward, to our loft in Tribeca and our gorgeous children. So what does it matter if there's a projector or not, and what does it matter if Teddy understands or not, and why do I even need to deal with it or bug him about it, what do I want with him, what do I want with any of this? Seriously strong weed, Jesus, my brain is full speed ahead.

❭

Other speakers come on, and then there's a formal dinner. Frank asks if I want to eat. I tell him that I don't, that I want to go up to my room. He objects and persuades me to keep drinking—at least he doesn't insist on eating—so we sit at the bar and laugh about the moment Wills thanked him and everyone turned to look at him. Then we talk about life and family and kids, and the conversation deepens and gets interesting and I forget everything else. He looks at me with eager eyes, fully engages in our talk, genuinely listens. The bar starts filling with guests who've finished their meal, and we figure we'd better leave so no one notices us. After all, people here know him. He goes to the restroom, and we decide to meet outside, under our tree. Before I leave the bar, Teddy walks in. Up until that moment, I'd somehow managed to evade him. He gives me a cold look. I smile at him.

"Nice speech," I compliment him and hate every cell in his body.

"Thank you."

I smile again and walk away. I find the joint where we'd hidden it, light it up, and wait for Frank.

So much booze, shouldn't smoke too much. Frank arrives, takes a little drag and then surprises me and asks if I'm willing to show him the movie, a private screening. I need to fetch my tablet so we say we'll meet at his room. I use the elevator on the other side, to avoid him noticing which floor I go to.

Once I'm alone in Teddy's room, I start by peeing, of course, and as I wash my hands I look in the mirror for a moment, even though I don't feel like seeing my face. I know what might happen with Frank tonight—or to be honest—what *will* happen with Frank tonight. What do I need that for?

I knock on Frank's door. He quickly opens and I enter. We look at each other and smile, realizing we're alone for the first time. I sit on his bed and switch on my tablet. Ready? Ready. Six minutes of pure joy. I watch it along with him, my knee slightly leaning on his elbow. He's enjoying the movie, applauds and gives compliments, first to the movie and then to the woman who made it. He says it's a shame everyone didn't get to see it tonight and I shrug my shoulders and stare at him, and he suddenly reaches out and caresses my face and looks at me in a way that triggers me and my stomach twitches from excitement. His gentleness, softness. I can feel how much he cares, how it matters to him. His hand stops. I look at him, he seems troubled. I think we need a minute. I go to his bathroom, consider whether to leave the door open but know it'll be too much for him, so I shut it. There's his deodorant. I pee and try to understand if there's an option of not sleeping with him. I guess there isn't, I guess I won't pass it up at this point. When I come back out, he's standing in the middle of the room, confused. I stand in front of him.

He looks tormented. I get him. I ask what'll be worse for him—if we go for it or if we drop it. He says it'll be worse if we drop it, says he needs it, so I just press him against the wall and kiss him. He's very eager, kisses me and kisses me and kisses me, and the chemistry between us fuels the lust. I sit on his bed again, the room's spinning so I lie on my back. He sits next to me and gently strokes me. I touch his wrist, pull up his sleeve and examine his arm, muscular with bulging veins. I hold his hand and he squeezes mine, I turn to my side and run my tongue over those beautiful veins, open my mouth and press it against his inner elbow, kiss that arm with softened lips. He breathes heavily and lets out a sigh that almost sounds like crying. I look up at him. He lies beside me and wants me to hug him. He places his head on my chest. This sort of thing would never happen with Teddy; he's never in a state where he needs me to hold him, that's not even an option. I'm actually supposed to feel that it's better this way, with Frank, with a young man who needs to lean on me, who needs me. But this is a serpentine feeling, because there's a part of me that wants to shove his head off me and get out of here. I silence that part so as not to hurt him, and I continue embracing him. Frank looks up at me and starts kissing me again, and our kiss is delicious and now, since we're in bed, he lies on top of me, and when I feel his whole body and his hard cock in his pants, I immediately really need him to fuck me. My desire pulls us in and things develop pretty fast. We take some clothes off, only what's necessary. I meet his cock, the fair and friendly thing that it is, not very enticing. Now I'm going to suck him off, because if he's made the effort to get to Disneyland, he should at least enjoy all the rides. I carefully press his balls down and put his cock in my mouth. It's smooth and tasty, and I suck him off good and with full intention and he groans and shouts and reacts very surprisingly for the type of guy he is. He says he doesn't have a condom and I say it's okay, but it makes me recall my bladder—which must have been waiting for this very moment, since it is quick to tell me: Hi there, thanks for finally thinking of me, don't you dare let anything in here or I'll give you hell tomorrow! I ignore it and spread my legs and tell him to fuck me, to fuck me hard, that he's allowed to fuck me as hard as he can. His cock goes inside me and it's nice, but I can't feel what I'm looking for. I tell him again to fuck me hard and he turns up the pace but not the intensity. He says he's about to come and I ask him to hold on so that we can keep going. He slows down and then stops to take a break, resting by my side. Our faces are close. We kiss again and get aroused again and he goes back in and immediately back out and comes on my thighs.

I assume that he'll turn off right away as most men do, but he leans on his elbow and looks at me. He asks if I came and I tell him I didn't, that maybe later when I'm alone and that I'll leave soon, but he objects and begs me to stay for the night and promises he'll caress me until I fall asleep, so I just take my dress off and get into bed and then get up again to pee and feel the sting and ask my bladder to leave me alone. On the way back to bed, he looks at my naked body and tells me that I'm so beautiful. I lie down next to him, and like a real man, a model cousin, he keeps his promise and caresses me until I fall asleep.

›

There's light outside. Is it morning? It takes me a moment to realize where I am and who's next to me, and another moment to feel the dreadful headache and recall the night that was and the evening that preceded it and the fight with Teddy and the infection. And Frank, who's still fast asleep. On the way to the bathroom I take out my phone from my purse; after all, I was gone for the whole night. But considering how Teddy was yesterday— it's no surprise that he didn't text me. The stinging hasn't gotten worse! At least that. I wash my face and drink water from the tap. As I pick up my dress from the floor, Frank starts waking up. His hair's messy and his face is swollen from sleep. I smile at him. He gestures for me to come closer. We hug sitting down, a warm hug, a continuation of sleep. His face is pressed against my neck, fingers gently gliding up my back. I close my eyes and give in to his touch, but it quickly becomes overly exciting and turns me on, which also testifies to his wanting it too, since this sort of feeling comes up only when it's mutual. I gently disconnect from him, tell him that I really needed it, as much as he did, and he nods his head with soft eyes and thanks me. I thank him too.

I leave his room and go up to Teddy's room. Open the door carefully, worried he's there but knowing he isn't. The room's tidy and Teddy's post-shower scent is still present. He left only a few minutes ago. Good, better off. I shower, washing Frank off my body. My thoughts wander between last night's events and total desolation, like a meditative state. And then, out of that nothingness, an idea arises. I get dressed and sit in front of my laptop. What's the time back home? Midday.

New email. Don't be scared. You have nothing to lose.

I write a generic cover letter, presenting myself as director for any project on offer. I make a list of all the producers I know back home, deliberate for a while about whom to send this to, and eventually send out eleven emails.

I go down to the dining room. When I enter, I see Teddy sitting on his own. I take a deep breath and walk over to his table, a short walk that for some reason feels both familiar and unfamiliar. When I get close enough to him, he looks up at me and smiles, then goes back to his phone.

"Good morning."

》

Michigan–Chicago, Chicago–back home. Teddy doesn't fly with us; he's staying in Michigan for an extra day with the rest of leadership. I feel relieved knowing he's not around. On the Chicago flight, once the seat belt sign lights up, I decide not to go to his place when we land.

I enter my neglected apartment. Midweek, noon. I come out to the roof to check on the plants. Some have been saved by the rain; most have passed away.

Where do you start? Where were you for six months, Noa? There's pain in my heart.

Do I at least have something smokable here? I find leftovers in one of the baggies, roll a joint. Text Roy to get me some weed. He replies that he's far away—he and Thomas are cat sitting in Jerusalem. Thanks for nothing. I'll have to find another source. Music. Bucket, rag, the floor cleaning fluid container's almost empty, go down to the store, buy a few more things since I'm already there. Carry all the shopping; two streets, three floors, key.

I clean my apartment for hours. It's been months since it's gotten this much care. It seems surprised—almost anguished—by the attention, as though it doesn't want to believe that it has a tenant who loves it, because maybe she'll disappear again, abandon and neglect it again. My phone rings.

"Hi, Dad."

"Noa? I wasn't sure when you're back. Are you still in America?"

"No, I'm back. I landed today."

He asks if it went well and I say it was fine. My heart drops when he asks how the movie screening went. I tell him it didn't work out in the end, and the little disappointment in his voice echoes within me and I feel the tears coming up, but I don't let them out. I don't usually share anything with him, but this time we'd happened to talk before I traveled, and maybe there was silence or maybe I got tired of how he asks loads of questions, so I told him I'd made a movie. In hindsight, it was a dumb idea. Don't worry, Father dear, just like you didn't get to be what you wanted—even though you had the necessary skills, the passion and the creativity—so too your daughter, a succession of failures. He asks if I'm coming by for Friday dinner, and I say I will. He's glad to hear that.

Text from Frank Clancy.

> Had to write you something,
> because I can't stop thinking
> about you. I'll stop, eventually,
> but not yet. Is it really possible
> you are thousands of miles
> away? I keep seeing you
> everywhere I look.

I'm aware of preferring to get something like that from Teddy right now, and still, Frank's message calms something within me. Knowing that he genuinely liked me, that I made a difference for him. Knowing that someone saw me: a man. Even if it's not the man I'd crowned as the alpha, and maybe this alpha's not who I thought he was, just like he's tried to tell me from the very beginning. I send Frank a reply and then text Tom, who says he has plenty of weed and tells me to come over right away and smoke with him—because he has no one to smoke with ever since Alison got pregnant. I get ready and leave, shut my clean apartment's door behind me, and in a strange and inexplicable way, I'm all right.

>

In the morning, I consider going for a swim, but it's so cold that I don't feel like wearing a bathing suit and getting in the water. Last night, Alison wasn't feeling well and stayed in bed, so I just sat with Tom, but she feels just fine this morning and wants to meet up for coffee. I run some errands and then meet her. She's in her second trimester and you can already tell. I put my hand on her little pregnant belly and think of Lara. My phone rings. Teddy Rosenfeld, slide to answer.

In the millisecond I see his name on the screen, something happens in my brain—a pure realization, like the deciphering of a code: This is how I need to talk to him right now. I get up from the table and step aside.

"Who's that calling me? Teddy Rosenfeld?"

It takes him a moment. "Him and no one else."

"Shame, someone else would be good."

"I agree." I can tell by his voice that he's reassembling for a conversation that's different from the one he'd expected. "How are you?"

"I'm good."

"Calmed down?"

This would probably annoy me if it were the usual Noa answering him. I ignore the question. "And you, how are you doing?"

"Fine, pretty beat."

"Beat, dying?"

"Dying, dead."

"Not that it would be the end of the world."

"It would be the end of me."

"What's the actual use of having you alive?"

He laughs. "No use. Where are you?"

"Having coffee."

"With who?"

"A friend."

"Which one?"

"Alison."

He falls silent for a moment. "All right. Come over afterward?"

"What for?"

"Confirm kill."

"That's tempting, I won't lie."

"Come over."

I take a deep breath, change my tone. "Really, what for, Teddy?"

"What do you mean 'what for'?" His tone changes too.

"What should I come for? You don't really want to talk to me. I don't know how to go on without talking about what happened there."

"All right, you'll get your talk. Come over."

I stay silent. I clearly know that I'll go, but judging by how he's talking, I already know I'll have an issue, and I also know it'll stay unresolved.

"Okay, I'll come by in a bit."

"Good." He sounds relieved, and then he adds, "Just get here already."

It's hard to hear him say 'just get here already' and instantly feel how much I miss him, how badly my body aches from wanting him to love me and hold me and fuck me and tell me things that only he knows how to tell me.

〉

It's not yet noon and I'm already standing outside his apartment. He opens the door and smiles. The revolting man from Michigan must have stayed in Michigan, because here's Teddy again.

"And you"—that's what I immediately say—"now that you're here and you've called me, what do *you* think about what happened there?" I ask this with the tone of a person who's trying to understand the nature of things, a person completely uninvolved in the matter.

"Do you want to come in?" He takes a little step back to make room for me. I walk in and he shuts the door behind me. I stay in the old, familiar entranceway.

"Because back there it seemed like *you* were the one who's angry with *me*, and that alone makes matters worse, Teddy. Just so you know."

"Why do we fly away together and all of a sudden our agreements just deteriorate?"

"What's deteriorated?"

"You're deteriorated."

"I'm deteriorated by you." I've had enough of him.

"Care to come in? Why are you staying by the door?" He turns and walks into the apartment.

I follow him. "Why were you like that? What happened there?"

"A mistake."

"What mistake?"

"All of it, everything." He gets irritated. "You coming with me, and that stupid movie I wish I hadn't even asked you for. I had so many things to deal with, Richard not coming there made it really hard on me. And you were insufferable."

"How was I insufferable?"

"Your behavior. Got a smoke?"

I take two cigarettes and hand him one; he takes it and goes out to the balcony. Here we go again. I follow him out.

"How did I behave?"

"Spoiled, rude, egocentric." Blood, sweat, tears.

"But don't you see that everything you're saying has to do with my reactions to you?"

"No, you were like that from the first minute." He lights his cigarette.

"False accusation."

"You think?" He inhales the smoke.

"It's not true."

"You needed me. All the time." Lord, kill me now.

"That's not true. And if you'd just said something, if you'd talked to me, told me it's hard on you—"

"Give me a break! I did tell you."

"No, you didn't. You told me you were busy, you didn't genuinely talk to me."

"Fine. Bottom line is that you screwed up because you didn't know how to be with me. And on top of that you bugged me with your fucking projector."

"How is the bottom line that I screwed up?" I lash out. "And why are you calling it 'your' projector?"

"Don't raise your voice."

"Why shouldn't I raise my voice? Now I'm also not allowed to raise my voice?"

"You're allowed."

I light my cigarette. "Tell me what happened there with my fucking projector, okay? Tell me the truth."

"You want the truth? What will you do with it, go home and cry?"

"What?" I don't understand him and I start feeling physically weak.

He finally deigns to start talking. "Nothing happened. The hotel's projector didn't work."

"Okay. You realize you didn't even bother telling me that, right?" He doesn't react so I keep going. "If something 'didn't work' then that's resolvable. Did you prefer not to show it?"

"I didn't care if we showed it or not, don't you get it? I didn't want to deal with it."

"But you weren't the one who needed to deal with it. Didn't Amanda know about it?"

"She did. She asked me if she should work on getting a new one, or whatever, and I told her to leave it alone."

"What? Why?" She asked him if she should take care of it, and he told her to leave it alone? "Why would you do that?"

"Because you pissed me off."

A current runs down my spine. "When did you tell her that?"

"After you pissed me off."

I stand in front of him, eyes focused, trying to absorb what I'm hearing. "On the day of the event?"

"Yes."

"You came into the room in the afternoon and told me it wasn't going to work out."

"Yes," he confirms. "And then I went downstairs, and she asked me, and I said no."

"Then that was before I locked you out of the room."

"Yes. That was very rude," he says without a shred of affection and stubs out his cigarette. "And you dare ask me if I fucked her." He turns and walks into the kitchen midconversation.

I put my burning cigarette in the ashtray and rush after him. "No, don't do that, that's not fair. That's how we always talk! You can't just—"

"Calling her 'duck-lady.'" He starts cutting up vegetables on a wooden board.

"It's just incredible to rediscover what a motherfucking asshole you are all over again." I lose it. "You always talk like that! That's just how we talk, so why turn it against me—"

"—Okay, you're right."

"'Our agreements just deteriorate'?"

"You're right."

"'You're deteriorated'?"

"You're right!" he raises his voice.

"About what?" I hear his and raise mine.

"It didn't bother me when you asked if I fucked her. I don't have a problem with that."

"Okay." Screeching halt.

"And that is how we talk, that's true."

Fuck. He's messing me up. And he knows it. I need to get my head together.

I return to my cigarette outside and see it's already smoked itself. I stub it out—a superfluous act—and think about how he told Amanda not to get a new projector, about the choice he'd made. I need to run the room-key fight in my head using this new information. I go back in, stand with my arms crossed at the entrance to the kitchen, right hand overlapping left elbow.

"Well, at least I'm not crazy."

"I wouldn't jump to conclusions."

"All those things you said back there, about me keeping you from working, about me holding on to the abandoned-child label, about my weed—you said all those insightful slanders *after* you'd already decided not to screen it."

"What you refer to as 'insightful slanders' is simply the truth, which apparently you can't handle very well, as expected. And *that* has nothing to do with your movie. That's irrelevant."

I let his words be the last words hanging in the air, and I keep quiet. I need to think about the meaning of all this. Where do I even start? I stare at him as he cuts the vegetables. CUT, CUT, CUT. Shame I'm not some martial artist who knows all these swift moves, so I could knock the knife from his hand and grab it and stab him. Where should I stab him? His neck? Where should I stab? Where should I stab? Nowhere.

"Why did you do it?"

"I told you why."

"No you didn't."

He gives me his dangerous look, the one that always comes up right before he's about to hit really hard. "Are you asking for more now? Is that what you're doing?"

I swallow. What do I want? Additional info? There is none. I have it all, it's just that his narrative isn't in sync with mine. "I want to understand you."

"Go ahead."

"Because that is not a nice thing to do."

"So what do you gather from that?" There's that look again.

"I need to think about it." I turn toward the living room. "Have you seen my weed case?"

"Yes. It's in the bedroom."

Here's the case.

His bedroom again. Better off staying here to make the joint, take a quiet moment to think about all these new insights.

He told me back there that I was causing drama, but he was the one making it all dramatic, and maybe the same thing happened with Lara? Maybe he's blaming her for his own drama. *With you I can talk.* Bullshit. Or maybe that confession in itself tells me that with me he allows himself to speak his pathetic truths. He could have saved me so much heartache. But that's not what he wanted.

He wanted you not to bother him—I get that. He wanted you not to need anything from him—I get that. He wanted you not to come to Michigan, he let you come because you asked. He came up with the movie idea so he'd have a reason to bring you along.

When did I lose him? During the weeks before the trip, I was like air around him, I didn't ask for anything, I fit myself to his needs. If I'm the one he can talk to, then why didn't he tell me not to come?

Don't you see the structure? Look:

The mistake will always come from you. Your desire, your passion, your action. He knows it's a mistake and he likes it when you take the wrong path, he likes to watch you fall into the pit. *You screwed up.*

What does that say about him? And he doesn't even know what pit you fell into, because he doesn't know about Frank. Or maybe he does and he's setting you up, that's also possible. Anything's possible when it comes to him. And this whole time you thought he wasn't playing with you.

The joint's ready. I look at my reflection in the big mirror in the bedroom, and only then do I realize I'm smiling. Why am I smiling? Am I relieved? I guess I prefer him to torment me rather than ignore me.

Yeah? Then what does that say about you?

On my way to the balcony, I get a whiff of Teddy's cooking and recall that I'm hungry. I walk past him and go out for a smoke. There's no need for me to answer him about what I've gathered from all this. I have a pile of answers, but the one on top is that I gathered that my answer isn't needed.

Knocking sound: Teddy's holding my phone against the glass door, showing me someone's calling.

"Who is it?" I walk over as the ringing stops.

"Roy." He hands me my phone and our fingers touch.

I call Roy back as I walk along the balcony rails. He picks up and it sounds like he's in a cheerful mood. He tells me that they're having a nice time in Jerusalem and asks if I can join them for a visit at Grandma's on Friday morning.

"Special occasion?" I'm suspicious.

"It's a surprise! Please don't ask me any questions."

I instinctively think that maybe it has something to do with Nurit, but then I push the thought away because Roy wouldn't put me through something like that. But what's the surprise?

"Are you eating?" Teddy asks as I walk back in. I see he's already set the table for me. During the meal I think about Frank. How will Teddy react if I decide to tell him? I list the possible reactions: either he gets angry and throws me out, or he punishes me, or he reacts indifferently and then I'll really feel like there's nothing between us. And there's the slight chance it'll interest him or arouse him. But in any case, in all scenarios, anything I say can and will be used against me in Teddy Rosenfeld's court of law.

So instead of saying something that will jeopardize me, I tell him that on Friday I need to be in Jerusalem.

"Take my car."

"Okay," I immediately agree without arguing, mainly so that we don't repeat ourselves.

9

Highway 1

+

Once you'll be mine again
If you'll ever be mine again
I'll show you what happened when you left
How painful it was and how painful you made it to be and how lonely
you made me and what it means to leave a girl and what it means to
leave a woman and what it means to leave me

»

On Friday, I wake up in despair. I feel the weight of it from the moment
I open my eyes. I'm alone in Teddy's bed, trying to hold on to the
dream I had, but can't. What happened there? It's like a certain truth
has been revealed to me, and now I know there's a truth, but I don't
know what it is.

I pull up the blanket and close my eyes again, running through the
replies I've gotten so far from the producers who received my solicita-
tion emails earlier in the week: "no new productions at the moment"; "I
thought you only do props?"; "Great to hear from you! Send your reel!";
"I just signed a director who also has no experience—so don't give up
trying!"; "I've got directors waiting in line here, honey"; et cetera. Then
I think about the ones who haven't bothered to reply, and eventually I
get out of bed.

Teddy's in his office. I'm on the balcony drinking my coffee and
smoking a joint, which unfortunately isn't numbing the notion that I

loathe this life, that my existence is unnecessary, that there's no chance for me to ever feel fine, that there never was.

I'm supposed to meet Roy at Grandma's in Jerusalem at 10:30 a.m. I do my best to be ready on time, but I end up leaving the apartment only a little after ten, which means I'm an hour late.

"Bye, Teddy, I'm leaving."

"Have a nice day."

'Have a nice day'—what are we, a bank teller and a customer?

I'm not doing well. I should tell my dad that I won't come for dinner. A meal with him and Mina is the last thing I can stomach right now. I'll make up some excuse.

I drive through the city hating everyone around me. The pedestrian light is red, but some skinny lady's crossing the road in a rush, blatantly disobeying traffic laws. Why would she do that? The man she was standing with keeps on waiting for the light to turn green. I think I know what's going on here: she decided to cross so she told him, Come on, and he didn't, but she crossed nevertheless; no, they talked about something and he pissed her off so badly that she preferred to risk her own life rather than stay standing next to him. She's right!

I'm on the highway to Jerusalem and a massive cargo truck shifts into my lane, behind me. Later on, there's a moment when we drive next to each other. Something about this Optimus Prime's proximity arouses me. I try to get a look at the driver, but the height difference makes it impossible. I'm definitely not doing well.

〉

Roy and Thomas are sitting very erect on my grandma's couch in her living room. This couch is too soft to sit on that stiffly—my grandma hasn't sat on it for years because it doesn't give any support. Irritating, the way they're sitting. They're both sporting the same haircut, similar beard length, and they generally resemble each other way too much. Thomas is holding Roy's hand. What's up with these two?

While Grandma's caretaker slowly helps her over to sit in front of us, we talk about the lawsuit. Roy tells me things seem to be working out and praises Werner the lawyer, or in my brother's words, "Teddy's slick silver fox."

The caretaker goes to her room and turns on the TV. The sounds of soap opera dialogue in a foreign language reach all the way to the living room. Thomas smiles and Roy announces with a festive tone that he has some good news: He and Thomas are getting married. They'll have a small wedding party here, and then they'll fly over to Austria to be legally wed there. Since Thomas is finishing up his affairs here pretty soon, Roy will be moving with him to Vienna.

My grandma reacts joyfully—as much as she's capable. I smile and try to put out some positive vibes, make an impression of being happy and excited, but the truth is I feel nothing. I look at them and see their genuine excitement, picture them fucking, imagine Thomas's European apartment and them eating breakfast together. A familiar and excep- tionally loathed sensation arises within and starts flooding through me; I feel like I'm losing my center. I try to push away the thought that I wish this whole thing weren't happening; I order myself to find a way of getting psyched this very minute, otherwise I'll be that old spinster who isn't delighting over her little brother's engagement.

I hug Roy, repeat the word 'congratulations' a few times. Behind his smile there's a look that I recognize: scared and tense; a look derived from my reaction. I congratulate Thomas warmly too, masking my shock with logistical questions.

Before I leave, I hug Grandma. She looks at me: one look through her thick glasses, brief and direct, aged eyes murky, and still—she sees. She sees how hard it is for me.

Roy and Thomas walk me downstairs. I light a cigarette. Thomas smiles at me.

"You know what I find incredible?" he asks, and I look at him with a smile, listening as he goes on. "You and Nurit are so much alike. Did you know that? I mean, you talk the same way. You have the same sense of humor."

Hold your tongue, don't react. Roy gets stressed and tells Thomas off: "I told you she wouldn't want to hear that, and I told you not to say anything."

Thomas quickly explains that he knows we're not in touch and that's precisely why it's so incredible that we're so similar, despite all the years gone by; that he thinks it's beautiful, that it testifies to the aspects that remained unharmed by everything that happened.

Go. Now.

I tell them I'm in a rush, hug them and leave.

I get in the car, start the engine and drive away. Thoughts tumble through my mind: he thinks Nurit and I are the same; same sense of humor—two little Hasidic girls cross the road—slender Thomas; Teddy; Roy in Vienna; Roy not here; Tamara Klein; wedding party; Teddy; Teddy in Michigan; I've got directors waiting in line here, honey; Dad and Mina; Grandma; same sense of humor?

At the final set of lights before the sloping road leading out to the highway, something happens in my brain. *Now leaving Jerusalem.*

+

You can keep on dreaming about babies you need to take care of, and they're too small compared with a normal baby, the size of a shoe at the most. And something always goes wrong—you can't find them or don't feed them, or they fall. But at the same time, all is well, somehow. It's not a nightmare, but rather like a rocky landscape with occasional sweet water reservoirs beneath.

But better off deconstructing the elements and seeing the baby in the dream as representing an aspect of my battered soul, and not just representing the baby I haven't had yet and who knows if I ever will.

》

"Your boss is outside." My dad's in front of me.

"What?" My voice is hoarse.

Roy peers from behind my dad. "Teddy's here."

"Let him in and leave the room."

My dad and Roy quickly follow my raspy orders and leave. A moment goes by and Teddy walks in.

"Well"—he smiles at me—"what was that good for?"

I see him and start crying. He sits down on the bed.

"Come here." He leans in toward me.

It hurts to move, but I slightly lift myself up, my face disappears into him and all the crying comes out, razor blades slicing me from within and I can't calm down, the crying only intensifies, shattering me into pieces.

"You'll be fine, you'll be fine. Everything will be fine," he says quietly, caressing my hair, pressing me into him.

"Something bad happened to me, Teddy," I say, choked up against his chest. "Something bad happened to me."

"I know. But you're here now, you're fine. You were lucky."

"I'm not fine . . ."

"This is considered fine, trust me. You know what could have happened to you? Relatively speaking, this isn't that bad."

I try to stop crying, disconnect from him and lean back on the pillow, look for a tissue. He gets up, walks around the room, finds a paper towel and hands it to me. The bed shifts when he sits back down and it hurts. I wipe my face and my nose with the coarse paper towel. I stop crying, but the tears are still streaming down.

"They need to operate," I quietly mumble.

"Yes, I had a word with the doctors here." He's speaking quietly too, close to me. "All right, surgery. Don't worry."

"They need to operate on the thigh, insert a titanium rod. Three incisions. I blacked out when they pushed my thigh back into place in the ambulance."

"Poor girl."

"And your car . . . shit." I cover my face with my right hand.

"Who gives a fuck?"

"I wrecked it."

"You didn't wreck it and don't give it another thought. It doesn't matter, except for the fact that if this had happened with your car, you wouldn't be here right now. So I'm very happy you were driving mine. Are you in pain?"

"How did you find out?"

"The police called."

"Shit. I'm sorry."

"No, don't be."

I point at the bruise on my forehead and my bloodshot eye, and the cut on my lip that hurts immensely, maybe even more than my leg.

"What will I do, Teddy? Look at me, look at my face."

"I see it. You're beautiful."

"Look at my body," I go on, "I don't want this. I don't understand how—"

"I know. It's hard."

I'm flooded by genuine panic, a strong feeling that something terrible happened, that my life will never be the same again.

"I don't want any of this! I don't want it, you understand what I'm saying to you?! I don't want it! I don't want it!" my broken voice screams.

My dad walks in. "Sorry to disturb . . . Noa? I heard you from the hallway. What are we going to do?"

I have no way of supporting my dad's anxiety right now. I look at Teddy and see his eyes quickly shifting to my dad and immediately back to me. When his eyes come across mine, I already know that I don't need to do anything.

"She'll be fine, you've got a strong kid," Teddy calms my dad down. "Let's wait till we hear from the surgeon."

"We've already met outside the room," my dad explains to me and points at Teddy, "so we've introduced ourselves already, just so you know. You need anything? Is there something I can do? Mina's on her way with some home-cooked food. She started straightaway, said you probably won't like the hospital food."

"Great, that's very good, you need to eat," Teddy replies on my behalf and turns to my dad again. "Food will be helpful."

"Good, great. Well, I didn't mean to interrupt you. I'm right outside in the hallway, and Mina will get here real soon."

"Thank you," I say quietly and look at Teddy.

My dad keeps going. "Are you hungry? I can get a plate of something from the nurses. No? Never mind, I won't disturb you. I'm right outside."

He leaves, and Teddy leans in, his face close to mine.

"Better off with the hospital food," I mutter wickedly. At least the crying has stopped.

"Never mind, let him help. You won't eat anything anyway."

We're close. He carefully kisses me on the undamaged side of my lips and then on my cheek, and again.

"There you are," he says.

"I'm scared of the surgery."

"Don't be, everything will be fine. Don't worry."

"Yeah, we've heard all about your 'don't worry.'"

He smiles at me with those teeth I love and that's a little comforting. "The main thing is that you're here and your fucked-up mind has remained intact."

"Yes."

"A good friend of mine recommended the surgeon who'll perform your operation. I wanted my friend to do the surgery himself, but he's up north and said you're better off not switching hospitals."

"Thank you, I didn't know you've already—" A sharp pain rises from my left knee, through my thigh and all the way to my lower back, momentarily paralyzing me.

"You in pain?"

"Yeah, it hurts." Tears come out.

He places a warm hand on my face and looks at me. I see the empathy in his eyes.

"The morphine's not helping?" He gently raises my arm. "You need to press this button."

"I know, but something isn't working."

"I'll go get them to come fix it. You shouldn't be suffering this much at this point." He gets up. "Be right back."

He leaves the room, and I realize that I have a long recovery process ahead of me, and I'm scared that something very bad has happened to my leg and that I'll never be the same as I was. I don't know how to gather the strength to deal with all this.

Thank God for Teddy.

>

Nighttime. I wake up, I'm in the ward. Teddy is not here. Maybe he left long ago? They asked everyone to leave. I was heavily sedated, guess I fell asleep straightaway.

I want to text him but even reaching my phone is a mission, so when I finally have it in my hand—I just call him. I hear the ringing tone and take another look at the screen. It's 3:18 a.m. That's not good. I don't manage to hang up in time.

"Noa." His voice. "You up?"

"Sorry, the time." My words are slurred.

"No, no problem." He takes a second. "How you doing?"

I didn't think speaking would be so hard for me. I hear him sitting up, rustling sounds and then a brief cough.

"You still a monster?"

He manages to amuse me. It's worth the pain in my lip as it stretches into a smile. "Maybe," I say quietly.

We stay silent. I want to tell him that I don't want to be here. But I can't organize my thoughts into a coherent sentence. "It will pass, I promise," he says. "I'll help you through this."

"Thomas. I can see Thomas. What he told me."

"What did he tell you?"

"And they're getting married."

"Yes, I know, Roy told me."

I stare ahead into the dark room, light seeping in from the hallway. Were my eyes closed up till now? Someone comes in. Night nurse? She asks if everything's all right. She has an accent. She checks my IV, moves things around, draws the curtain. Teddy's still on the line.

"Teddy."

"Yes?"

"Someone's here."

"Who is it? Thomas again?"

Another painful smile. "No. A nurse."

"Try to go back to sleep, call me when you wake up."

"Bye."

"Now let's get you to pee." The nurse turns on a little light and brings the designated pan to the bed. "Here, let's move the blanket for you. Just like that. Now lift your pelvis. Just the pelvis. No, no, you're moving your thigh! Don't move it. Don't move it. Just the pelvis, lift it. Yes, very good. There you go, sweetie."

She places the cold plastic underneath me. I look at her. She has beautiful dark eyes. She smiles at me.

"Go," she says.

"Soon."

"Then I'll come back in a few minutes. Okay?" She's nice to me.

"Yes. Thank you."

I stay alone. I only now realize that I'm alone in this room. How can that be?

I'm tired. I need to pee.

Go.

❯

I think I hear a rooster. Because it's morning? Why would they have a rooster here? I'm nauseated. Recollecting yesterday: each moment gets a single frame, but since I only have a few, the whole thing plays in my mind on a maddening loop, like a television news broadcast reporting on a disaster—without any additional information.

Light flickers on my phone. I pick up.

"How did you sleep?" Teddy's voice sounds distant.

"Don't know. I don't know if I slept." I speak so slowly.

"You're stoned. More than usual. That's good, better off that way."

"Don't know."

"I'm coming over, what should I bring?"

"Don't know. Nothing."

"Getting you some coffee, and something to eat. Phone charger. Decent tissues. And you want your tablet, or laptop? It's right here next to me."

My laptop is next to him and I'm not. My things are at his apartment and I'm at the hospital. I close my eyes and that immediately gets me deep inside, to a place from which I can no longer talk.

"Noa? Noa, are you with me?"

I make a huge effort to open my eyes.

"Never mind," Teddy says. "See you soon."

〉

By the time he arrives I'm already less of a shadow of myself, or at least less of a doped-up shadow of myself. The coffee reminds me there's a whole world out there. Teddy's sitting on a chair in front of me, focused on his phone.

"Sorry, I'll just be a minute, trying to close up something urgent."

I close my eyes. Sharon. I need to talk to Sharon. I'll call her soon. Teddy talks to me.

"Tomorrow," he says.

"Tomorrow," I repeat after him and think about the cold air of the operating theater, all the white light in the world. "Feel like smoking."

"Go ahead."

"Right."

"What will they do? Throw us out? Make us pay a fine?"

"It's inconsiderate of other patients."

"That's true."

"And inconsiderate of the staff."

"Listen, about tomorrow. I'll cut my trip short this week, but I have two meetings I need to attend. I'll be with you after the surgery and fly out at night, and I'll try to get back earlier."

"I forgot all about London."

"Yeah." He goes back to his phone. "Let's see how it goes."

"No. Why should you cut your trip short?"

He looks at me, then back to his phone. I wait for him to say something, but realize he isn't going to discuss the matter any further, he just wanted to let me know. I'll let it go. I want to be after.

>

White bright light. So cold. They're busy around me. We're all in the same room, but we have different status: they are people, I'm a body. The bed is warm. I think I'm scared. I'm in good hands. I'm all right. Am I—

>

I open my eyes. Teddy's still sitting on the armchair near my bed, but we're in a different room. He looks at me and takes off his glasses. I think he's smiling.

"Teddy?"

"Yes?"

"When's the surgery?"

"You're after it."

"When did you get here?"

"A while ago." Now he's really smiling. "Go back to sleep."

I stare ahead. I feel distant. Far from myself. As though I've been reduced to the bare minimum, and I'm a minuscule size compared with the rest of my body, like a person in a huge church: even if they scream with all their might their voice won't be heard outside. The window's open and I can see treetops. When I look at Teddy again, I realize he's been looking at me this whole time.

"How did the surgery go?" I ask slowly.

"It went well, very well. They're pleased."

"Did you talk to my dad?"

"Sure, I talk to him every couple of hours."

"Thank you. Why are you smiling, Teddy?"

"Because this is the fourth time we've had this conversation." His smile is sweet and his eyes are laughing.

"Senile old fools," I say and smile and fall asleep again.

>

A day after the surgery. Can't move. The IV drip has a steady pace: drop—one two three—drop. And again. Everything's closing in on me, Planet Earth is blue and there's nothing I can do. The helplessness is so extreme that it gradually morphs into claustrophobia.

12:43 a.m. I get a text. I reach my hand and lift the phone, hold it in front of my face. My eyes take a moment to adjust. Message from Teddy Rosenfeld.

> How you hanging in
>
> So so
>
> Managed to rest
>
> Anguish
>
> Understandable

I imagine him sitting and typing and understanding. Far from me, elsewhere.

> How's London?
>
> Fine . you feeling down
>
> Yes
>
> Once youre home youll
> feel better

Home?

> Youll smoke

What's going to happen now? What am I supposed to do when I get out of here? He's typing another message.

> Whered you go

I feel pulses in my leg's artery, around the foreign object they've inserted inside my thigh.

> Teddy
>
> What

I type slowly, letter by letter, hate myself for writing this, but I send it anyway.

> This is hard for me

Something within me shifted during that accident, and I haven't figured out what it is yet. This time, he's the one stalling his reply. I stare at the screen. I see he's typing.

> I know . I love you

I can't believe my eyes. This has never happened to me. From the day we met, he's never said it and surely never wrote it in black and white, in pixel on a touchscreen.

I text back:

> Now it's less hard

He replies:

> Maybe for you !

I smile. He loves me.

>

Two days after the surgery. Sharon's on her way to visit me at the hospital. While I wait for her, Teddy calls.

"I'm coming back tomorrow."

"When are you landing?"

"Early morning. I'll go by my place and then I'll come and get you."

"Where am I going?"

"My place."

I fill my lungs with air. "That's what you want?"

"Yes."

"Okay. Thank you." What can I say? "Is it because of the whole loving me thing and all that?"

He laughs. Success.

"Yes," he confirms.

"I didn't know."

"You do now."

My finger gently touches the cut on my lip. "I'll find a way to destroy it."

"I'm sure you will."

"Also, I formally declare that I'm not getting my hopes up or anything sick like that."

"Attagirl." I hear him smiling.

》

When someone dies, the Jewish custom is for the mourners to congregate at home for seven days of mourning. But the truth is that the real mourning process starts only once the seven days end. And so it is in my case too, though the death wasn't a death, only the possibility of death.

From the moment we step into his apartment after he picks me up from the hospital, seven days of wondrous grace: I have a man and I love him and he takes care of me and I'm important to him.

This sudden utopia with Teddy is saving me, but only mentally. Physically, I'm shattered. The pain is endless. I take very strong painkillers, time passes differently from how it usually does, and I feel like I'm inside a misty cloud. Every movement's tricky, everything's cumbersome. Lying down to sitting, sitting to standing and back down again. Brief walks between rooms, daring to put some weight on my leg.

Teddy's working from home. He's busy as always, but now he's busy right next to me. We're at each other's side, all day and all night and all the time. I know what he's doing every single minute, I can tell when he is tired, hungry. Happy. We laugh, kiss a little, but touch a lot. Sometimes it's arousing, but it doesn't develop into sex, except for one night when he's in bed by my side, and I seem agitated to him:

"You in pain?"

"No, I'm fine. The painkillers haven't worn off yet."

"So what's with the restless legs? Leg, in your case."

"Restless vagina, perhaps."

"Poor you."

"Yes, poor me. I can't make myself come. No angle."

He puts down his book and takes off his glasses, then turns and looks at me, amused, apparently. "I find it very sexy, how helpless you are."

I shift my eyes to him, my mouth slightly open in a taunting manner. "Do you?"

"Why don't you reach out to me and kindly ask for my assistance?"

Fucking tease.

"I'm an independent woman, that's why."

He sits up and peels the blanket off me, revealing both of my legs, along with the off-white bandage. The Good, the Bad, and the Ugly.

"Dependent," he diagnoses with a decisive tone.

I smile but I'm too unnerved to really be amused, so I keep the cold attitude. "All right. So how about this: I'll pay you to give me some oral pleasure."

He laughs, enjoying me. "How much do you pay?"

"Unfortunately for you, the amount will be determined solely according to performance and outcomes."

"I see."

"Your mission, should you choose to accept it."

"I choose to accept it. I could use the money."

I smile and as he is positioning himself, I realize that I'd just talked the talk, but I can't really walk the walk. I'm not even close to being aroused, it's just my body that's demanding, not my mind. He's getting ready, reaching for my underwear.

I look at the ceiling. "This is so not sexy for me."

"Right." He lets go and rises. "Why would it be?"

I look back at him. He stands up and takes the beer bottle from his nightstand, gulping down a few sips. I keep still, but my eyes follow him. He walks around the bed, over to my side, puts down the bottle and stands tall above me.

"Yeah, you shouldn't have paid a dime for that." He takes my neck with one hand, fingers pointing down and wrist pushing against my chin, forcing me to look back up at the ceiling. "It's not your pussy I should be going for." He changes his grip so that he can use his thumb and finger to press my mouth open. His face is high above me; his free hand is braced against the headboard. He brings his face close to mine, his fingers tightening on my cheeks and he shoves his tongue inside my mouth. My tongue responds to his and he starts licking it and kissing me and I kiss him back. He pulls away, still holding my face—"I missed you"—then kisses me again until my heart starts pounding. He lets go of my face and sits on the bed with his back to me, his hand lightly grazing my underwear on its way down my good leg and all the way up again, but this time bypassing my pussy. He does it again, and then puts his fingers right over my clit.

"Warm and swollen." He pushes the underwear to one side, revealing me. "I'm going to smell you now." He changes his position, revealing me again, pushing his face between my legs and breathing in deeply, quietly saying to himself or to my pussy, "You're too much." He licks me and starts going down on me, softly and then hard and then nothing and then hard again, and every change gets me further and more into it, until I'm so turned on that I can't help it and start moving my pelvis—and here's the pain. I instantly flinch and tense up. He stops.

"Shit," I mutter, and a wave of anger is flooding me. "Fuck. Fuck!"

"Take it easy."

"I hate it!" I put my hands on my face. "I just really hate it!"

"We'll find a way, we've just started. We'll get you there."

"I can't come if I can't move. I can't do it."

He sits up and looks at me with a soft smile on his face. "You can come only if you're the one doing the fucking. That's okay, that's usually how it goes, just like every other man."

I give him the middle finger.

He laughs and says, "Okay. Now, free of charge, I'm going to come on your face."

>

Symbiosis is dangerous, I know. The codependency relieves the aloneness, or at least it creates an illusion of relief. I give in to the situation, allow myself to forget what I'm like without him. For instance, I can't recall what I eat when I'm not with him or if I eat at all. Or how I sleep when he's not beside me.

And he's turning out to be a skilled symbiont, though facultative—he has a choice and isn't dependent, but still chooses to interact.

And so, in a weird way, I find myself freer with him now than I've ever been. What am I free of? The burden of proof?

»

Two weeks after the surgery there's an issue with one of the incisions on my leg. I'm in pain. Teddy wants to get a doctor to come for a home visit, but the surgeon who'd treated me at the hospital asks Teddy to bring me in for a checkup.

We take his loaner there. Even though the pain's constantly on my mind, I manage to notice the beautiful day outside. The passenger seat is set all the way back, and I still find it hard to sit. Teddy's phone rings, and since his speaker doesn't work in this car, he answers the call and presses the phone against his ear.

"Yes."

I can't hear what's being said on the other end. I look at his fingers on the steering wheel, his hand. Type "a man's hand" on Wikipedia and you'll get a page with an image of Teddy's hand on the steering wheel.

"Send it, send it to me." (   ) "What? No, no, fine. Bye." (   ) "All right, bye."

He hangs up.

When we get to the hospital, I suddenly feel some genuine distress. We wait for the doctor to call me in.

"You want something to drink, or some food?"

"No, thank you." I'm disgusted by the mere thought.

"All right, I'm going for a moment, will you be okay? I'll get you some water." Up until this very second, I was sure he'd go in with me to see the doctor.

"Yeah. Yeah, sure," I say quickly, since I don't want him to realize I've forgotten how to take care of myself.

He puts a hand on my shoulder for a second, then walks away, quick steps.

"An infection," the doctor rules and gives me a prescription for antibiotics. For some reason he's not as nice to me as he was before the surgery. There's a hostile edge to his polite manners, and he gives me the feeling that the infection's somehow my fault. He stamps the prescription hastily.

Where is he? Maybe now he'll leave me? Abandon me at the hospital and walk away for good, *Bitter Moon* style?

I text him.

> Done, I'm outside
>
> Call me

I call him.

"Where are you? Outside where?"

"Outside the doctor's office."

"Fine, then wait there, I'm coming. What did he say, an infection?"

›

We drive and don't talk much. Once we reach his parking lot, he turns off the engine and looks at me.

"And now I want you to tell me precisely what happened there."

"Where, at the doctor's?"

"No."

"Then what do you mean 'there'? What are you talking about?"

"Highway 1, two weeks ago."

"What?"

"What happened there, what were you doing there?"

"I don't understand what you're asking. You know what I was doing there, I was heading back from my grandma's."

"Noa."

"What?"

"Were you asleep at the wheel?"

"Yes, you know I was, why are you asking it like that?"

He falls silent and looks at me inquisitively. When I realize what he's thinking, I feel like all the blood running through my veins has been sucked out of me all at once.

"I fell asleep." I look at him with wide, confused eyes.

"What state were you in when you got in the car?"

"Pretty tired I guess."

"You can't keep telling me that."

"Telling you what? I was tired and pissed off too, right." I'm dizzy.

"How pissed off were you?"

"I don't know. Can we please go upstairs?"

"No. Can you please tell me what was going through your mind?"

"Teddy—"

"All right, you know what? Tell me what *you* think happened." His finger presses onto my shoulder. "If you do know, deep down. I can't figure out if you're conscious of it or not."

"Conscious of what? Why are you suddenly asking all this?"

"Because you were talking."

"To who?"

"Shouting."

"When—What?"

"You were shouting in the car right before you crashed into the wall, under that bridge."

"What? What are you talking about?"

"My car has a dash cam with an advanced EDR. Like on airplanes, like black boxes on a plane."

"What?" My heart's pounding like crazy. What is he saying? I wasn't shouting, I fell asleep. I fell asleep!

"Yes, I just got it. Not much to see, but there's audio."

"You listened to it? What did you hear?"

"You! I heard you."

I suddenly feel intense nausea and there's ringing in my ears, distant but incredibly loud. I instinctively open the car door, shove myself out but my injured leg hinders me halfway through, and I start to puke. Teddy quickly gets out and walks around to my side, frees my leg and pulls me out and I puke in the parking lot, bent down over the ground, and he's holding me, and I puke and puke, and then manage to stop and he lifts me back into the car. I'm sitting on the passenger seat with my legs out. My entire body's shaking. He crouches down and puts his hands on my knees.

"Is that it?"

I nod my head slowly. He grabs a bottle from the car, pours some water into his hand and cleans my face, then hands me the bottle. I wash out my mouth and then drink, look at him. When he sees I'm done, he takes the bottle and washes the puke off the asphalt with the rest of the water.

"Let's go up. Wait, I'll get the crutches out."

I don't entirely understand what just happened here, but I have a bad feeling, like an inner voice saying, You've just passed the point of no return.

>

We enter the apartment. He leaves me alone and goes to his office. I go to shower, still using a crutch. The water streams around the aluminum, lifting a corner of the sticker attached to the crutch and I want to peel it off. That's it. The good days are over, I know that; symbiosis terminated. I press the sticker to the bottom of the soap dispenser, somewhere even Betty can't see.

I dress slowly and sit down, leaning against the back of the bed, my wet hair still dripping onto my shoulders. Can't cry, can't sleep, can't leave, can't be.

He walks into the bedroom. "How are you?"

"Don't know. Okay."

He sits on the bed and examines me with a troubled, frozen look. I look him in the eye.

"I wasn't trying to die. Even if I wanted to, which, it's true, sometimes I do, I could never really choose it. It's sick. It's—I'm not there."

"Okay," he speaks slowly. "I won't have you, no matter what, no matter when, ever reaching that state again. Is that clear?" He sounds both harsh and soft.

"I didn't think that that's what happened."

"All right. I believe you."

"And you? You think that's what happened?"

"I don't know." He runs his hand through his hair. "But I do know you didn't fall asleep. That's not what happened. And I also know you got into the car in an unstable state, after Roy had told you they were getting married."

"A very pathetic narrative you're suggesting here."

He looks at me. "You wrote it."

"Can't remember what happened in the car before the accident. I remember some of my thoughts, and I felt like shit and I was mad, okay. But, I don't know, there's a chunk of time missing." I lower my eyes, staring at the edges of the pillow next to me. "I don't get it. How come you only now got the recording?"

"What does it matter?" He gets impatient but still explains: "They didn't find it to begin with. They had to search, and after they found it, it took those morons a good few days to recover the data."

"How come they didn't find it straightaway?"

"It flew off during the collision."

I stare ahead and then look at him again. "Why didn't you say anything about it?"

"Why would I say anything? You think I knew what they'd find there?"

He waited for those morons to send him a recording of me during the accident. A camera with a recording system in the car. That possibility never crossed my mind, ever. Flew off during the collision, they had to search for it. Where did they find it? Something strange is going on. I'm used to him keeping me in the dark, but now he knows things about me that even I don't know about myself.

He notices I've drifted off with my thoughts. "I'm going back to my office." He uses the moment to leave the room.

My head's exploding, I don't understand anything. Like what did he hear on the recording? Do I want to hear it? Will I hear the car flipping over? Or me screaming? Did I scream? What did I say? What does it sound like afterward? Feel sick again. I guess he genuinely doesn't know whether I somehow did it intentionally. And now I don't know either.

And I feel like I don't trust him. He's here, in the other room, and I can go over and ask him whatever I want to. But I don't want to.

›

In the middle of the night, I wake up from a terrible dream, which reabsorbs into my subconsciousness in a millisecond—and I can't hold on to any of it. Teddy's asleep next to me, he's dressed as though he didn't intend on going to bed, just lay down to rest. His arm's across his face. I turn my back to him.

"Noa," I hear him saying, and I sit up at once, which causes a splitting pain in my thigh. It's still dark out. My shirt's drenched in sweat.

"Yes?" I say, confused.

"You were shouting in your sleep. Come here." He takes me in his arms and hugs me. His fingers gently stroke the side of my face. I take off my wet shirt, return to his shoulder and close my eyes.

I don't remember the next detail-laden dream either, except for me walking on the street with Teddy or actually just passing by him, and he's walking with his dad, who's a bigger Teddy, and next to them walks Teddy's dad, another one.

›

I have a treatment session in the morning with Dawn, a physiotherapist who was already here twice last week at Teddy's demand.

She helps me make her a coffee while Teddy's in the shower. When he comes out, dressed and ready for his day, we're already midsession. He walks over to the treatment bed situated in the middle of the living room.

"I'm heading out, Noa." He puts his hand on the back of my neck.

"Okay."

"I'll be back soon." He slightly bends down near my ear and quietly says, "You're not leaving the house."

Maybe I'm in a horror movie. I squint, but I can't react since we're not alone and in any case he's already walking away.

After the session, I want to smoke a joint and think about yesterday, but Dawn, who commutes here from another city, asks to stick around for a while until her next appointment. I postpone the joint. I'm not sure whether to hang out with her, and she's already had a coffee, so we sit down and have some toast together, and it's awkward. Toward the end of the makeshift meal, Teddy comes home. I feel uncomfortable and tired. I smoke and get back into bed. It's noon.

I wake up shortly after 6:00 p.m., it's almost dark out. I hear voices talking somewhere in the house. A man's voice, but it's not Teddy. I continue lying in the darkness of the bedroom. They're laughing. I recognize that laugh, it's Richard Harrington. So even if I wanted to go out, I can't. How about that. Maybe the order 'You're not leaving the room' has come into effect while I was asleep. I check my phone and can't find any new orders. Still, I stay put.

I can't think straight.

After a few minutes go by, I text Teddy.

> Hi
>
> Youre up
>
> Yes
>
> Come say hi to Richard
>
> He knows I'm here?
>
> Yes
>
> So he knows about us?
>
> Yes

He knows about us. How long has he known about us? How come I don't know about us?

Should I get up? No, I don't feel like it. Maybe I actually do want to be ordered not to leave the room. But I do feel like smoking. How can I go out? How can I show my face out there? I'm a wreck. What will he see, Mr. Harrington? That charming young woman from the wedding who's now turned into a pathetic lump of nothing that his partner just can't seem to get rid of?

I lift myself up. Walk over to wash my face, one step at a time. Brush my teeth. Spit. Examine my face; all the bruises from the accident have healed by now. Change into some clean clothes. My hair's still messy, but never mind.

The voices get louder as I near the living room. They're sitting at the big table, Teddy with his back to me. Richard sees me and immediately gets up. Teddy turns his head and looks at me.

"There she is, our lovely Miss Simon!" Richard walks around the table and very naturally envelops me into a huge bear hug.

"You scared the hell out of us . . ." he says with a smile, and I—unfortunately—start to cry. The tears come out, I hide my face with my hand, still wrapped within a clenching hug that's getting tighter by the minute, and he whispers calming words and I feel his beard on my forehead and think about his kids, his daughter, so lucky to have that kind of dad. I manage to calm down and I pull back, grab on to the crutches that have patiently waited under my arms this whole time.

"Sorry." I wipe away my tears, then look up and see Teddy still seated, elbows leaning against the armrests as he reclines, observing me with soft eyes.

"Sorry for what? Cut yourself some slack, of course you're crying. It's good that you're crying!" Richard declares and turns to Teddy. "Tell her that it's a good thing she's crying."

"I'm dying for a smoke," I say.

"You two and your holy smoke!" He laughs and goes back to his seat and his whiskey.

I grab the cigarette pack from the table and pull one out.

"You can smoke here, sit down." Teddy pulls up a chair for me.

I lean my crutches on the table and slowly take a seat, light up and breathe in the smoke. What a magnificent cigarette.

"I need a tissue," I mumble.

"I'll get it." Teddy gets up. "Want some coffee?"

He hands me a box of tissues and I grab one and then point at the whiskey bottle. He nods and goes to the kitchen.

"Hey, kiddo"—Richard leans in—"you have no idea how much I get what you're going through right now. Mainly the trauma, more than the physical aspects. It's trauma, no doubt about it."

I wonder if he knows about the recording and, if so, if he knows what's on it. I smile at him. "Thank you, Richard."

"Not an easy recovery."

"She's doing good, she's recovering fast," Teddy says to Richard as he places a heavy glass in front of me. "She'll be fine in no time."

"Easy does it." Richard says the opposite of what his partner just said, maintaining their usual balance.

Teddy pours me a drink and sits back down on his chair, smiles at me. I smile too. Richard shifts his eyes between us. "The gang at the office all send you their warm regards."

"Thank you . . . Do they know I'm here?" I ask with a candor that somewhat surprises me. "The gang?" I repeat his choice of words with an amused tone.

"No," Richard says dismissively, and I glance at Teddy's stoic expression. "I wouldn't think so. They know you're recovering from an accident."

"How's your daughter, and your granddaughter?"

"Oh they're fantastic." He smiles lovingly. "We're all in seventh heaven."

I ask him to show me photos of his granddaughter. He holds his phone and we look at them together. Teddy watches us from the side.

"And I hear Judith's getting a grandchild soon too, right?" Richard puts his phone down.

"Right. Tom and Alison." I smile.

"Well! That's great. Very exciting." He gives Teddy a taunting look and adds, "You're next!"

Teddy smiles. "It's way past your bedtime, Harrington, you're starting to talk nonsense."

Richard and I laugh, and I turn to Richard and speak loudly and with clear diction, "We're going to take you home now, all right?"

We all laugh. I look at Teddy and he gives me a look I know all too well but can't quite define; maybe the look of someone all-knowing, someone who already knows how this will all end.

⟩

In the morning I wake up and don't feel like getting out of bed. Though last night was nice, I don't feel like seeing him. Is he even around? What day is it today? I think it's Tuesday.

Are you home?

No

Good. I'm better off if he's not here. I just want to be by myself. He adds:

Good morning

Good morning.

I don't feel anything, or more like I feel nothing.

Actually, why shouldn't I snort a bit of cocaine right now? I get off the bed, my leg hurts and my body's limp, but I'm already used to the movements and compensations of my right side, and Dawn's treatments are helping. It's been only two days and the infection is almost gone.

I take out my little tin box, grab a teaspoon that's set next to a mug that had yesterday's tea, and I use the edge of the teaspoon to scratch out the remnants from the box and snort them. I stay in the bedroom, watch a disturbing morning talk show and snort some more, because why the hell not? It's Tuesday!

"Dogs love being with someone authoritative. They only feel comfortable with authority," the dog expert on the morning show says. The dog that's with her in the studio starts barking. I turn the TV off, but the dog's still barking. It sounds almost like he's inside the house. Have I finally lost it? I shift from lying down to sitting up and then standing. My walk is slow and awkward, especially in the mornings. When I reach the living room, I see Xerox.

"Was that you barking?"

Well, if Xerox is here, that means Milo is too. What's Milo doing here first thing in the morning? He wasn't here last night.

"Milo?" I falter through the hallway toward his room. The door's shut.

"Huh . . ." I hear a sleepy voice from inside the room.

"Sorry! I woke you up," I say through the door. "Go back to sleep and we'll never mention this again," I add and hear him laughing.

"Come on in."

I open the door and stay standing there, looking in. "It's dark in here."

"Yeah, I'll get up soon, I'll open up." His head is on the pillow and his soft hair is messy.

"When did you get here? At night?"

"Yeah."

"In the middle of the night?"

"Yeah, like two in the morning, I think."

"Why? Everything okay with Daria?"

He sits up heavily. "No. Everything's really *not okay* with Daria."

"What happened? Never mind, come to the living room, let's have some coffee."

"I don't like coffee."

"Then what? Hot chocolate?"

"I'm not a four-year-old."

"Okay! Then what do you drink in the morning?"

"I don't know. Water?"

"Are you asking me what you drink in the morning?"

"I don't drink anything in the morning."

"No, people drink when they get up. I'll make you some tea. Have some tea."

"Okay, I'll be right there."

"What about Xerox? Should I give him anything?" I ask as I walk toward the living room.

"Yeah, can you feed him?" he shouts from his room.

I limp out to the balcony and pour food from a large bag into his bowl. Xerox chews up the dry food.

"A fan of chicken remnants, are you?"

This coke is pretty intense. I hope Milo won't notice I'm coked up. But what are the chances of him noticing? The guy doesn't even know what he drinks first thing in the morning.

I'm standing in the kitchen making us our coffee and tea when Milo walks in, heavy and despaired and sweet as ever. Xerox excitedly runs back and forth from me to Milo, to the living room, the balcony and back again.

"Shit, what time is it? I've got to take him out."

"Quarter past ten."

So far, I've complied with the führer's 'You're not leaving the house' order, but I now decide to join their walk. I put on an oversized sweatshirt and wide flip-flops. I need help putting the sock on my left foot and Milo gives me a hand. It's a bit intimate, but we get over it.

"So what happened?" I ask him when we reach the street. I lean on one crutch and light a smoke with my other hand.

"What? With Daria? I think it's over. Finished."

That reminds me of how Teddy talked about Lara. "Why?"

"Because she doesn't love me anymore."

"No way."

"No way?"

"Not the way I see it, no. If you love someone, then you'll always love them. It doesn't mean she wants you as she used to," I say, and then worry it might have been too harsh on the kid.

"Good for her."

"But if she doesn't want you anymore, then what can you do? She doesn't."

He falls silent and I feel like I'm doing a very shitty job at this. Xerox pees on a tree on the boulevard. I take a drag.

"What I'm trying to say is"—how can I explain what I mean?—"let's say I'm asparagus, and someone doesn't like asparagus. So what can I do? I'm still asparagus, if he's doesn't like me—then there's nothing I can do about it."

"I thought we were going to fly to South America together."

"Why would you do that? What are you, some pensioner traveling with his wife? Go and travel alone, meet people, spend time with yourself. That's the fun part!" I haven't traveled a day in my life, surely not on my own. "No having to consider other people's wishes, upset stomachs and sleeping bags and I don't know what, traveling . . . stuff."

"I don't get what you're saying."

Good thing I'm not a mother. I think about Monique, about how she'd hinted to me back then that she didn't like Daria all that much.

"I'm saying that right now you're sad about what's happening with Daria, and by the way you two may very well get back together, but if you don't, it's fine, because in any case you should be a bit more free, for a twenty-one-year-old, instead of 'marrying' your high school sweetheart this early on."

"I didn't know her in high school, I only met her after graduation. She served with a friend of mine in the army."

"Fine, your army sweetheart."

"She wasn't with me in the army."

"Okay, Milo, I get it!" I must have said that loudly, because he's giving me a somewhat frightened look. "You're not getting any of what I'm saying?"

"I get that you think that if she doesn't want me then it doesn't matter, even if it really hurts right now. And something about asparagus, but I don't remember what." He smiles.

I laugh and then ask carefully, "But why doesn't it matter? Do you get that part?"

"Because there's nothing I can do if she doesn't want me, because I am what I am?"

"Yes!" I say joyfully and proudly. "You're Milo! You get to stick around with you, so you're getting the best deal!"

He gives a shy smile and we turn to walk back to the house. My eyes fill with tears.

At home, I roll a joint to take the edge off the coke. Milo comes out to the balcony.

"What are you smoking?"

"Weed."

"Can I have a drag?"

"Really? You smoke? I didn't know." I hand it to him.

"Yeah, sometimes. A social smoker." He sits down, takes a drag and inhales the smoke.

"Does Teddy know you smoke?"

"Yeah, sure."

"And Monique?"

"Yeah. I even smoked with her. She's fine with it."

"It's great that you don't have to hide it."

We fall silent.

"Daria's my best friend," he announces to himself and to me.

"Yes, that's really harsh. That's the shittiest part about it."

Suddenly he starts crying. I immediately feel I'm about to cry too, but I hold back my irrelevant tears and get a grip on myself for his sake. His body's trembling from the crying and I'm flooded with anger toward Daria for not doing it right. There are ways to leave someone softly. Still, it doesn't matter, he needs to hurt. I put my hand on his shoulder.

"It'll pass."

He continues weeping quietly. I go inside and grab the tissue box left over from last night on the big table. Go back out to the balcony, offer him a tissue and sit next to him.

"You want to tell me what happened last night? How long has it seemed like it's ending?"

He sniffles. "I don't know, recently she's kind of different?" Is he asking or saying? "And yesterday we had a stupid argument, and then she just told me she's had enough of me, that I'm too nice and it pisses her off and that she's sorry she's saying it like that. But it sucks."

"And you? What do you want?"

"I wanted us to continue. Like, stay a couple."

"Yes. And the trip was already planned out?"

"No, because she never knows what she wants. We argued about that too now, I mean yesterday."

"Give her some time away from you. It'll do you some good too."

He's not crying anymore, just sitting there staring, a little stoned; he leans down and pets Xerox, who's lying next to him.

"How about a movie?" I ask, offering up a lighter activity.

"Yeah, okay."

We watch a movie, then binge on an entire season of a new series. We get high and eat.

At some point I text Teddy.

> Milo's here, he and Daria split
> up (for now)
>
> Saw him at night . how is he
>
> Sad. I'm keeping him company
>
> Jealous .Thanks Noa
>
> You don't need to thank me.

And I add:

He's a real sweetheart

He is so are you

›

Milo leaves in the evening, and I lie down in Teddy's bed and watch TV. I hear him coming home and stay lying down because I've had enough of dealing with my leg for today. I know he's had a long day and I can only guess he's beat. He's got nothing for me.

He walks into the room. I look at him. Yes, beat.

"How are you?" he asks.

"Fine."

"Where's Milo?"

"Meeting Ben for a beer."

"Right. Good." He takes off his jacket and unbuttons his sleeves. "How's he doing?"

"Still hasn't taken it all in."

"Yeah, makes sense." He takes off his wristwatch and places it on the bedside table.

There's a brief moment of silence.

"Teddy Rosenfeld." I say his full name for no apparent reason and look at him. "You busy?"

"Very," he says, and stands near the bed. "Did you talk to him a bit?"

"Yes, I tried to cheer him up. Gave him some advice."

"All right. I'm not sure you should be dishing out advice given your state." This one surprises me, whips right into me and paralyzes me and he continues: "Don't want to give him any ideas."

I look at him. He can tell that I'm insulted.

"I'm glad you spent the day together, and I'm sure you helped him. I was just kidding."

"No, you weren't," I say quietly.

He sits next to me on the bed. "I was. I don't trust you when it comes to you, but with him, I'm sure you did a great job."

I nod my head. "You know I can't stand you?"

He raises his right hand and rubs his face, then suddenly reaches it toward me and grabs my neck, leans in and kisses me. I don't cooperate, but he knows exactly what to do in order to change that; I try to push him, and he leaves my neck and grabs my hand instead and now he's got both my arms pinned down.

"Let me ask you this." His face is serious, just a bit of light coming from the little lamp. "Have you taken the time to think about what you did?"

I keep quiet and he continues.

"Have you taken the time to think what it would mean to the people in your life, if you'd gone all the way? Huh?" He tightens his grip since I'm trying to resist again. "What would it do to Roy? To your father? To your grandmother, your grandma? Would you really allow yourself to blacken her final years like that? And what about your friends? What about Sharon? What would it do to her, losing you?"

I want to tell him that I don't know if I did it on purpose, but I stay quiet because I also don't know that I didn't do it on purpose; I just don't know. And he might know more than I do. He loosens his grip but stays close to me, and I realize that he's genuinely talking with me right now, and that he wants and needs me to say something.

"No, I have not, I have not taken the time to think about it," I say dryly.

He nods his head. "And me? Did you think about me? About what it would do to my life, to have something like that happen while you're under my watch?" His eyes pierce holes through me.

Is that what I was supposed to think about?

"I didn't think about it because I don't know what to think about it. I don't know what happened."

"You know you didn't fall asleep. I told you what I've heard."

"You didn't really tell me."

"You want to hear for yourself?"

"No," I quickly say and my eyes escape his. "Because if that's what it is, it's horrific."

"It's horrific," he repeats after me, to emphasize what he thinks I'm not getting.

He demands my look, and when my eyes return to his he kisses me again and then backs away a little bit and looks at me, gently shakes his head as though saying, I give up.

"You have any idea what I'd think about you, if you'd died out there? How I'd remember you, after all this?"

"No."

"No. You wouldn't want me to remember you like that, because that's fucked up. Way too fucked up, Noa. Even for me."

10

Golden Gate Bridge

»

If things were normal, after everything Teddy's said I'd most likely sink all the way down to the bottom of my muddy soul. But things aren't normal, because Milo's here. So instead of introspection, I just pass the time with him. Day after day for a week. Slow walks with Xerox, joints, TV shows, food. I do my physio exercises while he's sprawled beside me with his phone. Weather's nice, beautiful days of early spring.

I learn a few things about Milo: he has a great sense of humor; he's not fast like Teddy and Adrian, but he's able to delve deep into complex matters; he's sensitive toward others; he's insecure and sometimes immature; he takes good care of his dog; and he has the cutest laugh I've ever heard from the day I was born and all the way till now.

Luckily I'm in a good mood when Teddy notifies me one morning: "I talked to Monique last night, I'm taking Milo to visit her for a few days."

My laptop's open in front of me, I close it and place it next to me on the bed.

"Okay. What do you mean 'taking Milo'? She's in Copenhagen, that's a lot of miles for 'taking.'"

"Yes, got a flight this evening." He goes into the walk-in closet.

I've already gotten used to hanging out with Milo, and now I'll have to part from him. But what matters is Milo, and I understand if he needs to be with his mother. "Is he happy about going?"

"What's that?" He takes some shirts off the rack and puts them in a pile on the bed.

"You packing already?"

"Yeah, I won't have time later. What were you asking?"

"If he's happy about going."

"He doesn't know yet. I'll tell him when he gets up."

Of course he doesn't know. His dad's Teddy Rosenfeld, deciding for him, not even bothering to tell him. And he'll probably never know that he doesn't know, that it's not him calling the shots.

"So you'll be away for a few days too." I put my hand on the pants piling up next to me on the bed.

"Yes."

"Cool. I'm sure you'll have a good time." I make an effort to sound positive and show that I'm not anxious about him leaving me here without him, and even worse—without Milo. "I'll watch over Xerox."

"No, Xerox is staying with his five-star dog sitter."

"Why?"

"Because I don't want to leave him here. You can hardly take care of yourself, so you'll take care of the dog now? But don't worry, you're not staying on your own, I'm getting you a chaperone."

"Sorry, what was that?"

"Someone to sit here, make sure you're not harming yourself."

"Stop it."

"Stop what?"

"You really think you're getting someone to watch me?"

"Yes."

"No, I'll leave."

"Then leave. If you're staying here—then not by yourself." He piles the clothes in the suitcase with the familiar motions of someone who has done this a million times.

"No, I won't have that."

"Why not? What's the problem? We'll get you someone nice enough—won't carry any weapons, of course, seeing as I'm not an idiot, but with a proper cock so he can fuck you the way you like it."

"Charming. You do see the twisted pathway leading from wanting to watch over me all the way to a proper cock."

"I see the pathway and I don't see what's twisted about it. But fine, whatever you want."

"What I want is for no one to watch me, what aren't you getting—"

"What am *I* not getting, that's what you're asking?"

"I don't need supervision."

"And what assurance do I have that you won't sink into some depression and decide to do something stupid?"

"I've gone through too much shit this past month to do anything stupid."

"And if you don't answer the phone when I call? What, I'll have to send Matt over to check on you?"

"No. No Matt. You're not sending anyone over."

He moves the suitcase to the armchair and goes into the bathroom.

"I'll settle for you texting me every hour on the hour," he says from the bathroom.

"Text you what? Like notify you that I'm alive?"

"Yes."

"This is such bullshit, honestly."

"It is what it is." He comes back out and puts his toiletry bag next to the suitcase.

Better off texting him than having to live with a chaperone. "How about every two hours?" I try to tilt the terms my way.

"No." He shuts the bedroom door.

"I feel like rebelling."

"No, that's not what I'm doing here." He finally deigns to approach me. "I seriously won't have it. I'm telling you."

"Because you're worried?"

"Yes." He picks up my laptop and puts it aside.

I give him an amused look. "Really?"

"What is it, you don't believe me?"

"No."

"All right. You don't believe me, and I don't trust your judgment. Sounds about right, your average couple." He sits down next to me.

"We're a couple?"

"Fuck no." He smiles at me, shoves the blanket away and reveals my thigh. I look at his hand caressing me. When he touches me like that, I can allow myself to ask things.

"Why are you only telling me about this trip now?"

"When was I supposed to tell you?"

"Never mind." I have to choose my battles. "How can you say that you're worried, and at the same time you tell me 'then leave'?"

"I'm not letting you leave. What are you talking about? You're not going anywhere."

"You said so."

"I wouldn't have let you. Not an option."

I laugh. "So I'm actually held captive here?"

"You can look at it that way, why not?" He pulls the entire blanket aside. "And now, let me fuck you."

"Why?"

"Because that's what I want, that's why."

He takes off my underwear in one swift yet careful move, then pulls me so I'm half seated and takes off my shirt and holds my face with both hands and kisses me, backs off for a moment and just looks at me. And then it starts.

His mouth on mine, his hands hold me, and I kiss him back and feel a swell of heat pouring from him to me. What do we have here? He loves me, that's what we have here. He has no way of hiding it, he's not even trying. He moves the pillows from behind me and lays me down on the sheet, then uses the pillows to set up my leg in a safe posture. He stands up and looks at my naked body, takes off his pants and underwear and lies on top of me, leans on his elbows and kisses my neck. I shove my hand down and grab his cock, tighten my fingers around it. He shifts his weight to his left elbow, his right hand goes between my legs and I spread as much as I can manage and feel his cock going in deep—and we both release moans at the same time.

A month and a half.

Six weeks of not feeling him this way. Both his elbows are on the bed, his hands hold my face, and he looks at me and then looks down. He's looking at himself fucking me. He puts one hand on my lower stomach and slides it down and presses so that every time his cock goes in, I feel it even more, and he doesn't stop looking at me so I look back at him and we kiss and I love him, especially when he's fucking me, especially like this.

He stops, and I stop too and just feel him and smell him and want him.

"I really am worried about you. Even if you don't believe me."

"Okay. Then I'll take the every-hour-on-the-hour deal."

>

11:00 am I'm alive

Good

They took the night flight. I'm home alone.

12:00 pm I'm alive

Thank God

I'm sitting in the living room. The house is empty and quiet, warm light. The night was exhausting; my dreams exasperated me and I woke up drenched in sweat again. What will I do here on my own for five days?

Now that I think about it, I haven't been on my own for a long time. I calculate the days, count back a week until I reach the day I went to the doctor, which is the day he got the recording. I haven't been alone for a minute since. But he did leave. He left the morning after, and Dawn was here. Dawn! Dawn was here, but she left only after he came back! How have I only just realized this?

Can you talk?

Yes call

He picks up. "Hi."

"Did you tell Dawn to stay with me till you got back?"

"Who?"

"Dawn. The physio—"

"Yeah, yeah, Dawn. What about her?"

"The day she was here, did you tell her to stay until you got back?"

"Yes. Why? What's the problem?"

"You're fucked up, that's the problem."

"Yes, all right, is that what you called to tell me?"

"Yes."

"Glad we had this talk. We're in the suburbs, in Nico's new house. You should see the view from his backyard. Amazing. I'll tell Milo to send you a photo." Someone says something to him. "Noa, we'll talk later."

"Okay, bye."

He asked Dawn not to leave me alone. Embarrassing. That's the only thought in my head, that it's embarrassing.

1:00 pm I'm alive

Very good

My dad calls. "Hello? I can't hear a thing. Hello?"

"Hi, Dad."

"Noa? Can you hear me?"

"Yes. And you?"

"Yeah, I can hear you."

"Good."

"How are you? How are things? How are you feeling? How's the pain?"

I give some trivial replies, and then he gets to the crux of the matter.

"Listen, I've actually got some good news. Maybe it'll cheer you up."

Why assume I need cheering up?

"Nurit—" He coughs. "She's decided to withdraw that whole apartment thing, she told me—she called me last night, but it was late, so I couldn't—"

I interrupt him. "I don't care about it, leave me out of it."

"What? No, she's retracting," he continues explaining as though I'm not getting it. "She wants it to be in your name too. That's a good thing, Noa. I don't know, maybe the accident knocked some sense into her."

"Yes." I'm starting to get pissed off. "And now in return for her generosity she wants me to meet her?"

"No, she didn't mention anything like that."

"All right, you do realize you're just pestering me—I mean, that she's pestering me, through you."

"Why would you say that? I understand this isn't your top priority right now, and that you're recovering and all, but I thought you'd be glad to hear that the whole thing's off the table. That's all."

I stay quiet. No point trying to explain to him that she's just resolved a problem she herself had created. I listen to another thirty seconds of sentence beginnings, and the moment he stops for air I say some good-byes and hang up. I take a deep breath and put my injured leg in the robotic contraption Teddy got me, which is meant to compensate for the lack of movement.

"If you're not a chaperone, then I don't know who is—am I right or am I right?" I tell the robot physiotherapist. His humming is the only sound in the apartment. "Right."

At 2:00 p.m. I don't need to notify Teddy I'm alive, since a few minutes beforehand he asks me to call him.

"Listen, I need you to do something. Matt's coming over in a bit, I need you to give him the key to the King George apartment."

"Okay. Why?"

"There's a problem there, burst pipe, I don't know exactly. I want him to go over there and check it out for me."

"I can go too."

"What for?"

"To see what's happening there, to help out."

He thinks for a moment. "And what about your leg? Will you man-age?"

"Yeah, yes. Of course." I'm glad to have a task, though slightly con-cerned about going back to his mother's eerie apartment.

"Okay, you can join him if you want. When you get there, look for Shlomo, the neighbor, he'll help you if you need anything."

"Okay."

"You know which key it is? It's hanging at the entrance, the one with the yellow key chain."

"Right." I get up and go look for the key.

"Wait—Milo, come here a sec, take my phone, send Noa Shlomo Alffassi's number, here, Noa, Milo's going to send you Shlomo's num-ber, okay? Found the key?"

"Yes."

"All right. How you feeling? You miss me?"

﹥

The burst pipe is indeed inside Teddy's mother's wall, but most of the water is leaking into the downstairs neighbor's apartment, and she's reacting to the situation with disproportionate hysteria. I help her sweep the water out, maneuvering between the crutch and the mop and using my finest diplomatic tone to calm her down, promising we'll compensate her for any damages. I think it was a good idea to come here, mainly because Matt seems to get on the lady's nerves, which is understandable.

Shlomo the neighbor also tries to calm her down; after all, he loves Teddy and wants to keep a good relationship with him. He excitedly tells me how ten years ago, his daughter had to undergo a complex surgery and the insurance didn't cover it or they weren't even insured, and how one day, Shlomo bumped into Teddy in the stairwell and cried about the terrible situation they were in, and then Teddy just told him he'll fund the entire treatment.

"You have to understand—he's as charitable as they get!" His aged hand clenches into a fist and then rises up to wipe a drop of spit from his lower lip. "Are you wedded to his son?"

While I wait for the plumber, I bring Teddy up to speed. Matt goes out to get a coffee for me and a burrito for him—he reacts to stressful situations with hunger, or so he says. I walk around all alone in the stifling apartment, feeling something different from what I felt before.

On the little bedside table, under a layer of dust, her things rest in peace: lip balm, medication, a handkerchief, two cases for glasses (one of them empty), a tube of hand cream, a little leatherbound notepad with a miniature Parker pen peering from inside. I pick up the notepad, my fingers leaving round marks in the dust.

This place needs to be taken apart; she needs to be allowed to leave. That's what she'd have wanted I think.

>

> 10:00 am I'm alive
>
> No word from you for 8 hours
>
> I was asleep!

Time goes by slowly.

I watch movie after movie, series after series, no longer choosing the content, whatever's in front of me goes. I come out to the living room, stroll around the deserted home. Walk into Teddy's office, look through stuff. Find a photo album: photos of a young Teddy with Alice and baby Adrian. Two pages later and I start feeling incredibly melancholic, so instead of diving into his memories, I shut the album and leave the room. Text back and forth with Sharon, she says she'll come visit later on in the week.

Roy texts me a link to a song we used to listen to together, it's about knowing there's always somewhere to come back to. I listen to it and get a bit emotional. At least he and Thomas are living in my apartment in the meantime, until I recover. That helps me feel less guilty about my reaction to their "till death do us part" announcement. To be honest, the accident that followed that announcement also makes me feel guilty.

Or maybe pathetic.

I once heard about someone who tried to commit suicide by jumping off the Golden Gate Bridge but ended up surviving. He said that a moment after his hands let go of the rail, he felt this huge regret. How come I don't recall feeling like that?

>

> 5:00 pm I'm alive

I'm lying on the living room rug, closely observing the couch's leg. There's direct sun at this hour, and it's lighting the corner formed between the floor and the wooden leg of the couch. It almost looks like a miniature street corner.

I don't know what I've done but it doesn't feel right. I should start figuring out what happened.

It's not something that started that same day. I need to go back to the starting point. Which of the points is the starting one?

There's an easy one. I sit up and open the calendar on my phone. If I cross-reference our texts and the calendar, I believe I'll be able to reconstruct a whole lot.

September 15—this is when we met.

Yes. I now know what I need to do during these coming days.

《

It's mid-September and I'm in the middle of a rough patch.

》

By the time they return from Denmark, it seems like the storm's over. I don't tell him that I'm writing, that I really am conducting research, but he must have noticed that I'm busy and in a better mood since he loosens his grip. He's busy with his own things and I start to calm down, thinking that we're back to the way things were and we're okay, until this one night when he says something that's definitely not okay.

Maybe I misheard him?

"You did what?"

"I had coffee with your mom today," he repeats the same sentence, which turns out I'd heard just fine the first time around.

He had coffee with 'your mom' today! No, this is not happening. I rise from my sprawled position on the couch and sit up.

"What do you mean you had coffee with her? Why would you have coffee with her, what are you talking about?"

"It's not that complicated. Need me to say it again?" He stands in the middle of the living room.

"Are you joking?"

"No. Not joking."

"What?" Blood rushes up and pulses through my temples as I realize this is real. "Why did you meet her? What the fuck? Why did you do that?!" I'm furious, and then I start thinking that maybe this has something to do with my dad or actually with the accident. "Did she call you after my accident?"

"No. She didn't call me."

"Then what?"

"I was the one who called her."

"*You* called *her*?"

"Yes."

"After the accident? At the hospital, during the surgery?"

"No, it has nothing to do with your accident."

"Then what are you talking about? You just picked up the phone? 'Hey, Nurit, it's Noa's dad here'?"

"What was that?" He caught my slip of the tongue. "No, I didn't introduce myself as your dad." He's not smiling, but he's obviously pleased about my slip.

"Great."

"So you want to hear about it?" He sits down on the armchair in front of me.

I stare at him with a frozen face; my heart's pounding and I'm hot. "When did you call her? Today?"

"No, a while back."

"What's 'a while back'? When?" I'm about to die.

"When did I call her?" He thinks for a moment. "December. Late December."

"December?! It's March! No, you really are a sick individual, I mean, what the fuck?" I suddenly realize. "Roy! After Roy came over here!"

"Yes," he confirms dryly, refusing to get riled up.

I feel little pinpricks all over my body, skin tightening. "That was ages ago. Why did you only meet her today?"

"I met her today too."

"What did you just say? What was that? No, no, this is not happening."

"Today was the third time."

I'm trying to calm down because I feel violence starting to take over. "Why didn't you tell me about it before?"

"I didn't want to."

"You didn't want to. You do know there's literally nothing worse you could have done to me. Do you realize that?"

"No. I don't see it that way. On the contrary."

"You're an asshole. You don't do that, you don't do something like that, Teddy, you should never—You abusive, egotistical, scumbag, motherfucking piece of shit, you should never, fifty-five years on this planet weren't enough for you to realize you don't meddle in people's— And what were you thinking, that you'd force me to get back in touch with her? That you're saving me? What is it that goes through that vain, megalomaniac brain of yours?"

"You should know that she's quite an exceptional woman."

"Just fucking die already!"

"Really. You'd love her. You're missing out on a mom you'd love."

"You're so out of line right now there's hardly any goddamn line left."

"Keep it down. You think I'm not mad at her?"

"You're mad at her! Oh, thank you, I'm so very grateful! Why are you mad at her? She's exceptional! Why would anyone ever be mad at that exceptional, charming woman?"

"I'm mad at her because you're so profoundly wounded."

"All right, why don't you take your self-righteous, protective bullshit and stick it right back in your ego—"

"That's enough."

"I am done with you, Teddy—I've finally built trust—"

"Enough, Noa."

"I've finally built trust with you—"

"I said that's enough!" He shuts me up and starts talking at a fast pace: "You've trusted me since day one, from the first minute, from the first fuck, and you know it, so don't bullshit me!" He crams all those words in one breath.

Doesn't matter how angry I am with him and how justified it is, the moment he raises his voice I instinctively recoil. I look at him with pure loathing, biting my lip, not knowing what to do with myself. "Doing something like that shows that you just don't know me, that you don't understand who I am."

"Oh I understand who you are all right, believe me."

"The third time . . . You've met her three times! And what exactly did you do? Sit there and talk about us? About how we fuck? What?"

"We talked about a lot of things. Not just about you. She wants to be in touch with you, so even sitting there talking to me about politics means something to her. What don't you get? It's just another way of reaching you. And yes, she talks to me about needing to know what's happening with you, and your dad won't do it and Roy absolutely refuses to talk about you, because he lives in constant fear that you'll sever ties with him too if he dares to mention even the smallest thing."

The way he's describing me makes my anger morph into injury. I get up from the couch. "Well, okay, I get it. Maybe I really should sever ties with Roy for giving you her number." I walk toward the big table.

He ignores my comment and my walking away. "And she asks about you, of course, carefully."

I'm looking for my phone, but for some reason it's not on the table. "Asks what? If I'm grateful about her retracting her decision to not include me in the apartment inheritance thing?"

"I don't know anything about an apartment or inheritance. What are you talking about?"

"Never mind." I take a deep breath. She asks about me and he tells her. They have their own bond, words have been uttered, she knows things about me, she knows because Teddy told her. What does she know? I find my phone on the kitchen counter but can't remember why I'd looked for it and what I'm supposed to do with it.

He walks into the kitchen, stands facing me, towering and calm. "What's the deal with the inheritance? She wanted to put it in Roy's name?"

I ignore the questions. "What does she know about me? What did you tell her about me?"

"What do you think I did? I told her you're sweet and brilliant and talented, that you're one of a kind. That you're incredibly hurt, that even I can't shift that place inside you."

"Oh yeah?" I look him right in the eye, hoping that all my hatred will pour into him and destroy his internal organs.

"Yes." Sadly he survives and looks back at me.

"And why do you need to shift anything inside me?" The tears are about to burst out.

"Because I care about you, what do you mean 'why'?"

I press my hands over my treacherous eyes. "I will not forgive you for this."

"I understand that."

"You don't do something like that." I look down.

"You didn't leave much choice. They're all terrified of you."

I look back at him with raging eyes. "Shame you're not."

"Good thing I'm not." He smiles softly.

"Why did you meet her? You're mine! You're not supposed to meet her, and behind my back no less, and three times! And you hide it from me for three months! I can't even look at you." I walk around him and leave the kitchen and continue all the way to the entrance and then out the door, slamming it behind me, but it immediately opens again.

"Noa." He follows me out.

I press for the elevator. The tears are running down my face and I have nothing and I don't care about anything anymore and I just want to go home—not even sure where that is—maybe with Sharon, I don't know, I'm alone in the world, now more than ever, there's no one. The elevator arrives and opens but I don't go in, just slowly slide down the wall till I reach the floor and cry into my hands. He stands next to me, leaning against the wall. The crying doesn't cease, I have no control over it. It comes up in massive waves, a flood carrying an old, inexplicable pain along with it; it's not a common pain. You might say it's the lord of all pain.

Teddy keeps standing there, occasionally says my name or asks for us to go back in, but mostly just stands there. The winds are blowing from opposite sides: my need for him to stay next to me and absorb all the anguish collides with a wall of anger, a clear awareness of complete, absolute, terminal abandonment. I think of all the words I've written about all that's happened to me with Teddy, and how I made everything revolve around him. I'm even angry at my words right now, loathing my need for them. I knew nothing would come out of this.

I don't know how long we stay there, but at some point the elevator opens. I leave my hands on my face, can't deal with anyone right now, but then I feel something warm and wet on my hand and recognize Xerox's nails tapping on the floor and the rustle of his leash.

"What happened to Noa? Is she crying?" It's Milo.

Teddy doesn't answer, maybe gestures with a look. I can't see them, but I hear Teddy going back into the apartment. Milo leans down and puts his hand on my knee. "What happened?"

My crying intensifies and I'm embarrassed to have him see me like this.

"Why are you crying?" he asks gently. "Let's go inside?"

"I don't want to see him right now," I quietly say, and I don't care that it's not a nice thing to say to a kid about his dad.

"Let's go to my room, he won't go in there." Milo must know his dad better than I thought.

I know that I have nowhere else to go. I slowly get up, and we go into the apartment and walk straight to Milo's room. I don't see Teddy but I hear the TV from his room and I know precisely what position he's lying down in. What I don't know is how he's feeling, and if he's capable of feeling at all.

On the balcony on Milo's side, I'm protected from Teddy. Milo tries to roll us a joint, but he can't hack it.

"Here, hand it over."

What do I do? Why did he meet her? I hate him, I really do. I want to get the fuck out of here. I'm tired. What's the time? It's 11:43 p.m. already. I'm not going to sleep in the same bed as him. No way. I can sleep in the upstairs guest room, but it'll be difficult to get up there with my leg, and there's no bathroom there either. My throat hurts, my neck too. Just what I needed now. I'd really like some hot tea, but I won't go to the kitchen because I don't want to see him.

Where did they meet, Teddy and Nurit?

I haven't seen her in years, she must have aged.

I feel sick.

❭

In the morning I wake up on the couch in Milo's room. He's asleep a few feet away from me, in his bed. Teddy didn't come in at night but he's here now. He shifts me aside and sits next to me.

He talks quietly so that Milo doesn't wake up. "Made you coffee, come have some." I stay lying down and look at him. My throat hurts, it hurts to swallow.

"You slept on the couch here?" He quickly glances around the room. "Yes."

"All right. How are you?" he asks and immediately continues: "Come to the living room, I want to talk to you. I'm leaving soon, I need to get to the office."

"Then leave, we have nothing to talk about."

"Noa."

"No, it's— You went too far. And you dare tell me that I'm fucked up?"

"Come outside." He puts his hand on me, over the blanket.

"I can't believe you did that to me."

"All right, better start believing it." His tone is harsh even when he speaks quietly. "And go meet her already. Don't you see how you're tormenting yourself? You've executed your ten-year-old self's decision beautifully, well done you, but it's been twenty-five years. It's unacceptable."

"Leave me alone."

"No. And by the way, it'll make everyone's lives easier. Your dad and Roy, you really think you're doing anyone any good this way?"

"Well don't you just know everything, Teddy." I give him a look full of contempt.

"That's enough," he reprimands me, and for a minute he even manages to make me feel like I'm the one in the wrong here. "I need to go, I'll talk to you later," he says and leaves.

>

My head hurts.

There's a note on the kitchen counter. I approach it and see 'Nurit' in Teddy's handwriting and a number underneath it. Fucking gross. At least he didn't text me her contact details (with a profile picture of him and her smiling at the camera).

When did Teddy ask Roy for her number? When Roy came over they didn't spend a single moment alone without me. So Teddy called him afterward? What did he say to him? And why didn't Roy tell me about it? So actually, Roy knows they've met. I'm losing my mind.

I make some tea and text Roy.

> Why did you give Nurit's number
> to Teddy and why didn't you tell
> me about it

I even send it without a question mark. There, he's typing.

Typing . . .

Typing . . .

Come on, send a reply already. Asshole. I'll smoke a cigarette even though I feel like shit.

> Good morning to you too!
> Because he asked and also told
> me in his own way not to tell you.
> And since I owe him lots and lots
> of money, I do whatever he says,
> thank you very much! And sorry.

Moron. Not only does he know they're meeting, but he's also aware of the fact that I had no idea. That makes the whole thing even worse! What does it mean, 'in his own way'? I try to imagine their conversation:

Hi Roy, it's Teddy. / Teddy! How are you? / I'm great, swell, no troubles here. Listen kiddo— / Yeah? / Send me Nurit's number. I want to talk to her. / Our mom, Nurit? / Yes. I just want to control everything and everyone. / Aye aye, Captain! No questions asked, sending it over to you ASAP! / All right, and let's keep this between us, it'll be our sick little secret—

All right, this isn't doing me any good.

I need to plan my moves, but I feel horrendous so I take some pain-killers and lie down on Teddy's neatly made bed, just for a short rest, until the drugs kick in.

I wake up after 3:00 p.m. I'm sick, no doubt about it. Great, no problem, why not? My face is burning, my muscles hurt, my neck's stiff and my existence sucks.

Texts from Teddy are waiting on my phone:

> 1:54 pm How are you
>
> 2:02 pm Call me
>
> 2:04 pm Noa

I should reply. I'll make some tea first.

Milo and Xerox must have gone out. I wait for the water to boil and try to phrase a reply.

> I slept, I don't feel well. |

No. Don't want to be sick and weak and pathetic and dependent.

> Everything's fine|

Bullshit.

> Hope you die|
>
> Fuck you|
>
> Why did you meet her? Why did you do that to me? What kind of a fucking asshole does that? |

Eventually I reply:

> Fine, was sleeping

Bullshit.

What do I do?

How can it be that I had no idea they've been talking for three months now? Just like with Lara, when I found out they talk every day. How come I never hear him talking to her?

And now this. I don't want to be here.

I'll pack my things and leave. Where will I go? Anywhere, as long as I'm not here. Roy and Thomas are at my apartment, the last thing I want is to go there, let alone hang out with those two right now. But I'm not staying here, I'm even better off at my dad and Mina's. Okay, maybe not. Tom and Alison's? Don't feel like entering a couple dynamic, especially when she's pregnant. Should I go to Sharon's? The mere thought of the commotion at her place . . . I'll go to my place, my brother and Thomas can figure something out.

My leg's hurting more than ever, of course. My body's telling me it prefers to stay here, but I shut off, take some more painkillers—momentarily consider downing the entire pack and maybe even all the painkillers in the apartment, but now even dying isn't allowed here. Where's my bag? In the closet, Betty must have put it there. Teddy likes it when everything's in its place. Betty likes it when Teddy's pleased. Teddy and Betty may very well share a burial plot, funeral times to be announced.

There, my clothes are in my bag. I limp toward the bathroom, and I actually have only a toothbrush and some makeup here and everything else is his, even the deodorant I use is his. Back to the room. Shoes. Straighten the blanket. Text from Teddy.

>   Call me

I pack the laptop and call him.

"Hi." I try to summon positive energy in my tone.

"Were you sleeping?"

"Yes."

"Okay. How are you?"

"Next question." I can't be completely inauthentic, otherwise he'll be onto me straightaway.

He takes a breath. "You don't need to be so angry."

"Why not?"

"Because it doesn't get you anywhere."

He makes my blood boil, but I can't get into it with him right now. Need to buy some time, that's all. "We'll talk when you get here."

"All right. I'll be back later."

I think I've got everything. Goodbye, sweet home, you're wonderful but your owner isn't, so I have to leave. I place the key on the console by the entrance. There's the rug we fucked on—bye to you too.

Turn the alarm on and shut the door behind me.

298 | MAYA KESSLER

>

I'm out.

The sun's not that strong anymore, the street's got that much-hated afternoon energy. Where do I limp from here? Where do I sleep? I call Roy, but he doesn't pick up, of course. Some brother. I hate him for not picking up. Must be scared of me, lousy coward. How could he be in on this? Is he even aware of the fact that without me he'd never have gotten Teddy's help? Ungrateful brat.

I think about Teddy walking in, seeing I'm not there. I was so wrong to get into this relationship with him. And I thought I was so clever. There's a taxi.

I give him my address and recall that day when we got into a taxi and he came over to my place and we fucked for the first time. I even remember the smell. I'm jealous of past-me, of the reality I had back then. Enough, it's over and done with. Do I even have a key to my place? Suddenly I'm not sure. Have I taken my set of keys? Yes, after I took Teddy's key off it. My apartment key's not on it—of course! Because I gave it to Roy, who wanted Thomas to have it and swore he'd copy it and give it back. Fuck! Call Roy again, no answer. Texting Roy:

Where are you???

And wait to see if he's seen it. Nothing.

"Excuse me." I lean toward the driver, the scent of his sweat managing to penetrate my blocked nose.

"What?"

"When we get there I need you to wait, because I don't have a key, so we might have to go to a different address."

"Traffic jam's not moving right now. When we get there you can talk to me about when we get there."

A kid running away from home doesn't have to deal with puny things like heavy traffic or stinking taxi drivers. I don't have Thomas's number, let's hope he's home. It was a bad idea to take the painkillers on an empty stomach, now I feel nauseated too.

"We're here," the driver says.

"One sec, I need to go up and make sure someone's home."

I reach for the door handle, but only then it hits me that I didn't take into account all the stairs and the state of my leg, and now I feel stupid. What was I thinking? No intercom, the only way to see if someone's home is to go upstairs and knock on the door. The driver has nowhere to pull over and a row of cars is gathering behind us. Someone honks.

"I can't stop here."

"Then never mind, just go."

"'Go'? Go where?"

"I don't know, start by freeing up the road for them. Ride around the block for a minute."

He grumbles and starts driving and I call Roy but he still doesn't pick up. I call Sharon.

"Where am I going?" the driver asks in a crude tone.

"West."

"Now west? Then what did we drive through all that traffic for?"

I feel like screaming at him to just shut up, that I'm paying him and if one more person mistreats me I'll slaughter them, but instead of attacking I discover a whole new side of myself and simply don't answer him.

"Hey honey." Unlike Roy, my loyal Sharon picks up the phone, sounds of children in the background.

"Shar, are you home? I'm coming over."

"Hell yeah! Sure, come over. Is everything okay?"

I give the driver her address and lean back. It's almost 6:00 p.m. Teddy hasn't tried to reach me, which means he's not home yet. I guess he's fine with me simmering for the last few hours within the nightmare scenario he's concocted. Must be stalling at the office to delay the moment he'll have to see me again. Don't worry, problem solved.

It takes a while, but the taxi eventually makes it west. When we arrive on Sharon's street, my phone starts ringing. It's Roy. I quickly answer it, growling at him.

"Thank you so much for getting back to me and for taking the key to my apartment and for not answering so when I got there I couldn't go in or even go all the way up to check if Thomas was there."

"What, what, what? What are you talking about? Why are you shouting at me?"

"And what were you thinking giving Teddy her number, and why didn't you tell me something that important? And this was three months ago! You knew he was meeting her, how could you keep this from me?!"

"What are you talking about? I just gave him her number!"

The taxi stops. "We're here. Should I drive back to the east side now?"

"I'm in a taxi, just got to Sharon's place and I need to get out. I'll call you."

"Call me? What's going on? Did we make plans for today? I'm in Jerusalem, I've got rehearsals here all day."

"Right, I've got to go, call you back."

I pay the driver—I don't care how expensive it's turned out to be—and cumbersomely get out of the taxi, pulling my bag out behind me. The driver looks back and sees the crutches in the back seat. He quickly unbuckles himself and gets out, reaches me and pulls the crutches out.

"Sorry, I didn't see you had these, didn't notice when you got in."

In the stairwell I feel that my leg's better now, but the walking's still slow. The farther up I get, the louder the noise from her apartment is. Sharon opens the door with little Elijah in her arms; the kids run up to see who's arrived.

"You should have told me, I'd have come down to give you a hand." Sharon puts the squirt down and he crawls away. She takes my bag. "How you doing?"

I go in, hug the kids and try to protect my leg. "Shit."

"What should I make you? Want some porridge, yummy yummy in the tummy?" We laugh and five-year-old Ariel pulls me by the hand toward her room as Dori runs after us. My phone rings and I pull it out of my jacket pocket. It's Teddy. Ariel loudly chatters about the little pony house. My phone keeps ringing. Don't pick up. I sit down on Ariel's bed; Dori joins me and shows off his flashlight. Ariel pulls it out of his hand and he gets upset and starts crying. I give it back to him and keep her busy with her ponies.

I don't know what to say to him. In a way I'm hoping that he isn't home yet, and if he is home then maybe he hasn't noticed my stuff's gone. I'm not calling him back, I decide as I diligently recite the lines my pony's been given by Ariel the director—I'm not calling him because I don't want to say what I have to say. So what's left?

Sharon gets the kids to sit down to eat: Elijah repeatedly knocks his plastic spoon on the tray, Dori eats quietly and occasionally inserts his spoon into a crack in his seat, getting it all dirty. Ariel doesn't want to eat, she wants to jump rope. Sharon tries to entice her to sit down but it falls on deaf ears, and then Dori gets up from the table and joins Ariel.

I go out to the balcony and light a cigarette. The painkillers are wearing off and the pain is resurfacing. Joe, Sharon's husband, comes home and she immediately hands Elijah over and comes out to the balcony with a cup of coffee. "Give me a drag."

"Better have your own, I think I'm a little sick." I hand her the pack.

"Then forget it, I'm better off not smoking. How's the leg? I thought you weren't even leaving the house."

"I hardly was. But I had to get out of there."

"What is it, you two had a fight and you walked out?"

"No, I left without him knowing, after he left for work."

"Mom!" from inside.

"Work it out!" she shouts, and quietly adds, "You have reached Mom, please call back during office hours." Sharon has a sour-toned voice, which is my favorite voice of all voices. "So what's happening? What happened?"

"Last night he told me he's been meeting Nurit behind my back for a few months."

"Get out! No fucking way!" Sharon reacts with shock just like I needed her to.

"Mom!" from inside again, and I try to figure out which one of them is calling her, but Sharon ignores the shouts. "Okay, give me a cigarette. I can't fucking believe this."

"Right?"

"Why is he meeting her?" She lights her cigarette. "Trying to mediate, or what? Who does he think he is?"

Joe peers out at the balcony from inside. "Look who's here! To what do we owe the honor?"

"Hey!" I'm glad to see him.

Sharon maintains the inertia of questions: "And what do you mean 'a few months'? Does it have something to do with the accident?"

"Mom! My tooth fell out! My tooth fell out!" Ariel crams herself between Joe and the doorframe and manages to wriggle out, then proudly presents us with her little mouth, now missing a front tooth. It's her first time and we're all excited about it, but then she gets upset by all the attention and starts crying. Joe takes Dori and Elijah to the bathroom, Sharon and I try to calm Ariel down, and I find my little tin box—thoroughly empty of its original contents, of course—give it a rinse and hand it to Ariel so she can keep her tooth in it.

Sharon bursts out laughing when she hears what the box was previously used for. The commotion continues until they're all tucked in for the night. When the living room lights get turned off there's finally silence, except for the washing machine's vigorous spin cycle. I go over to my phone, which hasn't been abandoned this long for weeks now.

He didn't try me again. I suddenly feel weird. Maybe I shouldn't have taken my stuff? The chaos here had distracted me from feeling sick, and now I sense the weight again. I want to lie down. Where will I sleep here?

>

I'm lying on the couch Sharon's fixed up for me. The whole place is asleep. I'm supposed to be sleeping too, but I'm too sad. I can't see what's left for me. Here they are, in a home full of a family they've made, kids they've created from their own reproductive cells. What have I done this past year? What have I done for the past ten years? Where has it gotten me?

Here comes the accident again.

Maybe I would have been better off dying there—although then I wouldn't have had Teddy's outburst of love during the days following the hospitalization. But what kind of love do we have here if he goes behind my back and does something like that?

"Honey?" Sharon's familiar voice whispers in the dark.

"Aren't you asleep?" I ask quietly.

"No. Want some more tea?"

"Yes. And a cigarette."

"But of course. Come on."

We're on the balcony again, but now there are no disruptions, just me and Sharon and hot tea. She rolls herself a cigarette in the dark and asks how Teddy has given himself permission to meddle in my life so aggressively. We try to figure it out. She says that she can see the good intention, but she has to go through the anger first—just like me.

"But that's not the main thing here." I say, "And I know that, and still can't get myself to focus on it. And every time I try, my brain rushes straight back to all the meaningless details."

"Yes, I get that. What's the main thing then?"

"I don't know." I try to organize my thoughts out loud: "They met. He didn't tell me about it. Okay, whatever. And what's next? What does it even mean? Because if I don't want to see her then it shouldn't matter to me."

"Of course it should matter to you." She blows on her tea to cool it down. "It should matter to you either way. But do you want to? Do you want to see her?"

"Ew, no. Just the mere thought and I can't breathe."

"Just like back in grade school." Sharon smiles.

"What, with the breathing?"

"Yeah, when you used to get those short-of-breath episodes all the time."

"And Zeligowski kept kicking me out of class for breathing too loudly."

We both laugh and she says, "Poor thing, that was horrible."

"It was horrible. I was such a screwed-up kid."

"True that."

"And what does she even want? What sort of relationship does she have in mind? Because I can't just sit next to her and talk or hug her." The thought of her hugging me makes me feel deeply uncomfortable.

"No. No hugging, I totally get that."

"I don't know her, I don't know us." I cough and then sip my tea. "Ariel lost a tooth today. Did I ever lose my first tooth? Did Nurit give me a little box to put it in? Did she also have a dubious little tin box to spare?"

Sharon looks at me lovingly.

"I know that she couldn't stand her life. I've been thinking about it and blaming her and getting angry at her for years. Now that I think about it, if I were in her shoes, I couldn't stand that life either."

"Yeah."

"I'm just tired of the whole thing. Tired of the blaming too."

"Then maybe you should meet her." She rips off a dry leaf from a potted plant. "That way at least you can control the narrative."

"Maybe." I shrug my shoulders. I've got to go lie down again. "He's such a goddamn motherfucking piece of shit."

〉

I'm under the covers again, but sleep isn't showing the slightest bit of interest in me and I can't breathe and my mind won't let go.

And say we meet, then what? And say I sit with her and we talk— then what about?

Life? Men?

Teddy?

What does she think about him? She can probably see that he's something else. She likes him, no doubt about it. He must have charmed her; not only did he reach out to her, but he even kept his word and granted her some access to me. I bet she adores him. How did she feel when her phone rang? A man's coarse voice about to change her life.

Nurit, hi, this is Teddy, I'm Noa's friend. (Is that how he introduced himself?)

And she said:

----- ----- ----- ----- ----- -----?

No. Can't do it. No idea how to imagine her reply. What kind of voice does she even have? What kind of things does she say?

I'm sad. I'm angry at Teddy for choosing to do this. He's destroyed his relationship with me as far as I'm concerned. The sadness amplifies my need to talk to him, but it's already late at night. And I haven't called him back so he must be pissed off.

Teddy.

The way he picked me up from the hospital that day to take me to his place—breezing through the discharge process, the staff hypnotized by him. In the hospital elevator, he leans down and whispers in my ear, "If you happen to think I'm not dying to fuck your brains out in this wheelchair, then you've got it very wrong." He straightens up, but I gesture for him to lean back down so he can hear me.

"My brain's already fucked."

"Still some work to be done."

I smile. He does too.

On the way home he orders a ridiculous amount of food. I use the crutches and we go upstairs. When we enter the apartment, I say I want to shower. He goes with me and we try to figure out how I'm supposed to do it because it's hard for me to stand. At least the bandages covering the stitches are waterproof. I slowly undress and he helps me, making a real effort and kneeling down. I straighten up and lean on the crutches and he nears his face to my stomach, strokes it and closes his eyes and breathes deeply.

"I missed this."

"No, no, get away, I smell like hospital."

I'm standing naked in front of him with a huge bruise around my bloodshot eye and a deep cut on my lip, all on the same side of my face. He gets up, dressed and tall, and all the pain of the first few days after surgery just vanishes into thin air.

"Can you handle standing like that for a minute?"

I nod my head, and he unbuttons his shirt and takes off his pants.

"All right, let's get you in."

I stand inside his spacious shower and he's standing there with me, barefoot, in his underwear and undershirt, soaping me and getting wet. The water's warm and feels nice and the soap has that lovely familiar scent. I want to wash the hospital off me, the operation theater, the accident. He helps me shampoo my hair. When we finish, he wraps me up in a towel and carefully leads me to the bed, where my clean clothes await me. I dry myself sitting down, and he dresses me and gets my leg in a good position, and I slowly lie back.

He goes out of the room and returns with an ashtray, lights a cigarette and hands it to me. He sits in front of me on the bed and listens to everything I tell him. Then the doorbell rings, food's here. I stay alone for a few moments, look around.

He comes back in. "I'm bringing your food over here."

"Teddy."

"What?"

"Wait, come here for a minute."

He sits in front of me, close, his hand holding the back of my neck. He kisses me. Carefully. A long, meaningful kiss. I feel like he's been waiting—from the moment he got the call about the accident—he's been waiting to kiss me already.

"You really are something." He runs his thumb over the cut on my lip. "Doesn't it hurt?"

Our faces remain close. I lean in and kiss him again, a little kiss. He looks at me; his hand gently moves over my good leg.

"What about all the fucking-my-brains-out I was promised?" I ask even though it's clear that there's no way for my body to be in a state of fucking right now, and even if I could—I don't have an ounce of strength, as though all the life's been sucked out of me.

"When it happens—you'll know." He makes us laugh and heads to the kitchen.

12:58 a.m., I type a message to Teddy:

I couldn't stay|

No. That won't do; it's pointless, he won't have it.

1 a.m., and I automatically type:

I'm alive

I'll try to go to sleep, my eyes feel heavy. I don't even manage to put the phone down and he's already texted back.

Where are you

I don't miss a beat. Just reply.

> At Sharon's
>
> Wheres that
>
> It's west. Talk tomorrow?
>
> Should I come get you
>
> No
>
> Okay . Noa

How come he uses a full stop, and then even adds my name? How am I supposed to read that? And since when does he agree with my choices?

Great, even better. Leave it. Go to sleep.

A plane flies through the sky, sounds incredibly close, near landing.

+

I remember her putting makeup on in front of the mirror in the bathroom with the old tiles and the green Formica. She's about to go out. They're both going out, we're staying with the babysitter. I want to come up with something to tell her, something she'll find interesting. I stand inside the shower. It's strange, being in there with my clothes on, but I want to show her all the figures in the stains on the marble partition that separates the shower and the bathtub. There's the smelling man, he's small and white and looks like he has his hands behind his back as he leans down for a whiff, and there's the woman who can't stand straight because she has one leg shorter than the other, and there's the bear I love because he smiles. She leans down to be the same height as me, to see it from up close.

›

"Is that a little foot in my ribs?! Who's there? I'll eat you up!"

Elijah laughs and rolls over the couch.

"I told you not to wake her up!" Sharon tells him off quietly. "Sorry, honey, go back to sleep."

"No problem. Why, what time is it?"

"Six."

"Which six?"

"A.M.!"

I'll admit there's something about kids first thing in the morning that is so sweet that I genuinely enjoy them, but I absolutely don't get how people do this on a daily basis. I cover myself up again, but then I feel my throat hurting and decide to get out of bed to make some tea.

Everyone heads out pretty quickly, and I stay alone in the empty apartment, thinking I might go back to sleep. Even though Sharon asked me not to touch anything, I tidy up the house a bit, make their beds, wash the dishes from breakfast, put toys back in their place, fold the blanket and place it neatly over the couch.

Roy calls. "What was yesterday all about? Thanks for getting back to me like you said."

"Sorry, I was dealing with shit, but I shouldn't have shouted at you."

"You didn't tell me you wanted to come over; if I had known I'd have left you a key." He's using his self-righteous, placating tone.

"Yeah well, it wasn't planned."

"Okay, no problem."

Like there's no problem. "You do understand how wrong it is, what you did, right?"

"What do you want? You really think he couldn't have gotten her number without me?"

"Why didn't you tell me he asked?!" Yesterday's anger is resurfacing.

"Because he told me not to! Stop it, Noa, you know that this is between you two, and I'm asking you not to drag me into it, I feel uncomfortable about him as it is."

"How do you think it makes me feel to suddenly find out they've been meeting?! And that you've known about it and didn't say anything! Does that sound reasonable to you?"

"What do you mean 'meeting'? What are you talking about?"

"He's met her! A few times now."

"Really? I had no idea! She hasn't said anything about it to me."

"Goddamn it." I'm exhausted by this whole thing.

"Okay, I'm sorry I gave him her number and didn't tell you about it."

"Why didn't you tell me?"

"Because he told me not to."

"How did he say it?"

"I don't remember."

"Come on!" I lash out again.

"I swear! I don't remember! 'Let me talk to her about it,' something along those lines. It made total sense at the time."

"You know what? Whatever. Let's just drop it."

"Okay." He takes a breath. "Jesus. So what, you want to go back to your place? Should we vacate?"

"No, no. It won't be comfortable for me anyway, I don't know what I was thinking."

"But can you just explain what's happening?"

"Roy, just leave it. I'll be fine. But get me a key to the apartment, I want to have one."

"I need to make a copy."

"Then make a fucking copy!"

"Okay! I will. Sorry."

"Bye." I hang up without waiting for his goodbye.

Where will I go? Please figure something out. Tidy the kids' kitchenette: little plates go on the shelf, pile all the cups on this tray right here, their sink's full! The distress climbs up from my stomach to my chest and continues upward in the form of a headache. I need to call Teddy.

"Hey." He picks up and I can't decipher his mood. I try to talk but find it difficult, I pause, and he continues before I manage anything. "Why did you leave your key here?"

"Because I don't want to be at your place anymore."

"I see. All right. You took your things too," he notes.

"Yes. I'm sorry." Why am I apologizing? He's the one who's betrayed me. "What don't you get?"

"I get it all, darling." 'Darling'? Is he mad? He's mad. Fine. I'm mad too.

"Then why are you asking?"

"Because I think you're not right in the head, that's why I'm asking!" He surprises me and attacks, raises his voice. "You don't want to be at my place? Fine. Where will you go? Back to your apartment on the third floor with no elevator? Stay over at Sharon's?"

Interestingly enough, unlike me, he's not forgotten the whole stairs thing.

"I don't know yet. I'll tell you where I am, I'm not disappearing."

"Not disappearing," he repeats after me with contempt. "Forget it, you know what? I'll book you a hotel room, where do you want to go? I'd rather have you stay at a hotel than wander around like this."

I don't recognize him. I mean, I do, but something's changed. What's different?

"I don't need a hotel."

"We'll get you a hotel on the beach."

"Just stop it, let me go." That's what I'm asking for?

"We'll get a room on the first floor, worst case you'll crush your other leg." And he keeps going.

"Stop it."

He falls silent and I hear him taking a deep breath. I know what his face looks like right now, every inch of it.

"All right," he says sharply and my body gets tense. "I'm stopping."

Don't hang up, don't hang up without saying anything—the wish is quicker than the rationale, but it has zero influence on reality. He hangs up.

〉

At noon, everyone gets back home, it's Friday so it's a shorter day. I have a fever, so Sharon moves Ariel to the boys' room and prepares her bed for me.

I sleep for hours, beneath a chain of little animals. A hanging zebra sways back and forth throughout the entire day.

Two missed calls from my dad. Sharon makes me some soup, doesn't want me taking medication on an empty stomach. At night they go out for dinner, come back, and put the kids to bed. Not a word from Teddy, there is no Teddy. Not a word from Noa, there is no Noa, there is only body aches and wanting to disappear. There is no him and there should be no me.

11

A Mom for a Mom

»

On Sunday morning—after two days of crashing at Sharon's—I'm still not healthy, but I feel better. Everyone leaves and I shower and try to figure out what to do. All I get out of my brain is: Can't deal with it. Can't deal with having nowhere to go. Can't deal with wanting to go back to his place. Can't deal with him.

He hasn't reached out since the last time we spoke. He's probably on his way to the office now. Do you understand that you're not supposed to continue wondering where he is and what he's doing. Do you understand that this is it? He's given up, you've given up, he betrayed your trust, you left, you told him to stop and he did. He stopped.

I wipe the steam off the mirror to discover that I look horrendous. Not that I expected any differently. I'm pale and my eyes are swollen.

I get dressed. Tidy up. Put pencils back in their boxes, arrange them by color, and stop when my phone starts ringing. It's Ronny, the producer I'd taken on for the Delmar filming.

She tells me about a new project, the director who was supposed to do it had to cancel last minute, so Ronny thought of me. She says it's an easy gig, a TV show for kids, and the scripts aren't all that great. She asks if I can come in for a meeting with the producer.

"When?"

"Tomorrow, let me know by tonight if you can make it."

Another call comes in. I glance at my phone: It's Teddy. He's calling me. I feel dizzy and also slightly relieved, which immediately annoys me. After I finish talking to Ronny, I call him.

"You still at Sharon's?" No hello. I can hear he's driving.

"Yes."

"Where's that?"

"What does it matter?"

"I want to see you, can I see you?"

I wet my dry lips. "Since when do you ask me that?"

"Where are you? What's the address?" He's impatient.

"Teddy."

"Text me the address. Bye." He hangs up.

I guess he didn't stop after all. I send him the address.

He calls from downstairs. "I'm here, where's the entrance?"

I open the door for him. He comes in and shuts it behind him, breathless from climbing the stairs. First thing he does is stand in front of me and reach his hand out, grab my face and turn it to him. He looks at me. I see his brown eyes examining me, and I think that maybe there's too much light and he'll see that I'm not pretty. He doesn't let go, still breathing heavily.

"Finally had enough of me?" he asks and I feel my body reacting to his question, way more than I'd have liked.

"I didn't leave because I'd had enough of you." I take his hand off me.

"Yeah, yeah, I know why you left, but that's not how it works." He turns for a moment and looks around the vast loft. "Nice place."

"Yes."

We're still standing by the entrance. He takes a couple of steps toward the kitchen, looks at the photos on the fridge. "Is that Sharon?"

"Yes." It's strange that I've never introduced them. "What do you mean 'that's not how it works'?"

His eyes shift from the photo back to me. "What's up, are you sick?"

"Yes, I was. But I'm better today."

He stands close to me, almost touching me, but not. "Still angry?" His fingers hover over my arm.

"Yes, obviously." I feel the attraction again; now it's not only my body, but also my brain.

"You don't look angry."

"I am angry, among other things."

"What other things? What else? Hopeless? Maybe I'll fuck you a little bit?"

"A little bit."

"All right, let's get you home."

"No."

"Yes, I'm taking you home, that's what I came for."

"You said you're stopping."

"Yes, I did. But then I thought: this is my favorite part. Why would I stop?"

"Because I asked you to."

"So you asked me to. And I'm supposed to believe you?"

I look at him and stay quiet. Why should he believe me, really?

He nods his head. "Yeah, thought so. Look"—he gets right in front of me—"let me make it clear. These things you do, I'm not bothered. You piss me off, that's for sure, but you have a lot more leeway than you realize."

"Some leeway. Don't you understand that I don't want it this way?"

"What way?"

"You deciding for me, that way." The rage starts rising up again. "It's my life! My family!"

"It's your life, your family, your mom. Yes. Say it, say 'my mom.' Can't you say it?"

"Why would you allow yourself to bring that up again, and like that? What do you want from me?"

"I want you not to piss me off, that's what I want. Let's go, where's your stuff?" He looks around and mumbles to himself, "You and your drama, why did I ever think there'd be less drama with you?"

What is he doing here? Why am I not putting up a fight? The dizziness intensifies and I need to lie down. I limp to the couch and sit down, lie on my side over the cushions and close my eyes. I hear him approaching. He sits down next to me. He gently strokes my head, shifts a strand of hair from my face and tucks it behind my ear. I keep my eyes closed.

"They own this place?"

"No. Rented."

"Should really buy something like this."

"Go ahead."

"Is it for sale?"

"How should I know?"

"I don't know. Ask them."

"I don't want to."

"Fine, then don't."

"You can get all the information you want without me having to ask anyone anything."

"True."

"And you're intrusive, and controlling."

"Also true." He gently cups my face; his hand's warm and his touch calms me.

"And I won't forgive you for what you did."

"I know." He means it.

His hand glides from my face to my throat and he holds my jaw. I open my eyes and look at him. He bites his lip; his other hand lies over my chest and slides down and halts on my stomach.

"I don't need you to forgive me"—he leans down and kisses my neck—"I need you to stop running away."

And all at once I feel that familiar urge but a great sadness too, and I can't tell which of them is reigning. His hands are on me, and he pulls me out of my resistance until my hands touch his face and I'm suddenly hugging him and pressing him to me tightly, with all my might, giving an outlet to the anger and passion and intimacy created by what he chose to do with me. I feel him wanting me and the pulse between my legs rises, a rush of blood, microscopic particles carrying electric charges into the infiniteness of my body. I'm so detached from my body, mainly connecting through my pussy. Use your head, not your pussy.

He sits up, keeping his hands on me. "I need to fuck you."

"Fuck me 'a little bit'?"

"No. Not a little bit."

My hand grabs his cock over his pants. "There's your cock."

"Right where you left it. Let's go home."

"No, no. Just leave me alone."

"Not going to happen. Come on, get up." He stands up and slightly pulls me until I sit up. He gives me a CEO kind of look, a look that tells me he's already moved on and I'm the one stalling. I know I have no choice. But I stay seated, talking quietly.

"Why? Why do you tell me I cause drama if you're the one who gets us into this fucking soap opera situation? How am I the one responsible for all the drama?" I look up into his eyes, genuinely asking.

"Yes, you're right."

"What?"

"You're right. Your drama's justified."

"You want to fuck me so bad that you tell me I'm right?"

"No. You really are right. I get why this is difficult," he says in a serious tone, honest.

"And you still chose to do it."

"Right."

"Why?"

"Don't ask me that, you won't like my answer. Can we go? If I stay here a minute longer, I'm buying this place." He pulls me up to standing.

I look at him. "I want to understand why you call her and meet her even though you know it's hard on me."

"Because I can."

"Because you can?"

"Yes. Because I can."

"That's your answer? That's not a real answer. What does that even mean?"

"Noa, sweetheart"—he holds my face—"I called her and met her because it felt like the right thing to do. This is what I can do. This is what I can give you. You get it? Can you get that through that stubborn head of yours? Look at me, hey, look at me."

"Yes."

My eyes fill with tears; my treacherous nose starts running and he wipes it with his thumb and doesn't care, and adds with an authoritative tone, "Don't torment yourself. Do what you need to do. And now, let's get you home."

〉

After Teddy helps me tidy Ariel's room, and after I call Sharon to thank her and let her know I'm leaving her safe house, we get in the car and drive away.

"Here's your key," he says when we enter his apartment and points at it, still right where I'd left it. Xerox rushes out of the living room.

"Is Milo home?" I ask.

"No."

"Wasn't nice of me, not telling him I was leaving."

"That's what's bothering you, not telling Milo?"

He goes in and puts my bag on one of the chairs. I look at him. I suddenly feel hot and have difficulty breathing. I'm sweating and my clothes feel heavy; my hands takes my shirt off. He pulls me into him. My body hurts and I'm dazed, but the need's awoken and now I won't give it up. Xerox sits down and watches us.

"Come here," he says and his hands are on me and it feels so good and my body clings to him and we're already in the bedroom and I want to meet my cock, there it is, what a beautiful cock, the most beautiful cock in the world. Come here, cock, but I can't put you in my mouth right now, I can't breathe through my nose, and I can't bend down. I lie back on the bed submissively. His fingers glide up my thigh and there they are, right between my legs, over my underwear. He gently presses and I spread my legs or they spread themselves—I think that even if I ordered them to close they'd still open as wide as they possibly could. He lets out a deep sigh, he's incredibly turned on, his cock's here beside me, huge and hard, I stroke it. His fingers move my underwear aside, I see him descending and I raise my arms, and then I feel his mouth on my pussy, he's licking me and I feel how badly he wants this in every move he makes. Now I really have to, I can come with the mouth but I want the cock, where's the cock?

"Fuck me already," I say, and in return he flips me onto my stomach.

"That's what you want?"

"Yes."

"Yes. I brought you back here and now I'm going to fuck you."

His cock goes in and it's crazy good all at once, and then he starts and within a minute he gets into a strong and fast pace, thrusting further and further into me, and it accelerates the heart rate and all the particles are charged and I moan and shout despite the pain in my throat, and he's fucking me hard and then not very fast but just at the right pace. He's in control of me, he's in control of himself too—"I'm fucking you now, I have to fuck you, your pussy, your ass"—his words surround us. "I'm crazy about you, what are you doing?"

I pull myself out from beneath him and push him onto his back and overcome my leg and congestion and manage to reach his cock and suck him off, cupping his balls, holding him, but then I get really hot and dizzy and I lie on my back, on the bed next to him.

"Need to drink."

"I'll get you some water."

I nod and he sits up, and when he gets up and leaves the bed I watch him go and think that he's old and fat. I follow the oh-so-familiar lines of the ceiling. Am I back?

›

He doesn't stop fucking me for hours. The anger toward him surfaces and he feels me angry and hateful and it works him up, so that every time I even start to think about stopping, there's a hand or a movement or eyes that bring me back. I come and then I come again.

Afterward we lie in bed. I feel very heavy, as though my body's sinking into the mattress. The sickness, the exhaustion, the fight and its consequences, the fucking—everything's adding further weight. I know I need to sleep, but we haven't had a real talk yet. I look at him. "All right, so tell me about your stupid meetings."

He sits up. "No, I'm not up for that."

This reaction confuses me; he was the one who wanted to tell me, and I was the one who didn't want to hear it. And now he's not up for it?

"I think we're done talking about it." He's already up and getting his pants on.

"But I want to know what happened."

"I told you."

"No, you didn't tell me. I want to know more."

"Yeah, well. Then go ask her."

How low can you go?

"This is wrong. This is seriously wrong. No, this is un-fucking-believable." I plummet back to lying down and rub my face in despair. "Every time I think I've finally reached the edge of the nightmare that you are, another goddamned part suddenly appears."

He stands towering above me. "What makes you think you've reached the edge?"

"You. You're usually what makes me think I've reached the edge."

"Me?"

"Stop being such a clever prick and just be honest with me. Why did you wait? Why didn't you tell me after the first meeting?"

"I'm going to make you some soup."

>

While we sit at the table eating the soup, Milo comes home and joins us. "Everything okay between you two?" he whispers to me while Teddy goes to the kitchen to get another bowl.

"I don't think so," I answer quietly.

He scratches his neck and gives me a puzzled look. "So you'll kiss and make up with him?"

I smile and Teddy comes back.

"What did you say to her?" he asks Milo.

"Nothing." Milo quickly changes the subject. "Noa, you know I'm thinking about moving to my mom's for a while?"

"Oh yeah? To live in Copenhagen?"

"Yeah, she might know someone with a job for me, and I think I actually feel like it?"

He tells me some more about his plan. It sounds like a good idea. I ask if Xerox will join him too.

"Dad says we can bring him there, yeah."

"Get yourself situated, we'll bring him over," Teddy confirms.

"You see?" I turn to Teddy. "That's how it's done."

"That's how what's done?"

"You don't just notify after the deed, after the decision's been made. You talk through the process."

"Yeah, Dad," Milo joins my ranks. "You could learn a lot from me."

That sentence gets a genuine smile on Teddy's face, his eyes are happy. They shift from Milo to me and back. "That's right, I can learn a lot from you. And from you too."

Thing is, he really does mean it. It's incredible that he can be like that just a moment after he shut the door in my face. Is that how in control he is, that he can decide when to feel and when not to? How is that even possible? We're talking about a master here, that's old news, but this time I think I can see the whole of his complexity, down to the very last detail, and it's glorious and sickening and fascinating.

After the soup, Teddy goes into his office to make a call, and I go back to the bedroom. I text Ronny to let her know I can make the meeting, and then I text Richard and ask if he's free to talk.

He calls straightaway.

"How are you doing?" he asks.

I tell him about the thoughts I'm having regarding my future in the company and about what I'd really like to do.

To my great delight, he gets me; he knows they don't have much to offer me, not the way he'd hoped to begin with, anyway. So we decide not to decide anything right now and for me to keep him posted.

"So you guys can stop paying me."

He laughs his typical Harrington laugh. "That's out of my hands, I'm afraid. Teddy's thing. What does he say?"

"I don't know."

"He doesn't know about it?"

"No," I confess and immediately explain, "I don't really think it matters to him."

Richard falls silent for a moment. I have no idea what he's about to say.

"Yes, I guess you're right. But talk to him."

❭

This is the first morning I don't feel sick. Relief. I'm getting ready for the meeting. When I come out to the living room, I find Teddy there, still home.

"Going somewhere?" He looks at me, surprised to see me dressed and ready. Rightly so. Where would I go?

"I have a meeting."

"All right," he says and doesn't ask anything.

I grab the coffee jar from the shelf, pour three heaping teaspoons into the paper filter.

"When's your meeting?" He does ask something after all.

"In two hours."

"Want to grab a coffee with me downstairs?"

I think, Yes, Teddy. Of course I want to grab a coffee with you. All day every day all I want is to sit with you at a café and talk, but you never want to or never have the time for it.

"Why not?" I say casually.

It's a beautiful day outside, the air's filled with a pleasant scent. We walk slowly so that my leg can keep up. I still like walking through the streets with him; still proud to be by his side, still enjoy coming across strangers' looks, catching that brief moment when their eyes shift from him to me. Not that there's anything exceptional or unique about us, not that they know what kind of shit he puts me through.

We're in line at the café.

"Teddy?"

"What?" He points at a cheese pastry. "Want one?"

"Yes, thank you. I talked to Richard yesterday. I told him that I want to try and get back into the industry again, as a director this time."

"All right."

He orders, and we wait on the side.

"So we discussed putting my position at Delmar on hold for now."

"What do you mean 'on hold'?"

"It means not paying me anymore, for example."

"You still officially work for us."

"Then you can fire me."

"I can't fire you, you're on sick leave."

"You're not under legal obligation, my sick days are long gone."

"I'm aware of that."

"Then why are you still paying me?"

"Because I feel like it."

Our coffee's ready. We go outside and sit by one of the tables.

"Pass me one." He points at my cigarettes. "You rather I stop paying you and you live on social security?"

"No, of course not. But yes, sure I do." I hand him a cigarette and he gives me a serious look and then suddenly smiles. "What?" I ask.

"Nothing." He takes the lighter from my hand.

He doesn't want to tell me what made him smile. Will he ever stop having this influence on me?

"Consider it a bonus for the pitch film you made." He lights the cigarette and hands me the lighter. "And I'm glad you're taking a step toward something that's more interesting for you. What's the matter?" he asks, because I'm staring at him.

"You're making me confused."

"Why?"

"I don't know. I've not really been working for a while now, but it's not like I have anything else yet, and I don't know if I even will, or when."

"So what's the problem? This way you don't need to let your finances determine what project you take on."

"I don't determine what project I take on either way. I'm not there yet."

He looks at me and then something changes in his expression; as if he'd moved on to think about something else. "All right. You figure it out. But I'm not going to stop paying you."

"Then what am I supposed to do in return?"

"Nothing."

I light a cigarette and look at the street. He reaches over and caresses the back of my neck. I consider telling him about the meeting and decide against it. I don't know any of the details as it is. All I know is that the producer's named Sugerman, but everyone calls him Sugar.

>

At Sugar's office, his assistant and I are sitting next to each other in front of his desk. The walls are covered with posters of TV shows he's produced; folders, a wilting potted plant, a Superman doll peering through a pile of papers on Sugar's desk—the only thing missing is Sugar.

"It's multicam, okay?" the assistant asks and looks back down at her papers.

"Yes." I nod.

She glances at me again; her glasses make her eyes look smaller. "You know how to work with multicam?"

"Yes."

"Excellent. Sugar's going to be here any minute and then we can start. What happened to your leg?"

I give her a vague reply, and once she resumes reading her papers I text Ronny.

> Didn't you say you'd be coming to the meeting?
>
> No way, I'm juggling three shows here

Sugar's 'any minute' takes nearly half an hour, but eventually he shows up, fashionably victimized from head to toe. After a formal introduction and a handshake that leaves my hand with a perfumed masculine scent of the foulest kind, he asks if I've read the scripts. I explain that I got the call from Ronny only yesterday and haven't been sent anything yet.

"Right." Sugar pushes himself slightly away from the desk. "So it's a teen show, very sweet, current, thrilling, romantic. Forty-one episodes, fifty shooting days, filming somewhere between eighteen to twenty-two airtime minutes per day, which comes out to around eighteen scenes a day."

"And we need to work super efficiently to make it all happen," Sugar's assistant adds when she notices my dumbfounded look.

"I understand you don't have any experience with this kind of show, so to be honest, chances are we won't be able to take the risk with you. But Ronny really pressed me, so I said fuck it, get you in the room, see what you have to say."

Is he waiting to see what I have to say right this second? What do I have to say? He's still waiting so I better say something. "Sounds easy."

Sugar laughs and peers into his takeaway coffee to see if there's something left.

"It's anything but easy." The assistant tries to keep the conversation going, adding a smile to clarify she got the joke.

"Okay, let me read the scripts."

"Sure, but how about this." Sugar reclines and crosses his arms. "Why should I hire you?"

"Why should you hire me?"

"Yes."

"In general?"

"Yes."

What in the name of Christ Almighty does this Sugar-man want from me? What kind of question is that?

"Well, I guess there are people who are more experienced, more professional, and, uh, generally better than I am," I pause and he waits for my *but*, "And probably cheaper too." I end my pitch.

Sugar looks at me, baffled. "Right. Okay! We'll send the scripts over to you. And most importantly"—he turns to his assistant—"did she sign an NDA?"

When I leave the place I feel dirty. Not just because of the way my hand smells now and not just because I know this was redundant and they're never going to let me direct this project, but also because I know that even if I wanted to, I wouldn't be able to do it. Who would? What am I missing?

>

The next day, it's already evening time and there's still zero scripts in my mailbox. I text Sugar's assistant and she confirms they've decided not to go ahead with me for now. Teddy comes home and I sit with him while he eats.

"Did you call her?" he asks.

I'm surprised he's raising the Nurit subject again. "No."

"Then call her already, what are you waiting for?"

I look to the side, toward the window. Last hues of sunset. I think about the things he said at Sharon's place. Some were comforting, some were just simply cruel.

"Say, how come you're not vacating the King George apartment?"

"How come you think that's relevant?"

My eyes return to him. "Your mother's apartment."

"Yes, I get it." Takes a bite. "Logistics."

"Yeah, right."

"I don't have the time, you know that."

"But I do. I have plenty of time. And you're paying me as it is, so this way it'll be justified."

He looks at me. "What is it now, Noa? A mom for a mom?"

"A mom for a mother."

"Give me a break."

"I know where the key is, it's hanging right over there, the one with the yellow key chain. I'll go there, I'll solve your logistics. That way we'll both be solving problems for each other."

He gets up and starts clearing the table, lights a cigarette indoors. "The problem with dealing with you and your childhood is that you get all infantile. What do you want with that apartment?"

"I want you to clear it. To let it go."

"Promise I will, once I get the time."

"Don't you trust me with it?"

"I trust you. Nothing to do with trust."

"You do? Good. I'll grab the key." I get up because I feel like taking my bizarre idea to the next level immediately.

"It won't be productive this way, I need to be there. What good will it do if you're there on your own?" He's speaking from the kitchen, so he doesn't notice I'm already at the entryway.

"There." I return with the key in my hand as he comes out of the kitchen.

"What are you doing?" He ashes his cigarette and looks at me.

"Got it. I'll take care of it."

"All right. You really showed me, well done. Now put the key back."

"No, I'm being serious. I'm going to do it."

"You're not going to do it. Find something else to bug me about, okay?"

"No. I'm doing it."

"Fine," he says dismissively.

"All I need is two or three weeks, and it'll be behind you."

"Have you lost your mind? You have no idea how much stuff is in there."

"I do have an idea, I was there when that pipe burst."

"This isn't something you can do on your own, especially with your leg. And I need to go over everything, there's my dad's boxes too, it's a lot of stuff."

"I'll go through everything and save some boxes for you, whatever seems important—"

"No, no, I won't have that."

"—and I'll get rid of the rest. Throw it away or donate a bunch of things. You can donate the apartment too, if you don't need it."

"I don't appreciate this manipulation."

"This is not manipulation."

"Then what is this?"

"This is what I can do. Because I can. Right?"

"Right." He's getting pissed off. "Didn't you just say you were going to look for a job?"

"What does that have to do with it?"

"Then go find yourself a job and get off my back."

"Why are you so against this?"

"Because it's completely irrelevant for you to do it."

"You're never going to do it, don't you see? And if anyone's going to do it for you, then it's probably me. Who else would you send over there?"

"I'll take care of it when the time comes."

"The time will never come! You're scared of parting with it."

"Why would I be scared?"

"Because you're a coward," I announce and immediately add, "And a liar."

"What does that have anything to do with this?"

"It's one thing to lie to me, but you're lying to yourself too. Do you believe your own excuses? That apartment's been like that for seven years now. People are homeless and you keep that place with the lousy excuse of a busy schedule? I call bullshit."

"Fine, you want to clear out her apartment? Go ahead, no problem." He's really angry now and I'm proud of myself for getting him to this state. "Another thing you want to fail at? Go right ahead. You'll give up within a day, but this time you won't have me to blame."

"Fabulous." I'm not letting him mess with my head.

"You're insufferable."

"Learned from the best."

〉

The following morning I arrive at the sleepy downtown building.

I enter the apartment and shut the door behind me. The smell's intense. I open the windows, stand in the middle of the living room and look around. An ocean of belongings. What was I thinking? What sort of person volunteers to do something like this, and without anyone even wanting them to? I look at Henia's photograph, hanging on the opposite wall. Another thing I want to fail at? I'll show your son what I'm really made of.

I work in the stifling apartment for hours. Smoking joints, listening to music—but not all the time. My clothes are covered in dust and so is my hair. There's something revolting about it. I occasionally get shivers of discomfort, as though I'm seeing something that I'm not supposed to see, or as though I'm being someone I'm not supposed to be. At first I wash my hands every ten minutes, but at some point I get tired of that, and I also get grossed out by using the towel hanging by the sink, so I go down to the convenience store and buy a pack of silicone gloves, paper towels, large garbage bags, cigarettes, a bottle of ouzo, and two bottles of water.

The sorting process presents some difficult decisions. The goal is to gather a few boxes of photo albums and sentimental items, and fill the rest of the boxes with items to donate.

I fill bags with trash, bags with clothes to donate. I don't even bother opening boxes of George's that are labeled "clothes" or "books," I just drag them to the living room corner I've designated for donations. Henia and George are co-donating their belongings. Finally they can co-something again.

Dealing with the shoes is especially gross. And generally speaking, I have a hard time with the closets. The putrid smell, the sense of voyeurism that on the one hand runs currents of curiosity through me and on the other fills me with emptiness. Then, suddenly and all at once, I can't keep going. That's enough for today. I'll come back tomorrow.

⟩

When I enter Teddy's apartment, there's still some light outside. Milo's with a friend on the balcony. I wave to him from afar, and he waves back and smiles at me. I go to the bedroom, smelling the weighty, dusty day on myself. I'm surprised to find Teddy there, lying in bed. I stop and look at him. Haven't spoken to him all day. He called me but I didn't pick up. Maybe I felt I'm allowed to ignore him when I'm at his mother's place.

"Where were you? King George?"

"Yes. How come you're in bed?"

"Pulled my back."

I give him a look lacking all empathy and start undressing.

"How are you feeling?" he asks.

"Much better. Even though there's a ton of dust there."

"What were you doing there?"

"I told you, starting to take it all apart."

"How did you get there? Taxi?"

"Yes."

"What are you taking apart? What are you doing exactly?"

"Clearing out, sorting, packing. Your mother's things, mainly. You know, packing up a home." I take off my shirt and then my bra. "Opening drawers and taking stuff out, emptying out wardrobes and all of that. There's loads of work, but I'll do it."

"I don't want you to do it." He rubs his forehead in irritation.

"It's got to be done."

"Says who?"

"Common sense."

"Now you decide to use your common sense? How come you haven't used it for the last six months?"

"Going to shower," I say and go into the bathroom, leaving the door open.

"Just drop it, will you?" he shouts from his sprawled position on the vast bed.

"In too deep!" I shout back.

I do everything double: shampoo twice, soap my body twice, wash my face twice. I finish and go to the wardrobe, put on some shorts and an old T-shirt. He's watching the news, foot fidgeting restlessly, the worry vein right next to his eye bulging. He seems angry and exhausted.

"Are you hungry?" I ask.

"Yes."

"I'll go see what's in the fridge. Do you want something?"

"Yes."

I ask Milo and his friend if they want to eat too, and I make us all sandwiches. Then I go back to the room.

"Here"—I hand him a plate—"and here's a beer and a glass."

"Thank you." He rises up and complains, "Can't even sit up, goddamn mothercunting back."

He leans on a pillow and groans with pain. I sit in front of him and take a bite of my sandwich.

"Noa."

"What?"

"Not sure I feel comfortable with this whole apartment thing."

"I'm sure you don't." I drink straight out of the bottle. "But that's what's happening."

>

I wake up in the morning with a softer attitude. He's no longer in bed. I turn onto my side and look at the view through the window. It takes me a minute, but then I recall Henia's apartment and get excited, like a kid waking up and remembering he got a new bike yesterday, and today it's all his. I feel like having some coffee and quickly going back there, to continue the good work. Teddy comes into the bedroom, dressed in sweats. According to his walk, his state hasn't improved.

"You up already?"

"Yeah, just woke up. How's your back?"

"Awful."

He goes into the bathroom, letting out exaggerated moans with every move he makes, it's almost comical. I get off the bed and follow him into the bathroom. He spreads shaving foam over his face in round movements.

"If you honestly don't want me to do it, then tell me."

He glances at me through the mirror. "And then how will you keep the symmetry of your revenge?" He runs the razor blade up his jawline, a clear path forming through the white foam.

"I don't want to force it on you."

"Could've fooled me. And what about your leg?"

"It's fine, as you can see."

"Yes." He rinses the razor blade and nears it to his face again. A pleasant, familiar scent fills the room.

"I used to try not to burden you, but now it's not my top priority, not burdening you."

"Yes, I can tell. And it does burden me."

"Still, I need to know that this is something you want—"

"Yes, yes. All right." He cuts me off.

"—So . . ." I'm still with the previous sentence's leftovers.

"So what?"

"Nothing, go ahead," I say.

"So, fine. I've had enough of this bullshit. You really want to do this?"

"Yes."

"Then go ahead, do it. Better to keep you busy than getting on my nerves. Just put some things aside for me, paperwork, don't throw away anything that seems important. Photo albums . . . beats me. I don't even know what's in there."

"Everything. All the things that people keep in their home."

He finishes shaving, leans over the sink and washes off the remainder of the foam in swift moves.

"You're insane to want to do it, I'm telling you. Something's seriously wrong with you."

"Good. I'm going to make some coffee."

》

That's how the days go on. Teddy and I hardly meet. He gets injections for his back and quickly recovers, goes back to long days at the office. He doesn't come to the King George apartment, and at a certain point he stops asking me about it too. Typical. I prefer it that way.

I like the power of routine, the duplicated time softening the present. I go through little moments that lead to big moments. For instance, coming out of the elevator and opening the door and feeling the hundreds of times Henia had done those exact same actions. Momentarily fusing with her in my mind, in my intentions, in the respect that I have for her and for myself, through her.

Sometimes I share my decisions with her or even talk to her for a while, until I get self-conscious about it and stop.

"Look at that, I'm packing up your kitchen a night before Passover dinner. You can treat it as a spring-clean for the holidays, and you must be delighted. Teddy's invited to Alice's. Adrian will be there, and he'll take Milo with him, that way Teddy will spend this important night with both his boys. Doesn't matter where Teddy's going, I'm out of fucks to give." She's used to me talking shit about Teddy. I'm supposed to be in the suburbs for the festive dinner. If I don't show up it'll be rude toward my family—Dad, Mina and a few of her faded relatives, and Roy, who's bringing Thomas. But I don't want to go. There or anywhere. Maybe I'll come here, to the apartment. "Want to have Passover dinner together, Henia? We can invite George too, if it's acceptable for divorcees to celebrate holidays together in the next life. Up to you. Doesn't matter to me."

I sit down on a chair in the narrow kitchen. The cupboards are open, some of the shelves are empty and some are still completely full. Each dish was placed there years ago. Henia's hand reached into the darkness of the cupboard and placed down a mug, and it hasn't been reclaimed till this very day. I light up a joint.

Where's Nurit having her Passover dinner?

There were years that I still knew, years that I'd hear of her whereabouts from Grandma. But that was ages ago, and even Grandma doesn't bother coming for holiday dinners anymore, the mere thought exhausts her. The mere thought of her exhaustion exhausts me.

I could call her. Nurit.

Yeah?

Could I?

What for?

What do I have to say to her?

Let's call and find out.

No. What a weird thought.

I don't even have her number. That really is strange, not even having her number. Wonder if he knew that when he'd left that fucking note. In any case, the note's not here. But this is a rare moment, a moment when I'm ready to call her, a moment when I'm capable of it. I don't want to ask anyone for her number. "We'll just drop it." I say out loud, to keep Henia in the loop.

From the moment I announce to myself that I'm capable of it, I can't let it go, of course, and in no time at all I go back to my phone. The fact that I don't have her number is so idiotic that I can't bear it. I text Milo, he's a no-questions-asked type of guy.

> Do you happen to be home plus awake?
>
> Yeah what's up
>
> There's a note somewhere with the name Nurit on it and a phone number. I think it's on the shelf by the kitchen window.
>
> Think I found it sending it now
>
> Thanks Babycakes
>
> Y'welcome Babycakes

All right.

Deep breath.

"You have reached the voicemail box of . . ." That familiar voice—maybe she's someone's mother too.

Back to the kitchen cupboards.

Noon. Second try. This time she picks up.

"Hello?"

"Hi, it's Noa," I say in a flat tone and my stomach turns.

"Noa? My Noa?" Her voice is low and much raspier than I'd imagined, so much so it almost distracts me from being called 'her Noa.' She continues in my silence. "I'm so happy to hear your voice! So happy. I can't believe it. How are you?"

She speaks slowly and a little full-on—not full-on, but rather clearly. I can hear the excitement in her voice, but I'm surprised to hear confidence there too.

"I'm fine." I must sound like a stranger to her. "Do you want to meet?"

"Of course! Of course I do. I would love that."

"Okay." Suddenly I can't remember what my plan was, what I'm supposed to say.

"I'm very happy you called. Wow, my heart's pounding, I swear, you have no idea how excited I am right now. I think I need to sit down."

"Yes, we haven't spoken in years." I'm as quiet and strong as rein-forced concrete.

"Yes. Well, never mind," she reprimands herself for losing her focus. "I can—Wait, you mean now? I can come anywhere you tell me to, or we can plan for another day, up to you."

I look around the messy apartment, boxes everywhere, the lives of people I never met. Now? Bring her over to Henia's? It suddenly makes sense to me. I dealt with her so much during the past few hours, maybe it would be better off to meet as soon as possible and get it over with.

"Yeah, maybe now."

"Yeah? Okay, I'm fine with that. I mean, I'll drop anything to come meet you. Where are you?"

"I'm downtown."

"Wait, excuse me, I'll just note it down. Where's the pen? One min-ute." I hear her shifting things around. "Yes, I'm writing it down."

No. I'm not bringing her here. I don't want to bring her here, because she knows Teddy. I find that repulsive. Or maybe not repulsive, maybe just bizarre.

"So, downtown where?" she asks.

Reconsidering. Wait a minute. I need a minute.

If I stay quiet she'll know I'm unsure. I need to say something.

"Actually, on second thought, maybe we can do tomorrow."

"Yes, of course. Yes."

"Maybe in the morning, does that work for you?"

"Whatever you say, sure. Whenever you say."

"Because it's Passover night, so maybe you'd need the morning for errands and stuff."

"So what? Not a problem."

"Okay, so I'll text you where and when."

"Great! Absolutely great. Good, okay, Noa . . ."

"So bye for now."

"Okay. Bye, bye, goodbye."

I hang up. A loud sigh comes out of me and causes me to feel embarrassed in front of Henia, who's staring at me from the photo on the wall in her usual way. What the fuck was that?

I feel bad. Not physically—but bad, like a bad girl. Like a kidnapper coming to feed his hostage.

This is what Teddy talked about. This is what he was trying to tell me.

Why are you crying now?

Nothing new here. If anything, there's something good. No, there's nothing good. I'm no good—I'm bad, rotten, hollow, worthless. Teddy's no good. No point there, no future there. Probably not even love.

Why did I call her? She was odd. She must be feeling tormented right now, like me. Poor woman. Gave birth to two kids, only ended up with one. Stop crying.

I have nothing. I've gotten nowhere. I come from nothing and I'm going nowhere, just like he said. And now he's brought me back to my mother. That's what he's done. Just because he can.

I stop crying when the doorbell rings; the downstairs neighbor wants to know when she'll get the check for the damages from the leak. I know for a fact she received the money that very day. She peers into the apartment, says she heard I'm clearing it out, and of course she's heard all the banging and the dragging, and at least she doesn't say she heard the call to my estranged mother and the crying that followed. Maybe she could have heard herself ringing the doorbell, if she'd have just stayed downstairs.

"Yes." Teddy picks up, sounds busy.

"The downstairs neighbor's here," I say and she nods, confirming she is the downstairs neighbor. "She's asking about her check."

"Let me talk to her."

I hand her my phone, repulsed by the thought of her mouth on it.

"Hello?" she almost yells.

Teddy speaks to her; she bursts into laughter, a strident laugh, the kind she must be hiding from the world, and once you hear it you immediately get why she should be hiding it. Her tone sweetens. What is he telling her, that idiot?

She hands me back the contaminated phone and leaves. I try to sterilize the poor device with an expired eyeglass cleaner spray.

I get a tip from the boss:

> Don't let her in again
>
> What did you tell her that made her laugh?
>
> You don't want to know
>
> You might be right.
>
> Am always
>
> Rarely.

Come to think of it, he doesn't know that I talked to Nurit. I'll tell him later, face-to-face.

›

I'm so tired. I almost fall asleep in the taxi back to the city center.

It's rather late and Teddy's home already. He's on the bed, still dressed, busy with his phone in his usual position. "I thought you ended up sleeping over there."

"Hoped, maybe." I take my shoes off.

"No, I prefer for you not to sleep there."

"Fine."

"I prefer for you to sleep here." He points at my side of his bed.

I'm completely drained so I don't play along. I feel distant from him, for some reason. Like I'm angry but can't recall why. "I'm going for a shower."

"Wait, wait, come here."

"What?" I approach him.

"Sit down for a second."

"I'm filthy from all your mother's dust and dirt," I say and immediately regret it, since it came out nasty and I don't understand why I said it. That's not even how I feel—after all these days at her place, she's become much more than just Teddy's mother to me. In return for my slip of the tongue, I obediently sit down right where he wanted me to.

"You need me to thank you for doing this? I need instructions, I'm not used to being in this position."

"No, no. That's not what I want."

"You need to hear that I appreciate it?"

"No, I don't need you to appreciate it now. Maybe someday."

"You want me to get someone to work with you over there?"

"I don't know, is he hot?" I ask tiredly.

"Total knockout."

"Good, can I go shower now?"

"Wait." He grabs my arm before I manage to get up. "We're having Passover drinks at the office tomorrow and I want you to come."

"I don't even work there anymore. Why do you need me to come?"

"Because you still work there officially. So come say hi."

"Fine." I get up and head toward the bathroom. Still dressed, I sit down to pee. I gaze at the floor pattern and suddenly realize that I haven't told him yet. How could I forget something like that?

"Teddy."

"What?" he replies from the bedroom.

"I called her."

"What?" Sounds like he's getting off the bed. "What did you say?" He walks into the bathroom.

"I called her."

"Seriously?" he asks with genuine joy, surprised.

"Yes."

"You don't say . . ." He smiles with proud eyes. "How was it?"

"Disgusting," I reply without thinking and his smile widens with love, all the way to those sweet canines.

"'Disgusting' sounds like a good start."

"She wanted to meet straightaway and I almost said yes, but then I reconsidered and told her we'll meet tomorrow."

"I'm very happy to hear that."

I rise and get my underwear and pants back on, even though I'm supposed to take them off. "This doesn't mean I'm not angry at you for what you did."

"You can stay angry."

"Yes, but I'm tired of being angry at you for it."

"Need a new reason? I can get something going." He scratches under his eye.

"No."

"Good."

"I don't know where I should meet her."

He thinks for a minute. "You don't want to do it here?"

"Here? No." My finger plays with the drops around the sink, stretching them out into lines.

"Then tell her to meet you somewhere, go sit at an outdoor café, so you two can smoke."

"She smokes?" How surprising!

"Yes. Weed too," he adds with a smile.

"Liar."

"I swear."

"Liar! No way."

He looks at me. "I'm crazy about you. You know that, right?"

"No." I can't help but smile.

"All right." He's standing in front of me and we're both smiling, and the shape of our love can be sensed, the negative space of his face in front of mine.

And then his phone rings.

He goes out of the bathroom to answer the call, and I finally take my clothes off. This is the moment I wait for every day, the bathing ceremony in his extravagant shower with the dark tiles and the strong water pressure. I put my hand in to see if the water's hot, but then I pick up a sliver of his conversation, so I turn off the water to hear it better.

"Fine, I'll talk to her."

Then silence again. "If that's what you think, yes."

I wrap a towel around me and come out to the bedroom. He's standing with his back to me.

"Yes, I understand," he says and turns around, sees me and keeps his eyes on me as he listens. (.... ... .) "Okay, I'll talk to her." Who will he talk to? (.... .. ..) "You're right. Yes. Okay. Okay."

Who's right? He hangs up and looks at me, lets out a sharp sigh.
"Who was that?"
"Lara's mom. Lara gave birth, six weeks early."
My blood freezes. "That's not good."
"No. I have to go."
"Okay. Of course. Is Lara all right? The baby . . . ?"
"I hope so. I don't know, I need to be there."

I'm standing under the stream of hot water, thoughts rushing through my mind, body steady in place. Lara's baby might be in danger. The fragility of this life, I can't stand it. That alone is enough to make you not want to take the risk. I hope nothing bad happens to her, I hope she gets through it. Teddy's going there now. What will he do? What can he do? The helplessness of it all. Lara's probably lying there, one big trauma. I don't know what happened at the birth, if it was natural or if they operated or what. I don't know Lara either, after all, I've never met her. But that doesn't matter right now.

The water runs, disappearing down the drain.

Little baby girl. Be strong. Please be strong. Please. Please. Please.

+

I can remember only a little bit of the good things. For example, I have a vague memory of a rainy Saturday: we're alone in the living room, early-morning hours. She's hugging me and I feel safe, softness, bliss. The kind of moment you can press pause and say, Everything's fine now.

I guess there were other good moments like that one, but I probably don't remember them, because when I had to go on living without her, remembering them was too painful. But sometimes I wish I could go back there, befriend that possibility, that I have a mother and that she loves me very much.

〉

He doesn't come home that night. The moment I wake up, I check to see if there's a new message from him. Before I fell asleep—in front of the TV, which is still on—he texted me that it'll be fine. That's all, no details and no reply when I asked for further info.

No new messages.

What's happening?

In a bit

His reply amplifies my tension. I get ready to leave and wait to hear from him. Try to figure out if I'll go to my dad's tonight. I suddenly feel wrong bailing on them. Hope Henia won't be too disappointed.

Once I'm ready to go, I call him. "Can you talk?"

"Yeah, wait a second, I'll go out." He puts the phone away and I hear rustling sounds. "I'll be right back. But leave it for now, wait for the checkup. One minute."

I hear him walking. Squeaky door, people talking.

"How's it going there? How's Lara? How's the baby?"

"It's complicated. Lara's fine physically. Mentally—I'm not so sure. But she'll be all right."

"Okay."

"The baby, she's not stable, still in the NICU. All sorts of complications, too early to tell. They're running tests, she's on antibiotics. Tiny thing, you can't imagine the size of her, can't believe that it's a person."

I hear the click of his lighter, then the first drag of a cigarette.

"How was the labor? Who was with her, with Lara?"

"It was a difficult one. Had complications and ended up going for a C-section."

"Shit."

"Yeah. Yes, it's harsh. Nothing we can do, it'll pass," he says, and I recall how he told me the same thing after the accident. He allows the difficulty to be present, and at the same time he manages to give convincing, fatherly encouragement. I'm glad she's not alone, that he's there for her.

"Who else is there?"

"Her parents were here all night, her sister came this morning. The baby's father, he was here too, left a little while ago."

"First time meeting him?"

"Yes."

"What's he like?"

"Nice guy. Polite. Cooperative."

"Cooperative." I smile. "How very Teddy of you. How's he reacting to the whole thing?"

"He's pretty much petrified. Feel bad for the guy."

I fall silent and feel the difficulty penetrating my bones, milliseconds of complete sympathy with their fears. "What a nightmare."

"As long as they manage to stabilize the little one, everything will be all right."

"And how are you?"

"Me?"

"Yes. Did you get any sleep?"

"No." He coughs. "No, I'm fine. I need to help her through this, she's a little shocked. Not quite with it, Lara."

"Yes, it's good that you're there. Should I bring you anything?"

"No, no. I don't need anything. Thank you. What about you?"

"I'm fine."

"You meeting Nurit?"

"I don't know. What does it matter now?"

"What does it matter? What do you think, that because of Lara I'll be neglecting my mission?"

I smile to myself. "Your lifelong mission. What about the office drinks? Can you skip it?"

"No, I can't. I'll see you there, and do me a favor, don't talk to anyone there about putting jobs on hold or any other inventions of yours. Okay?"

"Okay."

"All right. I'm going back in. Go meet her! Call me after. Bye."

〉

We decide to meet at 11:00 a.m., at a café I almost never go to.

"Hi," I say with a hesitant tone as I approach her table.

She gets up when she sees me, we're the same height. Yes, she's aged, but she's still pretty, in her own way. Resembles the woman I remembered: body's changed, but the style's remained the same. She doesn't dare touch me. Her eyes are getting teary, and she holds it back and returns to her chair as I sit down in front of her.

"Gosh! You're so beautiful!" She covers her face in excitement.

"Thank you . . ." I'm embarrassed, I look for somewhere to hang my bag but the chair's backrest is round and I have nowhere to put it. I leave it on my lap.

"Do you want something to drink? You want coffee?" she asks and it's the first time our eyes truly meet. Eyes never change. They age and blur, but their look remains the same.

"Yes, coffee."

"There's the waiter, one sec, let's call him over." She tries to catch his attention and I watch her as she waves to him. She's dressed in a short-sleeved blouse, a thin shawl wrapped around her shoulders. Her arm, I remember it, despite the years gone by. I examine the changed skin, loose and distant from the muscles, beauty marks and sunspots everywhere. "There, he saw me."

After the waiter takes our order—and gets a chilly look from me for his opening line "What can I get you girls?"—we look at each other; she smiles, I'm cautious.

"Where do we start?" That's me being the first to talk.

"Anything . . . Whatever you feel like."

"I don't know." I give up looking for a solution and place my bag on the ground.

"Maybe I can tell you some things, how about that?" she suggests.

"Okay."

"This is so overwhelming for me. I don't want to burden you with my excitement on the one hand, but on the other hand I have to, you know, say it, because that's the truth . . ."

"I know, that's fine."

"How do you feel? How are you recovering?"

"I'm okay, it's taking longer than I expected. I was sick too, better now." Not quite clear to me why I chose to share that.

"Yeah, the body always weakens during recovery."

"Yes."

Silence again, so I look for cigarettes in my bag, but I stop the search when she starts talking so that she doesn't think I'm not listening.

"I'm prepared—I'm prepared for you to be the one who sets the pace and, I don't know, it's important for me to tell you that I haven't come here with any expectations or anything. I just feel it's such a shame, not a day, not a day goes by without it hurting." All at once she breaks down into quiet weeping, repeatedly raises her hand in dismissal. "Sorry, I'm sorry, I really promised myself not to cry in front of you, it'll stop soon."

"It's all right that you're crying," I say and I'm concrete again, don't feel a thing, completely sheltered from what's happening in front of me, as though it has nothing to do with me.

"I'm sorry." She pulls herself together, wipes her nose with a tissue she's been clenching in her fist this whole time. "Okay then, let me tell you a little bit about myself."

I light a cigarette, and she tells me things about her: where she's been, what she's been up to, never remarried, had all sorts of boyfriends, nothing for a few years now, retiring next year. After a few minutes of her talking and me listening and reacting nicely and without judgment, I decide to dare and bring it up: "There is something I need to say, something that made me upset."

"Okay." She fills her lungs with air. "Is it about the apartment, the inheritance?"

"No. I don't care about that."

"I can only imagine you were upset about it, Noa, and I was actually glad you called so I could explain—"

"That's not what I'm talking about."

"Still—"

"And that's not what I want to talk about."

She stops her gush of words. "Then what were you upset about?"

"That you met with Teddy."

"That I met with Teddy?" She slightly straightens up.

"Yes."

"Who are you upset with?" she asks, and it's only then that I realize that considering our history, I have no right to be angry at her for it, which leaves my anger solely toward Teddy.

"I'm angry about you two meeting without me knowing about it," I try to find a way to obscure my accusations. "Didn't you ask him whether I knew about it?"

"I did, the first time we talked, I asked him if you knew about it. Not on the phone, I mean when we actually met. He didn't tell you about our meetings this whole time?"

"No. Just now."

Got to be careful when divulging details about Teddy, since anything to do with me has to stay protected and unexposed right now. She tells me that he called her, that she deliberated about it and he persuaded her to meet him.

"So that's it, I said yes." She briefly checks my reaction, and continues, "Actually, from the moment he called I knew I wanted to meet him, and I was obviously very excited, because I told myself that maybe through him we could find a way to talk."

"Well it worked, unfortunately," I say and she shrinks with insult, presses her lips together and looks aside and I quickly clarify: "Not 'unfortunately' about us meeting, I guess that had to happen—maybe it would have happened either way—I'm just not comfortable with the notion that me meeting you means it worked for him." So in order not to insult her, I sacrifice intimate intel about my power struggle with Teddy.

"Maybe you just wanted to feel that it came from you, that it's your choice to make," she plainly suggests another option.

The waiter arrives and serves us our coffee. She just smiles at him, doesn't touch her mug.

"You must have been terribly angry. Oh my." She looks at me with sympathetic eyes. "Listen, everything's out of my control here, it's so difficult and so delicate. You're dear to me. Sometimes I even differentiate between my relationship with you and my relationship with our tragedy. As though there's a separation, I can just think of you as you, not even in the context of me."

"I have no idea what to do with that," I say even though I understand what she means, and I'm a little glad to hear it.

"I know, I know. This is just me saying that I don't blame you. You don't have to do anything, really."

"No, I do. I need to hear you, for you to tell me what happened, the way you see it. I guess it's inevitable. Your coffee's getting cold."

"I like drinking it cold." What's there to like about that? "Yes. Whatever you want. Sure. I was waiting—I've been waiting to tell my side for years. All this time I felt that my side of the story had no legitimacy, that I'd lost my rights," she says and her eyes stay fixed on mine, but her head shakes in slight neurotic movements, as though gesturing 'no' ad infinitum.

I look at her and see something: this is a person who has been traumatized. What part of it did she bring on herself? And what's my part in the hell she's gone through? While these thoughts rush through my mind, my leg starts twitching. She notices.

"There's so much to talk about, I don't know where to start, right? Do you feel the same?" She finally sips her coffee.

"Yes." I'm getting tense and that makes me think about smoking a joint, and from there I associate to Roy. "What do you say about Thomas?"

"What do I say about Thomas?" she repeats after me, buying some time. "He seems great, I don't have much to say about him, really. He's very, very nice."

"And how does Roy seem to you?"

"Roy . . ." She smiles softly. One smile of hers is all it takes for me to see who Roy is to her, I can feel the twenty-five years of their relationship having developed, and I left myself behind. "Well, first of all, I'm happy for him. But I was quite surprised."

"How come?"

"Look, he's been in and out of relationships for years now, right? And at a crazy pace. And then suddenly this Swiss guy appears—"

"—Austrian."

"Yes, yes, Austrian, sorry. So, I was surprised it continued and got very serious very quickly. I hope that they make it work, that he won't get disappointed."

"Grandma likes Thomas."

"Yes, well," she says dismissively, and seems impatient for the first time since we sat down, "she says whatever's convenient for her to say."

"Okay," I deflect.

"And of course I'm sad about him moving abroad," she continues, "but I just want him to be happy. Both of you. That's what I always wanted, even in the harshest, most hostile moments."

I lean down and take my phone out of my bag. No texts or missed calls. Nurit looks at me somewhat tensely.

"Do you need to be somewhere?" she asks.

"We're having Passover drinks at the office, but it's only in an hour. I feel like smoking a joint. Teddy told me you smoke weed too, but I didn't believe him."

She lets out a genuine laugh, a sweet one. A warm feeling rises within me.

"What is it?" I want to understand what's making her laugh.

"Why didn't you believe him? Yes, I smoke. I like to smoke, it relaxes me. But I make a mess of rolling, I always need someone to roll it for me. Roy usually makes them for me. I don't need much, just a drag here and there. Sometimes I keep the same cigarette for days."

"If Roy's bringing you weed, then that means we've been smoking the same stuff all these years."

"Well . . ."

"That's the one thing we've got!"

"There you have it!" She's genuinely happy I've found something that connects us. "Wait, do you have anything on you?"

"Yeah, I have one prerolled. Prerolled by me."

"Oh yeah? Okay!" She looks at the café's little garden. "But we won't smoke it here, right?"

"No, let's get the check."

"Wait, I'm paying, let me pay." She picks up her bag and rummages through it, a big bag filled with too many unnecessary things.

Behind the café is a bridge, and beneath it is a little garden with a hilltop, a set of stairs to climb up all the way to a lone tree. There's a kind of privacy here, which makes me think about the number of indecent acts this tree was forced to witness.

We go up and sit on the bench. I light up the joint, take a drag and pass it to her. She takes a drag, closes her mouth with the smoke inside, holds it in, then exhales and hands it back to me. Our fingers touch. I think about the fact that it's her sitting next to me. Two strong, opposing currents soar within: intense existential nausea—like the knowledge that everything is absolutely unbearable—and, at the same time, excitement, like arriving, like what we feel when we arrive.

We look at each other, realizing we've just shared a silence, each to her own thoughts. Her eyes are soft, and I suppose mine have softened too.

"Noa." She says my name, and it slashes through my heart like a blade, but it does the same to her, so we just sit there and suffer together.

"You know what Teddy told me?" She suddenly brings up his name and I feel his power, the anchor that he is for me. "He told me . . . One of the things he said, before I'd even dreamed that you and I would actually meet, he said, 'Nurit, don't you be apologetic with Noa.' He told me not to show weakness with you."

"That's what he said?"

"Yes, I swear. He told me, 'You go see her and face her and don't be scared of her.'"

"Good thing he didn't post a tutorial 'How to Handle Noa.'"

"Look, I get what he was saying," she continues, missing my joke. "I understand that. But it's very hard finding the right balance. Really."

"Where did you meet?"

"A little café near my place."

"Okay. And how did it go?"

"I was the first to get there . . ."

"Yes."

"And I was really excited. This woman was sitting at a table next to me, and I asked her for a cigarette. I waited. And the thing is, I had no idea what he looked like." She smiles.

"You didn't google him?"

"No, I didn't even know his last name. Nothing."

"He didn't introduce himself?"

"He did, but when he spoke to me on the phone for the first time, I didn't quite, you know—it took me a minute to understand who he was, so I didn't catch his full name."

"Yeah, okay. So he suddenly shows up and you see a fat man, pretty fat, beautiful and impressive." I word it for her, or check to see if my description captures her perspective.

"To be honest, the moment I saw him, I knew it was him. First I had to put a face to the voice on the phone. And then I had to think of him as your boyfriend."

"'Your boyfriend.'" I smile in embarrassment. "I doubt he'd introduce himself that way."

"He didn't, that was my assumption . . . Oh, what do I know? How do you call him? Your man? Your partner?"

"I don't know. So? Keep going."

"And you can imagine, after ten minutes, I already felt like I could open up to him. He made me feel very comfortable."

"You remember what he said?"

"Oh yeah, of course I remember. He told me you've been in his life for a few months now, that he knows you're not in touch with me. He said he thought that you were missing out on something, so he decided to go and see for himself who your mother is. He also told me a lot about his sons, and his relationship with Adrian and the complexities—"

A loud burst of music interrupts her, it's her phone. She delves into the bag again, trying to find it.

"Sorry, just a minute." She finds the phone and holds it away to see who's calling. "Hello?" ("Nurit, hi, it's Albert!") "Yes, Albert! You're there? Can you leave it by the door?"

She gives some instructions over the phone, and I try to process what

I've just learned: Teddy told her about his relationship with Adrian. He doesn't talk to me about it, but he tells her? Should I find out what she knows? No. I don't want that. I glance at Nurit, examine her face while she's busy with her call. I think about how she'll feel afterward, and wonder about her evening. Then I think about the Passover dinner in the suburbs; Teddy; Lara and her family; the little baby girl. I'm glad Nurit and I met, but I think that's enough for now. I check the time. I need to get to the office soon.

When she finishes the call, I tell her that I have to leave. We say we'll meet up again.

Before we say goodbye we don't hug, but for a brief moment she sends out her hand and touches my face, a light caress.

12

The Protocol

》

The last time I was at the office was two months ago. The meeting with Nurit is still echoing inside me, and now I have to see everyone, including Teddy, who'll surely want me to give him a full report or at least award him an accolade for his contribution to making his own dream come true.

In the elevator, I look down at my leg. It's gotten better during the last few days.

26th floor.

When I step out I can immediately sense the festive vibe in the air. I look through the glass doors and see the decorations and the lobby filled with people, drinking and chattering loudly. From the moment I walk in, everyone greets me and asks how I'm doing. It's nice and all but also awkward. There's Teddy on the couch in the midst of a lively chitchat with a few colleagues, swells of laughter and pats on the back. Naomi appears and we hug excitedly. She apologizes for not having visited, and I tell her there was no need—not that I would have told her I was recovering at Teddy's place. In the corner of my eye I can tell he's noticed me. Our eyes briefly meet, and then I look at Naomi again and we go to grab a drink.

Already with a glass in hand, our eyes meet again and he gestures for me to approach him. I sit on the couch's armrest next to him, and he grabs my elbow and pulls me so that I lean down to him, creating a little space for a private conversation within the surrounding commotion.

"How was it?" he asks quietly.

"I'll tell you later. Not now," I reply even quieter. "How's Lara? What's happening there?"

"Better. The kid's improving."

"Really? That's great!" What a relief.

"I'm heading back there soon. And now back to you." He's more intense than usual. "How come you won't tell me now?"

"How come you're like this already? When did you start drinking?"

"Too early. Come on, how did it go?"

"Okay. Complicated."

"Yes."

I stay silent for a moment and watch him.

"Well?" he urges me, and I don't know what he expects me to say.

"You opened up to her much more than you do with me," I say quickly and quietly. "You shut me out, but not her. She could ask you whatever she wanted, and you answered everything, right?"

"You finally meet your mother after all these years"—I can smell the alcohol on him and, as always, it attracts me—"and that's what matters to you? The way *I* talked to her?"

"Among other things, yes. I also had to deal with the fact that you two met—what did you think would happen?"

"I thought that for once in your life, what really matters would matter to you."

"Okay, let's not do this now."

"I spoke to her as one parent to another," he insists on continuing.

"No, it's more than that."

"One parent to another," he emphasizes again, convinced of his own argument.

"Right. And what if I never have any children? So I won't be a 'parent,' and then what?"

"That's not the point."

"That's right. And there is nothing new here either. Just makes me think about why you need—or why we need—for you not to see me as an equal. That's all."

If he wasn't drunk he'd have stopped this quiet little chat ages ago, but for some sick reason he goes on. "Had a good talk, you two?"

"Yes, yeah, good talk."

"Good, that's what matters, the rest's not important—Phil, where you going? Get me a refill, will you, Phil?"

"Why?" I ask, but my question dissipates into the air as Phil pours Teddy some more whiskey and then says hi to me while leaning forward and giving me a restrained hug.

"What are you having? Need a refill?" Teddy takes the glass from my hand, makes sure Phil tends to me too.

"Why is the rest not important?" I say once the coast is clear.

"Because! What I do or how I talk to you or not isn't important."

"You're not the one to decide that."

"I am. Come on, let's go smoke."

He rises up theatrically, entertaining the people around us, and then we head to his office. We go in and he walks over to his desk, hands me a cigarette and pulls another one out of the pack for himself. I keep my distance; he's leaning on the window, giving me a look I know all too well.

"You don't really talk to me. You fuck me, that you do. Guess it's either-or for you."

"I do fuck you," he agrees.

"And even that's only once a decade."

He smiles, and I continue in a serious and matter-of-fact tone. "That's the position I'm in, and that's how you like it. You say it yourself. And as soon as I try to climb out, even the fucking stops."

"And what position is that?"

"Underneath you."

"Anywhere else you rather be? You made every effort to put yourself in that exact position."

I fall silent, blow the smoke out through the open window. "I know."

He nods his head, smokes and keeps his eyes on me.

"Has Lara started recovering?" I walk up to the ashtray on the table. "Yes."

"Has she been with the baby yet?"

"They let her hold her, the little one's connected to all those electrodes and tubes."

"What a nightmare." I rub my forehead. "At least she held her. I can't even imagine how she's feeling right now."

"Everything will be fine." He leans toward the table to stub out his cigarette and I place my hand on his neck. He eyes me.

"Let's go back out there." I take my hand away and stub out my cigarette. He stays standing close to me and moves only once I turn and start walking away.

I forgot my glass in Teddy's office, so I walk over to the bar in the middle of the lobby. I won't make it to King George today, I was naive to think I'd manage it on such a busy day, and I still have Passover dinner ahead of me. I text Roy.

> How are you getting to Dad's?
>
> Don't know yet . . . You?

Of course he doesn't know, why would he ever plan ahead? Hailey passes by me and gives a dramatic halt.

"Hey there! What's up? Where have you been hiding?"

"Hi. I had an accident."

"Yeah, obviously, everyone knows that. But that was ages ago, wasn't it?"

I smile, hoping the conversation will naturally die down without me having to acknowledge her remark, but I guess that silence triggers the next level with her—like a video game boss—seeing as now she's upping her audacity:

"Everything all right with Teddy?"

What's that supposed to mean? "How so?"

"I don't know, I saw you two having quite the talk over there. I thought that maybe you pulled a Jamie," she says with a wink, supposedly aimed to amuse me.

"Ah, no," I answer dismissively, feeling uncomfortable.

"So you still work here, officially?" She won't leave me alone, this horrible woman.

"Yes. Why?"

"You haven't been here for a while, we were wondering," so now she's a 'we,' "And the way you two were talking over there reminded me of him and Jamie."

I look at her and have no idea what to say. I suddenly recall how Adrian and I were standing and talking on his birthday, right where we're standing now. And this time I'm in Adrian's shoes, because maybe this is how he feels when he tries to have a conversation with someone.

"I don't really understand what you want." I say what Adrian might have said.

"What do you mean?" she replies with a question.

"I don't know why it reminded you of Jamie," I say even though I do know.

"Oops . . . I didn't mean to say anything I shouldn't have."

"Oops, you did it again?"

She laughs and grabs my arm—"You jokester, I missed your banter!"— and finally walks away. With all due respect to Richard, even though he's the one who got me here, I seriously don't understand his process when it comes to personnel. I wonder how he decided to hire me. What happened back there at the wedding? There's Richard, I can ask him.

"Of course I remember!" Richard is glad to reminisce. "I was impressed by the brilliant movie you'd made for them. The bride and groom were hugging you near the screen, and Teddy pointed at you and told me, 'She's the one who made the movie, call her over, maybe she'll be good for those Delmar movies of yours.'"

"And the rest is history," I add with a smile to hide my surprise at this new bit of information.

"Right you are!" Richard warmly presses my cheeks.

That despicable Teddy! I'm crazy about him. I need to revise my protocol, I think and smile to myself, and suddenly I get an idea to use my time in the office to print what I've written. Been itching to have it in my hands for days now.

I look for Maureen and find her in the kitchenette with her ass in the air as she leans down to get some paper cups from the bottom of the cupboard. She's surprised to discover me standing behind her when she rises back up, squeals, but then returns to her usual tone.

"What's up, Noa?" she pulls the wrapper off the paper cups.

"All good, how are you?"

"Great! How's the leg?"

"Much better. Hey, can I print something? I mean, where can I print something? My laptop's not here."

"Sure!" She's nicer than ever. "Email it to me, I'll print it for you."

No way, I can't send her that.

"Thanks. If there's a free computer I could use for a few minutes that would be best."

"You can use mine."

She leads me to her desk, and her neat and elongated nails speedily tap her password in. She resumes her party chores, and I go into my document and prepare it for printing. Teddy passes by me on his way to his office, then halts and takes a few steps back.

"Cancel all my meetings for today," he says, using his Teddy-to-Maureen tone, "and schedule one with you, in thirty minutes."

I look up and nod obediently, cooperating with my poker face on. He thanks me and goes into his office. I send the document for printing and quickly rush to the printer, don't want this falling into the wrong hands. It's only when I stand next to the printer as it spews the pages out that I realize how much I've written. The last page comes out, Golden Gate Bridge. I pick up the pile, loving its weight in my hands, and put it in my bag. I go back to Maureen's desk and delete the file without the option of recovery.

Thirty minutes later and there's hardly anyone left in the office. I may have had too much to drink. I look for Teddy and find him in his office, sitting by his desk.

"You going back to the hospital?" I say as I walk in.

"Yeah, in a bit." He's in a great mood, gives me a pleased look. "Want to come with me?"

"Hardy-fucking-har." I lean on the desk in order to maintain my balance. "What's with the glee? Lara's lying there in agony."

"Fully aware of that. I'll head there soon, what do you want me to do?"

"I don't know. What can you do?"

"Not much."

356 | MAYA KESSLER

"Okay." I check the time. "I might need a rest before dinner."

He reclines. "You have a meeting scheduled with me."

"I'll cancel."

"Sit down." He points at the chair in front of him, but I stay standing. "How are you getting to your dad's?"

"Don't know yet, Roy has no idea about anything as usual. Just clueless."

"Evil sister."

"No, I'm not an evil sister."

"Take my car, we're staying in town."

"But I can't drive yet."

"Roy can drive."

"No license. Maybe Thomas can drive. Whatever. Riveting discussion." I stare at him with a bored look and stretch my arms back. "Thank you. I almost forgot to say thank you."

He looks at my body. "Been a decade already?"

"At least."

"Noa." He shifts to a more lucid tone. "Will you sit down?"

"What for?"

"I want us to renegotiate our agreement."

Woah, now. "Okay." I sit down. How irresponsible of me to drink this much without eating anything, and how irresponsible of me to negotiate agreements in this state. What's he even talking about?

"What are your demands?" he begins.

"What are you offering?" I play along, unsure of where this is heading.

"At this stage—nothing."

"This is how you start a negotiation?"

"Of course. Always. What are your demands?"

"All right." I decide to reply seriously, despite feeling dazed. "Talk to me as your equal."

"Yes."

"Don't meddle in my life in a way that I can't control."

"Yes."

"Fuck me at least twice a decade."

"Define 'decade.'"

I think for a moment. "Ten days."

"Yes."

"Does 'yes' mean you're agreeing to the terms?"

"No. 'Yes' means I'm listening."

I fall silent for a moment. "Let me love you."

"Yes."

"That's pretty much it."

"Okay, I see. You're my equal, no meddling if you have no control over it, up the fucking by fifty percent, allow for loving," he summarizes quickly, and I understand how someone like him can run a huge firm when he's drunk for a considerable amount of the time. Impressive.

"Yes," I confirm. "And what are your demands?"

"Simple—no harming or putting yourself at risk, stay in touch with your mom, don't ask me to have a kid with you, don't get on my nerves—and you're welcome to stay with me until someone more interesting comes into your life. Or until I kick you out." He smiles. "Whichever one comes first. What do you say? We got a deal?"

I look at him, taking in everything he's said.

"Well?" He's waiting for an answer.

"I would have signed this straightaway back in the first week."

"And how about the last?" He smiles again.

"I need to think about it."

"Fair enough. Let me know, and if you decide to go for it, then you can leave your apartment and move into mine."

My heart skips a beat. I smile at him and he smiles back.

"Blow minding," I say in an amused tone, and then ask for real, "What is this? Is that what you want?"

"Yes. I like having you around."

"Didn't see that coming."

"Don't get too excited, this agreement's very bad for you."

›

A few minutes before we leave Teddy's apartment to attend our separate holiday meals, I'm standing in the kitchen, dressed and ready to go. Milo's sitting on the floor, sulking and playing tug-of-war with Xerox. Teddy's already back from the hospital and he's ready to head out.

"Where are they?" Teddy asks me. "You taking traffic into account?"

"They're late," I reply.

"I don't feel like going," Milo grumbles.

"Tough luck," Teddy dismisses him impatiently.

"I don't feel like leaving Xerox alone."

"Why, because it's the holidays?" I ask Milo with a smile.

"Yeah." He smiles too. "He doesn't like to be alone during the holidays."

"Why aren't you taking him to Alice's?"

"She's got cats," Milo mumbles with contempt.

"I can take him with me," I suggest and turn to Teddy. "Can he go in your car, or is it bad for the upholstery?"

"Sure he can, I don't care about the upholstery. Good, Noa takes Xerox, problem solved. C'mon, up you get, Milo, taxi's downstairs."

"I'd rather have Passover dinner with Noa and Xerox."

"Not an option. You're leaving the country in a week, so you're coming. Now get off your ass, get up!"

Milo rises and Teddy looks at me and smiles. I smile back at him.

The car windows are open and Xerox pops his head out into the wind, the potent scent of springtime. A quiet song plays on the radio. I look at Thomas's skinny hand on the steering wheel. Ever since he shared his insight about the resemblance between me and Nurit, I'm not his biggest fan. But I act like everything's normal so as not to make things heavy. Roy's sitting next to him. He turns back and gives me a look full of love.

"What do you want?" I ask.

"I'm proud of you, you know that?" He's talking about Nurit.

"Silence! I don't want to hear it," I tell him with a diminishing big-sister tone.

"Excuse me?! I'm allowed to say things too, you know."

"Why is that? Because you cooperated with the Forces of Evil? If anything, you're even less allowed."

"No. Because I'm your brother! Dickhead." He ends the conversation, then goes on babbling to Thomas about the costumes that the theater company's making for their wedding party or engagement banquet or whatever. I pet Xerox.

Mina's family sings the holiday songs differently from how my family used to sing them before the divorce. Roy and I look at each other and smile. Thomas seems fascinated, and I wonder if he's capable of being critical of the situation or if we simply seem exotic to him.

I go to the kitchen and open one of the bottles of wine Teddy's sent with me, a gift for my dad. Xerox circles around and sits down next to me. What an intense day: Nurit, Lara, the office, Teddy. And now this family shindig.

Did he actually ask me to move in with him?

Because what, things are going my way now? Xerox looks up at the ceiling. He's surely never come across such bright fluorescent lights before, must be shocked, the poor thing.

When I get back I see that the living room lights are on. That means Teddy's home. Xerox rushes in to look for Milo.

"How was it?" Teddy asks, sprawled on the couch.

"Is Milo home?"

"No."

It's only now that I feel how much I longed to get back to him, back to my place. His bare feet are on the table, one on top of the other, legs straight. His gorgeous feet. I kneel on the rug, lean down and press my face to his foot. He looks at me.

"You're beautiful," he declares. "Why are you smiling?"

"You haven't said that for a while now."

"You're right. But I see it every day, you being beautiful."

"How was yours?"

"Nice enough."

I kiss his foot, close my eyes. Xerox returns to us, disappointed about Milo being out. He sits down next to me and puts his face on Teddy's leg, gets a stroke in return.

>

After the holiday we rest for a few days. I take advantage of Milo still being around to spend time with him before he leaves for Denmark. Teddy's offer's still on the table.

It's Monday and I need to get back to King George. I want to pick up some cardboard boxes from a warehouse in the industrial quarter and decide to drive for the first time since the accident. I'm a bit tense at first, but that wears off pretty quickly.

As I stand in front of the warehouse shelves, deliberating between various box sizes, my phone rings. Unknown caller.

"Noa?" A young man's voice on the other end. "Hi, this is Leo, I got your number from Goldie."

Goldie's a seasoned producer I used to work with. She was one of the people I'd emailed when I was in Michigan; "I thought you only do props" was her. It's noisy around me, so I go deeper into the warehouse to hear him better.

Leo tells me he's producing a new comedy for TV, and I assume he wants me to do the props so I've already run the whole thing in my mind and reached the conclusion that I should take it, but then he explains that the network prefers a female director. *Director.*

"Well, I'm a female, so we're already off to a great start," I say and he chuckles and says that this is awkward for him too.

"And when I say that the network 'prefers,' I actually mean 'demands.'"

Now it's my turn to chuckle. I tell him that I'm interested, and he asks me to send him my details and bio.

"The schedule's super tight, so we need to finalize scripts ASAP. So after you read them, we'll get you to come in and meet the creator—how does that sound?"

I tell him that sounds great, and we say goodbye.

"What is this, running an office over here?" one of the warehouse employees, the receding-hairline-ponytail type, asks me while pushing a heavy cart. "Watch it, coming through."

"But why do you insist on constantly pushing your carts through my office?!" I ask as I step aside to make room for him.

He looks up at me. "Some smile you got there! That smile's why I keep coming through here—how do you like them apples?"

»

A week later, on the last day of April, the mission's accomplished: the King George apartment is completely cleared out. I wait for Teddy downstairs at his mother's building, thinking of all the days I've spent here—sorting, packing, donating, dragging heaped garbage bags to the dumpsters, calling and scheduling, napping on the couch while surrounded by the huge mess.

We take the elevator up and I look at him, incredibly excited. He gives me a little smile.

"Gentlemen and gentlemen . . . after three suspenseful weeks . . . give it up for . . . the King George apartment!" I open the door and gesture for him to walk in before me. He goes in, plants himself in one spot and looks around the empty apartment.

"Who did the cleaning?" He asks the most insignificant question possible.

"I did."

"I'd have gotten you a cleaning service, you psycho."

I look at him with contempt. He wanders around the vacant rooms, utterly silent.

"Well done?" I suggest some phrasing.

"Yes. Well done." He takes it.

"Does it feel strange?"

"Little bit." He looks at me and I see something vulnerable in his eyes, but then he says, "It's okay."

"I know," I say and move on to practical matters. "This is where

I gathered boxes for you to go through, these are your mom's and these are your dad's. And someone's coming to pick up that table next week."

"All right. You did good."

"Thank you."

"Impressive."

"The pleasure's all mine."

"The place is all yours."

"No, pleasure's mine, place is yours."

"Not anymore it isn't."

"What do you mean?"

"It's yours now."

"What's that?"

"All yours."

Does he mean what I think he means? My heart starts racing. "No. What does that even mean? Absolutely not."

"It just is."

"No, no, no . . . I can't."

"Afraid you have no choice. You think you can tell me what to do with my money?"

"Teddy, this is pissing me off now, stop it. That's not why I did it, you're giving me a headache with this shit."

He laughs, peers toward the kitchen. What the fuck? How does he always twist everything around?

He stands at the entrance to the bedroom. "How did you manage to get her giant bed out?"

"I found someone who dismantled it and took it." I lean on the wall in the narrow hallway. He stands facing me.

"What?" He's smiling.

"You know what."

"What's the matter? You told me to donate it."

"Right."

"So, what's wrong? I'm donating it to you."

"No! Not to me!"

"Why not? Got some financial safety net you never told me about?"

"That has nothing to do with this."

"Your parents don't have enough money and never will."

My heart's pounding and I'm starting to tremble. "Is this because of the whole thing with Nurit's apartment and Roy?"

"Completely unrelated, I don't know any of the details there. And anyway, how much are you going to get from that apartment? They have no way of supporting you, I know that much."

"Fine, I'm supporting me."

"Yes, that's good, that's what you should be doing. But you have nothing and that's not good, so now you've got this. At least that."

"What are you talking about? No one just gifts apartments. Who does that? There's Adrian and there's Milo, it's all good. This is theirs to have one day."

"You're worried about them? You sweet thing." He shifts from the hallway toward the living room. "Their future's all set for them, Noa. Way beyond this little apartment, trust me. In any case, monster, this is my decision, and if you don't want it then go ahead and donate it yourself, because it's yours."

I don't know what to do with myself. I look around and silence the inner voice that wants to celebrate this wonderful, insane news, this unfathomable gift. No, this is too much. "I don't know what to say."

"Thank you?"

"This isn't real. People don't just give away million-dollar apartments, with all due respect."

"One-point-four," he says while peering into an empty closet, "if you want to be precise."

"What?— Okay, this doesn't make any sense, and I don't want to be precise. I won't accept this."

"No one's asking you."

"That's not why I did this. I did it for you."

"You did it to piss me off," he reminds me who I'm dealing with here.

"That was my starting point, true, that was my initial muse," I admit. "But then I kept going for you."

"I know."

"Then please don't give it to me."

He stands in the middle of the empty living room and looks at me. "You know you're the only person I brought here, since she died?"

"What do you mean?"

"Just you. Matt was here once, and then again when you came with him. That's it."

"Lara, the boys?"

"No one."

I take a deep breath. "So why me?"

He thinks for a moment. "I don't know."

"Did you know I'd react this way? That this is what I'd do?"

"No. Didn't even cross my mind."

That moves me, and I nod my head at him with a look that says I realize the great honor bestowed upon me.

»

("Are you coming?") I can hear Lara's voice through his phone as we sit at the big table having breakfast. I spread butter on my toast.

"In a bit," he tells her, and I hope I manage to hear some more. "Is that it? They're getting your discharge papers?" ("Yeah. I think. They took the   ) "I'll be there in a bit." (   )

"Okay. Bye."

He gets up. "Need a ride to your meeting?"

"No, thanks."

I open the huge folder that's accompanied me for the past few days, the scripts for the comedy series inside it, dividers separating the episodes.

›

At Leo the producer's office, I open the folder. "So I've jotted down all of my comments and ideas and questions." I recline on the chair.

"Wow, not bad!" Leo pulls the folder over to him and quickly browses through it, and I think he's at least a decade younger than me. "I see you did your homework. Greg, do you prefer the comments on file or printed?" He looks up at the creator, who's leisurely sitting on the chair next to me, seems to be around my age, sporting a T-shirt.

"I have a file of it, I can send it over to you," I quickly say.

"Okay, let's have a look, don't hog it," Greg reprimands Leo and pulls the folder over to him. He browses through the pages and pauses on one of the comments in the first episode. A conversation ensues about that comment, and even before we discuss the project as a whole, we're already sucked into all the little details. I can immediately tell that Greg and I can work well together, the dialogue between us is just as it should be between two collaborators. I feel a huge relief.

Leo uses the moment to sneak out of the room for a phone call, and Greg and I continue talking.

"Well done for writing this. It's good," I compliment him. "Very glad to be directing it."

"Thank you." He puts the folder down and looks at me. "You do know we've met before."

That surprises me. It always feels strange when someone recognizes me but I don't recognize them. "Where did we meet?"

"You don't remember?"

"No, and I think you're confusing me with someone else, because I'd remember."

"It was a long time ago."

I look at him, shaking my head with an embarrassed smile. "Well?"

"Backwoods Kids summer camp, back in the nineties."

My eyes widen. "No way!"

"Way."

"Greg!"

"Remember anything?"

"Of course!"

"I remember you perfectly."

"This is unbelievable. I remember a Greg from that camp, but I didn't connect him to you."

He smiles. "What do you remember from there?"

"All sorts of stuff."

"You remember how your mom came for a visit?"

Slight chills run down my spine. I'm surprised he remembers that. "Yes."

"And she brought lemon popsicles for everyone."

"Apricot. It was apricot popsicles. They were orange."

"No, it was lemon popsicles."

"No."

"I swear."

"No way."

"Lemon."

"Apricot."

"I'll find a photo."

"Why, did you take a selfie with it?"

"No. I guess there's no proof of it happening, you'll have to take my word for it."

"This is insane . . . Greg!" I lightly shove his arm. "How crazy."

"Noa. Thought about you for years."

"Really? How come?"

He thinks for a moment, a gentle smile. "I don't know, there was something off about you, you weren't like the other girls."

Leo comes back into the room and sits down in front of us.

"You think our weighty history's going to get in the way of us working together?" I ask Greg.

"No, not at all. On the contrary."

Leo looks concerned. "What weighty history?"

"You familiar with Backwoods Kids?" I ask.

"Never heard of it. Who produced it? Which network?"

Greg and I look at Leo and smile.

❯

When I leave the meeting I have a text from Nurit awaiting me. Strange feeling. I'm not used to getting texts from her. Wonder if she remembers which flavor those popsicles were.

> Hi Noa , I'm reaching out to see if you'll come up to Jerusalem wit me , next week to visit grandma? It'll make her happy , its important. And I'd really like it too of course .

Go visit Grandma with her? The first instinct is resistance. I light a smoke. Jerusalem again, plus going there with Nurit, being there with her. But I know Grandma needs to see us and I know it's okay, that I can do it, that I'm going to do it.

》

"Here are the clothes from the dryer." I put a pile of warm clothes on Milo's bed.

"Oh man, I forgot all about those!" Milo unzips his suitcase.

"How did you forget? I reminded you at least twice. Never mind, you've got enough room in there."

I sit down on his bed and fold the remaining clothes. Teddy stands at the entrance to the room.

"Can we get going?" he asks Milo and then looks at me. "I'll meet you at the bar. Text me the address."

Tonight is Thomas and Roy's engagement party. Teddy's taking Milo to the airport and then he'll join me. It'll be the first time he's coming with me to one of my events. Milo battles the zipper; I lean on the suitcase to help him.

"Let's go. Got your passport?" Teddy asks and leaves the room without waiting for an answer. Milo and I are alone.

"Got your passport?" Milo repeats after his father with a smile, rolling his eyes.

"Got your passport!" I say and stand facing him.

"Babycakes!" He spreads his arms to the sides, inviting me in for a hug.

"Babycakes!" I embrace him tightly. "I'll miss you."

"I'll miss you too. Watch over him."

"I will." I stay with the hug and lean my head slightly back. "You mean Teddy, right?"

"I mean Xerox."

We hug again.

❭

When I get to the bar, Roy leaps onto me and starts crying, genuinely crying, tears and all. I hug him and smell his familiar scent, a scent that always makes me a little uncomfortable, because that's what nature does with biological siblings.

"Why are you crying? Why do you always have to cry?"

"You are a cold, soulless, and emotionally stunted individual. Just so you know."

"You're really starting to get all bridezilla up in here."

"So, what do you think?" He takes a step back and presents his extravagant clothes, then calls Thomas over so I can see their matching outfits.

"Ravishing!" I say.

I give Thomas a loose hug and go to the bar for a drink. I sit on one of the barstools and look around to see who's come to congratulate the royal couple. Luckily, Nurit's not supposed to come tonight. Otherwise I wouldn't have invited Teddy.

Roy has a very tight clique, childhood friends. I actually like them. I even slept with one of them once, Ethan, and there he is, walking in, hand in hand with a brunette sporting thick glasses, looks like a Goody Two-shoes. My phone rings: it's Teddy.

"Is that it? He's off?" I lean forward, putting a hand on my other ear to block the noise.

"Yes."

"Did you get my text with the address?"

"Yes, Noa, but I'm not coming."

I fall silent for a moment. "Why not?"

"Not in the mood."

He must be sad about saying goodbye to Milo. But I really want him to be here.

"I understand. But it's important for me that you come," I venture.

He stays quiet, and I hope he's reconsidering.

"I know. Sorry."

How disappointing. "Okay."

"Have fun. Send my regards."

Can't handle disappointment right now, but I can't help myself. Can't handle not helping myself either.

I'm past the second drink by the time Ethan comes over to say hi. It's uncomfortable when he hugs me since my face is smack in front of his girlfriend. I quickly release myself from the hug, which he interprets as rejection and asks if I'm a snob now. He introduces his girlfriend, who turns out to be his wife. She's a medical intern. Along with the future doctor, he also brought a water bottle spiked with synthetic psychoactive substances, and I think that a little bit of liquid Molly can only do the opposite of harm, so I drink the maximum amount one can gulp without seeming inconsiderate toward others.

Two cigarettes and eight mundane conversations later, I can already feel it taking effect, so I go back to the bottle to have another sip. Ethan must have had quite a bit, since he's disproportionately happy about my asking for a top-up. I stand next to him and think that maybe Teddy will still make it here after all. I check my phone. No texts from him, but got one from Nurit.

> Hi Noa, sorry for disturbing you
> at Roy's party. If you can pick me
> up tomorrow that would be great
> but if it doesn't work out then we
> can meet in Jerusalem .

Nothing I want more than to think about the Jerusalem trip right now! I'm too intoxicated.

I imagine us sitting at Grandma's. I reply that I'll pick her up. It makes sense. They had to endure me all these years, it's about time I start making it up to them. It's high time. When all is said and done, out of the two of us, I'm the one who's caused the most damage to this miserable family. I should drink some more.

The evening starts out with around twenty guests, but by the end there's just a small group of us left, and we decide to continue the night somewhere else. We walk down the main street, laughing. Thomas and Roy are skipping at the front, elated. The drugs have made me carefree and happy; the disappointment from earlier has crammed itself into a hidden corner and I don't care anymore about Teddy not coming. Better off.

We continue down the street, find another bar. There are loads of people outside, and our group scatters throughout the crowd. We sit down on the edge of the sidewalk amid the commotion, Ethan, the medical intern, and I.

"I need water. You've got to get me some water, stat." That's the intern, but Ethan's folded like a noodle and won't stop laughing, and we realize he's in no state to care for his young wife, so I get up and tell them I'll get some water.

Quite the mission I've taken upon myself! The stupid waiters are crazy busy, Roy and Thomas are nowhere to be seen, the bar's packed and I can't get to the bartenders. I look around. I see Buy the Way, a convenience store, across the street. I somehow manage to cross the road and approach the store when suddenly he passes by me, walking fast, doesn't notice me.

My mind is trying to calculate my moves but my first instinct overrides: "Adrian!"

He stops and turns to see who's calling him. His mouth's slightly open, which makes him seem confused.

"Adrian!" I call him again, walking toward him until he notices me, and reacts with a single nod of the head.

"Hi, what are you doing here?" he asks and looks to the side, maybe checking to see if Teddy's around too.

"I'm here with my brother and his friends."

"Ah," he says awkwardly, and then raises his hand with hesitation and adds, "Bye," and before I know it he's already got his back to me, walking away. I look at the other side of the road for a moment, searching for the giggler and his thirsty intern, then turn and look in the direction Adrian's heading and see him disappearing around the corner. I have to stop him. I rush after him, reach the turn and continue into an alleyway until I see him down the street. "Adrian, wait a minute!"

He looks back and stops when he sees me. I walk quickly, fully aware of my heavy leg. "Wait a minute," I repeat, breathless, even though he's already stopped. He stands there, frozen, looks at me with an embarrassed gaze of a kid who doesn't understand what he did wrong. His eyes scurry, searching for refuge.

"Sorry, one second." I bend down and lean my arms on my thighs, trying to catch my breath.

"You're not in shape."

I look up. "I haven't been in shape for a single day in my entire life." I straighten and stare at him; he stays silent and waits. "I wanted to talk to you for a minute."

"What about?" His eyes finally fix on mine. "What for?"

"What do you mean?"

"What's there to talk about?" He looks to the side again.

"I don't know. Just . . . stuff. Like, hi."

"We already said hi." He's being difficult.

"Milo left tonight."

"I know."

He's not going to cooperate, and I feel silly and can't quite understand what I want from him, but I better get it together and fast. "Listen, I'm a little bit drunk right now, so maybe I'm being totally out of line—"

"You're fine," he mumbles.

"I know we hardly know each other, but I always feel like something's bothering you."

"So?" He shrugs his shoulders, and I can tell by his reaction that I'm right.

"So, I wanted to ask you about it. And maybe I'll get an answer, maybe you will want to tell me. Because I want to know."

"No." He suddenly gives a slight smile—but not a soft smile, rather an angry one. "You don't want to know."

"I do."

"You're his, what do you want from me?" he says, revealing the same thing he'd shown me during our brief encounter on his birthday.

I look at him, the streetlight's casting a shadow on his face. "Can't you believe that I care?"

"About what?"

"About you, and how you feel."

"No. I don't know. Why would you care?"

"Because. I mean, am I supposed to just ignore you? Pretend like I don't see that there's an issue?"

"I don't get why it matters to you." He glances in the direction he was heading.

"It just does. I want to know what's on your mind. Why you're angry."

He stays silent for a moment, looks at the sidewalk. I wait patiently.

"You're actually a nice one. Why are you with him? What do you see in him? Because it's definitely not the money. I imagine there's loads of rich men around who aren't fat liars like him."

His toxicity toward Teddy brings up contrasting feelings within me, but I follow his lead. "Yes, I know he's a liar." I look at him closely, my jaw tightening from all the drugs.

"At least that."

" 'You're actually a nice one,' " I quote him. "Compared to who? Lara?"

At the sound of her name, he waves his hand dismissively. "What does it matter?"

"I thought you didn't like her."

"Is that what he told you?"

"No, he doesn't tell me anything. Milo told me something like that once, said you weren't fond of Lara."

"Well, that makes sense. That's probably what he told Milo. What do you know about Lara?"

"Not much."

"Yes, because you're kept in the dark, just like everyone else." Is he starting to enjoy this?

"Right." I nod my head and my phone starts ringing. I glance at the screen and see it's Roy, then quickly silence the call.

Adrian withdraws again. "Okay. I think I'll go now, before we say something we might regret, all right?" He wants to say something, even though he might regret it.

"No, not all right. Who are you trying to protect?"

"Myself," he says with a slightly raised voice, and then it hits me—he must be drunk too, but I haven't noticed it up till now because he's so withheld.

"I don't understand." I give him a look that demands an explanation. He stalls and I keep the look going and watch as it starts taking effect and I feel like he just needs a little push. "Make me understand."

"Ever asked him how he met Lara?"

"No."

"Why not?"

"Because he barely talks to me about her. He wouldn't answer that."

"Are you really that uninformed? You're his girlfriend, aren't you?"

"How did he meet Lara?"

"Through me."

"Through you? She was your girlfriend?"

"No, but I was in love with her for a pretty long time. She was a colleague of mine. And I'm sorry, I still don't see the point in telling you any of this."

"How does 'out of pity' sound?"

That makes him laugh: all at once a smile overtakes his face, vanquishing the harsh expression. "You really do deserve some pity."

"That's right, they even say I tried to harm myself!" I give something back to him for the information he's divulged.

"Yes, so I've heard." He looks at me and it seems like he appreciates my sharing. "Pity."

"Who told you?"

"About your accident? My mom."

"And what did she tell you?"

"That he thinks you tried to kill yourself. That's what he told my mother."

"You see?"

"I know. You think I don't know?"

"Wait, but did he know you were into her?" I bring us back on track.

"Probably. She used to come over with me to his place back when I lived there."

"Yes. So I guess he knew."

"She constantly wanted to hang out with me. Looking back, I can see why." He looks at me and there's some light on his face now, and I see the pain in his eyes. "I realized a few things in hindsight. For

374 | MAYA KESSLER

instance, we'd hang out and then she'd say good night and leave, and I'd go to sleep, and then she'd come back and have sex with him. That's my father. That's who he is."

How incredibly fucked up. "That's who he is," I repeat after him, and it feels weird to relate to his experience and at the same time to know precisely what Lara felt when she came back to fuck Teddy, and even—in a sick way—to feel jealous of her.

"Yeah." He stays in his candid mode for a moment longer, finally someone listening to him, someone from his father's camp.

"How did it come out?"

He blinks in a sort of slight spasm, which reminds me of the first time I met him. "What?"

"Did he tell you?"

"No, much worse." He smiles bitterly, seems to be enjoying shocking me. "Lara did."

"Lara told you? Jesus. And what did he do?"

"Married her?" he says sarcastically. "Since that's what he ended up doing."

"Right, but did he talk to you about it?"

He looks down at the sidewalk and shakes his head. "He sat me down for a talk," he reports in a dry tone. "It was after Lara had spoken to me, after she told me they were in love, and that they weren't getting married because he didn't want to tell me, and so she asked me for my blessing." He says that last sentence with repulsion.

I feel him opening up, and I can't abandon him now. "Idiots. And what did Teddy say when he sat you down for a talk?"

"He said it's for me to decide if I found it acceptable or not."

"For you to decide? No way." What have they done to this kid? "Did your mother know about the whole thing?"

"No, why would she?"

"Do you know about Lara being in the hospital? And the baby and all that?"

"Yes." He gives me a look I completely understand: the look of a kid who knows he's right to be angry on the one hand, but feels guilty on the other, as though his anger's played some part in the catastrophe. "I have to go, I need to be somewhere."

"Okay. Thank you for telling me, Adrian. Should I keep this between us?"

He thinks for a moment. "No." He's already turning to leave. "Now you know. So do whatever the hell you want with it. Good night."

Now I know. I'll do whatever the hell I want with it.

"Where are you guys?"

"Where are we?!" Roy's at his most dramatic when he's drunk and stoned. "You're insane! We thought you got run over! I've already called all the hospitals, and I'm about to call the morgue if you'll just clear the line for me, please!"

"Shut up. I bumped into someone I know. Where you at?"

I find them back at that bar. Hard to miss them—after all, only two out of all these people look like they've just finished their swan song at the Eurovision finals. After a cigarette I feel like I need to be alone, so I say goodbye to everyone and leave.

›

Hit the ground again. Walk it back.

I can understand some of it; I can understand falling in love, I can understand wanting and crossing the line, I can even understand crossing that specific, incredibly problematic line. But the secrecy, it won't leave me be. Where does that put us? What's the point?

Main road. Piles of fresh newspapers waiting outside the stores.

Lines have been crossed, yes. And the damage is done.

›

Dawn breaks through the sky. I take the elevator up to the apartment, quietly walk in. Xerox is waiting at the entrance. After I pee, I feed him and then stand in the kitchen and drink some water.

Here's the living room. This is where it happened, this is where he met Lara when she came to hang out with Adrian. This is where he fell in love, this is where he fucked her. What kind of idiot does that? And what kind of idiot gets jealous about it?

I slowly walk up to his bed, sit down carefully and observe him. He's not hers anymore. He's not mine either. His sleep is shallow, and I guess he feels my presence because he's opening his eyes.

"How was it?" he asks and sits up, drinks some soda out of a glass bottle next to him, puts his glasses on and quickly glances at his phone.

"It was fun."

"Good."

He takes off his glasses and puts the back of his hand on his forehead. I reach out my hand and caress his inner arm, which attracts me even when it's attached to a disgraceful man who can do something like that to his own son. He looks at me with distant eyes. I know something he doesn't know I know.

"Is this how she'd come into your room at night?"

"Who?" He's even more beautiful when he's just woken up.

"Lara, while Adrian was asleep in his room."

His eyes are surprised, examining me. He's almost motionless, but judging by the way his mouth is closed, I can tell he's tense.

"Who told you that?" He can be scary in these kinds of moments. I'm not scared anymore.

"You want to tell me yourself?"

"No."

"Why not?"

"Not proud of the whole thing. Who did you talk to?"

"So when you're not proud, you don't tell?"

"Where's this coming from?"

"Did she fall in love with you?"

He sighs. "Noa."

"Did she fall in love with you?" I ask again so he knows I'm not going to give up this time.

"Yes. Madly," he says coldly. "Sound familiar?"

I ignore his remark but note that he's detected an opportunity to hurt me. "And you fell for her?"

"Madly." And what could be more painful than his truth? "Who did you talk to? Tell me."

"Not a lot of people know about it, right?"

"Right. Did you talk to Lara?" He takes a shot in the dark.

"No. Adrian."

"Adrian? Adrian told you that? I doubt it."

"Yes, he did."

"What were you doing talking to him?"

"What have you done?"

"What are you asking? What do you want to know?"

"Who you are and what you do and what you're capable of."

"Okay, I think you got a pretty clear picture of it all. Can you move, I want to get up." I shift aside and he sits up, puts his feet down on the colorful rug beneath his bed.

"I was hoping the picture wasn't all that clear."

"You're judging me for something very complicated, which involves other people, people you don't know," he says as he walks into the bathroom.

"I'm not judging yet, just asking you what happened." I stand at the entrance.

"And then you'll do the judging?"

"Yes. Did you know how Adrian felt about her?"

He pees and falls silent for a moment, as though considering whether to even continue this conversation. "Nothing was said explicitly, but I saw the way he looked at her and how he behaved when she was around, yes."

"So you saw he was in love with her."

"Of course he was in love with her, come on. Who wouldn't be? But it was irrelevant, she never wanted him." He flushes.

Anger rises within me. "She didn't want him. But she did want you."

"That's right." He breaks the wave with his cockiness, and the anger's gushing through me now, flooding.

"What do you mean 'that's right'? He's your son. How fucked up can a person get?"

"She's older than him."

"So what?"

"So nothing. She wasn't interested." He leans down to wash his face over the sink.

"Did you try to stop it from happening?"

"Of course I did. I couldn't help it, just couldn't."

"Why not?"

"Because I wanted her. And she wouldn't give up." He glances at me through the mirror. "Just like you."

"You like it when we don't give up."

"I do. And so do you."

He walks over to the kitchen and I follow him and Xerox follows me. The sky outside is grayish blue, deep hues. The apartment's dark; he turns on a little light and starts brewing some coffee.

"Then why didn't it end with some discreet fuck and then call it a day? How come she got more?" I think I'm getting confused and injecting myself into it. Or is he the one doing that? In any case, he sniffs it out straightaway, the motherfucker.

"'How come she got more?' How come you got more?"

"But I wasn't Adrian's."

"All right, give me a break. She wasn't Adrian's either."

He stands there, not budging, his eyes fixed on me. When I was preparing for this carnage on my way here, I'd assumed that he wouldn't account for his actions. But that's not what's happening. He lights a cigarette.

"And now you tell me. Tell me what you did. Did you go talk to him?"

"I bumped into him on the street and tried to talk to him, yes. And even managed to, a bit."

He goes quiet, closes his eyes and exhales, as though trying to calm himself down. "You must have driven him crazy until he told you."

"Yeah, a little bit."

"Wish you hadn't."

"Why?"

"Because it's unnecessary. In case you haven't noticed, Lara and I aren't together anymore. And that has to do with Adrian too."

"Sounds to me like it has more to do with you than with Adrian."

"Fine." He loses his patience. "I don't care what it sounds like to you. Didn't we agree that you won't get on my nerves?"

I look at him. I'm tired. "Yes. You're right."

"Then get off my case and leave me alone."

"Okay." I lean on the kitchen counter, holding my head in my hands. "I'll leave you alone."

We're quiet. He stubs out his cigarette and takes the moka pot off the stove.

I stare at the swirls on the wooden counter, speaking with my face down. "I'm done."

"Done getting on my nerves?"

"No. I'm done with this." I say with my eyes still on the swirls.

"Okay." He pours the coffee and a pleasant scent surrounds us.

"Had enough."

"Enough of what? Enough of me? Because of Lara?"

"No." I rise. "Because you could have told me. And you didn't. Not just this, everything else too. Because that's the way you operate, that's your MO. What you choose to divulge and what you don't, and when."

He doesn't take his eyes off me. His lips are shut, maybe he's even biting them from the inside; his arms are crossed and his body is on the defense.

But his eyes, his eyes are with me, mine, he's genuinely listening to everything I'm saying. "And how long can I stay with you and be kept in the dark? Not knowing shit, not knowing what you're up to? See, that's your freedom, right there, it's defined by the boundaries you set for the people around you."

His look shifts to the side and then returns to me. "Never thought of it that way."

"But you like it." I smile. "You like it that way. But it's not good for me."

He lets all the air out in one sharp sigh. "I know."

"It's dangerous for me. That's why I suited you so well, your pattern. I can understand why."

"Me too. You tired?"

I look at him. I forgot he's also my friend. "Very."

"Then go to bed. You can leave me tomorrow."

"I have that stupid Jerusalem thing tomorrow."

"It's not stupid, it's important. Then leave me the day after tomorrow, okay? Go to sleep."

I look at him. He's right, I want to sleep. He turns me around and leads me to the bedroom, helps me undress even though I don't need help and puts me to bed.

"When should I wake you up?"

"Ten o'clock."

"You don't have long to sleep. This is how you're going to Jerusalem?"

"Yes. Promise that I won't do what I did last time."

"Right. Since when do you admit to that? This is new to me." He covers me with his blanket and looks at me from above.

"I've been researching it. See that over there?" I point at the little table. "The papers?"

He shifts his eyes to the pile of white pages. "Is that your research?"

I put my head down on the pillow, smile and close my eyes. "And don't think for a minute that I'm not jealous."

"Of who?" Sounds like he's walking away from the bed.

"Of Lara."

"Lara? After all of that, you're jealous of her? Then who's fucked up here, care to tell me, monster?"

With my eyes shut, I raise my hand, indicating that it's me, I'm fucked up. I hear him mumbling to himself as he leaves the room.

"This kind of shit, first thing in the morning, you fucking cunt, at least make me some coffee next time, wake me up with a cup of coffee before you start your witch hunt. Come on, Xerox, I'll take you out for a walk because you're a good boy."

›

My phone won't stop ringing. I wake up to a splitting headache. The phone won't let up.

"Hey."

"Get up, been trying to wake you up for nearly an hour."

"Shit, sorry, what time is it?"

"Eleven."

"Fuck. Why did I agree to do this with her the morning after the party?"

"Because she asked you and you wanted to say yes."

"Right." I use all my strength to sit up. "I'm dead."

"Told Matt to take you. He's waiting downstairs. When you're ready just go down."

"But I'm supposed to pick her up."

"Then have Matt drive you there and pick her up. What's the problem?"

"It'll be awkward."

"Get over it."

I somehow manage to get out of bed. "Fuck! Fucking hangover. I'm dying."

He laughs. "Moved from dead to dying. See? You're better already."

"What will you do in Jerusalem now? I'm sorry," I tell Matt after he allows me to sit in the back because the windows there are darker.

"I'll go to the market. My cousin's there, just around the corner from your grandma's place."

He continues talking about his cousin until we stop in front of Nurit's building. The back door opens and Nurit appears. So much light.

"What's this, Noa, a chauffeur?" She sits down next to me and leans forward toward Matt. "Hi there, nice to meet you."

I introduce them and quickly explain how we got to this situation. She smiles and nods her head, but doesn't say a thing, then she looks out the window. She's careful not to slip. I put my sunglasses back on and look through my window.

The ride's calm, we occasionally talk a little. She asks about the party, I tell her about it and show her some photos.

The bright letters at the city entrance: *Welcome to Jerusalem*. Matt drops us off outside my grandma's building. We're standing on the sidewalk and I look up, and to my surprise I see Grandma by the window, watching us.

"Look." I point up.

"Is that her standing by the window?" Nurit tries to see and then swaps glasses. "How silly, why would she be waiting by the window?"

When we go in, Nurit and Grandma hug in the same way Grandma and I usually do, lovingly yet restrained. Limited edition hug. Then Grandma hugs me and says some things about the accident and the great fortune we've had.

"Mother," Nurit says with full diction and I realize that I clearly remember the way she speaks to my grandma, "I brought you some ginger cookies as well as the social security paperwork for you to sign."

They deal with some bureaucracy for a while, a slight argument ensues, and I watch them from the couch. It warms my heart, that familiar tension between them, and even though I thought I would sympathize with Grandma, I find myself occasionally siding with Nurit. I tend to feel frustrated by my grandma's compulsions too.

Afterward, Grandma needs the restroom. Her caretaker takes her, and Nurit goes with them, even though her help really isn't necessary; maybe she feels guilty about someone else nursing her mother, so when she's here she tries to get involved.

After Grandma's back in her seat, she looks at the two of us through the narrow crevices beneath her weighty eyelids.

"Seeing the two of you here together . . ." she says and shakes her head heavily, doesn't complete the sentence. Nurit doesn't react, which I think is out of character, but she stays quiet and there's silence all around.

And then I see my grandma crying. She wipes her tears with her skinny finger, and Nurit leans over and hands her a tissue. I don't think I've ever seen her cry before.

How can I make them happy? I tell them that I'm about to direct a TV show.

"Seriously?" Nurit asks. "Did you write it?"

"No. I wish."

"Well, that's still great!" she quickly adds. "Right? This is something you want, isn't it?"

"Wait a minute," Grandma says and shifts her squinted look from Nurit to me. "I don't understand."

"She's going to be directing a TV show." Nurit enunciates each word.

"On national TV?" Grandma asks me, her eyes wide.

"On national TV, Grandma," I say with a smile and look at Nurit. She smiles too.

>

"Where are you headed? The office?" Matt asks after we drop Nurit off back at her place. "Works for me because I have to go by there anyway."

"Okay," I say and think that maybe it would be a good idea to see Teddy for a moment after everything that happened over the past twenty-four hours.

I go up to the office with Matt, only to find out Teddy's not even there.

"He went out for lunch," Maureen says, "but I have no idea where or who with."

"Okay." I thank her and get out of there, dazed as can be.

Where are you? |

I don't send it because I think I know where he is. I walk down the street, cross the road and go into one of his favorite restaurants. The hostess asks if I have a table booked and I peer inside and see that familiar back. I tell her I'm joining someone and walk in.

Luckily for me he's on his own, sitting there going through contracts or whatever. I sit down in the chair across from him, and only then do I see what he's reading. He puts the pages down and looks at me.

I smile. "Any good?" I ask.

He smiles too. "Yes."

"How's Teddy?"

"Not as charming as Richard."

My heart's pounding wildly and my smile widens. I put my hand over my face to try to hide it. "Who gave you permission to read it?" I mumble through my hand. Can't hide my smiling eyes.

"You did."

"And what do you say?"

"What do I say, Noa?"

"Yes, that's precisely what I want to know." I put my hand down. "What do you say?"

"I say it's good." He looks at me. "You sure can write. You're good."

My heart's pushing through my rib cage, as though trying to get out of me and cross the table and reach him. "Thank you."

"What are you so pleased about?" He laughs, and I think that he might be feeling pleased too.

"I'm happy that you read it. How does it feel?"

"It's a great pleasure to get to know you without you getting in my way."

I laugh. "That's a nice thing to say."

"You describe things incredibly precisely. Certain things of mine too, I guess."

I nod my head and smile. He returns a smiling nod.

"And the fucking, how did I describe the fucking?"

He breathes in and goes serious, leans back. "With terrifying precision."

Happiness gushes all the way to the depths of my soul. "Yeah?"

"Yes."

"Then my job here is done!"

He finishes the last sip of wine in his glass. "I guess mine is too."

"Thank you," I say and I mean everything, everything he's given me. "And, Teddy, about King George—"

He raises his hand and stops me. "It's already happening. Save it, Noa, it's not up for discussion, I'm telling you. Don't waste your energy."

"You seriously expect me to accept that?"

"Absolutely. Yes. I demand it."

"What kind of demand is that?" I ask, but I won't get an answer since he just smiles at me with those beloved teeth. Knowing they won't be mine anymore is unbearable. Those hands, those eyes, the arms, the scent. The scent. No, what will I do without it? And that cock.

"What about your cock?"

"What about it?"

"How are we doing this? Joint custody?"

He laughs. "I'll miss your humor."

"I'll miss your everything."

"Why didn't you tell me you let Frank Clancy fuck you?"

My eyes shift in embarrassment. "It didn't seem to be of interest to you at the time. Why?" I look at him again. "Does it matter?"

"No. It's fine."

"Thought so."

"I'll kill him. But it's fine."

I smile, give it a minute to sink in. "So, generally speaking, you could say I've made it, I'm right where you wanted me to be."

"Yes."

"So are you happy?"

"No."

"And who's the next one after me?"

"You said there's no one after you."

"That's right."

"So, no one."

"Sometimes it's convenient that you're a liar."

He smiles at me. He's beautiful.

"Teddy"—I love him so very much—"I'll come visit."

"I'll let you in."

How do you part from a love like this? Who in the world can walk away from such a thing?

Teddy. That's who. If I could have just become him. I look at his smile and I smile too. I suddenly realize something, very clearly: "You'll get over this, won't you?"

He looks at me and answers quietly: "Yes, afraid so. I'll get over it."

I take a breath. "Then so will I."

"I know." He smiles.

A waiter towers above us and asks me, "Would you like a menu?"

"No thank you."

"Check, please," Teddy says, and then tilts his head toward me. "She'll get it."

I'm surprised. I nod to the waiter in approval.

"Noa," he says when the waiter leaves us.

"What?"

"Will you let me have you?"

I try to understand but I can't. "Meaning what?"

"Meaning just that."

"I already did."

"I know, but right now, will you let me have you right now?"

I look at him. "You mean you want to fuck?"

"Yes."

"Right now?"

"Yes."

I lean back, but it feels like my heart stays in place. "And then what?"

He looks at me and smiles, "And then again."

+

And this is what Nurit wrote me:

When you were about two years old, maybe almost three, we were sitting in the waiting room at the doctor's office. There were a few other people there, sitting quietly and waiting for their turns.

You were wandering around them. Suddenly one of them, a fat man, got up to grab a magazine, and you came up behind him and hugged him. He froze in his spot, paused for a moment, and out of embarrassment—and before I could even see his surprised look—I told him, "Sorry!" with an apologetic smile, and then turned to you and said, "Noa, what are you doing?"

And you answered me immediately, without hesitation:

"But Mommy, I love him."

» THANK YOU

Ori Ravin › Tzvi Gutter › Lee Oren › Asaf Danziger › Dafi Grossman ›
Oded Ben Yehuda › Matan Shalita › Ran Hartstein › Itamar Heifetz ›
Kariv Aviaz › Shahar Rodrig › Maya Thomas › Alma Cohen Vardi ›
Willehad Eilers › Alona Rivka Cohen › Nili Landesman › Maya Sela ›
Netta Gurevitch › Neta Hoter › Dr. Haggai Sharon › Avi Shomer ›
Hannah Solmor › Lucia Marquez › Guy Ben Nun › Alexander Valik ›
Aaron Barnett › Gil Tevet › Yehoshua Ziv › Dalia & Eran Ravin ›
Shachar Stern › Avital Barak › Michal Geller › Einat Schreiber ›
Keren Friedland › Dorit Ben Shoshan › Shlomo Cohen ›
Elliot R. Kessler & Adam R. Kessler + my mom: Ruta Cohen

The Deborah Harris Agency » my editor & agent Jessica Kasmer-Jacobs ›
Margo Shickmanter & the team at Avid Reader: Amy Guay › Allison Green ›
Alex Primiani › Caroline McGregor › Eva Kerins › Alison Forner ›
Paul Dippolito › Jonathan Evans › Alicia Brancato › Cait Lamborne ›
Dominick Montalto › Tony Newfield › Nancy Tan › Meryll Preposi

Maya Kessler is a writer, film director, and producer. Kessler studied arts in the Rietveld Academy in Amsterdam. She currently works as a filmmaker for a global oncology company, alongside writing and developing original content for the international television market. *Rosenfeld* is her first novel.